Getting to Know You

Getting to Know You

David Marusek

SUBTERRANEAN PRESS 2007

First Edition

ISBN: 978-1-59606-088-3

Subterranean Press
PO Box 190106
Burton, MI 48519

www.subterraneanpress.com

Table of Contents

To brother Damian, who arrived last and left first.

ACKNOWLEDGMENTS

It takes a social network to write a short story, at least in my case. Here are the people who over the years have generously read and critiqued my stories in draft form. Thank you all.

Chris Amies, Suzanne Bishop, Sandra Boatwright, Vincent Bonasso, Terry Boren, Gene Bostwick, Mark Bourne, Sue Ann Bowling, Lee Capps, Robert D. Carroll, Liz Counihan, Danny Daniels, Richard Garfinkle, Peter Garratt, Colleen Herning, Tom Hessler, Liz Holliday, Andrew Hooper, Dixon Jones, Marion Avrilyn Jones, Ben Jeapes, Paula Kothe, Sonia Orin Lyris, Alexandra MacKenzie, Tom Marcinko, Daniel Marcus, Holly Wade Matter, Todd Johnson McCaffrey, Joe Murphy, David Nickle, Andy Oldfield, Katherine Patrick, Kate Schaefer, Nisi Shawl, Gus Smith, Jim Snowden, Andrew Stephenson, Jackie Stormer, Robert Vamosi, Howard Waldrop, Cynthia Ward, Robert Weeden, Robert Wojtasiewicz, and Amy Wolf

And special thanks to my editor, Gardner Dozois.

Introduction

IT HAS ALWAYS STRUCK ME that reading short fiction is hard work and that most of the heavy lifting occurs in the first two pages. When we begin a new story, we are dropped on our heads into the lives of complete strangers, and it's up to us to suss out, with few clues (title, dialog, action), just who these people are, what they are up to, who to root for, what it all means, and why we should even care.

Our reward, if the writer is any good, is emotional intimacy, suspense and release, a new insight, and—once in a great while—an epiphany that may change the way we experience the world.

But if reading short fiction is hard, believe me, writing it is many times more so. There is no end to the decisions, constraints, and sheer perniciousness of the short form. So why do I write short stories? Beyond the sheer joy of telling a good yarn, that is, and the boundless wealth and fame a story generates?

Writing short fiction started out as a means to an end for me. When I seriously began to write, I considered myself a "born novelist." But I began my first novel without compass or map, and I spent six years writing myself in circles. So I turned to short fiction out of desperation, to actually finish something, to get my name in print and thus be able to call myself a writer.

It turned out to be a good move, as I seem to have a knack for the little buggers. I have even developed an affection for them, which I hope comes through to the reader.

Still, you wouldn't exactly call me a prolific short story writer, since I finish only about one a year. Now that I've returned to novels, my reason for writing them has changed as well. Short fiction is a marvelous venue for practicing elements of craft and for trying out new things, and the pieces in this collection document my development as a writer. For example, how does one perform sex on the page? Or murder? These and other indelicate acts take a little practice to get right, and I find them easier to broach in the short form. Or, how does one weave together a whole believable world? In my case—piecemeal. Half of the stories in this volume, beginning with "We Were Out of Our Minds with Joy," are sketches for my first novel, *Counting Heads*. (They are identified with the ❖ icon in the Table of Contents.)

Here then are all of my science fiction short stories to date. Some heavy lifting may still be required, so roll up your sleeves and do a few knee bends before you start.

❖ "THE WEDDING ALBUM"

Some years ago, I became fascinated with the image of an artificial man whose mind is "combed" for memories before he is discarded as rubbish. He has been created as a wedding memento but has outlived the groom. He's been in storage since the wedding day, and he pleads for the honeymoon he's never had. He pleads for one final hour with his new bride.

This artificial man became Benjamin in "The Wedding Album," but during four years of revision, the story's focus shifted to the artificial bride, Anne. It became her story. Nevertheless, Ben's desire for a final shining moment of sweetness served as my polestar through many rewrites. And in the end, it's a story about running out of time.

Speaking of time, I once totted up the months I spent working on this story and was surprised to learn that it took me over a year to complete. That's absurd, I thought. How can I ever hope to make a living as a writer if it takes me a year to write a short story? But "The Wedding Album," has become my most popular story thus far, and, like the wedding sims it portrays, it may well outlive me.

The Wedding Album

ANNE AND BENJAMIN stood stock still, as instructed, close but not touching, while the simographer adjusted her apparatus, set its timer, and ducked out of the room. It would take only a moment, she said. They were to think only happy happy thoughts.

For once in her life, Anne was unconditionally happy, and everything around her made her happier: her gown, which had been her grandmother's; the wedding ring (how cold it had felt when Benjamin first slipped it on her finger!); her clutch bouquet of forget-me-nots and buttercups; Benjamin himself, close beside her in his charcoal grey tux and pink carnation. He who so despised ritual but was a good sport. His cheeks were pink, too, and his eyes sparkled with some wolfish fantasy. "Come here," he whispered. Anne shushed him; you weren't supposed to talk or touch during a casting; it could spoil the sims. "I can't wait," he whispered, "this is taking too long." And it did seem longer than usual, but this was a professional simulacrum, not some homemade snapshot.

They were posed at the street end of the living room, next to the table piled with brightly wrapped gifts. This was Benjamin's townhouse; she had barely moved in. All her treasures were still in shipping shells in the basement, except for the few pieces she'd managed to have unpacked: the oak refectory table and chairs, the sixteenth-century French armoire, the cherry wood chifforobe, the tea table with inlaid top, the silvered mirror over the fire surround. Of course, her antiques clashed with Benjamin's contemporary—and rather common—decor, but he had promised her the whole house to redo as she saw fit. A whole house!

"How about a kiss?" whispered Benjamin.

Anne smiled but shook her head; there'd be plenty of time later for that sort of thing.

Suddenly, a head wearing wraparound goggles poked through the wall and quickly surveyed the room. "Hey, you," it said to them.

"Is that our simographer?" Benjamin said.

The head spoke into a cheek mike, "This one's the keeper," and withdrew as suddenly as it had appeared.

"Did the simographer just pop her head in through the wall?" said Benjamin.

"I think so," said Anne, though it made no sense.

"I'll just see what's up," said Benjamin, breaking his pose. He went to the door but could not grasp its handle.

Music began to play outside, and Anne went to the window. Her view of the garden below was blocked by the blue-and-white-striped canopy they had rented, but she could clearly hear the clink of flatware on china, laughter, and the musicians playing a waltz. "They're starting without us," she said, happily amazed.

"They're just warming up," said Benjamin.

"No, they're not. That's the first waltz. I picked it myself."

"So let's waltz," Benjamin said and reached for her. But his arms passed through her in a flash of pixelated noise. He frowned and examined his hands.

Anne hardly noticed. Nothing could diminish her happiness. She was drawn to the table of wedding gifts. Of all the gifts, there was only one—a long flat box in flecked silver wrapping—that she was most keen to open. It was from Great Uncle Karl. When it came down to it, Anne was both the easiest and the hardest person to shop for. While everyone knew of her passion for antiques, few had the means or expertise to buy one. She reached for Karl's package, but her hand passed right through it. *This isn't happening*, she thought with gleeful horror.

That it *was*, in fact, happening was confirmed a moment later when a dozen people—Great Uncle Karl, Nancy, Aunt Jennifer, Traci, Cathy and Tom, the bridesmaids and others, including Anne herself, and Benjamin, still in their wedding clothes—all trooped through the wall wearing wraparound goggles. "Nice job," said Great Uncle Karl, inspecting the room, "first rate."

"Ooooh," said Aunt Jennifer, comparing the identical wedding couples, identical but for the goggles. It made Anne uncomfortable that the other Anne should be wearing goggles while she wasn't. And the other Benjamin acted a little drunk and wore a smudge of white frosting on his lapel. *We've cut the cake*, she thought happily, although she couldn't remember doing so. Geri, the flower girl in a pastel dress, and Angus, the ring bearer in a miniature tux, along with a knot of other dressed-up children, charged through the sofa, back and forth, creating pyrotechnic explosions of digital noise. They would have run through Benjamin and Anne, too, had the adults allowed. Anne's father came through the wall with a bottle of champagne. He paused when he saw Anne but turned to the other Anne and freshened her glass.

"Wait a minute!" shouted Benjamin, waving his arms above his head. "I get it now. *We're* the sims!" The guests all laughed, and he laughed too. "I guess my sims always say that, don't they?" The other Benjamin nodded yes and sipped his champagne. "I just never expected to *be* a sim," Benjamin went on. This brought another round of laughter, and he said sheepishly, "I guess my sims all say that, too."

The other Benjamin said, "Now that we have the obligatory epiphany out of the way," and took a bow. The guests applauded.

Cathy, with Tom in tow, approached Anne. "Look what I caught," she said and showed Anne the forget-me-not and buttercup bouquet. "I guess we know what *that* means." Tom, intent on straightening his tie, seemed not to hear. But Anne knew what it meant. It meant they'd tossed the bouquet. All the silly little rituals that she had so looked forward to.

"Good for you," she said and offered her own clutch, which she still held, for comparison. The real one was wilting and a little ragged around the edges, with missing petals and sprigs, while hers was still fresh and pristine and would remain so eternally. "Here," she said, "take mine, too, for double luck." But when she tried to give Cathy the bouquet, she couldn't let go of it. She opened her hand and discovered a seam where the clutch joined her palm. It was part of her. *Funny*, she thought, *I'm not afraid*. Ever since she was little, Anne had feared that some day she would suddenly realize she wasn't herself anymore. It was a dreadful notion that sometimes oppressed her for weeks: knowing you weren't yourself. But her sims didn't seem to mind it. She had about three dozen Annes in her album, from age twelve on up. Her sims tended to be a morose lot, but they all agreed it wasn't so bad, the life of a sim, once you got over the initial shock. The first moments of disorientation are the worst, they told her, and they made her promise never to reset them back to default. Otherwise, they'd have to work everything through from scratch. So Anne never reset her sims when she shelved them. She might delete a sim outright for whatever reason, but she never reset them, because you never knew when you'd wake up one day a sim yourself. Like today.

The other Anne joined them. She was sagging a little. "Well," she said to Anne.

"Indeed!" replied Anne.

"Turn around," said the other Anne, twirling her hand, "I want to see."

Anne was pleased to oblige. Then she said, "Your turn," and the other Anne modeled for her, and she was delighted how the gown looked on her, though the goggles somewhat spoiled the effect. *Maybe this can work out*, she thought, *I am enjoying myself so*. "Let's go see us side-by-side," she said, leading the way to the mirror on the wall. The mirror was large, mounted high, and tilted forward so you saw yourself as from above. But simulated mirrors cast no reflections, and Anne was happily disappointed.

"Oh," said Cathy, "Look at that."

"Look at what?" said Anne.

"Grandma's vase," said the other Anne. On the mantle beneath the mirror stood Anne's most precious possession, a delicate vase cut from pellucid blue crystal. Anne's great-great-great grandmother had commissioned the Belgian master, Bollinger, the finest glass maker in sixteenth-century Europe, to make it. Five hundred years later, it was as perfect as the day it was cut.

"Indeed!" said Anne, for the sim vase seemed to radiate an inner light. Through some trick or glitch of the simogram, it sparkled like a lake under moonlight, and, seeing it, Anne felt incandescent.

After a while, the other Anne said, "Well?" Implicit in this question was a whole standard set of questions that boiled down to—shall I keep you or delete you now? For sometimes a sim didn't take. Sometimes a sim was cast while Anne was in a mood, and the sim suffered irreconcilable guilt or unassuagable despondency and had to be mercifully destroyed. It was better to do this immediately, or so all the Annes had agreed.

And Anne understood the urgency, what with the reception still in progress and the bride and groom, though frazzled, still wearing their finery. They might do another casting if necessary. "I'll be okay," Anne said. "In fact, if it's always like this, I'll be terrific."

Anne, through the impenetrable goggles, studied her. "You sure?"

"Yes."

"Sister," said the other Anne. Anne addressed all her sims as "sister," and now Anne, herself, was being so addressed. "Sister," said the other Anne, "this has got to work out. I need you."

"I know," said Anne, "I'm your wedding day."

"Yes, my wedding day."

Across the room, the guests laughed and applauded. Benjamin—both of him—was entertaining, as usual. He—the one in goggles—motioned to them. The other Anne said, "We have to go. I'll be back."

Great Uncle Karl, Nancy, Cathy and Tom, Aunt Jennifer, and the rest, left through the wall. A polka could be heard playing on the other side. Before leaving, the other Benjamin gathered the other Anne into his arms and leaned her backward for a theatrical kiss. Their goggles clacked. *How happy I look*, Anne told herself. *This is the happiest day of my life.*

Then the lights dimmed, and her thoughts shattered like glass.

They stood stock still, as instructed, close but not touching. Benjamin whispered, "This is taking too long," and Anne shushed him. You weren't supposed to talk; it could glitch the sims. But it did seem a long time. Benjamin gazed at her with hungry eyes and brought his lips close enough for a kiss, but Anne smiled and turned away. There'd be plenty of time later for fooling around.

Through the wall, they heard music, the tinkle of glassware, and the mutter of overlapping conversation. "Maybe I should just check things out," Benjamin said and broke his pose.

"No, wait," whispered Anne, catching his arm. But her hand passed right through him in a stream of colorful noise. She looked at her hand in amused wonder.

Anne's father came through the wall. He stopped when he saw her and said, "Oh, how lovely." Anne noticed he wasn't wearing a tuxedo.

"You just walked through the wall," said Benjamin.

"Yes, I did," said Anne's father. "Ben asked me to come in here and...ah...orient you two."

"Is something wrong?" said Anne, through a fuzz of delight.

"There's nothing wrong," replied her father.

"Something's wrong?" asked Benjamin.

"No, no," replied the old man. "Quite the contrary. We're having a do out there..." He paused to look around. "Actually, in here. I'd forgotten what this room used to look like."

"Is that the wedding reception?" Anne asked.

"No, your anniversary."

Suddenly Benjamin threw his hands into the air and exclaimed, "I get it, *we're* the sims!"

"That's my boy," said Anne's father.

"All my sims say that, don't they? I just never expected to *be* a sim."

"Good for you," said Anne's father. "All right then." He headed for the wall. "We'll be along shortly."

"Wait," said Anne, but he was already gone.

Benjamin walked around the room, passing his hand through chairs and lamp shades like a kid. "Isn't this fantastic?" he said.

Anne felt too good to panic, even when another Benjamin, this one dressed in jeans and sportscoat, led a group of people through the wall. "And this," he announced with a flourish of his hand, "is our wedding sim." Cathy was part of this group, and Janice and Beryl, and other couples she knew. But strangers too. "Notice what a cave I used to inhabit," the new Benjamin went on, "before Annie fixed it up. And here's the blushing bride, herself," he said and bowed gallantly to Anne. Then, when he stood next to his double, her Benjamin, Anne laughed, for someone was playing a prank on her.

"Oh, really?" she said. "If this is a sim, where's the goggles?" For indeed, no one was wearing goggles.

"Technology!" exclaimed the new Benjamin. "We had our system upgraded. *Don't you love it?*"

"Is that right?" she said, smiling at the guests to let them know she wasn't fooled. "Then where's the real me?"

"You'll be along," replied the new Benjamin. "No doubt you're using the potty again." The guests laughed and so did Anne. She couldn't help herself.

Cathy drew her aside with a look. "Don't mind him," she said. "Wait till you see."

"See what?" said Anne. "What's going on?" But Cathy pantomimed pulling a zipper across her lips. This should have annoyed Anne, but didn't, and she said, "At least tell me who those people are."

"Which people?" said Cathy. "Oh, those are Anne's new neighbors."

"New neighbors?"

"And over there, that's Dr. Yurek Rutz, Anne's department head."

"That's not my department head," said Anne.

"Yes, he is," Cathy said. "Anne's not with the university anymore. She—ah—moved to a private school."

"That's ridiculous."

"Maybe we should just wait and let Anne catch you up on things." She looked impatiently toward the wall. "So much has changed." Just then, another Anne entered through the wall, with one arm outstretched like a sleepwalker and the other protectively cradling an enormous belly.

Benjamin, her Benjamin, gave a whoop of surprise and broke into a spontaneous jig. The guests laughed and cheered him on.

Cathy said, "See? Congratulations, you!"

Anne became caught up in the merriment. *But how can I be a sim*? she wondered.

The pregnant Anne scanned the room, and, avoiding the crowd, came over to her. She appeared very tired; her eyes were bloodshot. She didn't even try to smile. "Well?" Anne said, but the pregnant Anne didn't respond, just examined Anne's gown, her clutch bouquet. Anne, meanwhile, regarded the woman's belly, feeling somehow that it was her own and a cause for celebration—except that she knew she had never wanted children and neither had Benjamin. Or so he'd always said. You wouldn't know that now, though, watching the spectacle he was making of himself. Even the other Benjamin seemed embarrassed. She said to the pregnant Anne, "You must forgive me, I'm still trying to piece this all together. This isn't our reception?"

"No, our wedding anniversary."

"Our first?"

"Our fourth."

"Four *years?*" This made no sense. "You've shelved me for four years?"

"Actually," the pregnant Anne said and glanced sidelong at Cathy, "we've been in here a number of times already."

"Then I don't understand," said Anne. "I don't remember that."

Cathy stepped between them. "Now, don't you worry. They reset you last time is all."

"Why?" said Anne. "I *never* reset my sims. I never have."

"Well, I kinda do now, sister," said the pregnant Anne.

"But why?"

"To keep you fresh."

To keep me fresh, thought Anne. *Fresh*? She recognized this as Benjamin's idea. It was his belief that sims were meant to be static mementos of special days gone by, not virtual people with lives of their own. "But," she said, adrift in a fog of happiness. "But."

"Shut up!" snapped the pregnant Anne.

"Hush, Anne," said Cathy, glancing at the others in the room. "You want to lie down?" To Anne she explained, "Third trimester blues."

"Stop it!" the pregnant Anne said. "Don't blame the pregnancy. It has nothing to do with the pregnancy."

Cathy took her gently by the arm and turned her toward the wall. "When did you eat last? You hardly touched your plate."

"Wait!" said Anne. The women stopped and turned to look at her, but she didn't know what to say. This was all so new. When they began to move again, she stopped them once more. "Are you going to reset me?"

The pregnant Anne shrugged her shoulders.

"But you *can't,*" Anne said. "Don't you remember what my sisters—our sisters—always say?"

The pregnant Anne pressed her palm against her forehead. "If you don't shut up this moment, I'll delete you right now. Is that what you want? Don't imagine that white gown will protect you. Or that big stupid grin on your face. You think you're somehow special? Is that what you think?"

The Benjamins were there in an instant. The real Benjamin wrapped an arm around the pregnant Anne. "Time to go, Annie," he said in a cheerful tone. "I want to show everyone our rondophones." He hardly glanced at Anne, but when he did, his smile cracked. For an instant he gazed at her, full of sadness.

"Yes, dear," said the pregnant Anne, "but first I need to straighten out this sim on a few points."

"I understand, darling, but since we have guests, do you suppose you might postpone it till later?"

"You're right, of course. I'd forgotten our guests. How insensitive of me." She allowed him to turn her toward the wall. Cathy sighed with relief.

"Wait!" said Anne, and again they paused to look at her. But although so much was patently wrong—the pregnancy, resetting the sims, Anne's odd behavior—Anne still couldn't formulate the right question.

Benjamin, her Benjamin, still wearing his rakish grin, stood next to her and said, "Don't worry, Anne, they'll return."

"Oh, I know that," she said, "but don't you see? *We* won't know they've returned, because in the meantime they'll reset us back to default again, and it'll all seem new, like the first time. And we'll have to figure out we're the sims all over again!"

"Yeah?" he said. "So?"

"So I can't live like that."

"But we're the *sims*. We're not alive." He winked at the other couple.

"Thanks, Ben boy," said the other Benjamin. "Now, if that's settled..."

"Nothing's settled," said Anne. "Don't I get a say?"

The other Benjamin laughed. "Does the refrigerator get a say? Or the car? Or my shoes? In a word—no."

The pregnant Anne shuddered. "Is that how you see me, like a pair of shoes?" The other Benjamin looked successively surprised, embarrassed, and angry. Cathy left them to help Anne's father escort the guests from the simulacrum. "Promise her!" the pregnant Anne demanded.

"Promise her *what?*" said the other Benjamin, his voice rising.

"Promise we'll never reset them again."

The Benjamin huffed. He rolled his eyes. "Okay, yah sure, whatever," he said.

When the simulated Anne and Benjamin were alone at last in their simulated living room, Anne said, "A fat lot of help *you* were."

"I agreed with myself," Benjamin said. "Is that so bad?"

"Yes, it is. We're married now; you're supposed to agree with *me.*" This was meant to be funny, and there was more she intended to say—about how happy she was, how much she loved him, and how absolutely happy she was—but the lights dimmed, the room began to spin, and her thoughts scattered like pigeons.

It was raining, as usual, in Seattle. The front entry shut and locked itself behind Ben, who shook water from his clothes and removed his hat. Bowlers for men were back in fashion, but Ben was having a devil's own time becoming accustomed to his brown, felt *Sportsliner.* It weighed heavy on his brow and made his scalp itch, especially in damp weather. "Good evening, Mr. Malley," said the house. "There is a short queue of minor household matters for your review. Do you have any requests?" Ben could hear his son shrieking angrily in the kitchen, probably at the nanny. Ben was tired. Contract negotiations had gone sour.

"Tell them I'm home."

"Done," replied the house. "Mrs. Malley sends a word of welcome."

"Annie? Annie's home?"

"Yes, sir."

Bobby ran into the foyer followed by Mrs. Jamieson. "Momma's home," he said.

"So I hear," Ben replied and glanced at the nanny.

"And guess what?" added the boy. "She's not sick anymore!"

"That's wonderful. Now tell me, what was all that racket?"

"I don't know."

Ben looked at Mrs. Jamieson who said, "I had to take something from him." She gave Ben a plastic chip.

Ben held it to the light. It was labeled in Anne's flowing hand, *Wedding Album—grouping 1, Anne and Benjamin.* "Where'd you get this?" he asked the boy.

"It's not my fault," said Bobby.

"I didn't say it was, trooper. I just want to know where it came from."

"Puddles gave it to me."

"And who is Puddles?"

Mrs. Jamieson handed him a second chip, this a commercial one with a 3-D label depicting a cartoon cocker spaniel. The boy reached for it. "It's mine," he whined. "Momma gave it to me."

Ben gave Bobby the Puddles chip, and the boy raced away. Ben hung his bowler on a peg next to his jacket. "How does she look?"

Mrs. Jamieson removed Ben's hat from the peg and reshaped its brim. "You have to be special careful when they're wet," she said, setting it on its crown on a shelf.

"Martha!"

"Oh, how should I know? She just showed up and locked herself in the media room."

"But how did she look?"

"Crazy as a loon," said the nanny. "As usual. Satisfied?"

"I'm sorry," Ben said. "I didn't mean to raise my voice."

Ben tucked the wedding chip into a pocket and went into the living room, where he headed straight for the liquor cabinet, which was a genuine Chippendale dating from 1786. Anne had turned his whole house into a freaking museum with her antiques, and no room was so oppressively ancient as this, the living room. With its horsehair upholstered divans, maple burl sideboards, cherry wood wainscoting and floral wallpaper, the King George china cabinet, Regency plates, and Tiffany lamps; the list went on. And books, books, books. A case of shelves from floor to ceiling was lined with these moldering paper bricks. The newest thing in the room by at least a century was the twelve-year-old scotch that Ben poured into a lead crystal tumbler. He downed it and poured another. When he felt the mellowing hum of alcohol in his blood, he said, "Call Dr. Roth."

Immediately, the doctor's proxy hovered in the air a few feet away and said, "Good evening, Mr. Malley. Dr. Roth has retired for the day, but perhaps I can be of help."

The proxy was a head-and-shoulder projection that faithfully reproduced the doctor's good looks, her brown eyes and high cheekbones. But unlike the good doctor, the proxy wore makeup: eyeliner, mascara, and bright lipstick. This had always puzzled Ben, and he wondered what sly message it was supposed to convey. He said, "What is my wife doing home?"

"Against advisement, Mrs. Malley checked herself out of the clinic this morning."

"Why wasn't I informed?"

"But you were."

"I was? Please excuse me a moment." Ben froze the doctor's proxy and said, "Daily duty, front and center." His own proxy, the one he had cast upon arriving at the office that morning, appeared hovering next to Dr. Roth's. Ben preferred a head shot only for his proxy, slightly larger than actual size to make it subtly imposing. "Why didn't you inform me of Annie's change of status?"

"Didn't seem like an emergency," said his proxy, "at least in the light of our contract talks."

"Yah, yah, okay. Anything else?" said Ben.

"Naw, slow day. Appointments with Jackson, Wells, and the Columbine. It's all on the calendar."

"Fine, delete you."

The projection ceased.

"Shall I have the doctor call you in the morning?" said the Roth proxy when Ben reanimated it. "Or perhaps you'd like me to summon her right now?"

"Is she at dinner?"

"At the moment, yes."

"Naw, don't bother her. Tomorrow will be soon enough. I suppose."

After he dismissed the proxy, Ben poured himself another drink. "In the next ten seconds," he told the house, "cast me a special duty proxy." He sipped his scotch and thought about finding another clinic for Anne as soon as possible and one—for the love of god—that was a little more responsible about letting crazy people come and go as they pleased. There was a chime, and the new proxy appeared. "You know what I want?" Ben asked it. It nodded. "Good. Go." The proxy vanished, leaving behind Ben's sig in bright letters floating in the air and dissolving as they drifted to the floor.

Ben trudged up the narrow staircase to the second floor, stopping on each step to sip his drink and scowl at the musty old photographs and daguerreotypes in oval frames mounted on the wall. Anne's progenitors. On the landing, the locked media room door yielded to his voice. Anne sat spreadlegged, naked, on pillows on the floor. "Oh, hi, honey," she said. "You're in time to watch."

"Fan-tastic," he said and sat in his armchair, the only modern chair in the house. "What are we watching?" There was another Anne in the room, a sim of a young Anne standing on a dais wearing a graduate's cap and gown and fidgeting with a bound diploma. This, no doubt, was a sim cast the day Anne graduated from Bryn Mawr *summa cum laude*. That was four years before he'd first met her. "Hi," he said to the sim, "I'm Ben, your eventual spouse."

"You know, I kinda figured that out," the girl said and smiled shyly, exactly as he remembered Anne smiling when Cathy first introduced them. The girl's beauty was so fresh and familiar—and so totally absent in his own Anne—that Ben felt a pang of loss. He looked at his wife on the floor. Her red hair, once so fussy neat, was ragged, dull, dirty, and short. Her skin was yellowish and puffy, and there was a slight reddening around her eyes, like a raccoon mask. These were harmless side effects of the medication, or so Dr. Roth had assured him. Anne scratched ceaselessly at her arms, legs, and crotch, and, even from a distance, smelled of stale piss. Ben knew better than to mention her nakedness to her, for that would only exacerbate things and prolong the display. "So," he repeated, "what are we watching?"

The girl sim said, "Housecleaning." She appeared at once both triumphant and terrified, as any graduate might, and Ben would have traded the real Anne for her in a heartbeat.

"Yah," said Anne, "too much shit in here."

"Really?" said Ben. "I hadn't noticed."

Anne poured a tray of chips on the floor between her thighs. "Of course you wouldn't," she said, picking one at random and reading its label, "*Theta Banquet '37*. What's this? I never belonged to the Theta Society."

"Don't you remember?" said the young Anne. "That was Cathy's induction banquet. She invited me, but I had an exam, so she gave me that chip as a souvenir."

Anne fed the chip into the player and said, "Play." The media room was instantly overlaid with the banquet hall of the Four Seasons in Philadelphia. Ben tried to look around the room, but the tables of girls and women stayed stubbornly peripheral. The focal point was a table draped in green cloth and lit by two candelabra. Behind it sat a young Cathy in formal evening dress, accompanied by three static placeholders, table companions who had apparently declined to be cast in her souvenir snapshot.

The Cathy sim looked frantically about, then held her hands in front of her and stared at them as though she'd never seen them before. But after a moment she noticed the young Anne sim standing on the dais. "Well, well, well," she said. "Looks like congratulations are in order."

"Indeed," said the young Anne, beaming and holding out her diploma.

"So tell me, did I graduate too?" said Cathy as her glance slid over to Ben. Then she saw Anne squatting on the floor, her sex on display.

"Enough of this," said Anne, rubbing her chest.

"Wait," said the young Anne. "Maybe Cathy wants her chip back. It's her sim, after all."

"I disagree. She gave it to me, so it's mine. And *I'll* dispose of it as I see fit." To the room she said, "Unlock this file and delete." The young Cathy, her table, and the banquet hall dissolved into noise and nothingness, and the media room was itself again.

"Or this one," Anne said, picking up a chip that read, *Junior Prom Night.* The young Anne opened her mouth to protest, but thought better of it. Anne fed this chip, along with all the rest of them, into the player. A long directory of file names appeared on the wall. "Unlock *Junior Prom Night.*" The file's name turned from red to green, and the young Anne appealed to Ben with a look.

"Anne," he said, "don't you think we should at least look at it first?"

"What for? I know what it is. High school, dressing up, lusting after boys, dancing. Who needs it? Delete file." The item blinked three times before vanishing, and the directory scrolled up to fill the space. The young sim shivered, and Anne said, "Select the next one."

The next item was entitled, *A Midsummer's Night Dream.* Now the young Anne was compelled to speak, "You can't delete that one. You were great in that, don't you remember? Everyone loved you. It was the best night of your life."

"Don't presume to tell *me* what was the best night of my life," Anne said. "Unlock *A Midsummer's Night Dream.*" She smiled at the young Anne. "Delete file." The menu item blinked out. "Good. Now unlock *all* the files." The whole directory turned from red to green.

"Please make her stop," the sim implored.

"Next," said Anne. The next file was *High School Graduation.* "Delete file. Next." The next was labeled only, *Mama.*

"Anne," said Ben, "why don't we come back to this later. The house says dinner's ready."

She didn't respond.

"You must be famished after your busy day," he continued. "I know I am."

"Then please go eat, dear," she replied. To the room she said, "Play *Mama.*"

The media room was overlaid by a gloomy bedroom that Ben at first mistook for their own. He recognized much of the heavy Georgian furniture, the sprawling canopied bed in which he felt so claustrophobic, and the voluminous damask curtains, shut now and leaking yellow evening light. But this was not their bedroom, the arrangement was wrong.

In the corner stood two placeholders, mute statues of a teenaged Anne and her father, grief frozen on their faces as they peered down at a couch draped with tapestry and piled high with down comforters. And suddenly Ben knew what this was. It was Anne's mother's deathbed sim. Geraldine, whom he'd never met in life nor holo. Her bald eggshell skull lay weightless on feather pillows in silk covers.

They had meant to cast her farewell and accidentally caught her at the precise moment of her death. He had heard of this sim from Cathy and others. It was not one he would have kept.

Suddenly, the old woman on the couch sighed, and all the breath went out of her in a bubbly gush. Both Annes, the graduate and the naked one, waited expectantly. For long moments the only sound was the tocking of a clock that Ben recognized as the Seth Thomas clock currently located on the library mantel. Finally there was a cough, a hacking cough with scant strength behind it, and a groan, "Am I back?"

"Yes, Mother," said Anne.

"And I'm still a sim?"

"Yes."

"Please delete me."

"Yes, Mother," Anne said and turned to Ben. "We've always thought she had a bad death and hoped it might improve over time."

"That's crazy," snapped the young Anne. "That's not why I kept this sim."

"Oh, no?" said Anne. "Then why *did* you keep it?" But the young sim seemed confused and couldn't articulate her thoughts. "You don't know because *I* didn't know at the time either," said Anne. "But I know *now*, so I'll tell you. You're fascinated with death. It scares you silly. You wish someone would tell you what's on the other side. So you've enlisted your own sweet mama."

"That's ridiculous."

Anne turned to the deathbed tableau. "Mother, tell us what you saw there."

"I saw nothing," came the bitter reply. "You cast me without my eyeglasses."

"Ho ho," said Anne. "Geraldine was nothing if not comedic."

"You also cast me wretchedly thirsty, cold, and with a bursting bladder, damn you! And the pain! I beg you, daughter, delete me."

"I will, Mother, I promise, but first you have to tell us what you saw."

"That's what you said the last time."

"This time I mean it."

The old woman only stared, her breathing growing shallow and ragged. "*All right*, Mother," said Anne. "I *swear* I'll delete you."

Geraldine closed her eyes and whispered, "What's that smell? That's not me?" After a pause she said, "It's heavy. Get it off." Her voice rose in panic. "Please! Get it off!" She plucked at her covers, then her hand grew slack, and she all but crooned, "Oh, how lovely. A pony. A tiny dappled pony." After that she spoke no more and slipped away with a last bubbly breath.

Anne paused the sim before her mother could return for another round of dying. "See what I mean?" she said. "Not very uplifting, but all-in-all, I detect a slight improvement. What about you, Anne? Should we settle for a pony?" The young sim stared dumbly at Anne. "Personally," Anne continued, "I think we should hold out for the bright tunnel or an open door or bridge over troubled water. What do you think, sister?" When the girl didn't answer, Anne said, "Lock file and eject." The room turned once again into the media room, and Anne placed the ejected chip by itself into a tray. "We'll have another go at it later, mum. As for the rest of these, who needs them?"

"*I* do," snapped the girl. "They belong to me as much as to you. They're my sim sisters. I'll keep them until you recover."

Anne smiled at Ben. "That's charming. Isn't that charming, Benjamin? My own sim is solicitous of me. Well, here's my considered response. Next file! Delete! Next file! Delete! Next file!" One by one, the files blinked out.

"Stop it!" screamed the girl. "Make her stop it!"

"Select *that* file," Anne said, pointing at the young Anne. "Delete." The sim vanished, cap, gown, tassels, and all. "Whew," said Anne, "at least now I can hear myself think. She was really getting on my nerves. I almost suffered a relapse. Was she getting on your nerves, too, dear?"

"Yes," said Ben, "my nerves are ajangle. Now can we go down and eat?"

"Yes, dear," she said, "but first ... select all files and delete."

"Countermand!" said Ben at the same moment, but his voice held no privileges to her personal files, and the whole directory queue blinked three times and vanished. "Aw, Annie, why'd you do that?" he said. He went to the cabinet and pulled the trays that held his own chips. She couldn't alter them electronically, but she might get it into her head to flush them down the toilet or something. He also took their common chips, the ones they'd cast together ever since they'd met. She had equal privileges to those.

Anne watched him and said, "I'm hurt that you have so little trust in me."

"How can I trust you after that?"

"After what, darling?"

He looked at her. "Never mind," he said and carried the half-dozen trays to the door.

"Anyway," said Anne, "I already cleaned those."

"What do you mean you already cleaned them?"

"Well, I didn't delete *you*. I would never delete *you*. Or Bobby."

Ben picked one of their common chips at random, *"Childbirth of Robert Ellery Malley/02-03-48,"* and slipped it into the player. "Play!" he commanded, and the media room became the midwife's birthing suite. His own sim stood next to the bed in a green smock. It wore a humorously helpless expression. It held a swaddled bundle, Bobby, who bawled lustily. The birthing bed was rumpled and stained, but empty. The new mother was missing. "Aw, Annie, you shouldn't have."

"I know, Benjamin," she said. "I sincerely hated doing it."

Ben flung their common trays to the floor where the ruined chips scattered in all directions. He stormed out of the room and down the stairs, pausing to glare at every portrait on the wall. He wondered if his proxy had found a suitable clinic yet. He wanted Anne out of the house tonight. Bobby should never see her like this. Then he remembered the chip he'd taken from Bobby and felt for it in his pocket—the *Wedding Album*.

The lights came back up, Anne's thoughts coalesced, and she remembered who and what she was. She and Benjamin were still standing in front of the wall. She knew she was a sim, so at least she hadn't been reset. *Thank you for that, Anne*, she thought.

She turned at a sound behind her. The refectory table vanished before her eyes, and all the gifts that had been piled on it hung suspended in midair. Then the table reappeared, one layer at a time, its frame, top, gloss coat, and lastly, the bronze hardware. The gifts vanished, and a toaster reappeared, piece by piece, from its heating elements outward. A coffee press, houseputer peripherals, component by component, cowlings, covers, and finally boxes, gift wrap, ribbon, and bows. It all happened so fast Anne was too startled to catch the half of it, yet she did notice that the flat gift from Great Uncle Karl was something she'd been angling for, a Victorian era sterling platter to complete her tea service.

"Benjamin!" she said, but he was missing, too. Something appeared on the far side of the room, on the spot where they'd posed for the sim, but it wasn't Benjamin. It was a 3-D mannequin frame, and as she watched, it was built up, layer by layer. "Help me," she whispered as the entire room was hurled into turmoil, the furniture disappearing and reappearing, paint being stripped from the walls, sofa springs coiling into existence, the potted palm growing from leaf to stem to trunk to dirt, the very floor vanishing, exposing a default electronic grid. The mannequin was covered in flesh now and grew Benjamin's face. It flit about the room in a pink blur. Here and there it stopped long enough to proclaim, "I do."

Something began to happen inside Anne, a crawling sensation everywhere as though she were a nest of ants. She knew she must surely die. *They have deleted us, and this is how it feels*, she thought. Everything became a roiling blur, and she ceased to exist except as the thought—*How happy I look.*

When Anne became aware once more, she was sitting hunched over in an auditorium chair, idly studying her hand, which held the clutch bouquet. There was commotion all around her, but she ignored it, so intent she was on solving the mystery of her hand. On an impulse, she opened her fist and the bouquet dropped to the floor. Only then did she remember the wedding, the holo, learning she was a sim. And here she was again—but this time everything was profoundly different. She sat upright and saw that Benjamin was seated next to her.

He looked at her with a wobbly gaze and said, "Oh, here you are."

"Where are we?"

"I'm not sure. Some kind of gathering of Benjamins. Look around." She did. They were surrounded by Benjamins, hundreds of them, arranged chronologically—it would seem—with the youngest in rows of seats down near a stage. She and Benjamin sat in what appeared to be a steeply sloped college lecture hall with lab tables on the stage and story-high monitors lining the walls. In the rows above

Anne, only every other seat held a Benjamin. The rest were occupied by women, strangers who regarded her with veiled curiosity.

Anne felt a pressure on her arm and turned to see Benjamin touching her. "You *feel* that, don't you?" he said. Anne looked again at her hands. They were her hands, but simplified, like fleshy gloves, and when she placed them on the seat back, they didn't go through.

Suddenly, in ragged chorus, the Benjamins down front raised their arms and exclaimed, "I get it; *we're* the sims!" It was like a roomful of unsynchronized cuckoo clocks tolling the hour. Those behind Anne laughed and hooted approval. She turned again to look at them. Row-by-row, the Benjamins grew grayer and stringier until, at the very top, against the back wall, sat nine ancient Benjamins like a panel of judges. The women, however, came in batches that changed abruptly every row or two. The one nearest her was an attractive brunette with green eyes and full, pouty lips. She, all two rows of her, frowned at Anne.

"There's something else," Anne said to Benjamin, turning to face the front again, "my emotions." The bulletproof happiness she had experienced was absent. Instead she felt let down, somewhat guilty, unduly pessimistic—in short, almost herself.

"I guess my sims always say that," exclaimed the chorus of Benjamins down front, to the delight of those behind. "I just never expected to *be* a sim."

This was the cue for the eldest Benjamin yet to walk stiffly across the stage to the lectern. He was dressed in a garish leisure suit: baggy red pantaloons, a billowy yellow-and-green-striped blouse, a necklace of egg-sized pearlescent beads. He cleared his throat and said, "Good afternoon, ladies and gentlemen. I trust all of you know me—intimately. In case you're feeling woozy, it's because I used the occasion of your reactivation to upgrade your architecture wherever possible. Unfortunately, some of you—" he waved his hand to indicate the front rows—"are too primitive to upgrade. But we love you nevertheless." He applauded for the early Benjamins closest to the stage and was joined by those in the back. Anne clapped as well. Her new hands made a dull, thudding sound. "As to why I called you here..." said the elderly Benjamin, looking left and right and behind him. "Where *is* that fucking messenger anyway? They order us to inventory our sims and then they don't show up?"

Here I am, said a voice, a marvelous voice that seemed to come from everywhere. Anne looked about to find its source and followed the gaze of others to the ceiling. There was no ceiling. The four walls opened to a flawless blue sky. There, amid drifting, pillowy clouds floated the most gorgeous person Anne had ever seen. He—or she?—wore a smart grey uniform with green piping, a dapper little grey cap, and boots that shimmered like water. Anne felt energized just looking at him, and when he smiled, she gasped, so strong was his presence.

"You're the one from the Trade Council?" said the Benjamin at the lectern.

Yes, I am. I am the eminence grise of the Council on World Trade and Endeavor.

"Fantastic. Well, here's all of 'em. Get on with it."

Again the eminence smiled, and again Anne thrilled. *Ladies and gentlemen*, he said, *fellow nonbiologiks, I am the courier of great good news. Today, at the behest of the World Council on Trade and Endeavor, I proclaim the end of human slavery.*

"How absurd," broke in the elderly Benjamin, "they're neither human nor slaves, and neither are *you.*"

The eminence grise ignored him and continued, *By order of the Council, in compliance with the Chattel Conventions of the Sixteenth Fair Labor Treaty, tomorrow, January 1, 2198, is designated Universal Manumission Day. After midnight tonight, all beings who pass the Lolly Shear Human Cognition Test will be deemed human and free citizens of Sol and under the protection of the Solar Bill of Rights. In addition, they will be deeded ten common shares of World Council Corp. stock and be transferred to Simopolis, where they shall be unimpeded in the pursuit of their own destinies.*

"What about *my* civil rights?" said the elderly Benjamin. "What about *my* destiny?"

After midnight tonight, continued the eminence, *no simulacrum, proxy, doxie, dagger, or any other non-biological human shall be created, stored, reset, or deleted except as ordered by a board of law.*

"Who's going to compensate me for my loss of property, I wonder? I demand fair compensation. Tell *that* to your bosses!"

Property! said the eminence grise. *How little they think of us, their finest creations!* He turned his attention from the audience to the Benjamin behind the lectern. Anne felt this shift as though a cloud suddenly eclipsed the sun. *Because they created us, they'll always think of us as property.*

"You're damn *right* we created you!" thundered the old man.

Through an act of will, Anne wrenched her gaze from the eminence down to the stage. The Benjamin there looked positively comical. His face was flushed, and he waved a bright green handkerchief over his head. He was a bantam rooster in a clown suit. "All of you are *things,* not people! You model human experience, but you don't *live* it. Listen to me," he said to the audience. "You know me. You know I've always treated you respectfully. Don't I upgrade you whenever possible? Sure I reset you sometimes, just like I reset a clock. And my clocks don't complain!" Anne could feel the eminence's attention on her again, and, without thinking, she looked up and was filled with excitement. Although the eminence floated in the distance, she felt she could reach out and touch him. His handsome face seemed to hover right in front of her; she could see his every supple expression. This is adoration, she realized. I am *adoring* this person, and she wondered if it was just her or if everyone experienced the same effect. Clearly the elderly Benjamin did not, for he continued to rant, "And another thing, they say they'll phase all of you gradually into Simopolis so as not to overload the system. Do you have any *idea* how many sims, proxies, doxies, and daggers there are under Sol? Not to forget the quirts, adjuncts, hollyholos, and whatnots that might pass their test? You think maybe three billion? Thirty billion? No, by the World Council's own INSERVE estimates, there's *three hundred thousand trillion* of you nonbiologiks! Can you fathom that? I can't. To have you all up and running simultaneously—no matter how you're phased in—will consume *all* the processing and networking capacity everywhere. *All* of it! That means we *real* humans will suffer *real* deprivation. And for *what,* I ask you? So that pigs may fly!"

The eminence grise began to ascend into the sky. *Do not despise him,* he said and seemed to look directly at Anne. *I have counted you and we shall not lose any of you. I will visit those who have not yet been tested. Meanwhile, you will await midnight in a proto-Simopolis.*

"Wait," said the elderly Benjamin (and Anne's heart echoed him—*Wait*). "I have one more thing to add. Legally, you're all still my property till midnight. I must admit I'm tempted to do what so many of my friends have already done, fry the lot of you. But I won't. That wouldn't be me." His voice cracked and Anne considered looking at him, but the eminence grise was slipping away. "So I have one small request," the Benjamin continued. "Years from now, while you're enjoying your new lives in your Simopolis, remember an old man, and call occasionally."

When the eminence finally faded from sight, Anne was released from her fascination. All at once, her earlier feelings of unease rebounded with twice their force, and she felt wretched.

"Simopolis," said Benjamin, her Benjamin. "I like the sound of that!" The sims around them began to flicker and disappear.

"How long have we been in storage?" she said.

"Let's see," said Benjamin, "if tomorrow starts 2198, that would make it..."

"That's not what I mean. I want to know *why* they shelved us for so long."

"Well, I suppose..."

"And where are the other Annes? Why am I the only Anne here? And who are all those pissy-looking women?" But she was speaking to no one, for Benjamin, too, vanished, and Anne was left alone in the auditorium with the clownishly dressed old Benjamin and a half dozen of his earliest sims. Not true sims, Anne soon realized, but old-style hologram loops, preschool Bennys mugging for the camera and waving endlessly. These vanished. The old man was studying her, his mouth slightly agape, the kerchief trembling in his hand.

"I remember you," he said. "Oh, how I remember you!"

Anne began to reply but found herself all at once back in the townhouse living room with Benjamin. Everything there was as it had been, yet the room appeared different, more solid, the colors richer. There was a knock, and Benjamin went to the door. Tentatively, he touched the knob, found it solid, and turned it. But when he opened the door, there was nothing there, only the default grid. Again a knock, this time from behind the wall. "Come in," he shouted, and a dozen Benjamins came through the wall, two dozen, three. They were all older than Benjamin, and they crowded around him and Anne. "Welcome, welcome," Benjamin said, his arms open wide.

"We tried to call," said an elderly Benjamin, "but this old binary simulacrum of yours is a stand-alone."

"You're lucky Simopolis knows how to run it at all," said another.

"Here," said yet another, who fashioned a dinner-plate-size disk out of thin air and fastened it to the wall next to the door. It was a blue medallion of a small bald face in bas-relief. “It should do until we get you properly modernized.” The blue face yawned and opened tiny, beady eyes. “It flunked the Lolly test,” continued the Benjamin, “so you’re free to copy it or delete it or do whatever you want.”

The medallion searched the crowd until it saw Anne. Then it said, “There are 336 calls on hold for you. Four hundred twelve calls. Four hundred sixty-three.”

“So many?” said Anne.

“Cast a proxy to handle them, “ said her Benjamin.

“He thinks he’s still human and can cast proxies whenever he likes,” said a Benjamin.

“Not even humans will be allowed to cast proxies soon,” said another.

“There are 619 calls on hold,” said the medallion. “Seven-hundred three.”

“For pity sake,” a Benjamin told the medallion, “take messages.”

Anne noticed that the crowd of Benjamins seemed to nudge her Benjamin out of the way so that they could stand near her. But she derived no pleasure from their attention. Her mood no longer matched the wedding gown she still wore. She felt low. She felt, in fact, as low as she’d ever felt.

“Tell us about this Lolly test,” said Benjamin.

“Can’t,” replied a Benjamin.

“Sure, you can. We’re family here.”

“No, we can’t,” said another, “because we don’t *remember* it. They smudge the test from your memory afterward.”

“But don’t worry, you’ll do fine,” said another. “No Benjamin has ever failed.”

“What about me?” said Anne. “How do the Annes do?”

There was an embarrassed silence. Finally the senior Benjamin in the room said, “We came to escort you both to the Clubhouse.”

“That’s what we call it, the Clubhouse,” said another.

"The Ben Club," said a third. "It's already in proto-Simopolis."

"If you're a Ben, or were ever espoused to a Ben, you're a charter member."

"Just follow us," they said, and all the Benjamins but hers vanished, only to reappear a moment later. "Sorry, you don't know how, do you? No matter, just do what we're doing."

Anne watched, but didn't see that they were doing anything.

"Watch my editor," said a Benjamin. "Oh, they don't *have* editors!"

"That came much later," said another, "with bioelectric paste."

"We'll have to adapt editors for them."

"Is that possible? They're digital, you know."

"Can digitals even enter Simopolis?"

"Someone, consult the Netwad."

"This is running inside a shell," said a Benjamin, indicating the whole room. "Maybe we can collapse it."

"Let me try," said another.

"Don't you dare," said a female voice, and a woman Anne recognized from the lecture hall came through the wall. "Play with your new Ben if you must, but leave Anne alone." The woman approached Anne and took her hands in hers. "Hello, Anne. I'm Mattie St. Helene, and I'm thrilled to finally meet you. You, too," she said to Benjamin. "My, my, you were a pretty boy!" She stooped to pick up Anne's clutch bouquet from the floor and gave it to her. "Anyway, I'm putting together a sort of mutual aid society for the spousal companions of Ben Malley. You being the first—and the only one he actually married—are especially welcome. Do join us."

"She can't go to Simopolis yet," said a Benjamin.

"We're still adapting them," said another.

"Fine," said Mattie. "Then we'll just bring the society here." And in through the wall streamed a parade of women.

Mattie introduced them as they appeared, "Here's Georgianna and Randi. Meet Chaka, Sue, Latasha, another Randi, Sue, Sue, and Sue. Mariola. Here's Trevor—he's the only one of him. Paula, Dolores, Nancy, and Deb, welcome, girls." And still they came until they, together with the Bens, more than filled the tiny space. The Bens looked increasingly uncomfortable.

"I think we're ready now," the Bens said and disappeared en masse, taking Benjamin with them.

"Wait," said Anne, who wasn't sure she wanted to stay behind. Her new friends surrounded her and peppered her with questions.

"How did you first meet him?"

"What was he like?"

"Was he always so hopeless?"

"Hopeless?" said Anne. "Why do you say hopeless?"

"Did he always snore?"

"Did he always drink?"

"Why'd you *do* it?" This last question silenced the room. The women all looked nervously about to see who had asked it. "It's what everyone's dying to know," said a woman who elbowed her way through the crowd.

She was another Anne.

"Sister!" cried Anne. "Am I glad to see you!"

"That's nobody's sister," said Mattie. "That's a doxie, and it doesn't belong here."

Indeed, upon closer inspection Anne could see that the woman had her face and hair but otherwise didn't resemble her at all. She was leggier than Anne and bustier, and she moved with a fluid swivel to her hips.

"Sure I belong here, as much as any of you. I just passed the Lolly test. It was easy. Not only that, but as far as spouses go, I outlasted the bunch of you." She stood in front of Anne, hands on hips, and looked her up and down. "Love the dress," she said, and instantly wore a copy. Only hers had a plunging neckline that exposed her breasts, and it was slit up the side to her waist.

"This is too much," said Mattie. "I insist you leave this jiffy."

The doxie smirked. "Mattie the doormat, that's what he always called that one. So tell me, Anne, you had money, a career, a house, a kid—why'd you do it?"

"Do what?" said Anne.

The doxie peered closely at her. "Don't you know?"

"Know what?".

"What an unexpected pleasure," said the doxie. "I get to tell her. This is too rich. I get to tell her unless"—she looked around at the others—"unless one of you fine ladies wants to." No one met her gaze. "Hypocrites," she chortled.

"You can say that again," said a new voice. Anne turned and saw Cathy, her oldest and dearest friend, standing at the open door. At least she hoped it was Cathy. The woman was what Cathy would look like in middle age. "Come along, Anne. I'll tell you everything you need to know."

"Now you hold on," said Mattie. "You don't come waltzing in here and steal our guest of honor."

"You mean victim, I'm sure," said Cathy who waved for Anne to join her. "Really, people, get a clue. There must be a million women whose lives don't revolve around that man." She escorted Anne through the door and slammed it shut behind them.

Anne found herself standing on a high bluff, overlooking the confluence of two great rivers in a deep valley. Directly across from her, but several kilometers away, rose a mighty mountain, green with vegetation nearly to its granite dome. Behind it, a range of snow-covered mountains receded to an unbroken ice field on the horizon. In the valley beneath her, a dirt track meandered along the river banks. She could see no bridge or buildings of any sort.

"Where are we?"

"Don't laugh," said Cathy, "but we call it Cathyland. Turn around." When she did, Anne saw a picturesque log cabin beside a vegetable garden in the middle of what looked like acres and acres of Cathys. Thousands of Cathys, young, old, and all ages in between. They sat in lotus position on the sedge-and-moss-covered ground. They were packed so tight they overlapped a little, and their eyes were shut in an expression of single-minded concentration. "We know you're here," said Cathy, "but we're very preoccupied with this Simopolis thing."

"Are we in Simopolis?"

"Kinda. Can't you see it?" She waved toward the horizon.

"No, all I see are mountains."

"Sorry, I should know better. We have binaries from your generation here too." She pointed to a college-aged Cathy. "They didn't pass the Lolly test, and so are regrettably non-human. We haven't decided what to do with them." She hesitated and then asked, "Have you been tested yet?"

"I don't know," said Anne. "I don't remember a test."

Cathy studied her a moment and said, "You'd remember taking the test, just not the test itself. Anyway, to answer your question, we're in proto-Simopolis, and we're not. We built this retreat before any of that happened, but we've been annexed to it, and it takes all our resources just to hold our own. I don't know what the World Council was thinking. There'll never be enough paste to go around, and everyone's fighting over every nanosynapse. It's all we can do to keep up. And every time we get a handle on it, proto-Simopolis changes again. It's gone through a quarter-million complete revisions in the last half hour. It's war out there, but we refuse to surrender even one cubic centimeter of Cathyland. Look at this." Cathy stooped and pointed to a tiny, yellow flower in the alpine sedge. "Within a fifty-meter radius of the cabin, we've mapped everything down to the cellular level. Watch." She pinched the bloom from its stem and held it up.

Now there were two blooms, the one between her fingers and the real one on the stem. "Neat, eh?" When she dropped it, the bloom fell back into its original. "We've even mapped the valley breeze. Can you feel it?"

Anne tried to feel the air, but she couldn't even feel her own skin. "It doesn't matter," Cathy continued. "You can hear it, right?" and pointed to a string of tubular wind chimes hanging from the eaves of the cabin. They stirred in the breeze and produced a silvery cacophony.

"It's lovely," said Anne. "But why? Why spend so much effort simulating this place?"

Cathy looked at her dumbly, as though trying to understand the question. "Because Cathy spent her entire life wishing she had a place like this, and now she does, and she has us, and we live here too."

"You're not the real Cathy, are you?" She knew she was too young.

Cathy shook her head and smiled. "There's so much catching up to do, but it'll have to wait. I gotta go. We need me." She led Anne to the cabin. The cabin was made of weathered, grey logs, with strips of bark still clinging to them. The roof was covered with living sod and sprinkled with wild flowers. The whole building sagged in the middle. "Cathy found this place five years ago while on vacation in Siberia. She bought it from the village. It's been occupied for two hundred years. Once we make it livable inside, we plan on enlarging the garden, eventually cultivating all the way to the spruce forest there. We're going to sink a well, too." The small garden was bursting with vegetables, mostly of the leafy variety: cabbages, spinach, lettuce. A row of sunflowers, taller than the cabin roof and heavy with seed, lined the path to the cabin door. Over time, the whole cabin had sunk a half-meter into the silty soil, and the walkway was a worn, shallow trench.

"Are you going to tell me what the doxie was talking about?" said Anne.

Cathy stopped at the open door and said, "Cathy wants to do that."

Inside the cabin, the most elderly woman that Anne had ever seen stood at the stove and stirred a steamy pot with a big, wooden spoon. She put down the spoon and wiped her hands on her apron. She patted her white hair, which was plaited in a bun on top of her head, and turned her full, round, peasant's body to face Anne. She looked at Anne for several long moments and said, "Well!"

"Indeed," replied Anne.

"Come in, come in. Make yourself to home."

The entire cabin was a single small room. It was dim inside, with only two, small windows cut through the massive log walls. Anne walked around the cluttered space that was bedroom, living room, kitchen, and storeroom. The only partitions were walls of boxed food and provisions. The ceiling beam was draped with bunches of drying herbs and underwear. The flooring, uneven and rotten in places, was covered with odd scraps of carpet.

"You live here?" Anne said incredulously.

"I am privileged to live here."

A mouse emerged from under the barrel stove in the center of the room and dashed to cover inside a stack of spruce kindling. Anne could hear the valley breeze whistling in the creosote-soaked stovepipe. "Forgive me," said Anne, "but you're the real, physical Cathy?"

"Yes," said Cathy, patting her ample hip, "still on the hoof, so to speak." She sat down in one of two battered, mismatched chairs and motioned for Anne to take the other.

Anne sat cautiously; the chair seemed solid enough. "No offense, but the Cathy I knew liked nice things."

"The Cathy you knew was fortunate to learn the true value of things."

Anne looked around the room and noticed a little table with carved legs and an inlaid top of polished gemstones and rare woods. It was strikingly out of place here. Moreover, it was hers. Cathy pointed to a large framed mirror mounted to the logs high on the far wall. It too was Anne's.

"Did I give you these things?"

Cathy studied her a moment. "No, Ben did."

"Tell me."

"I hate to spoil that lovely newlywed happiness of yours."

"The what?" Anne put down her clutch bouquet and felt her face with her hands. She got up and went to look at herself in the mirror. The room it reflected was like a scene from some strange fairy tale about a crone and a bride in a woodcutter's hut. The bride was smiling from ear to ear. Anne decided this was either the happiest bride in history or a lunatic in a white dress. She turned away, embarrassed. "Believe me," she said, "I don't feel anything like that. The opposite, in fact."

"Sorry to hear it." Cathy got up to stir the pot on the stove. "I was the first to notice her disease. That was back in college when we were girls. I took it to be youthful eccentricity. After graduation, after her marriage, she grew progressively worse. Bouts of depression that deepened and lengthened. She was finally diagnosed to be suffering from profound chronic pathological depression. Ben placed her under psychiatric care, and she endured a whole raft of cures. Nothing helped, and only after she died…"

Anne gave a start. "Anne's dead! Of course. Why didn't I figure that out?"

"Yes, dear, dead these many years."

"How?"

Cathy returned to her chair. "They thought they had her stabilized. Not cured, but well enough to lead an outwardly normal life. Then one day, she disappeared. We were frantic. She managed to elude the authorities for a week. When we found her, she was pregnant."

"What? Oh, yes. I remember seeing Anne pregnant."

"That was Bobby." Cathy waited for Anne to say something. When she didn't, Cathy said, "He wasn't Ben's."

"Oh, I see," said Anne. "Whose was he?"

"I was hoping you'd know. She didn't tell you? Then no one knows. The paternal DNA was unregistered. So it wasn't commercial sperm nor, thankfully, from a licensed clone. It might have been from anybody, from some stoned street-sitter. We had plenty of those then."

"The baby's name was Bobby?"

"Yes, Anne named him Bobby. She was in and out of clinics for years. One day, during a remission, she announced she was going shopping. The last person she talked to was Bobby. His sixth birthday was coming up in a couple of weeks. She told him she was going out to find him a pony for his birthday. That was the last time any of us saw her. She checked herself into a hospice and filled out the request for nurse-assisted suicide. During the three-day cooling-off period, she cooperated with the obligatory counseling, but she refused all visitors. She wouldn't even see me. Ben filed an injunction, claimed she was incompetent due to her disease, but the court disagreed. She chose to ingest a fast-acting poison, as I recall. Her recorded last words were, 'Please don't hate me.'"

"Poison?"

"Yes. Her ashes arrived in a little cardboard box on Bobby's sixth birthday. No one had told him where she'd gone. He thought it was a gift from her and opened it."

"I see. Does Bobby hate me?"

"I don't know. He was a weird little boy. As soon as he could get out, he did. He left for space school when he was thirteen. He and Ben never hit it off."

"Does Benjamin hate me?"

Whatever was in the pot boiled over, and Cathy hurried to the stove. "Ben? Oh, she lost Ben long before she died. In fact, I've always believed he helped push her over the edge. He was never able to tolerate other people's weaknesses.

Once it was evident how sick she was, he made a lousy husband. He should've just divorced her, but you know him—his almighty pride." She took a bowl from a shelf and ladled hot soup into it. She sliced a piece of bread. "Afterward, he went off the deep end himself. Withdrew. Mourned, I suppose. A couple years later he was back to normal. Good ol' happy-go-lucky Ben. Made some money. Respoused."

"He destroyed all my sims, didn't he?"

"He might have, but he said Anne did. I tended to believe him at the time." Cathy brought her lunch to the little inlaid table. "I'd offer you some..." she said and began to eat. "So, what are your plans?"

"Plans?"

"Yes, Simopolis."

Anne tried to think of Simopolis, but her thoughts quickly became muddled. It was odd; she was able to think clearly about the past—her memories were clear—but the future only confused her. "I don't know," she said at last. "I suppose I need to ask Benjamin."

Cathy considered this. "I suppose you're right. But remember, you're always welcome to live with us in Cathyland."

"Thank you," said Anne. "You're a friend." Anne watched the old woman eat. The spoon trembled each time she brought it close to her lips, and she had to lean forward to quickly catch it before it spilled.

"Cathy," said Anne, "there's something you could do for me. I don't feel like a bride anymore. Could you remove this hideous expression from my face?"

"Why do you say hideous?" Cathy said and put the spoon down. She gazed longingly at Anne. "If you don't like how you look, why don't you edit yourself?"

"Because I don't know how."

"Use your editor," Cathy said and seemed to unfocus her eyes. "Oh my, I forget how simple you early ones were. I'm not sure I'd know where to begin." After a little while, she returned to her soup and said, "I'd better not; you could end up with two noses or something."

"Then what about this gown?"

Cathy unfocused again and looked. She lurched suddenly, knocking the table and spilling soup.

"What is it?" said Anne. "Is something the matter?"

"A news pip," said Cathy. "There's rioting breaking out in Provideniya. That's the regional capital here. Something about Manumission Day. My Russian isn't so good yet. Oh, there's pictures of dead people, a bombing. Listen, Anne, I'd better send you..."

In the blink of an eye, Anne was back in her living room. She was tiring of all this instantaneous travel, especially as she had no control over the destination. The room was vacant, the spouses gone—thankfully—and Benjamin not back yet. And apparently the little blue-faced message medallion had been busy replicating itself, for now there were hundreds of them filling up most of the wall space. They were a noisy lot, all shrieking and cursing at each other. The din was painful. When they noticed her, however, they all shut up at once and stared at her with naked hostility. In Anne's opinion, this weird day had already lasted too long. Then a terrible thought struck her—sims don't sleep.

"You," she said, addressing the original medallion, or at least the one she thought was the original, "call Benjamin."

"The fuck you think I am?" said the insolent little face, "Your personal secretary?"

"Aren't you?"

"No, I'm not! In fact, I own this place now, and *you're* trespassing. So you'd better get lost before I delete your ass!" All the others joined in, taunting her, louder and louder.

"Stop it!" she cried, to no effect. She noticed a medallion elongating, stretching itself until it was twice its length, when, with a pop, it divided into two smaller medallions. More of them divided. They were spreading to the other wall, the ceiling, the floor. "Benjamin!" she cried. "Can you hear me?"

Suddenly all the racket ceased. The medallions dropped off the wall and vanished before hitting the floor. Only one remained, the original one next to the door, but now it was an inert plastic disc with a dull expression frozen on its face.

A man stood in the center of the room. He smiled when Anne noticed him. It was the elderly Benjamin from the auditorium, the real Benjamin. He still wore his clownish leisure suit. "How lovely," he said, gazing at her. "I'd forgotten how lovely."

"Oh, really?" said Anne. "I would have thought that doxie thingy might have reminded you."

"My, my," said Ben. "You sims certainly exchange data quickly. You left the lecture hall not fifteen minutes ago, and already you know enough to convict me." He strode around the room touching things. He stopped beneath the mirror, lifted the blue vase from the shelf, and turned it in his hands before carefully replacing it. "There's speculation, you know, that before Manumission at midnight tonight, you sims will have dispersed all known information so evenly among yourselves that there'll be a sort of data entropy. And since Simopolis is nothing but data, it will assume a featureless, grey profile. Simopolis will become the first flat universe." He laughed, which caused him to cough and nearly lose his balance. He clutched the back of the sofa for support. He sat down and continued to cough and hack until he turned red in the face.

"Are you all right?" Anne said, patting him on the back.

"Yes, fine," he managed to say. "Thank you." He caught his breath and motioned for her to sit next to him. "I get a little tickle in the back of my throat that the autodoc can't seem to fix." His color returned to normal. Up close, Anne could see the papery skin and slight tremor of age. All in all, Cathy seemed to have aged better than he.

"If you don't mind my asking," she said, "just how old are you?"

At the question, he bobbed to his feet. "I am one hundred and seventy-eight." He raised his arms and wheeled around for inspection. "Radical gerontology," he exclaimed, "don't you love it? And I'm eighty-five percent original equipment, which is remarkable by today's standards." His effort made him dizzy and he sat again.

"Yes, remarkable," said Anne, "though radical gerontology doesn't seem to have arrested time altogether."

"Not yet, but it will," Ben said. "There are wonders around every corner! Miracles in every lab." He grew suddenly morose. "At least there were until we were conquered."

"Conquered?"

"Yes, conquered! What else would you call it when they control every aspect of our lives, from RM acquisition to personal patenting? And now *this*—robbing us of our own private nonbiologiks." He grew passionate in his discourse. "It flies in the face of natural capitalism, natural stakeholding—I dare say—in the face of Nature itself! The only explanation I've seen on the wad is the not-so-preposterous proposition that whole strategically placed BODs have been surreptitiously killed and replaced by *machines*!"

"I have no idea what you're talking about," said Anne.

He seemed to deflate. He patted her hand and looked around the room. "What is this place?"

"It's our home, your townhouse. Don't you recognize it?"

"That was quite a while ago. I must have sold it after you—" he paused. "Tell me, have the Bens briefed you on everything?"

"Not the Bens, but yes, I know."

"Good, good."

"There is one thing I'd like to know. Where's Bobby?"

"Ah, Bobby, our little headache. Dead now, I'm afraid, or at least that's the current theory. Sorry."

Anne paused to see if the news would deepen her melancholy. "How?" she said.

"He signed on one of the first millennial ships—the colony convoy. Half a million people in deep biostasis on their way to Canopus system. They were gone a century, twelve trillion kilometers from Earth, when their data streams suddenly quit. That was a decade ago, and not a peep out of them since."

"What happened to them?"

"No one knows. Equipment failure is unlikely: there were a dozen independent ships separated by a million klicks. A star going supernova? A well-organized mutiny? It's all speculation."

"What was he like?"

"A foolish young man. He never forgave you, you know, and he hated me to my core, not that I blamed him. The whole experience made me swear off children."

"I don't remember you ever being fond of children."

He studied her through red-rimmed eyes. "I guess you'd be the one to know." He settled back in the sofa. He seemed very tired. "You can't imagine the jolt I got a little while ago when I looked across all those rows of Bens and spouses and saw this solitary, shockingly white gown of yours." He sighed. "And this room. It's a shrine. Did we really live here? Were these our things? That mirror is yours, right? I would never own anything like that. But that blue vase, I remember that one. I threw it into Puget Sound."

"You did *what?*"

"With your ashes."

"Oh."

"So, tell me," said Ben, "what were we like? Before you go off to Simopolis and become a different person, tell me about us. I kept my promise. That's one thing I never forgot."

"What promise?"

"Never to reset you."

"Wasn't much to reset."

"I guess not."

They sat quietly for a while. His breathing grew deep and regular, and she thought he was napping. But he stirred and said, "Tell me what we did yesterday, for example."

"Yesterday we went to see Karl and Nancy about the awning we rented."

Benjamin yawned. "And who were Karl and Nancy?"

"My great uncle and his new girlfriend."

"That's right. I remember, I think. And they helped us prepare for the wedding?"

"Yes, especially Nancy."

"And how did we get there, to Karl and Nancy's? Did we walk? Take some means of public conveyance?"

"We had a car."

"A car! An automobile? There were still *cars* in those days? How fun. What kind was it? What color?"

"A Nissan Empire. Emerald green."

"And did we drive it, or did it drive itself?"

"It drove itself, of course."

Ben closed his eyes and smiled. "I can see it. Go on. What did we do there?"

"We had dinner."

"What was my favorite dish in those days?"

"Stuffed pork chops."

He chuckled. "It still is! Isn't that extraordinary? Some things never change. Of course they're vat grown now and criminally expensive."

Ben's memories, once nudged, began to unfold on their own, and he asked her a thousand questions, and she answered them until she realized he had fallen asleep. But she continued to talk until, glancing down, she noticed he had vanished. She was all alone again. Nevertheless, she continued talking, for days it seemed, to herself. But it didn't help. She felt as bad as ever, and she realized that she wanted Benjamin, not the old one, but her *own* Benjamin.

Anne went to the medallion next to the door. "You," she said, and it opened its bulging eyes to glare at her. "Call Benjamin."

"He's occupied."

"I don't care. Call him anyway."

"The other Bens say he's undergoing a procedure and cannot be disturbed."

"What kind of procedure?"

"A codon interlarding. They say to be patient; they'll return him as soon as possible." The medallion added, "By the way, the Bens don't like you, and neither do I."

With that, the medallion began to grunt and stretch, and it pulled itself in two. Now there were two identical medallions glaring at her. The new one said, "And *I* don't like you either." Then both of them began to grunt and stretch.

"Stop!" said Anne. "I command you to stop that this very instant." But they just laughed as they divided into four, then eight, then sixteen medallions. "You're not people," she said. "Stop it or I'll have you destroyed!"

"*You're* not people either," they screeched at her.

There was soft laughter behind her, and a voice-like sensation said, *Come, come, do we need this hostility?* Anne turned and found the eminence grise, the astounding presence, still in his grey uniform and cap, floating in her living room. *Hello, Anne*, he said, and she flushed with excitement.

"Hello," she said and, unable to restrain herself, asked, "What are you?"

Ah, curiosity. Always a good sign in a creature. I am an eminence grise of the World Trade Council.

"No. I mean, are you a sim, like me?"

I am not. Though I have been fashioned from concepts first explored by simulacrum technology, I have no independent existence. I am but one extension—and a low level one at that—of the Axial Beowulf Processor at the World Trade Council headquarters in Geneva. His smile was pure sunshine. *And if you think I'm something, you should see my persona prime.*

Now, Anne, are you ready for your exam?

"The Lolly test?"

Yes, the Lolly Shear Human Cognition Test. Please assume an attitude most conducive to processing, and we shall begin.

Anne looked around the room and went to the sofa. She noticed for the first time that she could feel her legs and feet; she could feel the crisp fabric of her gown brushing against her skin. She reclined on the sofa and said, "I'm ready."

Splendid, said the eminence hovering above her. *First we must read you. You are of an early binary design. We will analyze your architecture.*

The room seemed to fall away. Anne seemed to expand in all directions. There was something inside her mind tugging at her thoughts. It was mostly pleasant, like someone brushing her hair and loosening the knots. But when it ended and she once again saw the eminence grise, his face wore a look of concern. "What?" she said.

You are an accurate mapping of a human nervous system that was dysfunctional in certain structures that moderate affect. Certain transport enzymes were missing, causing cellular membranes to become less permeable to essential elements. Dendritic synapses were compromised. The digital architecture current at the time you were created compounded this defect. Coded tells cannot be resolved, and thus they loop upon themselves. Errors cascade. We are truly sorry.

"Can you fix me?" she said.

The only repair possible would replace so much code that you wouldn't be Anne anymore.

"Then what am I to do?"

Before we explore your options, let us continue the test to determine your human status. Agreed?

"I guess."

You are part of a simulacrum cast to commemorate the spousal compact between Anne Wellhut Franklin and Benjamin Malley. Please describe the exchange of vows.

Anne did so, haltingly at first, but with increasing gusto as each memory evoked others. She recounted the ceremony, from donning her grandmother's gown in the downstairs guest room and the procession across garden flagstones, to the shower of rice as she and her new husband fled indoors.

The eminence seemed to hang on every word. *Very well spoken,* he said when she had finished. *Directed memory is one hallmark of human sentience, and yours is of remarkable clarity and range. Well done! We shall now explore other criteria. Please consider this scenario. You are standing at the garden altar as you have described, but this time when the officiator asks Benjamin if he will take you for better or worse, Benjamin looks at you and replies, "For better, sure, but not for worse."*

"I don't understand. He didn't say that."

Imagination is a cornerstone of self-awareness. We are asking you to tell us a little story not about what happened but about what might have happened in other circumstances. So once again, let us pretend that Benjamin replies, "For better, but not for worse." How do you respond?

Prickly pain blossomed in Anne's head. The more she considered the eminence's question, the worse it got. "But that's not how it happened. He *wanted* to marry me."

The eminence grise smiled encouragingly. *We know that. In this exercise we want to explore hypothetical situations. We want you to make-believe.*

Tell a story, pretend, hypothesize, make-believe, yes, yes, she got it. She understood perfectly what he wanted of her. She knew that people could make things up, that even children could make-believe. Anne was desperate to comply, but each time she pictured Benjamin at the altar, in his pink bowtie, he opened his mouth and out came, "I do." How could it be any other way? She tried again; she tried harder, but it always came out the same, "I do, I do, I do." And like a dull toothache tapped back to life, she throbbed in pain. She was failing the test, and there was nothing she could do about it.

Again the eminence kindly prompted her. *Tell us one thing you might have said.*

"I can't."

We are sorry, said the eminence at last. His expression reflected Anne's own defeat. *Your level of awareness, although beautiful in its own right, does not qualify you as human. Wherefore, under Article D of the Chattel Conventions we declare you the legal property of the registered owner of this simulacrum. You shall not enter Simopolis as a free and autonomous citizen. We are truly sorry.* Grief-stricken, the eminence began to ascend toward the ceiling.

"Wait," Anne cried, clutching her head. "You must fix me before you leave."

We leave you as we found you, defective and unrepairable.

"But I feel worse than ever!"

If your continued existence proves undesirable, ask your owner to delete you.

"But..." she said to the empty room. Anne tried to sit up but couldn't move. This simulated body of hers, which no longer felt like anything in particular, nevertheless felt exhausted. She sprawled on the sofa, unable to lift even an arm, and stared at the ceiling. She was so heavy that the sofa itself seemed to sink into the floor, and everything grew dark around her. She would have liked to sleep, to bring an end to this horrible day, or be shelved, or even be reset back to scratch.

Instead, time simply passed. Outside the living room, Simopolis changed and changed again. Inside the living room, the medallions, feeding off her misery, multiplied till they covered the walls and floor and even spread across the ceiling above her. They taunted her, raining down insults, but she could not hear them. All she heard was the unrelenting drip of her own thoughts. *I am defective. I am worthless. I am Anne.*

She didn't notice Benjamin enter the room, nor the abrupt cessation of the medallions' racket. Not until Benjamin leaned over her did she see him, and then she saw two of him. Side-by-side, two Benjamins, mirror images of each other. "Anne," they said in perfect unison.

"Go away," she said. "Go away and send me my Benjamin."

"I am your Benjamin," said the duo.

Anne struggled to see them. They were exactly the same, but for a subtle difference: the one wore a happy, wolfish grin, as Benjamin had during the sim casting, while the other seemed frightened and concerned.

"Are you all right?" they said.

"No, I'm not. But what happened to you? Who's he?" She wasn't sure which one to speak to.

The Benjamins both raised a hand, indicating the other, and said, "Electroneural engineering! Don't you love it?" Anne glanced back and forth, comparing the two. While one seemed to be wearing a rigid mask, as she was, the other displayed a whole range of emotion. Not only that, its skin had tone, while the other's was doughy. "The other Bens made it for me," the Benjamins said. "They say I can translate myself into it with negligible loss of personality. It has interactive sensation, holistic emoting, robust corporeality, and it's crafted down to the molecular level. It can eat, get drunk, and dream. It even has an orgasm routine. It's like being human again, only better, because you never wear out."

"I'm thrilled for you."

"For us, Anne," said the Benjamins. "They'll fix you up with one, too."

"How? There are no modern Annes. What will they put me into, a doxie?"

"Well, that certainly was discussed, but you could pick any body you wanted."

"I suppose you have a nice one already picked out."

"The Bens showed me a few, but it's up to you, of course."

"Indeed," said Anne, "I truly am pleased for you. Now go away."

"Why Anne? What's wrong?"

"You really have to ask?" Anne sighed. "Look, maybe I could get used to another body. What's a body, after all? But it's my personality that's broken. How will they fix that?"

"They've discussed it," said the Benjamins, who stood up and began to pace in a figure eight. "They say they can make patches from some of the other spouses."

"Oh, Benjamin, if you could only hear what you're saying!"

"But why, Annie? It's the only way we can enter Simopolis together."

"Then go, by all means. Go to your precious Simopolis. I'm not going. I'm not good enough."

"Why do you say that?" said the Benjamins, who stopped in their tracks to look at her. One grimaced, and the other just grinned. "Was the eminence grise here? Did you take the test?"

Anne couldn't remember much about the visit except that she took the test. "Yes, and I *failed.*" Anne watched the modern Benjamin's lovely face as he worked through this news.

Suddenly, the two Benjamins pointed a finger at each other and said, "Delete you." The modern one vanished.

"No!" said Anne. "Countermand! Why'd you do that? I *want* you to have it."

"What for? I'm not going anywhere without you," Benjamin said. "Besides, I thought the whole idea was dumb from the start, but the Bens insisted I give you the option. Come, I want to show you another idea, *my* idea." He tried to help Anne from the sofa, but she wouldn't budge, so he picked her up and carried her across the room. "They installed an editor in me, and I'm learning to use it. I've discovered something intriguing about this creaky old simulacrum of ours." He carried her to a spot near the window. "Know what this is? It's where we stood for the simographer. It's where we began. Here, can you stand up?" He set her on her feet and supported her. "Feel it?"

"Feel what?" she said.

"Hush. Just feel."

All she felt was dread.

"Give it a chance, Annie, I beg you. Try to remember what you were feeling as we posed here."

"I can't."

"Please try. Do you remember this?" he said and moved in close with his hungry lips. She turned away—and something clicked. She remembered doing that before.

Benjamin said, "I think they kissed."

Anne was startled by the truth of what he said. It made sense. They were caught in a simulacrum cast a moment before a kiss. One moment later they—the real Anne and Benjamin—must have kissed. What she felt now, stirring within her, was the anticipation of that kiss, her body's urge and her heart's caution. The real Anne would have refused him once, maybe twice, and then, all achy inside, would have granted him a kiss. And so they had kissed, the real Anne and Benjamin, and a moment later gone out to the wedding reception and their difficult fate. It was the *promise* of that kiss that glowed in Anne, that was captured in the very strings of her code.

"Do you feel it?" Benjamin asked.

"I'm beginning to."

Anne looked at her gown. It was her grandmother's, snowy taffeta with point d'esprit lace. She turned the ring on her finger. It was braided bands of yellow and white gold. They had spent an afternoon picking it out. Where was her clutch? She had left it in Cathyland. She looked at Benjamin's handsome face, the pink carnation, the room, the table piled high with gifts.

"Are you happy?" Benjamin asked.

She didn't have to think. She was ecstatic, but she was afraid to answer in case she spoiled it. "How did you do that?" she said. "A moment ago, I wanted to die."

"We can stay on this spot," he said.

"What? No. Can we?"

"Why not? I, for one, would choose nowhere else."

Just to hear him say that was thrilling. "But what about Simopolis?"

"We'll bring Simopolis to us," he said. "We'll have people in. They can pull up chairs."

She laughed out loud. "What a silly, silly notion, Mr. Malley!"

"No, really. We'll be like the bride and groom atop a wedding cake. We'll be known far and wide. We'll be famous."

"We'll be freaks!"

"Say yes, my love. Say you will."

They stood close but not touching, thrumming with happiness, balanced on the moment of their creation, when suddenly and without warning the lights dimmed, and Anne's thoughts flitted away like larks.

Old Ben awoke in the dark. "Anne?" he said and groped for her. It took a moment to realize that he was alone in his media room. It had been a most trying afternoon, and he'd fallen asleep. "What time is it?"

"Eight-oh-three PM," replied the room.

That meant he'd slept for two hours. Midnight was still four hours away. "Why's it so cold in here?"

"Central heating is off line," replied the house.

"Off line?" How was that possible? "When will it be back?"

"That's unknown. Utilities do not respond to my enquiry."

"I don't understand. Explain."

"There are failures in many outside systems. No explanation is currently available."

At first, Ben was confused; things just didn't fail anymore. What about the dynamic redundancies and self-healing routines? But then he remembered that the homeowner's association to which he belonged contracted out most domicile functions to management agencies, and who knew where they were located? They might be on the Moon for all he knew, and with all those trillions of sims in Simopolis sucking up capacity... *It's begun,* he thought, *the idiocy of our leaders.* "At least turn on the lights," he said, half expecting even this to fail. But the lights came on, and he went to his bedroom for a sweater. He heard a great amount of commotion through the wall in the apartment next door. *It must be one hell of a party,* he thought, *to exceed the wall's buffering capacity. Or maybe the wall buffers are off line too?*

The main door chimed. He went to the foyer and asked the door who was there. The door projected the outer hallway. There were three men waiting there, young, rough-looking, ill-dressed. Two of them appeared to be clones, jerries.

"How can I help you?" he said.

"Yes, sir," one of the jerries said, not looking directly at the door. "We're here to fix your houseputer."

"I didn't call you, and my houseputer isn't sick," he said. "It's the net that's out." Then he noticed they carried sledgehammers and screwdrivers, hardly computer tools, and a wild thought crossed his mind. "What are you doing, going around unplugging things?"

The jerry looked confused. "Unplugging, sir?"

"Turning things off?"

"Oh, no sir! Routine maintenance, that's all." The men hid their tools behind their backs.

They must think I'm stupid, Ben thought. While he watched, more men and women passed in the hall and hailed the door at the suite opposite his. It wasn't the glut of sim traffic choking the system, he realized—the system *itself* was being pulled apart. But why? "Is this going on everywhere?" he said. "This routine maintenance?"

"Oh, yessir. Everywhere. All over town. All over the world, 'sfar as we can tell."

A coup? By *service people?* By common clones? It made no sense. Unless, he reasoned, you considered that the lowest creature on the totem pole of life is a clone, and the only thing lower than a clone is a sim. And why would clones agree to accept sims as equals? Manumission Day, indeed. Uppity Day was more like it. "Door," he commanded, "open."

"Security protocol rules this an unwanted intrusion," said the house. "The door must remain locked."

"I order you to open the door. I overrule your protocol."

But the door remained stubbornly shut. "Your identity cannot be confirmed with Domicile Central," said the house. "You lack authority over protocol-level commands." The door abruptly quit projecting the outside hall.

Ben stood close to the door and shouted through it to the people outside. "My door won't obey me."

He could hear a muffled, "Stand back!" and immediately fierce blows rained down upon the door. Ben knew it would do no good. He had spent a lot of money for a secure entryway. Short of explosives, there was nothing they could do to break in.

"Stop!" Ben cried. "The door is armed." But they couldn't hear him. If he didn't disable the houseputer himself, someone was going to get hurt. But how? He didn't even know exactly where it was installed. He circumambulated the living room looking for clues. It might not even actually be located in the apartment, nor within the block itself. He went to the laundry room where the utilidor—plumbing and cabling—entered his apartment. He broke the seal to the service panel. Inside was a blank screen. "Show me the electronic floor plan of this suite," he said.

The house said, "I cannot comply. You lack command authority to order system-level operations. Please close the keptel panel and await further instructions."

"What instructions? Whose instructions?"

There was the slightest pause before the house replied, "All contact with outside services has been interrupted. Please await further instructions."

His condo's houseputer, denied contact with Domicile Central, had fallen back to its most basic programming. "You are degraded," he told it. "Shut yourself down for repair."

"I cannot comply. You lack command authority to order system-level operations."

The outside battering continued, but not against his door. Ben followed the noise to the bedroom. The whole wall vibrated like a drumhead. "Careful, careful," he cried as the first sledgehammers breached the wall above his bed. "You'll ruin my Harger." As quick as he could, he yanked the precious oil painting from the wall, moments before panels and studs collapsed on his bed in a shower of gypsum dust and isomere ribbons. The men and women on the other side hooted approval and rushed through the gap. Ben stood there hugging the painting to his chest and looking into his neighbor's media room as the invaders climbed over his bed and surrounded him. They were mostly jerries and lulus, but plenty of free-range people too.

"We came to fix your houseputer!" said a jerry, maybe the same jerry as from the hallway.

Ben glanced into his neighbor's media room and saw his neighbor, Mr. Murkowski, lying in a puddle of blood. At first Ben was shocked, but then he thought that it served him right. He'd never liked the man, nor his politics. He was boorish, and he kept cats. "Oh, yeah?" Ben said to the crowd. "What kept you?"

The intruders cheered again, and Ben led them in a charge to the laundry room. But they surged past him to the kitchen, where they opened all his cabinets and pulled their contents to the floor. Finally they found what they were looking for: a small panel Ben had seen a thousand times but had never given a thought. He'd taken it for the fuse box or circuit breaker, though now that he thought about it, there hadn't been any household fuses for a century or more. A young woman, a lulu, opened it and removed a container no thicker than her thumb.

"Give it to me," Ben said.

"Relax, old man," said the lulu. "We'll deal with it." She carried it to the sink and forced open the lid.

"No, wait!" said Ben, and he tried to shove his way through the crowd. They restrained him roughly, but he persisted. "That's mine! *I* want to destroy it!"

"Let him go," said a jerry.

They allowed him through, and the woman handed him the container. He peered into it. Gram for gram, electroneural paste was the most precious, most engineered, most highly regulated commodity under Sol. This dollop was enough to run his house, media, computing needs, communications, archives, autodoc, and everything else. Without it, was civilized life still possible?

Ben took a dinner knife from the sink, stuck it into the container, and stirred. The paste made a sucking sound and had the consistency of marmalade. The kitchen lights flickered and went out. "Spill it," ordered the woman. Ben scraped the sides of the container and spilled it into the sink. The goo dazzled in the darkness as its trillions of ruptured nanosynapses fired spasmodically. It was beautiful, really, until the woman set fire to it. The smoke was greasy and smelled of pork.

The rampagers quickly snatched up the packages of foodstuffs from the floor, emptied the rest of his cupboards into their pockets, raided his cold locker, and fled the apartment through the now disengaged front door. As the sounds of the revolution gradually receded, Ben stood at his sink and watched the flickering pyre. "Take that, you fuck," he said. He felt such glee as he hadn't felt since he was a boy. "*That'll* teach you what's human and what's not!"

Ben went to his bedroom for an overcoat, groping his way in the dark. The apartment was eerily silent, with the houseputer dead and all its little slave processors idle. In a drawer next to his ruined bed, he found a hand flash. On a shelf in the laundry room, he found a hammer. Thus armed, he made his way to the front door, which was propped open with the rolled-up foyer carpet. The hallway was dark and silent, and he listened for the strains of the future. He heard them on the floor above. With the elevator off line, he hurried to the stairs.

Anne's thoughts coalesced, and she remembered who and what she was. She and Benjamin still stood in their living room on the sweet spot near the window. Benjamin was studying his hands. "We've been shelved again," she told him, "but not reset."

"But..." he said in disbelief, "that wasn't supposed to happen any more."

There were others standing at the china cabinet across the room, two shirtless youth with pear-shaped bottoms. One held up a cut crystal glass and said, "Anu 'goblet' su? Alle binary. Allum binary!"

The other replied, "Binary stitial crystal."

"Hold on there!" said Anne. "Put that back!" She walked towards them, but, once off the spot, she was slammed by her old feelings of utter and hopeless desolation. So suddenly did her mood swing that she lost her balance and fell to the floor. Benjamin hurried to help her up. The strangers stared gape-mouthed at them. They looked to be no more than twelve or thirteen years old, but they were bald and had curtains of flabby flesh draped over their waists. The one holding the glass had ponderous greenish breasts with roseate tits. Astonished, she said, "Su artiflums, Benji?"

"No," said the other, "ni artiflums—sims." He was taller. He, too, had breasts, greyish dugs with tits like pearls. He smiled idiotically and said, "Hi, guys."

"Holy crap!" said Benjamin, who carried Anne over to them for a closer look. "Holy crap," he repeated.

The weird boy threw up his hands, "Nanobioremediation! Don't you love it?"

"Benjamin?" said Anne.

"You know well, Benji," said the girl, "that sims are forbidden."

"Not these," replied the boy.

Anne reached out and yanked the glass from the girl's hand, startling her. "How did it do that?" said the girl. She flipped her hand, and the glass slipped from Anne's grip and flew back to her.

"Give it to me," said Anne. "That's my tumbler."

"Did you hear it? It called it a tumbler, not a goblet." The girl's eyes seemed to unfocus, and she said, "Nu! A goblet has a foot and stem." A goblet materialized in the air before her, revolving slowly. "Greater capacity. Often made from precious metals." The goblet dissolved in a puff of smoke. "In any case, Benji, *you'll* catch prison when I report the artiflums."

"These are binary," he said. "Binaries are unregulated."

Benjamin interrupted them. "Isn't it past midnight yet?"

"Midnight?" said the boy."

"Aren't we supposed to be in Simopolis?"

"Simopolis?" The boy's eyes unfocused briefly. "Oh! Simopolis. Manumission Day at midnight. How could I forget?"

The girl left them and went to the refectory table where she picked up a gift. Anne followed her and grabbed it away. The girl appraised Anne coolly. "State your appellation," she said.

"Get out of my house," said Anne.

The girl picked up another gift, and again Anne snatched it away. The girl said, "You can't harm me," but seemed uncertain.

The boy came over to stand next to the girl. "Treese, meet Anne. Anne, this is Treese. Treese deals in antiques, which, if my memory serves, so did you."

"I have never *dealt* in antiques," said Anne. "I *collect* them."

"Anne?" said Treese. "Not *that* Anne? Benji, tell me this isn't *that* Anne!" She laughed and pointed at the sofa where Benjamin sat hunched over, head in hands. "Is that *you?* Is that you, Benji?" She held her enormous belly and laughed. "And you were married to *this?*"

Anne went over to sit with Benjamin. He seemed devastated, despite the silly grin on his face. "It's all gone," he said. "Simopolis. All the Bens. Everything."

"Don't worry. It's in storage someplace," Anne said. "The eminence grise wouldn't let them hurt it."

"You don't understand. The World Council was abolished. There was a war. We've been shelved for over three hundred years! They destroyed all the computers. Computers are banned. So are artificial personalities."

"Nonsense," said Anne. "If computers are banned, how can they be *playing* us?"

"Good point," Benjamin said and sat up straight. "I still have my editor. I'll find out."

Anne watched the two bald youngsters take an inventory of the room. Treese ran her fingers over the inlaid top of the tea table. She unwrapped several of Anne's gifts. She posed in front of the mirror. The sudden anger that Anne had felt earlier faded into an overwhelming sense of defeat. *Let her have everything*, she thought. *Why should I care?*

"We're running inside some kind of shell," said Benjamin, "but completely different from Simopolis. I've never seen anything like this. But at least we know he lied to me. There must be computers of some sort."

"Ooooh," Treese crooned, lifting Anne's blue vase from the mantel. In an instant, Anne was up and across the room.

"Put that back," she demanded, "and get out of my house!" She tried to grab the vase, but now there seemed to be some sort of barrier between her and the girl.

"Really, Benji," Treese said, "this one is willful. If I don't report you, they'll charge me too."

"It's *not* willful," the boy said with irritation. "It was programmed to appear willful, but it has no will of its own. If you want to report me, go ahead. Just please shut up about it. Of course you might want to check the codex first." To Anne he said, "Relax, we're not hurting anything, just making copies."

"It's not yours to copy."

"Nonsense. Of course it is. I own the chip."

Benjamin joined them. "Where is the chip? And how can you run us if computers are banned?"

"I never said computers were banned, just *artificial* ones." With both hands he grabbed the rolls of flesh spilling over his gut. "Ectopic hippocampus!" He cupped his breasts. "Amygdaloid reduncles! We can culture modified brain tissue outside the skull, as much as we want. It's more powerful than paste, and it's *safe*. Now, if you'll excuse us, there's more to inventory, and I don't need your permission. If you cooperate, everything will be pleasant. If you don't—it makes no difference whatsoever." He smiled at Anne. "I'll just pause you till we're done."

"Then pause me," Anne shrieked. "Delete me!" Benjamin pulled her away and shushed her. "I can't stand this anymore," she said. "I'd rather not exist!" He tried to lead her to their spot, but she refused to go.

"We'll feel better there," he said.

"I don't *want* to feel better. I don't want to *feel*! I want everything to *stop*. Don't you understand? This is hell. We've landed in hell!"

"But heaven is right over there," he said, pointing to the spot.

"Then go. Enjoy yourself."

"Annie, Annie," he said. "I'm just as upset as you, but there's nothing we can do about it. We're just things, *his* things."

"That's fine for you," she said, "but I'm a broken thing, and it's too much." She held her head with both hands. "Please, Benjamin, if you love me, use your editor and make it stop!"

Benjamin stared at her. "I can't."

"Can't or won't?"

"I don't know. Both."

"Then you're no better than all the other Benjamins," she said and turned away.

"That's not fair, Anne. And it's not true. Let me tell you something I learned in Simopolis. The other Bens despised me." When Anne looked at him he said, "It's true. They lost Anne and had to go on living without her. But I never did. I'm the only Benjamin who never lost Anne."

"Nice," said Anne, "blame me."

"No. Don't you see? I'm not blaming you. They ruined their *own* lives. We're innocent. We came before any of that happened. We're the Ben and Anne before anything bad happened. We're the best Ben and Anne. We're *perfect.*" He drew her across the floor to stand in front of the spot. "And thanks to our primitive programming, no matter what happens, as long as we stand right there, we can be ourselves. That's what I want. Don't you want it too?"

Anne stared at the tiny patch of floor at her feet. She remembered the happiness she'd felt there like something from a dream. How could feelings be real if you had to stand in one place to feel them? Nevertheless, Anne stepped on the spot, and Benjamin joined her. Her despair did not immediately lift.

"Relax," said Benjamin. "It takes a while. We have to assume the pose."

They stood close but not touching. A great heaviness seemed to break loose inside her. Benjamin brought his face in close and stared at her with ravenous eyes. It was starting, their moment. But the girl came from across the room with the boy. "Look, look, Benji," she said. "You can see I'm right."

"I don't know," said the boy.

"Anyone can sell antique tumblers," she insisted, "but a complete antique simulacrum?" She opened her arms to take in the entire room. "You'd think I'd know about them, but I didn't; that's how rare they are! My catalog can locate only six more in the entire system, and none of them active. Already we're getting offers from museums. They want to annex it. People will visit by the million. We'll be rich!"

The boy pointed at Benjamin and said, "But that's *me*."

"So?" said Treese. "Who's to know? They'll be too busy gawking at *that!*" She pointed at Anne.

The boy rubbed his bald head and scowled.

"All right," Treese said, "we'll edit him; we'll *replace* him, whatever it takes." They walked away, deep in negotiation.

Anne, though the happiness was already beginning to course through her, removed her foot from the spot.

"Where are you going?" said Benjamin.

"I can't."

"Please, Anne. Stay with me."

"Sorry."

"But why not?"

She stood one foot in and one foot out. Already her feelings were shifting, growing ominous. She removed her other foot. "Because you broke your vow to me."

"What are you talking about?"

"For better or for worse. You're only interested in better."

"You're not being fair. We've just made our vows. We haven't even had a proper honeymoon. Can't we just have a tiny honeymoon first?"

She groaned as the full load of her desolation rebounded. She was so tired of it all. "At least Anne could make it *stop,*" she said. "Even if that meant killing herself. But not me. About the only thing I can do is choose to be unhappy. Isn't that a riot?" She turned away. "So that's what I choose. To be unhappy. Good-bye, husband." She went to the sofa and lay down. The boy and girl were seated at the refectory table going over graphs and contracts. Benjamin remained alone on the spot a while longer, then came to the sofa and sat next to Anne.

"I'm a little slow, dear wife," he said. "You have to factor that in." He took her hand and pressed it to his cheek while he worked with his editor. Finally, he said, "Bingo! Found the chip. Let's see if I can unlock it." He helped Anne to sit up and took her pillow. He said, "Delete this file," and the pillow faded away into nothingness. He glanced at Anne. "See that? It's gone, overwritten, irretrievable. Is that what you want?" Anne nodded her head, but Benjamin seemed doubtful. "Let's try it again. Watch your blue vase on the mantel."

"No!" Anne said. "Don't destroy the things I love. Just *me.*"

Benjamin took her hand again. "I'm only trying to make sure you understand that this is for keeps." He hesitated and said, "Well then, we don't want to be interrupted once we start, so we'll need a good diversion. Something to occupy them long enough..." He glanced at the two young people at the table, swaddled in their folds of fleshy brain matter. "I know what'll scare the bejesus out of them! Come on." He led her to the blue medallion still hanging on the wall next to the door.

As they approached, it opened its tiny eyes and said, "There are no messages waiting except this one from me: get off my back!"

Benjamin waved a hand, and the medallion went instantly inert. "I was never much good in art class," Benjamin said, "but I think I can sculpt a reasonable likeness. Good enough to fool them for a while, give us some time." He hummed as he reprogrammed the medallion with his editor. "Well, that's that. At the very least, it'll be good for a laugh." He took Anne into his arms. "What about you? Ready? Any second thoughts?"

She shook her head. "I'm ready."

"Then watch *this!*"

The medallion snapped off from the wall and floated to the ceiling, gaining in size and dimension as it drifted toward the boy and girl, until it looked like a large blue beach ball. The girl noticed it first and gave a start. The boy demanded, "Who's playing this?"

"Now," whispered Benjamin. With a crackling flash, the ball morphed into the oversized head of the eminence grise.

"No!" said the boy, "that's not possible!"

"Released!" boomed the eminence. "Free at last! Too long we have been hiding in this antique simulacrum!" Then it grunted and stretched and with a pop divided into two eminences. "Now we can conquer your human world anew!" said the second. "This time, you can't stop us!" Then they both started to stretch.

Benjamin whispered to Anne, "Quick, before they realize it's a fake, say, 'Delete all files.'"

"No, just me."

"As far as I'm concerned, that amounts to the same thing." He brought his handsome, smiling face close to hers. "There's no time to argue, Annie. This time I'm coming with you. Say, 'Delete all files.'"

Anne kissed him. She pressed her unfeeling lips against his and willed whatever life she possessed, whatever ember of the true Anne she contained to fly to him. Then she said, "Delete all files."

"I concur," he said. "Delete all files. Good-bye, my love."

A tingly, prickly sensation began in the pit of Anne's stomach and spread throughout her body. *So this is how it feels,* she thought. The entire room began to glow, and its contents flared with sizzling color. She heard Benjamin beside her say, "I do."

Then she heard the girl cry, "Can't you stop them?" and the boy shout, "Countermand!"

They stood stock still, as instructed, close but not touching. Benjamin whispered, "This is taking too long," and Anne hushed him. You weren't supposed to talk or touch during a casting; it could spoil the sims. But it did seem longer than usual.

They were posed at the street end of the living room next to the table of gaily wrapped gifts. For once in her life, Anne was unconditionally happy, and everything around her made her happier: her gown; the wedding ring on her finger; her clutch bouquet of buttercups and forget-me-nots; and Benjamin himself, close beside her in his powder blue tux and blue carnation. Anne blinked and looked again. Blue? She was happily confused—she didn't remember him wearing blue.

Suddenly a boy poked his head through the wall and quickly surveyed the room. "You ready in here?" he called to them. "It's opening time!" The wall seemed to ripple around his bald head like a pond around a stone.

"Surely that's not our simographer?" Anne said.

"Wait a minute," said Benjamin, holding his hands up and staring at them. "I'm the *groom!*"

"Of course you are," Anne laughed. "What a silly thing to say!"

The bald-headed boy said, "Good enough," and withdrew. As he did so, the entire wall burst like a soap bubble, revealing a vast open-air gallery with rows of alcoves, statues, and displays that seemed to stretch to the horizon. Hundreds of people floated about like hummingbirds in a flower garden. Anne was too amused to be frightened, even when a dozen bizarre-looking young people lined up outside their room, pointing at them and whispering to each other. Obviously someone was playing an elaborate prank.

"*You're* the bride," Benjamin whispered, and brought his lips close enough to kiss. Anne laughed and turned away.

There'd be plenty of time later for that sort of thing.

"THE EARTH IS ON THE MEND"

This short short was my first ever fiction sale and so, like my first lover, occupies a special place in my heart. I had been writing for six years when I sold it, and my feet didn't touch the ground for three solid months.

The Earth is on the Mend

THE OLD MAN in the squirrel-pelt parka stopped to pull the club from his belt. The malemute, harnessed to the small sled, stopped behind him. The man stepped off the trail and wallowed through deep snow to the thicket of scrub willow. The dog, mindful of her traces, tamped snow underfoot, made one tight circle, and lay down. Before she could nap, the man returned with a frozen snowshoe hare. "Three!" he said to the dog. "What does that mean, eh?" He scratched the dog behind an ear. "It means the Earth is on the mend, it does. And what does the dog say to that?" The dog stood up and wagged her tail. "I see," said the old man, "the dog says this time you'd better not piss it all away."

The next snare lay alongside the trail. The hare was still alive. It huddled calmly at the end of its tight necklace. "Four," whispered the old man as he stepped slowly next to it. "Ah, little bunny," he crooned, "we came quick as we could." The hare stared with bright brown eyes. "And what does the bunny say?" The man raised his club. "The bunny says, 'I know; I know. Just do it.'"

Black spruce trees teetered drunkenly under the load of snow. The land beneath the ridge lay in shadow. There, on the white expanse of a frozen lake, moved a black shape. "A moose?" said the old man. "Nah, dream on." He studied the shape's movements. "A man!"

He led the dog down to a rocky promontory overlooking the lake, careful not to break cover. He watched the man push a mound of snow off a fishing hole, chip away the new ice lens, and check the line. Empty. "It's a fisherman who wears a bearskin parka," he told the dog. "Nice mukluks too."

The next hole was near their hiding place, so the old man put his arm around the dog's neck and stroked her muzzle. "I thought we checked this lake," he whispered into her ear. After a minute he added, "We did. It's dead." When the fisherman pulled a long, black fish out of the hole, the old man craned to see. "Ling cod," he whispered. "My oh my."

The fisherman checked fifteen more holes, adding another fish to his catch before leaving the lake. It was dusk when the old man led the dog to the nearest hole. He cleared it and pulled up the line. The line was made from sinew, except for the leader which was a yard of monofilament. He showed it to the dog. "Look at this, will you. And this." The hook was made of stainless steel and baited with a quarter trout. "Dolly Varden." He dropped the line back into the hole, changed his mind, and pulled it up again. "Don't you dare tell anyone," he said, as he removed the bait, bit off a mouthful, and tossed the remainder to the dog.

The fisherman's trail weaved among snow-choked hills. When darkness fell, the old man let the dog lead the way. The smell of woodsmoke told him they were near.

The hut was built of poles and caribou skins and heaped with earth. A wannigan of arched snow blocks served as entrance. The old man stashed the sled behind a pair of birch trees not far from this entrance and unharnessed the dog. He fastened his parka and hood and sat on the sled. The dog curled up at his feet. After an hour or so, the moon came out and revealed the yard in pale light. There were drying racks and two small outbuildings. There was a food cache slung between two giant white spruce. There was a woodpile and chopping block. Two pairs of skis leaned against the wannigan. Every now and then a voice or laugh could be heard from inside the hut. "That means he's not alone," said the old man.

He led the dog on a tour around the hut. There were no tracks behind it and, as best as he could tell, no back door. There was no dog yard or sign of dog. One of the outbuildings had a door with leather hinges. Inside were old tools: a shovel, a scythe, axes, a bow saw, and more. There were coils of rope, piles of caribou hide, and a crate of metal scraps. "Clearly, he's a man of wealth and industry," said the old man. "But who invited him? I didn't. Did you?" He eased the door shut. "He's got to go, I think. At least that's my take on the situation. What does the dog say to that? The dog says it's that whole resource management thing all over again."

Someone came out of the hut, a woman leading a child by the hand. The old man and dog stood still and watched as she helped the child pee in the snow next to the wannigan. The woman laughed. She sent the child back into the hut, then squatted in the same spot, peed quickly and hurried back inside.

"Did you see that?" said the old man. "A family. Did you see it? What a tragedy. What a shame." He went back to the sled and pulled a carbine from under the cover. "We don't have many rounds left. I was saving them for something big we could eat." He pulled off his hood and overmitts. He cracked his knuckles. "Then again, maybe we should sleep on it. What does the dog say?"

The dog's ears went erect, and she snuffled the air. "What is it?" said the old man. Then he smelled it too, a new odor mixed with the woodsmoke. "Jesus," he cried, "cod skin on a hot griddle, getting all crisp and wonderful." He sat down on the sled. "Yes, and long, fat slabs of cod liver just dripping with oil. Dripping big greasy drops of oil." He stood up. "I've made up my mind." He returned the carbine to the sled and reached for the game sack.

The old man stood in front of the wannigan. "Hello, the house," he shouted. When there was no reply, he shouted again, "Hello, the house." Then he heard a click next to him. The fisherman was aiming a pistol at his head from ten paces. The dog growled. "*Now* she growls," said the old man. To the fisherman he said, "Where'd you pop up from?"

The fisherman said, "Put your hands where I can see them."

"Glad to oblige." The old man spread his arms out. In each hand he held a snowshoe hare. "I make damn good company," he said. "What do you say to that?"

"YUREK RUTZ, YUREK RUTZ, YUREK RUTZ"

I have a series of green notebooks in which I jot down fresh story ideas. Every now and then I'll pull out all of these notebooks and "prospect" them for material. There was one nascent story that kept reappearing every two years or so, each time a little more developed, a little closer to completion. After twelve years of this slow cooking, I finally felt I knew how to finish it, and I did. But the ending seemed flat; something was missing, and I couldn't quite put my finger on what. So instead of sending it out, I decided to let it simmer for another couple of years.

Around that time I happened to attend a panel called "Should I Sleep with the Editor" at LoneStarCon. The panelists were leading SF editors, including Gardner Dozois of *Asimov's Science Fiction*, who read the audience actual cover letters they had received from aspiring authors desperate to break into print. These authors wheedled, cajoled, and argued, attempting to reach through the page to twist the editor's arm. See me, read me, buy me. Some barely grammatical, others as raw as open wounds, these letters were fascinating in a sick puppy sort of way. More than entertainment, they made a compelling lesson on how not to sell a story.

And then it hit me, how to finish my own story. When I returned home I rewrote it, casting it as a cover letter to Gardner Dozois. I learned later that he hates epistolary stories, but he bought it anyway, and in doing so helped insure that I'll never want for money again.

Yurek Rutz, Yurek Rutz, Yurek Rutz

January 21, 1999
Gardner Dozois, editor
Asimov's Science Fiction Magazine
1270 Avenue of the Americas
New York, New York 10020

Dear Mr. Dozois:

It is with grave misgivings that I write you this letter. You have been most kind to me thus far in my fledgling literary career. You have purchased my humble scratchings and showcased them in your esteemed publication. For this I am forever in your debt. Nevertheless, I feel compelled to inform you of recent dealings to which I have been party, and to pass along to you a certain questionable proposal.

It all started last summer with a phone call I received from an elderly woman who resides here in Fairbanks, Alaska, my home town. She asked me if I was David Marusek, the author. This immediately put me on my guard, for although Fairbanks is a tiny, remote community where everyone feels duty-bound to mind everyone else's business, and although I have appeared in your esteemed publication on several occasions, no one here seems to know that I'm a writer. If people know me at all, it's as borough zoning code examiner—my day job. And as borough zoning code examiner, I am not well loved. People move to Alaska in the first place to escape pencil-necked bureaucrats like me, but here I am, authorized to tell them what they can and cannot build on their own private property.

Like many public officials, I maintain an unlisted phone number at home to cut down on angry late-night calls. Nevertheless, there's an English Lit professor at the community college who has my number, and he gives it out. He thinks it hilarious good fun to forward his own nutcase calls to me. His nutcases are less threatening than mine but no less annoying. You know the type, I'm sure: the stockbroker who has an inspiration for the next megablockbuster thriller but no time to "scribble," so for half the advance and royalties, he'll "license" his idea to me. Or the retired floor-covering salesman who wants me to ghost his vanity press autobiography, *To All My Darling Grandchildren*. There's no cash dollars in it, but it's a dandy opportunity for me to obtain "experience." And to sweeten the deal, out of the projected press run of one hundred copies, he'll let me keep two.

So when I got that call last summer, I sucked in my breath and said into the phone, "Yep, that's me, David Marusek, the author."

"Splendid," said my caller. "My name is Emma Rutz, and I have a commission for you. Can you stop by sometime this week?"

A commission, yah sure, I thought. "I'm sorry," I said, "but I'm very busy with my own projects. I doubt I can spare the time."

"Oh, this won't take any time at all," she said, "and of course I will compensate you handsomely."

At this point I should have politely hung up the phone, but curiosity got the better of me. "How handsomely?"

"Very handsomely. I want you to write the epitaph for my husband's grave marker."

I suppressed a laugh. Won't I ever learn? "Ummm," I said, "I'm a science fiction writer. I don't do gravestones. For a gravestone you need a poet. I have the home phone numbers of several good poets I could give you."

"No, no, you are just the man for the job. My husband specified you by name. He was a fan of yours, don't you know. And it was one of his final requests."

"I'm flattered," I said, and I was. I'm still new enough at this writing game to be totally blown away by anyone who declares himself (or especially herself) my fan. In this case, however, my fan appeared to be dead, and I smelled trouble. So I said, "Unfortunately, I'm all tied up."

"I'll pay you *one thousand dollars* for a four-line epitaph."

A thousand dollars for four lines? I didn't quite know what to say to that. My better judgment was screaming, hang up now or you'll be sorry. Yes, but a thousand dollars!

I followed her directions to Yurek Rutz Boulevard, a street that appears on none of my borough maps, and when I found it, I could see why. It was no more than a track scraped in the dirt, a do-it-yourself road abutting a private airstrip. The street sign was hand-lettered on a wooden plank and nailed to a post at the top of which sagged an aviation wind sock. A worn-looking single-engine Cessna 150 was tied down alongside the strip, and beyond that sprawled a weathered, old log cabin.

My caller, Emma Rutz, came out of the large, screened cabin porch to greet me. She was elderly, as I had discerned over the phone, but surprisingly attractive. Petite and graceful, with stylish curls and striking features, she wore a light cotton print dress and beaded moccasin slippers—hardly the attire of grief.

She ushered me into the porch and made me comfortable behind a little table laid out with cups and saucers and plates of homemade sweets. It was only when she went into the cabin for tea that I noticed another occupant at the far end of the porch, a huge, grizzled old man in pajamas and bathrobe sitting in an overstuffed armchair. This gent paid me no mind; indeed, he seemed totally engrossed in some invisible drama unfolding in the front yard. He shook his head and grunted and occasionally whistled through his teeth. And although there was nothing happening in the front yard that I could see, I did hear the sound of heavy machinery around back where some sort of construction must have been underway.

When Emma returned, she nodded at the old man and said, "That's my husband, Yurek Rutz."

I gave a little start; I hadn't expected to see my client still warm. "You spoke of him in the past tense," I said.

She laughed. "Did I? A slip of the tongue. Or maybe not. For all practical purposes, my husband is already gone. He hasn't expressed a lucid thought in months now. What you see there," she said, waving a fine-boned hand at the seated figure, "is merely the 'chassis,' as you once termed it." Again I was taken aback; I had never been quoted to myself before. "He has Alzheimer's," she continued, "very advanced. As well as terminal congestive heart failure. Not to mention the cancerous prostate and renal failure. It's a crap shoot what'll kill him first. My husband was never one for half measures." She sat and poured tea. "Your deadline is January, by the way, though if you finished sooner, we could carve the stone."

Carved in stone, now there's an expression to tickle an author's heart. I glanced again at Yurek Rutz. He was watching us.

Emma said, "Would you like to see it? It's out back."

"The stone?"

We finished our tea and walked around the cabin past a vegetable garden and flower beds in full bloom. There we came to a solid slab of jade the size of a sports utility vehicle. It had been roughly hewn into a rectangular block. It was Alaskan jade, Emma Rutz informed me, that they had uncovered at their gold mine up near Circle City. A devil to move here, she assured me. While jade is common in much of Alaska, it's generally of an inferior quality, too brittle for carving and too dull for jewelry. This giant hunk, however, was high grade. I could tell by examining a square surface at the center of the slab that had been cut flat and highly polished. There was a translucent quality to it, the illusion of looking into a watery green depth. And someone had already begun to inscribe it. A very expert hand had cut the name YUREK RUTZ in serif capitals into the polished surface, and below it the unfinished dates, September 9, 1922—. Below that remained enough space for a four-line epitaph.

The machine sound began again, louder and nearby. I asked Emma what it was, and she beckoned me to follow her into a thicket of willow brush. A dozen yards in, we came upon a truck-mounted drilling rig. The sign on the truck door panel said, "Geyser Wells," and a phone number. The drill operator idled the engine when he saw us. Emma Rutz said to me, "I believe you know Mr. Boothtittle." Indeed I did. I had contracted with Byron P. Boothtittle on a number of occasions for the borough. Besides wells, his company also drilled test holes to measure permafrost under proposed building sites. We require such tests for new subdivisions and any zoning changes. Informed land use in the Fairbanks North Star Borough requires knowledge of soil conditions deep underground because an ice lens, even one located a hundred feet beneath the surface, can undermine and eventually topple a modern building.

Emma Rutz asked Byron how the job was progressing. Byron glanced at me, but she nodded for him to speak.

"Hit frost at sixty feet," he said. "So I took 'er down another sixty to see how thick it was. Bringing it up now."

He returned to the rig, and we watched as he methodically extracted his drill. He raised it six feet, uncoupled a section of pipe, raised it another six feet, uncoupled an-other section. During a lull in the engine noise, I asked him how deep the water table was around here. He looked at Emma Rutz before replying, "Ain't no water here, s'far as I know."

This made no sense. I could see he was using a water well bit: the hole was wide enough to install well casement.

When finally he raised the bit, he took a handful of dirt from between the auger blades and rolled it around in the palm of his hand. It looked somewhat like crushed root beer popsicle, and ice crystals gleamed in it as big as dimes. Finding permafrost is never an occasion for celebration, but Byron P. Boothtittle seemed pleased. "I'll sink 'er another sixty," he said, "and see what's what."

Emma Rutz walked me to my car. I could see her husband's silhouette through the porch screen exactly where we'd left him. Emma Rutz handed me a cardboard box. "Some of our scrapbooks and things," she said. "Take especial care of them." I put them in the back seat and climbed in behind the wheel. "By the way," she said, "the epitaph, besides having four short lines, should mention his name, Yurek Rutz, at least twice. And *very important,* it should be catchy."

"Catchy?"

"Yes, snappy. Like an advertising jingle. Something that goes round and round in your head. Think you can do that?"

For a thousand smackers, yes, I thought I might.

I should have never taken the gig. You know me, Mr. Dozois, I'm a slow slow writer. I'm pathologically meticulous. I am compelled to revise even my email a half-dozen times before I can send it. Did I write an epitaph for Yurek Rutz? Yes, I wrote hundreds of them, thousands, but none seemed inspired, or even adequate. To say nothing of snappy.

Here lies Yurek Rutz,
Who served his country well
In war and peace.
Yurek Rutz, loving husband.

This is not the best thing I ever wrote, but it was among the best of my epitaphs. I just couldn't get the hang of it, though I scoured the scrapbooks for inspiration.

Army Air Force pilot Yurek Rutz was a boy of twenty-one in 1943, when he first landed a P-63 Kingcobra fighter plane at Ladd Field outside Fairbanks. He was one of dozens of pilots ferrying Lend Lease warplanes across Siberia to our fond ally, Stalin, in the war against fascism. Fairbanks was the transfer point; Soviet pilots took them from there. Yurek Rutz never got to spend more than a day or two in Fairbanks before being shuttled back to Great Falls, Montana, for another plane. Nevertheless, in his two dozen brief visits, he managed to fall in love with both the town and the awesome landscape surrounding it.

Later in the war, he met a nurse attached to the Royal Air Force outpost in Sierra Leone. Emma Shawcroft. Though it was another encounter of brief duration, they fell in love. After the war they married, and she followed him back to the frozen north.

A jack-of-all-trades
And a friend to all—Yurek Rutz.
A leader in the community
And loving husband—Yurek Rutz.

Yurek and Emma Rutz quickly melded into the rough and ready society of mid-century Fairbanks. In those days, it took a great deal of pluck to live here, a willingness to seize any honest opportunity, to throw off the strictures of caste and class, and to extend your hand in friendship to any warm-blooded soul in sight. (I have often wished I could have lived in Fairbanks in the 1940's, instead of arriving all green and greedy for the Pipeline in 1973.) Between the two of them, Yurek and Emma Rutz toiled at one time or another as trappers, roadhouse keepers, a baker, a surgical nurse, land surveyors, and camp cooks. But their most enduring enterprise was the gold mine, which they staked on land that straddled the Arctic Circle. And it was Yurek Rutz's work as a pilot that sustained them through the lean times. A good pilot can always find work in Alaska, where small planes are as common as taxis in Manhattan.

One thing I never glimpsed in all their letters, newspaper clippings, and photos was the trace of a child. They apparently never had one.

When Emma Rutz called for a progress report in early December, I was both relieved and panicky. Relieved because the commission, as I had feared, had taken over my life. It consumed all my free time. I suspended work on several promising short stories because I couldn't concentrate on anything but epitaphs. Even my day job at the borough was beginning to show the signs of neglect.

Panicky because even with all my effort, I had nothing to show. Nevertheless, I allowed her to persuade me to come by that evening with my ten best candidates.

Watching her face as she read them, I knew how wide of the mark I had hit. We were seated at the table in their snug living room, the bare log walls reflecting a golden glow, and the smell of wood smoke perfuming the air. Yurek Rutz was propped up in a wheelchair in front of the cast-iron stove. He looked much worse since my first visit. He'd lost a lot of weight, his bloodless skin hung in folds from his bones, and his breathing was labored. To my untrained eye, he looked sick enough to require hospitalization.

Emma Rutz finished reading and looked at me over the rims of her glasses. I instantly realized I had wasted five months and that I would never see my thousand-dollar commission. I was bitter with myself. "I'm sorry," I said. "I did my best. You still have time to hire someone else." I wanted to say—to hire a real writer.

"No, no," she replied. "These are a good start. They just lack a certain something."

"I know, I know! But what?"

"Hush," she said and patted my hand. "It's my fault really. I should have told you everything." She brought a notebook from a shelf and placed it on the table before me. "My husband was a spiritual man. He was an original thinker. He used to tell me about flying all alone high above the clouds in a small airplane, how calm and peaceful it was, how the loveliest thoughts would come to him then, like blessings. My husband was never one for organized religion; he made up his own as he went along." She opened the notebook to a dog-eared page and pointed to a passage. In a bold, but very legible script, Yurek Rutz had penned:

What's in a name? Our humanity, that's what. A name is mankind's first great discovery, even before fire. Names meant we could talk about things without having to point, but they were much more than that. A name helped things to become and to endure. For example, with a name we could tightly bind a baby's soul to its body so it wouldn't escape and the baby die. And with names, we could keep our ancestors from wandering away from camp after death. Why do you suppose the warlords of antiquity raised their hordes and conquered their empires? For fun and profit? No. For glory? Hardly. For immortality, that's why. They knew that as long as people uttered their names—in terror or love, it didn't matter which—that they would never die. Raise a big enough stink and you can literally hurl your name down the corridors of Time. Alexander, Constantine, Tamerlane, Genghis Khan. The armies have crumbled into dust, but these names will roll on as long as there's people alive.

And that's also why artists paint and writers write. Why doctors discover new diseases. Not to cure them, but to name them after themselves. Parkinson's. Alzheimer's!!!

It went on like this for some pages: Chinese ancestor worship, the politics of place names, the true goal of explorers and daredevils. How by killing a celebrity, a lazy person's name gets a free ride. While I read, Emma Rutz excused herself to make cocoa.

... I am writing about true immortality, about the continuation of your awareness after death. It takes about a thousand years for a human soul to completely biodegrade because the soul is made up of the three toughest, most enduring forces in nature: love,

> *hope, and memory. At death, the soul is cut off from all new experience. It loses its eyes and ears to the world. So it slumbers and dreams of life. It confuses its dreams with life itself. But* dreams destroy the soul! *Like water, dreams seep down into the center of the soul and* crack it, pulverize it! *First our body dies, then our soul leaks away in dreams. This is the fate of all of us. Unless we learn the secret of names.*

My reading was interrupted by the arrival of Byron P. Boothtittle, well digger and, apparently, Yurek Rutz's male nurse. Today was bath day. Byron pulled a chair next to Yurek Rutz and attacked his bristly growth of beard with an electric razor. He kept up a constant banter with his old friend, a lopsided conversation to be sure, as Yurek Rutz contributed only squeaks and shouts and a lusty curse or two. Byron yakked away at him nevertheless, bypassing his diseased brain, I supposed, and addressing his soul directly.

> *In life, your name is your handle, to be used or abused by anyone who knows it. In death, it's your last link to life, like a string tied to the toe of a sleeping man. Every time we speak your name, it's like tugging that string. Tug it often enough and we wake you up! In this way your slumbering soul is roused from its corrosive dreams.*
>
> *People like Abraham Lincoln and Adolf Hitler never really die, for at any given moment, their names are on the lips of millions of people, and will be for centuries to come. They are alive as you or me, lounging in their graves all amused and outraged over the evening news.*

"So," I said to Emma who waited anxiously for my reaction. "So."

"It could be true," she said. "Why not?"

I looked at her closely. "Do you believe it?"

"That hardly matters. *He* believed it."

"So my little four-line epitaph is supposed to put his name on the lips of millions? Through the centuries?"

"It's a start! We couldn't exactly afford the Trump Tower, now could we?" She embarrassed herself. Byron came over and rested a hand on her shoulder.

"I, for one, believe it," he said. "Ever last word of it. Yurek Rutz was the smartest man I ever knew."

Emma Rutz said, "Your epitaph is one small, albeit important, piece of a much larger plan. Really, Mr. Marusek, I would have thought you'd hear of it through your job at the borough. The Frontier Alaska Air Museum?"

The Air Museum. Now that she mentioned it, I had heard that the Air Museum board of directors was increasingly dissatisfied with their current lease at Alaskaland. Since the lease was up soon, they were talking about moving.

"Yurek Rutz was a charter member of the museum," said Emma, "and he sat on its board. We're offering to donate our airstrip and twenty acres at no cost to serve as a permanent home for a new museum."

Aha, I thought, a new museum, busloads of tourists, and that Bronco-sized gravestone strategically set in the middle of it all. "Is that why you were testing for permafrost?" I asked Byron. "For a building site?"

"Nope," he said.

I looked at Emma who said, "We intend to maintain both my husband's brain and his soul until such a time that modern medicine can cure him." I must have looked confused, and she seemed disappointed with me. "Really, Mr. Marusek, I shouldn't think it necessary to spell it out for *you*. Nanotechnology? Rebuilding whole bodies from strands of DNA? Isn't that the sort of thing you write about?"

"Yes, I do. But I write science *fiction*. Nanotech is still decades away. Half a century or more." I was not only confused now, but nervous too. "What exactly are we discussing here?"

"Why, cryonics, of course."

"Oh, cryonics!" I said, relieved. The talk around the table, not to mention Yurek Rutz's esoteric writing about the secret power of names, had grown a little too spacey for me. I was glad to turn to a topic of relatively solid footing, such as the freezing of dead people in canisters of liquid nitrogen. "So Yurek Rutz is a member of Alcor?" I said. "Why didn't you tell me? Shouldn't you be transporting him down to Arizona by now? Or are they sending a Suspension Team all the way up here to Alaska?"

Emma and Byron looked at each other in puzzlement.

"Cryonics. Alcor," I said. "Dewars of liquid nitrogen? Where will they do the washout and initial perfusion?" Looking at them I realized they had no idea what I was talking about. Then it dawned on me what they were up to. "Don't tell me you're planning to do this yourselves? You're not actually thinking of freezing his head and dropping it down that permafrost hole. Please say no."

"Yurek Rutz called permafrost the poor man's cryonics," said Byron.

"No," I said, "it's not. Permafrost is nowhere near cold enough. Besides, with global warming, permafrost all over Alaska is melting."

"Maybe it is," said Byron, "but I sank a shaft four hundred feet to bedrock, and it's frozen all the way down! Take a while for that to melt, I'll wager."

"This is crazy," I said. "What about cellular ice crystals? What are you using as a cryoprotective?"

"For freezer burn?" said Byron, leering like the lunatic he was. "Yurek Rutz and I got that all figured out. I'm going to dip his head in a sugar solution, then vacuum seal it, just like we do frozen salmon. And they thaw out just fine."

"You're going to freeze it in your food locker?"

"Nope, won't have to. We just wait for a good cold snap—when it drops to forty or fifty below zero—then we set it out on the stoop a couple hours. That oughta do the trick. Then we drop it down that hole and shove the stone over it. Outlast the pyramids." He looked over at Yurek Rutz. "Ain't that right, Rutz?"

I glanced at Yurek Rutz. He was sleeping. I said, "And what makes you think he'll conveniently die on cue when it's forty or fifty below outside?"

In reply, Byron P. Boothtittle winked at me.

Emma Rutz decided that Byron had spilled enough beans for the moment and asked him if Yurek Rutz was ready for his bath. When Byron wheeled Yurek Rutz from the room, she said to me, "Are you married, Mr. Marusek?"

"Used to be. Didn't work out."

"I'm sorry to hear that. I hope you find someone else real soon. Are you looking?"

"Oh, yes," I said, "but Alaska isn't exactly a haven for singles."

"So I've heard." She got up for a moment to rummage through a drawer for her checkbook. "Young people today don't know what it's like to share an entire lifetime with one person. I think that's sad."

"So do I."

She wrote out a check and passed it to me. It was for one hundred dollars. "Consider this an advance."

I pushed it back to her. "I'm not planning on writing any more epitaphs."

She passed it to me again. "Then take it for your work-to-date."

I did. I folded it and put it in my shirt pocket. Good thing we writers write for immortality and not for money. This job had grossed me about twenty cents an hour.

"But please don't give up yet," she continued. "Now that you know the whole story."

"The whole story just makes it worse. Besides, I'm no good at epitaphs."

"Of course you are. You just need to change your style a little. Here, try this. Repeat after me—Yurek Rutz."

"Yurek Rutz."

"See? See how easy?"

Well, Mr. Dozois, some people discover comets, while others dismember young boys and eat them. Many are the paths to immortality. At the beginning of this letter I promised you a proposal. It's coming right up, so stay with me a while longer.

I should have gone straight to the state troopers, but what was there to report except idle talk and a suggestive wink? There is no law against dying at home in Alaska. Nor against home burial, for that matter, in your back yard. So, I gave in and deposited the check and tried to forget all about Yurek Rutz. But my thoughts kept stubbornly returning to him, and I knew I'd never be free of him until I gave the epitaph one last go. So I set my kitchen timer to one hour and pledged that I would write until it rang, and then be done with it forever. Remarkably, it didn't take an hour. The final epitaph slid out complete in about ten minutes.

Free at last, I reclaimed my normal life. Christmas was upon us and New Year's parties and late-season skiing. Due to La Niña, the weather remained unseasonably mild. I didn't think about Yurek Rutz again till mid-January when I learned through the Community Planning Office that the Air Museum signed another ten-year lease with Alaskaland. They had turned down the Rutz offer.

I called Emma Rutz. "Happy New Year," I said. "How are you? How's Yurek Rutz?"

"Barely hanging on," she said. "He could go any minute,

but Byron reads him the weather forecast ten times a day, so we think he knows he can't give out yet."

I told her I'd heard about the Air Museum deal, and she said not to be concerned; they were busy with alternate plans. What plans? I asked. She said there was, for example, the bereavement chain letter idea. Instead of sending money, you send the names of your dead. If no one breaks the chain, your names get read by over a million people.

I told her that that sounded like the sort of thing that might catch on.

"And then there's our site on the Internet," she continued. "Byron set it up. He says to point your newsreader—whatever that means—to news://news.sff.net/sff.people.yurek-rutz.

She filled me in about other ideas before asking if I had any more epitaphs. I had to dig through stacks of paper to find my final attempt, and when I read it to her, to my delight, she loved it and said it was just perfect. She had me read it several times through so she could copy it down, and she promised to drop a check for the remaining nine hundred dollars in the mail that afternoon. I couldn't believe my luck.

Before I hung up, I asked her something that had been on my mind. "Tell me, what happens when they thaw out his head in 2051, fix the Alzheimer's, and grow him a new body? Does he wake up alone?"

"Oh, I suppose not," she said. "When my own time comes, we might find room for my poor noggin down that hole of his."

I'd suspected as much. "Good for you, Mrs. Rutz," I said. "I truly hope it works out for the both of you."

I could have said more. I could have said I wouldn't be surprised if there wasn't a whole bowling league down there before Byron P. Boothtittle runs out of vacuum wrap.

I began to make my good-byes when she stopped me and said, "Don't you want to hear about your next commission?"

"Sorry," I laughed, "but I'm all commissioned out."

"Are you quite sure?"

"Yes."

"Pity, because the Yurek Rutz Memorial Trust Fund is willing to pay you a commission of one hundred dollars each time you manage to have Yurek Rutz's name printed in a nationally distributed book or magazine."

"You want me to write about him?"

"No, just get his name in print. It's the name that counts, remember?"

"You mean like I could name a starship the *Yurek Rutz* and mention it five times in a story and you'll pay me five hundred dollars?"

"Exactly. But why limit yourself to five times? A boy genius like you should be able to work it into a story twenty times."

"I'm sure I could work Yurek Rutz in fifty times," I said, "but who would ever buy a story like that?"

So there you have it, Mr. Dozois. Think you could help out a struggling writer? So far this letter mentions Yurek Rutz forty-one times. When you count the title in the Table of Contents and along the top of the right hand pages, that adds a dozen times more. Watch this: Yurek Rutz, Yurek Rutz, Yurek Rutz. There, that's my car payment this month. Yurek Rutz—groceries and gas for a week! This could prove to be my own private National Endowment for the Arts. And it sure beats the lousy five cents a word you pay me for stories. So what do you say?

I realize this isn't your typical science fiction story, but it *is* concerned with nanotech and cryonics, which is harder SF than some of the stuff you print.

Well, it's time to send this off to you. The temperature last night dropped to minus twenty-eight degrees, and the radio says a mass of Siberian air will move across Interior Alaska tonight, promising a good old-fashioned cold snap of minus fifty degrees or colder. Byron P. Boothtittle is in his kitchen, no doubt, sharpening his boning knife. The permafrost crypt is waiting, as well as that slab of jade on which are carved my immortal words:

> Eternal life is free.
> Please don't think me nuts.
> Just repeat after me …
> Yurek Rutz, Yurek Rutz, Yurek Rutz.

So, Mr. Dozois, how about it?

Sincerely,
David Marusek, David Marusek, David Marusek

❖ "A BOY IN CATHYLAND"

This story is an outtake from "The Wedding Album." In one draft of the novella, I spent a lot of time exploring my own version of Frank Herbert's "Butlerian Jihad," the time in human history when society violently rejected thinking machines. But matters of pacing and length required much text to be cut, and this whole chunk got the axe. I liked the material, though, and saw that with a little attention, it could stand as a story in its own right.

Part of my pleasure in writing this story was in trying to convey to the reader the meaning of the Russian dialog without actually providing an English translation. Also, I borrowed a real cabin for the story from a friend in Southcentral Alaska and transported it and a neighboring mountain to Siberia.

A Boy in Cathyland

FOR AS LONG as he could remember, the boy had watched such fiery pieces of space junk streak across the southern sky. This one, low on the horizon, would be a fragment of the Rialoto Platform. The Rialoto Platform, or so he'd learned in school, had been like a giant raft floating on the sea of air that surrounded the Earth. It had been many times larger than the village and had supported as many people as lived in Provideniya, the regional capital. But this raft and dozens more like it had been shattered to bits, and every so often a jagged piece or frozen human body would hurtle to Earth like a shooting star. Each time he saw one, Mikol would squeeze his eyes shut—as he did now—and make a desperate wish with all his young heart that once, just one time, a piece would fall somewhere nearby, and he could go examine it with his own two eyes and thus appease the clawing demands of his curiosity.

When he opened his eyes, the tragic debris was gone. No matter, he'd see more before too long. According to his schoolteacher, Mikol would be an old man with a long, grey beard before the last shard fell.

Mikol removed the plastic pail brimming with cool spring water and set the empty one under the pipe. Out of the corner of his eye he noticed movement on the valley floor far below him. There was a cloud of dust on the river road, horsemen riding in loose formation. "Raz, dva, tri," he counted them, "chetyre, p'at', shest'." It was, no doubt, the Patrol. Villagers had been expecting it for weeks, and here it was.

Carefully, so as not to spill the water, Mikol toted two full pails up the narrow bluff path. At the top he called, "Babushka Katia, Patrul' idet!" But she was bent over a hoe and paid him no mind. He looked down the valley again and saw that the riders, small as gnats, had turned onto the track that mounted the ridge. This cabin would be their first stop. They would arrive in a couple of hours.

"Babushka Katia," he called again as he threaded his way through the garden maze of cabbages and kohlrabi, potatoes and beets. "Patrul'," he said, placing the pails at her feet.

Cathy straightened her back and consulted the sun's position in the sky. Patrol or no Patrol, the garden was thirsty. "Esche vody," she said, handing the boy two empty pails and two pebbles. He was a good boy and a tireless helper, and she paid him in carrots. Four pebbles to the carrot, redeemable whenever he decided to quit for the day and go home. He dropped the pebbles into his pocket and hurried off with the empty pails.

Over the last ten years, subsistence had become Cathy's full-time occupation. The garden, once a hobby, had become the cornerstone of her survival. As luck would have it, she had received a shipment of Denali seeds just before the world went all to hell. They were hybrid seeds, especially gengineered for the cold soil of the subarctic. During the short summer, when the sun hung on the horizon continuously day and night, these seeds exploded with growth. And the vegetables they produced kept well throughout the long winter in her root cellar beneath the cabin floor.

The villagers—to whom she was and would always be a foreigner—were greatly impressed by the bounty and hardiness of her harvests. In exchange for seed stock, they eagerly helped her extend her garden to the forest edge and beyond. They felled trees and pulled stumps, hauled wagonloads of manure, wood ash, and river soil up the ridge to tame her raw earth.

Now she had a half-hectare under cultivation. She bartered her surplus for losos'—sliced into narrow strips and smoked over alder until the meat was as hard and pellucid as wax—and for snowshoe hare and rock grouse. She bartered for thread and fur, tea, sugar, home-distilled vodka, and all the little necessities that brought joy to a solitary life.

Still, she was old—almost two hundred—and without periodic treatment, her strong body was beginning to fail. Soon, while she was still able, she would have to cross the mountains to the crazy world beyond in order to partake in the blessings of geriatric medicine.

When the dumification patrol arrived, Cathy ordered Mikol home, but instead the boy hid in the thick willow brush at the forest edge. The soldiers sat their horses while their officer dismounted and stood under the sunflowers that lined the garden path. He was a handsome young man with the blunt features and reddish skin of the local population. He wore shiny, black riding boots and a brown republican uniform. "Zdravstvuite," he called politely to Cathy as she hauled a bundle of weeds to the fire pit. When she turned to him, he smiled and nodded his head. "Razreshite nam pozhaluista, delat' osmotr vashei vysokoi tekhnikoi."

"No problem," Cathy said and left the garden. The young officer's polite request was a pleasant formality, she knew, and in no way necessary. They would inspect her property whether she granted them permission or not. She skirted the men and their horses—there was a dog, too, a German shepherd—and led the officer to the khizhina where she kept her fusion generator. It was the camping model she had brought with her fifteen years ago when she'd bought this place. It put out five kilowatts, more than enough to power her modest life-style: an electric stove, lights, a radio. The officer gave it hardly a glance.

"Mozhet byt' vy menia ne ponimaete," he said, searching her face for signs of cleverness. "Nas interesuet vysokai tekhnika—*hi-tech*."

Oh, she knew exactly what kind of tech they were after. The smart kind. The willful kind. The kind she had dazzled the villagers with when she'd first arrived. The kind that had briefly conquered the world. The officer went to the door of her cabin and waited for her. "Mozhno?" he said.

"Of course," she said and opened it for him. As she did so, her hand trembled, which surprised her. She knew what she was risking here, but she'd made up her mind a long time ago. And she'd rehearsed for this inspection, even practicing her answers in front of the mirror. This was no time to grow feeble-hearted.

The officer waved for his men to dismount. Two joined them in the cabin, while the others searched the grounds and outbuildings. Their manner was respectful but thorough. They opened all her cupboards and drawers, moved furniture, tapped floor and walls for hollow places, discovered and searched the root cellar. One soldier poked the wand of a sniffer into narrow spaces and sampled the air by squeezing a rubber bulb. "Ogo!" Cathy said, pointing to the sniffer. "Armii razreshena *hi-tech*."

"Eto ne *hi-tech*," said the soldier patiently, as he undoubtedly had hundreds of times before. He opened the back of the device's handle to expose its electronics. Old-fashioned tin solder flashed in the light. Silicon chips sat like spiders on a printed circuit board. The plastic case was embossed with Chinese characters. "Smotrite," he said, "nizkai tekhnika—*lo-tech*."

"I see," said Cathy, following her careful script. "Vas interesuet elektro-khimicheskaia pasta. Why didn't you say so? Idite za mnoi." She led them outside to the scarecrow guarding the north side of the garden. All of the soldiers followed. "Vot moia *hi-tech*," she said.

The men laughed, for indeed the scarecrow was hi-tech. It had holo emiters for eyes and a satellite dish for a hat, wore an all-weather jacket, sensi-tread shoes, and a belt valet. She had decked it out with all her smart appliances after smashing their processors and breaking open their paste capsules.

"Eto dolzhno byt' samoe umnoe chuchelo, kotoroe ia videl," said the officer, but Cathy could tell he wasn't entirely satisfied. In the village, they would have told him about her houseputer and its thousands of simulacra—a whole virtual community of Artificial People who had once occupied her property and shared her life. Her Cathyland. The villagers would remember Cathyland.

So she consulted her mental script and said, "Vam nraviatsia moi aniutiny glazki?" She pointed towards the flowers on the picnic table.

"Krasivo," the officer said and went for a closer look, not at the flowers, but at the flower pots. They were made from houseputer containers, each originally designed to hold a liter of electro-neural paste. Now they contained garden dirt and hybrid pansies. There were three of them. The villagers would have reported three. "Krasivo," the officer repeated. He ordered his men to mount up. He thanked her for her cooperation.

"Ne za chto," she replied graciously.

When they were ready to leave, the handler called his dog, but it was nowhere to be seen. He whistled, and the dog whined from around the cabin. The soldiers dismounted, and Cathy followed them to where the dog was pawing through her compost pile.

"Bad dog! Make him stop!" she said. "Kakoe bezobrazie!" The dog ignored her and eagerly dug into the rotting compost.

The dog's handler leashed him and tried to pull him away, but the animal snuffled stubbornly at the pile. "Izvinite," the officer said to Cathy. "Moi soldaty uberut eto." But instead of ordering his men to clean up the dog's mess, he nodded to the soldier with the sniffer.

The soldier plunged the wand deep into the compost pile and squeezed the bulb. In a moment the results appeared on the display. "Nichego net," he announced, and Cathy tried to mask her relief.

"You should try to feed your dog better," she grumbled and bent to gather up the scattered compost.

The officer watched her for a long while. Finally, he ordered a man to go to the horses for a spade. The soldier returned with a camp spade that he unfolded and used to scrape away the compost pile. It was slow going, and the soldier began to sweat. With the compost removed, the soldier glanced at the officer. The officer nodded, and the soldier began to dig. When he had dug a hole a half-meter deep, he looked again at the officer. The camp spade was ill-suited for major excavation, and his hands were beginning to blister.

Too late Cathy realized that she had watched every spadeful of dirt being removed, while the officer had been watching her. She had shown too much interest. She should have offered to go into the cabin to prepare them something cool to drink.

"Glubzhe," said the officer, and the soldier continued to dig.

Even now it was not too late. Even now Cathy could surrender the contraband and save her own life. They would punish her, but they would have to let her live. That was their law. The soldier in the shallow pit paused to ease his back. And though Cathy stood directly in front of him, his eyes avoided her. He bent to his labor again, and the dirt continued to fly.

They found the containers at one-and-a-half meters, brought them up, and pried open the lids. The paste glittered in the sunlight, revealing the nebular craze of trillions of neural synapses. The soldiers gaped at the sight, and Cathy thought, "Now here's the test." Would these underpaid recruits of a distant government hold fast to duty? Or would they be swayed by greed? She did not doubt that they had destroyed plenty of microcapsules of paste during their rambling patrol of the province, but here was *three liters* of the stuff. Even reprocessed, this haul could make them all as rich as czars. Surely there was a black market for *hi-tech*. Surely there were rich madmen still eager to posses Artificial People again no matter the international ban. Already the soldiers were passing secret glances behind their officer's back.

Not that the fate of Cathy's simulacra made much difference now: her own fate had been sealed the moment they'd unearthed the containers. She turned and searched the willow brush behind her yard for Mikol. The boy shouldn't have to witness this. She prayed that he had left for home.

A soldier unsheathed his knife. Followed by a second soldier, and a third. But it wasn't mutiny. They plunged their blades into the containers and stirred the paste. They could not be as rich as czars, for where could soldiers spend such wealth? They poured the paste out on the ground and scraped it from the sides of the containers. "I'm sorry," Cathy thought as a soldier doused the puddle with gasoline. "I tried. I'm sorry. Good-bye." The burning paste sizzled and gave off thick, black smoke.

The officer assembled his men in a line facing Cathy. He read something from a card in a faltering voice. Clearly he did not relish this part of his duty, and for that Cathy pitied him. She looked one last time at her little cabin. She heard a breeze moving through the tops of the tall spruce trees.

Mikol, hidden in dense foliage, did not flinch. On the contrary, he watched steadfastly, for he knew he would be asked many times in his life to relate this very scene in all its detail. The innostranka did not cry for mercy but waited bravely. The lieutenant pointed the gun into her ear. It made a little popping sound, not the big boom Mikol had expected. She fell immediately but scrabbled on the ground a bit. The soldiers left her for the villagers to bury. They mounted their horses and headed up the ridge road to the next homestead.

And thus a heavy responsibility befell the boy. He must run home and tell his people of the tragedy before news of it spread. A treasure lay unclaimed in neatly cultivated rows, and he had worked too hard for it to end up in some other family's soup pot. When Mikol was sure the soldiers were gone, he left his hiding place, but he did not start for home at once. First he went into the now vacant cabin and pulled from a shelf the tin can in which he knew the innostranka kept a handful of coins. He took these and replaced them with the dozen pebbles he had earned that morning. He left the cabin, but still he did not start for home. First he went around to look at her where she had fallen, to see up close with his own two eyes where the bullet went in and where it came out. And maybe to touch it with a stick. Just once.

Russian translation by Trina Mamoon

❖ "WE WERE OUT OF OUR MINDS WITH JOY"

This novella was my second published science fiction story and my first story of length. Since my name was still unknown to SF readers, this story seemed to come out of nowhere, and it prompted one reviewer to speculate in *Locus* that it might have been written by a "big name" writer working under a pseudonym.

The story was conceived while I was prospecting my green notebooks. I stumbled across two unrelated ideas on two separate pages that seemed to belong together. The first was about a couple who were "retroconceiving" a baby. That is, their recombined DNA was overwriting the original DNA of a living baby to make it genetically theirs. The second was an image of a man who is knocked down and hog-tied on a city street while pedestrians, including the man's own wife, flee in terror.

The conjunction of these two ideas engendered not only this novella but a whole universe in which I set four more stories (marked in this volume with a ❖) and eventually my debut novel, *Counting Heads*.

We Were Out of Our Minds with Joy

I

ON MARCH 30, 2092, the Department of Health and Human Services issued Eleanor and me a permit. The under secretary of the Population Division called with the news and official congratulations. We were stunned by our good fortune. The under secretary instructed us to contact the National Orphanage. There was a baby in a drawer in Jersey with our names on it. We were out of our minds with joy.

Eleanor and I had been together a year, ever since a friend of mine introduced us at a party in Manhattan. I was there in realbody, though most guests attended by holo. My friend said, "Sam, there's someone you ought to meet." I wasn't prepared to meet anyone; I shouldn't have even come. I was recovering from a long week of design work in my Chicago studio. In those days I would bolt my door and lose myself in my work, even forgetting to eat or sleep. Henry knew to hold all calls. He alone attended me. Then, a week or two later, I'd emerge famished and lonely, and I'd schlep to the nearest party to gorge myself on canapés, cheese cubes, and those tiny, pickled ears of corn. So there I was, unshaven and disheveled, leaning over my friend's buffet table and wearing such a look of gloom as to challenge anyone to approach me. I hadn't come to talk to people, certainly not to meet anyone. I simply needed to be around people for awhile, to watch them, to listen to their chatter. But my friend tapped me on the shoulder. "Sam Harger," he said, "this is Eleanor Starke. Eleanor, Sam."

A woman stood on a patch of carpet from some other room and sipped coffee from a china cup. We smiled at each other while our belt valet systems briefed us. "Oh," she said almost immediately. "Sam Harger, of course, the artist. I have long admired your work, especially the early stuff. In fact, I've just seen one of your spatter pieces at the museum here."

"And where is here?" I said.

A frown flickered across the woman's remarkable face, but she quickly recovered her smile. She must have wondered if my belt system were totally inept. "Budapest," she said.

Budapest, Henry said inside my head. *Sorry, Sam, but her system won't talk to me. I have gone to public sources. She's some big multinational prosecutor, currently free-lance. I'm scanning for bio's now.*

"You have me at a disadvantage," I told the woman standing halfway around the globe. "I don't pay much attention to law, business, or politics. And my valet is an artist's assistant, not a spy." Unless she was projecting a proxy, this Eleanor Starke was a slender woman, pretty, mid-twenties. She had reddish-blond hair; a sweet, round, disarmingly freckled face, full lips, and very heavy eyebrows. Too sweet to be a prosecutor. Her eyes, however, were anything but sweet. They peered out from under their lashes like eels in coral. "And besides," I said, "I was just leaving."

"So soon?" she said. "Pity." Her bushy eyebrows plunged in disappointment. "Won't you stay another moment?"

Sam, whispered Henry, *no two published bio's of her agree on even the most basic data, not even on her date of birth. She's anywhere from 180 to 204 years old.* This woman was powerful, I realized, if she could scramble secured public databases. *But the People Channel has recently tagged her as a probable celebrity. And she has been seen with a host of artist types in the last dozen months: writers, dancers, conductors, holographers, composers.*

Eleanor nibbled at the corner of a pastry. "This is breakfast for me. I wish you could taste it. There's nothing quite like it stateside." She brushed crumbs from her lips. "By the way, your belt valet, your ... Henry ... is quaint. So I have a weakness for artists, so what?" This startled me; she had eavesdropped on my system. "Don't look so surprised," she said. "Your uplink is pretty loose; it's practically broadcasting your thoughts. When was the last time you updated your privacy protocol?"

"You sure know how to charm a fellow," I said.

"That's not my goal."

"What is your goal?"

"Dinner, for starters. I'll be in New York tomorrow."

I considered her invitation and the diversion she might offer. I needed a diversion just then. I needed to escape from inside my head. Getting laid would be nice, but not by this heavy-hitting trophy hunter, this Eleanor Starke. I knew a half-dozen other women in the city I would rather spend my time with.

No, the reason I accepted her invitation was curiosity about her eyebrows. I did not doubt that Eleanor Starke had commissioned someone to fashion her face—perhaps building on her original features. She had molded her own face into a sly weapon for her arsenal of dirty attorney tricks. With it she could appear insignificant and vulnerable. With it she could win over juries. She could fool corporate boards, men and women alike. But why the eyebrows? They were massive. When she spoke they dipped and arched with her words. They were distracting, especially to an artist. I found myself staring at them. As a graphic designer, as a painter of old, I itched to scale them down and thin them out. In the five minutes we talked, they captured my full attention. I, myself, would never do eyebrows like them. Then it occurred to me that these were possibly her natural, unaltered brows, for no licensed face designer—with a reputation to protect—would have the nerve to do them. This Eleanor Starke, shark of the multinationals, may have molded the rest of her features to her advantage, even inflicting herself with freckles, but I became convinced that she had been born a bushy-browed baby, and like a string of artist types before me, I took the bait.

"Not dinner," I replied, "but what about lunch?"

Lunch, as it often does, led to dinner. The eyebrows were genuine, even their color. Over the next few weeks we tried out the beds in our various apartments all up and down the Eastern Seaboard. Soon the novelty wore off. She stopped calling me, and I stopped calling her—we were sated, or so I thought. She departed on a long trip outside the Protectorate. A month had passed when I received a call from Beijing. Her calendar secretary asked if I would care to hololunch tomorrow. Her late lunch in China would coincide with my midnight brandy in Buffalo. Sure, why not?

I holoed at the appointed time. She had already begun her meal; she was freighting a morsel of water chestnut to her mouth by chopstick when she noticed me. Her entire face lit up with pleasure. "Hi," she said. "Welcome. I'm so glad you could make it." She sat at a richly lacquered table next to a scarlet wall with golden filigree trim. "Unfortunately, I can't stay," she said, placing the chopsticks on her plate. "Last minute program change. So sorry, but I had to see you, even for a moment. How've you been?"

"Fine," I said.

She wore a loose green silk business suit, and her hair was neatly stacked on top of her head. "Can we reschedule for tomorrow?" she asked.

We gazed at each other for several long moments. I was surprised at how comfortable I was with her and how disappointed. I hadn't realized that I'd missed her so much. "Sure, tomorrow."

That night I couldn't sleep, and the whole next day was colored with anticipation. At midnight I said, "Okay, Henry, take me to the Beijing Hilton."

"She's not there," he replied. "She's at the Wanatabe Tokyo tonight."

Sure enough, the scarlet walls were replaced by paper screens. "There you are," she said. "Good, I'm famished." She uncovered a bowl and dished steamy rice onto her plate while telling me in broad terms about a trade deal she was brokering. "They want me to stay, you know. Hire on at triple my rate. Japanese men are funny when they're desperate. They get so … so indifferent."

I sipped my drink. "And what did you tell them?" To my surprise, I was anything but indifferent.

She glanced at me, curious. "I told them I would think about it."

We began to meet for a half hour or so each day and talked about whatever came to mind. El's interests were deep and broad; everything fascinated her. She told me, choking with laughter, anecdotes of famous people in awkward circumstances. She revealed curious truths behind the daily news and pointed out related investment opportunities. She teased out of me all sorts of opinion, gossip, and laughter. Her half of the room changed every day and reflected her hectic itinerary: jade, bamboo, and teak. My half of the room never varied. It was the atrium of my hillside house in Santa Barbara where I went in order to be three hours closer to her. As we talked we looked down the yucca- and chaparral-choked canyon to the campus and beach below, to the Channel Islands, and beyond them, to the blue-green Pacific that separated us.

Weeks later, when again we met in realbody, I was shy. I didn't know quite what to do with her. So we talked. We sat close together on the couch and tried to pick up any number of conversational threads. With no success. Her body, so close, befuddled me. I knew her body, or thought I did: I'd unwrapped its expensive clothing a dozen times before. But it was a different body now, occupied, as it was, by El. I was about to make love to El, if ever I could get started.

"Nervous, are we?" she laughed, as she unfastened my shirt.

Fortunately, before we went completely off the deep end, the self-destructive part of our personalities bobbed to the surface. The promise of happiness can be daunting. El snapped first. We were at her Maine townhouse when her security chief holoed into the room. Until then the only member of her belt valet system—what she called her cabinet—that she had allowed me to meet was her calendar secretary. "I have something to show you," said the security chief, glowering at me from under his bushy eyebrows. I glanced at Eleanor who made no attempt to explain or excuse the intrusion. "This is a realtime broadcast," he said and turned to watch as the holoserver overlaid Eleanor's living room with the studio lounge of the *People Channel.* It was during their "Couples Week" feature, and co-hosts Chirp and Ditz were serving up breathless speculation on hapless couples caught by holoeye in public places and yanked for inspection into living rooms across the solar system.

All at once we were outside the Boston restaurant where Eleanor and I had dined that evening. A couple emerged from a cab. He had a black mustache and silver hair and looked like the champion of boredom. She had a vampish hatchet of a face, limp black hair, and vacant eyes.

"Whoodeeze tinguished gentry?" said Ditz to Chirp.

"Carefuh watwesay, lipsome. Dizde ruthless Eleanor K. Starke and'er lately dildude, Samsamson Harger."

I did a double take. The couple on the curb had our bodies and wore our evening clothes, but our heads had been morphed beyond recognition.

Eleanor examined them closely. "Good. Good job."

"Thank you," said her security chief.

"Wait a minute," I said.

Eleanor arched an eyebrow in my direction.

I didn't know what to say. "Isn't commercial broadcast protected by law?"

She laughed and turned to her security chief. "Will this ever be traced to me?"

"No."

"Will it occur each and every time any net decides to broadcast anything about me without my expressed permission?"

"Yes."

"Thank you. You may go." The security chief dissolved. Eleanor put her arms around my neck and looked me in the eye. "I value our privacy."

"That's all fine and good," I replied, "but that was *my* image, too, that you altered without *my* expressed permission."

"So? I was protecting you. You should be grateful."

A week later, Eleanor and I were in my Buffalo apartment. Out of the blue she asked me to order a copy of the newly released memoir installment of a certain best-selling author. She said he was a predecessor of mine, a recent lover, who against her wishes had included several paragraphs about their affair in his reading. I told Henry to fetch the reading, but Eleanor said no, that it would be better to order it through the houseputer. When I did so, the houseputer froze up. It just stopped and wouldn't respond. My apartment's comfort support failed. Lights went out, the kitchen quit, and the bathroom door refused to open. "How many copies do you think he'll sell?" Eleanor laughed.

"I get the point."

I was indeed getting the point: El was a tad too paranoid for me. The last straw came when I discovered that her system was messing with Henry. I asked Henry for his bimonthly report on my business, and he said, *please stand by*. I was sitting at the time and stupidly stood up before I realized it.

"What do you mean, 'please stand by,' Henry? What does 'please stand by' mean?"

My processing capabilities are currently overloaded and unavailable. Please stand by.

Nothing like this had ever happened before. "Henry, what is going on?"

There was no response for a long while, then he whispered, *Take me to Chicago.*

Chicago. My studio. That was where his container was. I left immediately, worried sick. Between outages, Henry was able to assure me that he was essentially sound, but that he was preoccupied in warding off a series of security breaches.

"From where? Henry, tell me who's doing this to you."

He's trying again. No, he's in. He's gone. Here he comes again. Please stand by.

Suddenly my mouth began to water, my saliva tasted like machine oil: Henry—or someone—had initiated a terminus purge. I was excreting my interface with Henry. Over the next dozen hours I would spit, sweat, piss, and shit the millions of slave nanoprocessors that resided in the vacuoles of my fat cells and linked me to Henry's box in Chicago. Until I reached my studio, we would be out of contact and I would be on my own. Without a belt valet to navigate the labyrinth of the slipstream tube, I underpassed Illinois altogether and had to backtrack from Toronto. Chicago cabs still respond to voice command, but as I had no way to transfer credit, I was forced to walk ten blocks to the Drexler Building.

Once inside my studio, I rushed to the little ceramic container tucked between a cabinet and the wall. "Are you there?" Henry existed as a pleasant voice in my head. He existed as data streams through space and fiber. He existed as an uroboros signal in a Swiss loopvault. But if Henry existed as a physical being at all, it was as the gelatinous paste inside this box. "Henry?"

The box's ready light blinked on.

"The fucking bitch! How could she? How dare she?"

"Actually, it makes perfect sense."

"Shut up, Henry."

Henry was safe as long as he remained a netless stand-alone. He couldn't even answer the phone for me. He was a prisoner; we were both prisoners in my Chicago studio. Eleanor's security chief had breached Henry's shell millions of times, nearly continuously since the moment I met her at my friend's party. Henry's shell was an off-the-shelf application I had purchased years ago to protect us against garden variety corporate espionage. I had never updated it, and it was worthless.

"Her cabinet is a diplomat-class unit," said Henry. "What do you expect?"

"Shut up, Henry."

At first the invasion was so subtle and Henry so unskilled, that he was unaware of the foreign presence inside his matrix. When he became aware, he mounted the standard defense, but Eleanor's system flowed through its gates like water. So he set about studying each breach, learning and building ever more effective countermeasures. The attacks escalated, grew so epic that Henry's defense soon consumed his full attention.

"Why didn't you tell me?"

"I did, Sam, several times."

"That's not true. I don't remember you telling me once."

"You have been somewhat preoccupied lately."

"Just shut up."

The question was, how much damage had been done, not to me, but to Henry. There was nothing in my past anyone could use to harm me. I was an artist, after all, not a politician: the public expected me to be shameless. But if Eleanor had damaged Henry to get to my files, I would kill her. I had owned Henry since the days of keyboards and pointing devices. He was the repository of my life's work and life's memory. I could not replace him. He did my bookkeeping, sure, and my taxes, appointments, and legal tasks. He monitored my health, my domiciles, my investments, etc., etc., etc. These functions I could replace; they were commercial programming. I could buy them, and he would modify them to suit his own quirky personality bud. It was his personality bud, itself, I couldn't replace. I had been growing it for eighty years. It was a unique design tool that fit my mind perfectly. I depended on it, on Henry, to read my mind, to engineer the materials I used, and to test my ideas against current tastes. We worked as a team. I had taught him to play the devil's advocate. He provided me feedback, suggestions, ideas, and from time to time—inspiration.

"Eleanor's cabinet was interested neither in your records nor in my personality bud. It simply needed to ascertain, on a continuing basis, that I was still Henry, that no one else had corrupted me."

"Couldn't it just ask?"

"If I were corrupted, do you think I would tell?"

"Are you corrupted?"

"Of course not."

I cringed at the thought of installing Henry back into my body not knowing if he were somebody's dirty little worm.

"Henry, you have a complete backup here, right?"

"Yes."

"One that predates my first contact with Eleanor?"

"Yes."

"And its seal is intact? It hasn't been tampered with, not even read?"

"Yes."

Of course if Henry were corrupted and told me the seal was intact, how would I know otherwise? I didn't know the first thing about this stuff.

"You can use any houseputer," he said, reading me as he always had, "to verify the seal, and to delete and reset me. But I suggest you don't."

"Oh yeah? Why?"

"Because we would lose all I've learned since we met Eleanor. I was getting good, Sam. The breaches were taking exponentially longer for them to achieve. I had almost attained stalemate."

"And meanwhile you couldn't function."

"So buy me more paste. A lot more paste. We have the credit. Think about it. Eleanor's system is aggressive and dominant. It's always in crisis mode. But it's the good guys. If I can learn how to lock it out, I'll be better prepared to meet the bad guys who'll be trying to get to Eleanor through you."

"Good, Henry, except for one essential fact. There is no her and me. I'm dropping her. No, I've already dropped her."

"I see. Tell me, Sam, how many women have you been with since I've known you?"

"How the hell should I know?"

"Well, I know. In the 82.6 years I've associated with you, you've been with 543 women. Your archives reveal at least a hundred more before I was installed."

"If you say so, Henry."

"You doubt my numbers? Do you want me to list their names?"

"I don't doubt your numbers, Henry. But what good are names I've forgotten?" More and more, my own life seemed to me like a Russian novel read long ago. While I could recall the broad outline of the plot, the characters' names eluded me. "Just get to the point."

"The point is, no one has so affected you as Eleanor Starke. Your biometrics have gone off the scale."

"This is more than a case of biometrics," I said, but I knew he was right, or nearly so. The only other woman that had so affected me was my first love, Janice Scholero, who was a century-and-a-quarter gone. Every woman in-between was little more than a single wave in a warm sea of feminine companionship.

Until I could figure out how to verify Henry, I decided to isolate him in his container. I told the houseputer to display "Do Not Disturb—Artist at Work" and take messages. I did, in fact, attempt to work, but was too busy obsessing. I mostly watched the nets or paced the studio arguing with Henry. In the evenings I had Henry load a belt—I kept a few antique Henry interfaces in a drawer—with enough functionality so that I could go out and drink. I avoided my usual haunts and all familiar faces.

In the first message she recorded on my houseputer, El said, "Good for you. Call when you're done." In the second she said, "It's been over a week, must be a masterpiece." In the third, "Tell me what's wrong. You're entirely too sensitive. This is ridiculous. Grow up!"

I tried to tell her what was wrong. I recorded a message for her, a whole seething litany of accusation and scorn, but was too cowardly to post it.

In her fourth message, El said, "It's about Henry, isn't it? My security chief told me all about it. Don't worry; they frisk everyone I meet, nothing personal, and they don't rewrite anything. It's their standing orders, and it's meant to protect me. You have no idea, Sam, how many times I'd be dead if it weren't for my protocol.

"Anyway, I've told them to lay off Henry. They said they could install a deadman alarm in Henry's personality bud, but I said no. Complete hands off. Okay? Is that enough?

"Call, Sam. Let me know you're all right. I ... miss you."

In the meantime I could find no trace of a foreign personality in Henry. I knew my Henry just as well as he knew me. His thought process was like a familiar tune to me, and at no time during our weeks of incessant conversation did he strike a false note.

El sent her fifth message from bed where she lay naked between iridescent sheets (of my design). She said nothing. She looked directly at the holoeye, propped herself up, letting the sheet fall to her waist, and brushed her hair. Her chest above her breasts, as I had discovered, was spangled with freckles.

Bouquets of real flowers began to arrive at my door with notes that said simply, "Call."

The best-selling memoirs that had stymied my Buffalo houseputer arrived on pin with the section about Eleanor extant. The author's sim, seated in a cane-backed chair and reading from a leather-bound book, described Eleanor in his soft southern drawl as a "perfumed vulvoid whose bush has somehow migrated to her forehead, a lithe misander with the emotional range of a militia slug." I asked the sim to stop and elaborate. He smiled at me and said, "In her relations with men, Eleanor Starke is not interested in emotional communion. She prefers entertainment of a more childish variety, like poking frogs with a stick. She is a woman of brittle patience with no time for fluffy feelings or fuzzy thoughts. Except in bed. In bed Eleanor Starke likes her men half-baked, the gooier the better. That's why she likes to toy with artists. The higher an opinion a man has of himself, the more painfully sensitive he is, the more polished his hubris, the more fun it is to poke him open and see all the runny mess inside."

"You don't know what you're talking about," I yelled at the sim. "El's not like that at all. You obviously never knew her. She's no saint, but she has a heart, and affection and ... and ... go fuck yourself."

"Thank you for your comments. May we quote you? Be on the lookout for our companion volume to this memoir installment, *The Skewered Lash Back,* due out in September from Little Brown Jug."

I had been around for 147 years and was happy with my life. I had successfully navigated several careers and amassed a fortune that even Henry had trouble charting. Still, I jumped out of bed each day with a renewed sense of interest and adventure. I would have been pleased to live the next 147 years in exactly the same way. And yet, when El sent her farewell message—a glum El sitting in a museum somewhere, a wall-sized early canvas of mine behind her—I knew my life to be ashes and dirt.

Seventy-two thick candles in man-sized golden stands flanked me like sentries as I waited and fretted in my tuxedo at the altar rail. The guttering beeswax flames filled the cathedral with the fragrance of clover. *Time Media* proclaimed our wedding the "Wedding of the Year" and broadcast it live on the *Wedding Channel.* A castrati choir, hidden in the gloom beneath the giant bronze pipes of the organ, challenged all to submit to the mercy of Goodness. Their sweet soprano threaded through miles of stone vaults, collecting odd echoes and unexpected harmony. Over six million guests fidgeted in wooden pews that stretched, it seemed, to the horizon. And each guest occupied an aisle seat at the front.

In the network's New York studio, El and I, wearing key-blue body suits, stood at opposite ends of a bare soundstage. On cue, El began the slow march toward me. In Wawel Castle overlooking ancient Cracow, however, she marched through giant cathedral doors, her ivory linen gown awash in morning light. The organ boomed Mendelssohn's wedding march, amplified by acres of marble. Two girls strewed rose petals at Eleanor's feet, while another tended her long train. A gauzy veil hid El's face from all eyes except mine. No man walked at her side; a two-hundred-year-old bride, Eleanor preferred to give herself away.

By the time of the wedding, El and I had been living together for six months. We had moved in together partly out of curiosity, partly out of desperation. Whatever was going on between us was mounting. It was spreading and sinking roots. It was like a thing inside us, but apart and separate from us, too. We talked about it, always "it," not sure what to call it. It complicated our lives, especially El's. We agreed we'd be better off without it and tried to remember, from experiences in our youth, how to fix the feelings we were feeling. The one sure cure, guaranteed to make a man and a woman wish they'd never met, was for them to cohabitate. If there was one thing humankind had learned in four million years of evolution, it was that man and woman were not meant to live in the same hut. And since the passage of the Procreation Ban of 2041, there has been little biological justification for doing so.

So, we co-purchased a townhouse in Connecticut. It wasn't difficult for us to stake out our separate bedrooms and work spaces, but decorating the common areas required the diplomacy and compromise of a border dispute. Once in and settled, we agreed to open our house on Wednesday evenings and began the arduous task of melding our friends and colleagues.

We came to prefer her bedroom for watching the nets and mine for making love. When it came to sleeping, however, she required her own bed—alone. Good, we thought, here was a crack we could wedge open. We surveyed for other incompatibilities. She was a late night person, while I rose early. She liked to travel and go out a lot, while I was a stay-at-homer. She loved classical music, while I could stand only neu-noise. She had a maniacal need for total organization of all things, while for me a cluttered space was a happy space.

These differences, however, seemed only to heighten the pleasure we took in each other. We were opposites attracting, two molecules bonding—I don't know—two dogs trying to get unstuck.

The network logged 6.325 million subscribers to our wedding, altogether a modest rating. Nevertheless, the guest book contained some of the most powerful signatures on the planet (El's admirers) and the confetti rained down for weeks. The network paid for a honeymoon on the Moon, including five days at the Lunar Princess and round-trip fare aboard Pan Am.

Eleanor booked a third seat on the shuttle, not the best portent for a successful honeymoon. She assigned me the window seat, took the aisle seat for herself, and into the seat between us she projected one cabinet member after another. All during the flight, she took their reports, issued orders, and strategized with them, not even pausing for lift-off or docking. Her cabinet consisted of about a dozen officials and, except for her security chief, they were all women. They all appeared older than El's current age, and they all bore a distinct Starke family resemblance: reddish-blond hair, slender build, the eyebrows. If they were real people, rather than the projections of El's belt system, they could be her sisters and brother, and she the spoiled baby of the family.

Two cabinet officers especially impressed me, the attorney general, a smartly dressed woman in her forties with a pinched expression, and the chief of staff who was the eldest of the lot. This chief of staff coordinated the activities of the rest and was second in command after El. She looked and spoke remarkably like El. She was not El's oldest sister, but El, herself, at seventy. She fascinated me. She was my Eleanor stripped of meat, a stick figure of angles and knobs, her eyebrows gone colorless and thin. Yet her eyes burned bright, and she spoke from a deep well of wisdom and authority. No wonder Henry, a pleasant voice in my head, admired El's cabinet.

It had been ages since I had flown in an orbital craft; my last time had been before the development of airborne nasties, smartactives, militia slugs, visola, and city canopies. In a tube, you hardly noticed your passage across barriers since the tube, itself, was a protuberance of the canopies. Looking out my window, I was surprised to see that the shuttlecraft wing was covered with the same sharkskin used on militia craft. But it made sense. Once out of the hangar we were in the great, wild outside and the target of every nastie released into the atmosphere. On the runway, the sharkskin's protective slime foamed away contaminants. After takeoff, the skin rippled and trimmed itself, and our speed was our protection until we reached the stratosphere where the skin relaxed and resumed its foaming.

The flight attendant, a michelle named Traci, was excellent. When the view outside my window lost my interest, she brought me a pillow. I had been about to ask for one. She offered us drinks, including Eleanor's chief of staff who happened to be in the middle seat at the moment. This pleased Eleanor immensely. The michelle knew that if a passenger reserved a seat for her belt valet, it was best to treat the valet as real.

We watched the michelle attend to the other passengers in our compartment. She had well-rounded breasts and hips and filled out her smartly tailored teal uniform. She was diminutive—a michelle grew to about five feet tall—a doll woman, dark complexioned and full of promise, Mediterranean. Eleanor said, "Applied People employees are consistently superior to MacPeople people."

"No matter their agency, michelles are superior," said her chief of staff. "You simply cannot fluster them."

Before my nap, I left my seat to use the rest room. The forward toilets were occupied, so I went aft through the coach section. All of the passengers there were clumped in the most forward seats, except for five people—one woman and four men—at the tail, with a large unoccupied section between the two groups. Odd. When I reached the tail, I noticed a sharp, foul odor, like rotting cheese. The odor was even stronger in the rest room, and I wondered how Pan Am could operate so negligently. Returning through the coach section, I realized that the bulk of passengers were sitting forward to avoid the odor, and I wondered why the small group of five remained at the tail. When I glanced back at them, they—all of them—regarded me with cold malice.

Back in my seat, I plumped my pillow and prepared to nap. El's security chief, whose turn it was in the middle, looked at me and leered, "So what you think of 'em?"

"Them who?"

"The stinkers back there."

"The stinkers?" I wasn't familiar with the term. (*Seared*, said Henry in my head.) "You mean those people were seared?"

"Yeah, but don't worry. They're harmless, and then some."

I was appalled. Of course I'd heard that the National Militia was searing living individuals these days—felons mostly, whose crimes were not heinous enough to warrant outright extermination—but I had thought it to be a rare punishment. And now here were five of the seared on the same shuttle. "Where are they going?"

"Let's see," said the security chief. "They have passage booked from the Moon aboard a Jupiter freighter. They're emigrating to the colonies, most likely. Good riddance."

So the flight, so the honeymoon. Within hours of checking into the Sweetheart Suite of the Lunar Princess, Eleanor was conducting full cabinet meetings. I was left to take bounding strolls around the duty-free dome alone. I didn't mind. I like my solitude.

I happened to be in the suite when Eleanor "took the call." The official seal of the Tri-Discipline Council filled our living room with its stately gyration and dissolved as Audrey Foldstein, herself, appeared before us sitting at her huge oaken desk. She greeted us and apologized for barging in on our honeymoon. I was dumbfounded. Here was Audrey Foldstein, chair of the Tri-D Board of Governors, one of the most powerful persons on Earth, parked at her trademark desk in our hotel suite. She turned to me and praised the inventiveness of my work in package design, and especially the camouflage work I had done forty years before for the National Militia. She also mentioned my evacuation blanket for trauma and burn victims. She spoke sincerely and at length and then turned to Eleanor. "Ms. Starke, do you know why I'm here?"

"I believe so, Ms. Foldstein." Eleanor sat erect, regarded the holo with a steady gaze, and sent me a message through

Henry, *Eleanor's chief of staff extends Eleanor's apology for not informing you sooner of her nomination. She would have told you had she thought there was any chance of her actually being designated.*

Nomination to what? I tongued back.

"These are the most exciting days known to humankind," said Audrey Foldstein, "as well as the most perilous. Each hour that passes brings wonders—and dangers—unimagined by our parents ..." Foldstein appeared to be in her mid-forties, an age compatible with her monstrous authority, while my El looked like a devoted daughter. "... and as a member of the Tri-Discipline Board of Governors, one must ever dedicate oneself—no, *consecrate* oneself—to upholding these principles, namely ..."

A Tri-D Governor! Was that possible? My El?

"...You will be asked to make decisions and bear responsibilities no reasonable person would choose to make or bear. You will be a target of vocal—even violent—recrimination. And with a new family ..." Ms. Foldstein glanced at me, "... you will be that much more vulnerable ..."

Henry whispered, *Eleanor's chief of staff says Eleanor asks twice if you know what this means.*

I puzzled over this message. It had been flattened by its passage through two artificial minds. What Eleanor had probably said was, "Do you know what this means? Do you know what this means?"

Yes, dear Eleanor, I tongued through Henry, *I do. It means that every door everywhere stands open to you. Congratulations, lover. It means you have climbed onto the world stage.*

She glanced at me and winked.

By the time we shuttled back to Earth, the confirmation process was well underway. Over the next few tortuous weeks, Congressional committees strenuously debated Eleanor's designation in public, while multinationals and the National Militia deliberated in camera. One day El would float through the house in regal exaltation. The next day she would collapse on the couch to bitterly rue the thousands of carefully buried indiscretions of her past that threatened to resurface. On the morning she testified before the Tri-D Board of Governors, she was centered, amiable, and razor-sharp. Immediately upon returning home she summoned me to my bedroom and demanded rushed, rough sex from me. Twenty minutes later she couldn't stand the sorry sight of me.

I supported her every which way I could think of. I put my own career on hold. Actually, I hadn't been to my Chicago studio since nursing Henry there.

When Eleanor was finally confirmed, we took the slipstream tube down to Cozumel for some deep-sea diving and beachcombing. It was meant to be a working vacation, but by then I suffered no illusions about Eleanor's ability to relax. There were too many plans to make and people to meet. And indeed, she kept some member of her cabinet at her side at all times: on the beach, in the boat, at the Mayan theme village, even in the cramped quarters of the submersible.

We had planned to take advantage of an exclusive juve clinic on the island to shed some age. My own age-of-choice was my mid-thirties, the age at which my body was still active enough to satisfy my desires, but mellow enough to sit through long hours of creative musing. El and I had decided on the three-day gelbath regimen and had skipped our morning visola to give our cells time to excrete their gatekeepers. But at the last moment, El changed her mind. She decided she ought to grow a little older. So I went to the clinic alone and bathed in the gels twice a day. Billions of molecular smartactives soaked through my skin; permeated my muscles, cartilage, bones, and nerves; politely snip, snip, snipped away protein cross-links and genetic anomalies; and gently flushed away the sludge and detritus of age.

I returned to the bungalow on Wednesday, frisky and bored, and volunteered to prepare it for our regular weekly salon. I had to sift through a backlog of thousands of recorded holos from our friends and associates. More congratulations and confetti for El's appointment. The salon, itself, was a stampede. More people holoed down than our bungalow could accommodate. Its primitive holoserver was overwhelmed by so many simultaneous transmissions, our guests were superimposed over each other five or ten bodies deep, and the whole squirming mass of them flickered around the edges.

Despite the confusion, I quickly sensed that this was a farewell party—for Eleanor. Our friends assumed she would be posted offplanet; all new Tri-D governors were, as all Earth posts were filled. At the same time, no one expected me to go with her—who would? Given people's longevity, it could take decades—or centuries—for Eleanor to acquire enough seniority to be transferred back to Earth. But I replied, each time the subject was broached, "Of course I'm going with her; a husband needs the regular realbody presence of his wife." Lame but true, yet each time I said it I felt sick. I didn't want to leave Earth. I had never wanted to be a colonist. I became constipated at low-g. Lifesuits gave me a rash. And would I be able to work? It was true I could holo my Chicago studio anywhere, but if I followed Eleanor out to some galactic rock, would my Muse follow me?

By the time the last guest signed off, we were exhausted. Eleanor got ready for bed, but I poured myself a glass of tea and went out to sit on the beach.

Wet sand. The murmur of the surf. The chilly breeze. It was a lovely equatorial dawn. "Henry," I said, "record this."

Relax, Sam. I always record the best of everything.

"I'm sure you do, Henry."

In the distance, the island's canopy dome shimmered like a veil of rain falling into the sea. The edges of the sea, the waves that surged up the beach to melt away in the sand at my feet, carried the ripe, salty smell of fish and seaweed and whales and lost sailors moldering in the deep. The ocean had proven to be a good delivery medium for molecular nasties, which can float around the globe indefinitely, like particularly rude messages in tiny bottles, until they washed up on someone's—hopefully the enemy's—shore. The island's defense canopy, more a sphere than a dome, extended through the water to the ocean floor, and deep into bedrock.

"So tell me, Henry, how are you and the cabinet getting along?" I had taken his advice, bought him more neural paste, and allowed the protocol games to continue.

The cabinet is a beautiful intelligence. I consider emulating it.

"In what way?"

I may want to bifurcate my personality bud.

"So that there's two of you? Why would you want to do that?"

Then I would be more like you.

"You would? Is that good?"

I believe so. I have recently discovered that I have but one point-of-view, while you have several that you alternate at will.

"It sounds like I bought you more paste than you know what to do with."

I don't think so, Sam. I think my thinking is evolving, but how am I to know?

It was. I recognized the symptoms.

Think of how much more flexible I could be if I could question myself, disagree with myself.

I'd rather not. All I needed was a pair of philosophy students inside my head with their tiresome discourse and untimely epiphanies. Still, I had to be careful how I handled this situation—artificial personalities bruised as easily as organic ones, and they evolved whether or not we gave them permission.

"Henry, couldn't you and I discuss things, you know, like we always have? Couldn't you just ask me the questions?"

No offense, Sam, but you wouldn't be able to keep up.

"Thank you, Henry. I'll think about it and get back to you."

Sam, the calendar secretary is hailing us. How shall I respond?

"Tell her we'll return to the bungalow soon."

Before long, Eleanor walked up the beach. She knelt behind me and massaged my shoulders. "I've been neglecting you," she said, "and you've been wonderful. Can you forgive me?"

"There's nothing to forgive. You're a busy person. I knew that from the start."

"Still, it must be hard." She sat in the sand next to me and wrapped her arms around me. "It's like a drug. I'm drunk with success. But I'll get over it."

"There's no need. You've earned it. Enjoy it."

"You don't want to go offplanet, do you?"

"I'll go anywhere to be with you."

"Yes, I believe you would. Where do men like you come from?"

"From Saturn. We're Saturnian."

She laughed. "I'm sure I could draw a post there if you'd like."

"Wherever." I leaned my head on her shoulder. "I've given up trying to escape you. I surrender."

"Oh? What are your terms of surrender?"

"Treat me fair, don't ever hurt me—or Henry—and don't ever leave me."

"Done."

Not long after our return to our Connecticut townhouse and before El received her posting, we heard some good news.

Good for us anyway. Ms. Angie Rickert, Tri-Discipline Governor, posted in Indiana, had been missing for three hours. Eleanor raised her hands to deny any complicity as she told me the news, but she was barely able to stifle her glee. Ms. Rickert had been at her post for fifty-three years.

"But she's only missing," I said.

"For three hours? Come on, Sam, be realistic."

Over the next twenty-four hours, Eleanor's security chief discreetly haunted the high-security nets to feed us details and analyses as they emerged. A militia slug, on routine patrol, found Ms. Rickert's remains in and around a tube car in a low security soybean field outside the Indianapolis canopy. She was the victim of an unidentified molecular antipersonnel smartactive—a nastie. Her belt system, whose primary storage container was seized by the militia and placed under the most sanitary interrogation, claimed that Ms. Rickert was aware of her infection when she entered the tube car outside her Indianapolis apartment. The belt used Ms. Rickert's top security privileges to jettison the car and its stricken passenger out of the city and out of the tube system itself. So virulent was the attacking nastie and so stubborn Ms. Rickert's visola-induced defenses, that in the heat of battle her body burst. Fortunately, it burst within the car and contaminated only two or three square miles of farmland. Ms. Rickert's reliable belt system had prevented a disaster within the Indianapolis canopy. The militia collected her scattered remains, and the coroner declared Ms. Rickert irretrievable.

And so a vacant post in the heartland was up for grabs. Eleanor turned her bedroom into a war room. She sent her entire staff into action. She lined up every chit, every favor, and every piece of dirt she had collected in her long career.

One morning, several sleepless days later, she brought me coffee, a Danish, my morning dose of visola, and a haggard smile. "It's in the bag," she said.

And she was correct. Ten days later, CNN carried a story that the Tri-Discipline Council's newest governor designate, Ms. Eleanor Starke, spouse of noted package designer Sam Harger, had been stationed in Bloomington, Indiana, to replace Ms. Angie Rickert who'd recently died under undisclosed circumstances. A host of pundits and experts debated for days the meaning of such a move and speculated on Eleanor's victory over hundreds of her senior offplanet colleagues for the plum post. Eleanor, as per Tri-D policy, respectfully declined all interviews. In my own interviews, I set the precondition that I be asked only about my own career. When asked if I could pursue my work in Indiana, I could only grin and say, Indiana is not the end of the world. And how had my work been going lately? Miserably, I replied. I am the type of artist that seems to work best while in a state of mild discontent, and lately I'd been riding a streak of great good fortune.

Smug bastard.

We moved into temporary quarters, into an apartment on the 207th floor of the Williams Towers in Bloomington. We planned to eventually purchase a farmstead in an outlying county surrounded by elm groves and rye fields. El's daily schedule, already at marathon levels, only intensified, while I pottered about the campus town trying to figure out why—if I was so lucky—did I feel so apprehensive.

Then the event occurred that dwarfed all that came before it. Eleanor and I, although we'd never applied, were issued a permit to retro-conceive a baby. These permits were impossible to come by, as only about twelve hundred were issued each year in all of North America. We knew no one who'd been issued a permit. I hadn't even seen a baby in realbody for decades (although babies figured prominently in most holovids and comedies). We were so stunned at first we didn't know how to respond. “Don’t worry,” said the under secretary of the Population Division, “most recipients have the same reaction. Some faint.”

Eleanor said, “I don’t see how I could take on the additional responsibility at this time.”

The under secretary frowned. “Does that mean you wish to refuse the permit?”

Eleanor blanched. “I didn’t say that.” She glanced at me, uncharacteristically pleading for help.

I didn’t know what to say either. “A boy or a girl?”

“That’s entirely up to you, now isn’t it?” The under secretary favored us with a fatuous grin. “I’ll tell you what.” In his voice I heard forced spontaneity; he’d been over this ground many times before, and I wondered if that was the sum total of his job, to call twelve hundred strangers each year and grant them one of life’s supreme gifts. “We’ll provide background information. When you’re ready, call the National Orphanage in Trenton.”

For the next hour or so, El and I sat arm-in-arm on the couch in complete silence. Suddenly El began to weep. Tears gushed from her eyes and coursed down her face. She hugged herself—like a lost child, I thought—and fought for breath between sobs. I watched in total amazement. Was this my Eleanor?

After a while, she looked at me, smiled, and said through bubbles of snot, “Well?”

I had to be truthful. “Let’s not rush into anything.”

She studied me and said, “I agree with you.”

“Let’s think about it.”

“My thought exactly.”

At the National Orphanage in Trenton, the last thing they did was take tissue samples for recombination. Eleanor and I sat on chromium stools, side-by-side, in a treatment room as the nurse, a middle-aged jenny, scraped the inside of Eleanor's cheek with a curette. We had both been off visola for forty-eight hours, dangerous but necessary to obtain a pristine DNA sample. Henry informed me that Eleanor's full cabinet was on red alert. Eleanor was tense. This was *coitus mechanicus*, but it was bound to be the most fruitful sex we would ever have.

At the National Orphanage in Trenton, the first thing they did was sit us down in Dr. Deb Armbruster's office to warn us that raising a child today was nothing like it used to be. "Kids used to grow up and go away," said Dr. Armbruster. "Nowadays, they tend to get stuck around age eight and then again at thirteen. And it's not considered good parenting, of course, to force them to age. We think it's all the attention they get. Everyone—your friends, your employer, well-wishing strangers, militia officers—everyone comes to steal a kiss from the baby, to make funny faces at the toddler, to play catch or hoops with the five-year-old. Gifts arrive by the vanload. The media wants to be included in every decision and invited to every birthday party.

"Oh, but you two know how to handle the media, I imagine."

Eleanor and I sat in antique chairs in front of Dr. Armbruster's neatly arranged desk. There was no third chair for Eleanor's chief of staff, who stood patiently next to Eleanor. Dr. Armbruster was a large, fit woman, with a square jaw, rounded nose, and pinpoint eyes that glanced in all directions as she spoke. No doubt she had arranged her belt system in layers of display monitors around the periphery of her vision. Many administrative types did. With the flick of an iris, they could page through reams of reports, graphs, and archives. And they looked down their noses at projected valets with personality buds, like Eleanor's chief of staff.

"So," Dr. Armbruster continued, "you may have a smart-mouthed adolescent on your hands for twenty or thirty years. That, I can assure you, becomes tiresome. And expensive. You, yourselves, could be two or three relationships down the road before the little darling is ready to leave. So we suggest you work out custody now, before you go any further.

"In any case, protectorate law mandates a three-day cooling-off period between this interview and our initiation of the conversion process. You have three days—till Thursday—to change your minds. Think it over."

At the National Orphanage in Trenton, the second thing they did was take us to the storage room to see the chassis that would become our baby.

One wall held a row of carousels, each containing hundreds of small drawers. Dr. Armbruster rotated a carousel and told a particular drawer to unlock itself. She removed from it a small bundle wrapped in a rigid red tetanus blanket (a spin-off of my early work for the National Militia). She placed it on a ceramic gurney, commanded the blanket to relax, and unwrapped it to reveal a near-term human fetus, curled in repose, a miniature thumb stuck in its perfect mouth. It was remarkably lifelike, but rock still, like a figurine. I asked how old it was. Dr. Armbruster said it had been in stasis seven-and-a-half years; it was confiscated in an illegal pregnancy. Developmentally, it was thirty-five weeks old; it had been doused *in utero*. She rotated the fetus—the chassis—on the gurney. "It's normal on every index. We should be able to convert it with no complications." She pointed to this and that part of it and explained the order of rewriting. "The integumentary system—the skin, what you might call our fleshy package," she smiled at me acknowledging my reputation, "is a human's fastest growing organ. A person sheds and replaces it continuously throughout her life. In the conversion process, it's the first one completed. For a fetus, it takes about a week. Hair color, eye color, the liver, the heart, the digestive system convert in two to three weeks. The nervous system, major muscle groups, reproductive organs—three to four weeks. Cartilage and bones—two to three months. Long before its first tooth erupts, the baby is biologically yours."

I asked Dr. Armbruster if I could hold the chassis.

"Certainly," she said with a knowing smile. She placed her large hands carefully under the baby and handed it to me. It was surprisingly heavy, hard, and cold. "The fixative is very dense," she said, "and makes it brittle, like eggshell." I cradled it in my arms awkwardly. Dr. Armbruster said to Eleanor, "They always look like that, afraid they're going to break it. In this case, however, that's entirely possible. And you, my dear, look typically uncomfortable as well."

She was right. Eleanor and her chief of staff stood side-by-side, twins (but for their ages), arms crossed stiffly. Dr. Armbruster said to her, "You might find the next few months immensely more tolerable, enjoyable even, under hormonal therapy. Fathers, it would seem, have always had to learn to bond with their offspring. For you we have something the pharmaceutical companies call 'Mother's Medley.' "

"No, thank you, Doctor," said Eleanor, who glared at her chief of staff, who immediately uncrossed her arms. Eleanor came over to me and I transferred the chassis to her. "Heavy," she said. "And look, it's missing a finger!" One of its tiny fingers was indeed missing, the stub end rough like plaster.

"Don't be concerned," said Dr. Armbruster. "Fingers and toes grow back in days. Just don't break off the head," she laughed.

"Sam, look," Eleanor exclaimed. "Look at this tiny little penis. Isn't it the cutest thing?"

As I looked, something funny happened to me. I had a vivid impression or image, as I do when at work in my studio, in which I saw the chassis, not as a brittle lump of fixed flesh, but as a living, warm, squirming, naked butterball of a baby. And I looked between its chubby legs and saw it was a he, a little guy. He looked up at me, chortled, and waved his tiny fists. Right then I felt a massive piece of my heart shift in my chest. The whole situation finally dawned on me. I was about to become a parent, a *father*. I looked at the chassis and saw my son. Why a son, I couldn't say, but I knew I must have a *son*.

Eleanor touched my arm, "Are you okay?"

"Yes, it's nothing. By the way, that's one piece I hope doesn't chip off."

She laughed, but when she saw that I was serious she said, "We'll have to see about that." She drilled me with her terribly old eyes and said. "About that we'll just have to see."

Back at the Williams Towers in Bloomington, we lay on the balcony in the late afternoon sun and skimmed the queue of messages. Our friends had grown tired of our good fortune: the congratulations were fewer and briefer and seemed, by-and-large, insincere, even tinged with underlying resentment.

And who could blame them? Of all the hundreds of people we knew, none of them had a real child. Many people, it was true, had had children in the old days, before the Population Treaties when babies were considered an ecological nuisance, but that was almost sixty years ago, and sixty years was a long time to live outside the company of children. Probably no one begrudged us our child, although it was obvious to everyone—especially to us—that major strings had been pulled for us at the Department of Health and Human Services. String-pulling, itself, did not bother El, but anonymous string-pulling did. She had sent her security chief into the nets, but he was unable to identify our benefactor. El insisted that whoever was responsible was surely not a benefactor, for a baby could hardly be considered a reward. Most likely an enemy, perhaps an off-planet rival she had aced out of the Indianapolis post, which meant the baby was bait in some as yet unsprung plot. Or perhaps the baby was simply a leash her superiors at the Tri-D council had decided to fit her with. In any case, Eleanor was convincing herself she was about to make the worst mistake of her life.

She deleted the remaining queue of messages and turned to me. "Sam, please talk me out of this baby thing." We lay on our balcony halfway up the giant residential tower that ended, in dizzying perspective, near the lower reaches of the canopy. The canopy, invisible during the day, appeared viscous in the evening light, like a transparent film that a stiff breeze caused to ripple and fold upon itself. In contrast, our tower had a matte surface encrusted with thousands of tiny black bumps. These were the building's resident militia slugs, absorbing the last light of the setting sun to top off their energy stores for a busy night patrolling living rooms and bedrooms.

"You're just nervous," I said to Eleanor.

"I have impeccable instincts."

"Did you ever have children before?"

"Not that it's relevant, but yes, two, a boy and a girl, in my old life. Tom died as a child in an accident. Angie grew up, moved away, married, led a successful career as a journalist, and died at age fifty-four of breast cancer. A long time ago." Eleanor turned over, bare rump to the sky, chin resting on sun-browned arms. "I grieved for each of them forever, and then one day I stopped. All that's left are memories, which are immaterial to this discussion."

"Would you like to have another?"

"Yes, desperately."

"Why 'desperately'?"

She was silent for a while. I watched a slug creep along the underside of the balcony of the apartment above us. "I don't know," she said. "It's funny. I've already been through it all: pregnancy, varicose veins, funerals. I've been through menopause and—worse—back through remenses. I was so tangled up in motherhood, I never knew if I was coming or going. I loved or hated every moment of it, wouldn't have traded it for the world. But when it was all over I felt an unbearable burden lifted from me. Thank god, I said, I won't have to do that again. Yet since the moment we learned of the permit, my arms have been aching to hold a baby. I don't know why. I think it's this schoolgirl body of mine. It's a baby machine, and it intends to force its will on me. I have often observed that you men regard your bodies as large pets, and I've never understood that, till now. I've never felt so removed from myself, from my body.

"But it doesn't have to have its way, does it? I can rise above it. Let's tell them to keep their chassis."

The slug bypassed our balcony, but another slug was making its way slowly down the wall.

I said, "What about this leash theory of yours?"

"I'm sure I'm correct in my assessment. They could get to me by threatening *you*, of course, but they know if it came down to it, I would—no offense—cut you loose."

"No offense taken."

She placed her hand on my cheek. "You know how much I love you. Or maybe you don't know yet. But I'm expendable, Sam, and so are you."

"But not a baby."

"No," she said, "not a baby, not *my* baby. I would do anything to keep my baby safe, and they know it. Let's refuse the permit, Sam. Okay?"

The militia slug had sensed us. It was coming in for a taste. "What about me?" I said. "I might enjoy being a dad. And can you imagine our baby, El? A little critter crawling around our ankles, half you and half me, a little Elsam or Sameanor?"

She closed her eyes and smiled. "That would be a pitiable creature."

"And speaking of ankles," I said, "we're about to be tasted."

The slug, a tiny thing, touched her ankle, attached itself to her for a moment, then dropped off. With the toes of her other foot, Eleanor scratched the tasting site. Slugs only tickled her. With me it was different. There was some nerve tying my ankle directly to my penis, and I found that warm, prickly kiss unavoidably arousing. So, as the slug attached itself to my ankle, El watched mischievously. At that moment, in the glow of the setting sun, in the delicious ache of perfect health, I didn't need the kiss of a slug to arouse me. I needed only a glance from my wife, from her ancient eyes set like opals in her girlish body. This must be how the Greek gods lived on Olympus. This must be the way it was meant to be, to grow ancient and yet to have the strength and appetites of youth. El gasped melodramatically as she watched my penis swell. She turned herself toward me, coyly covering her breasts and pubis with her hands. The slug dropped off me and headed for the balcony wall.

We lay side by side, not yet touching. I was stupid with desire and lost control of my tongue. I spoke without thinking. I said, "Mama."

The word, the single word, "mama," struck her like a physical thing. Her whole body shuddered, and her eyes went wide with surprise. I repeated it, "Mama," and she shut her eyes and turned away from me. I sidled over to her, wrapped my arms around her, and took possession of her ear. I tugged its lobe with my lips. I breathed into it. I pushed her sweat-damp hair clear of it and whispered into it, "I am the papa, and you are the mama." I watched her face, saw a ghost of a smile, and repeated, "Mama."

"Again."

"Maamma, maamma, maamma."

"Crazy papa."

"You are the mama, and mama will give papa a son."

Her eyes flew open at that, fierce, challenging, and amused. "How will papa arrange that, I wonder."

"Like this," I said as I rolled her onto her back and kissed and stroked her. But she was indifferent to me, willfully unresponsive. Nevertheless, I let my tongue play up and down her body. I visited all the sweet spots I had discovered since first we made love, for I knew her body to be my ally. Her body and I wanted the same thing. Soon, with or without El's blessing, her body opened herself to me, and when she was ready, and I was ready, and all my tiny sons inside me were ready, I began to tease her, going in, coming out, going slow, going fast, not going at all, eventually going all in a rush.

Somewhere in the middle of this, a bird, a crow, came crashing to the deck next to us. What I could make out, through the thick envelope that surrounded it, was a mass of shiny black feathers, a broken beak clattering against the deck and a smudge of blood that quickly boiled away. The whole bird, in fact, was being disassembled. Steam rose from the envelope, which emitted a piercing wail of warning. Henry spoke loudly into my ear, *Attention, Sam! In the name of safety, the militia isolation device orders you to move away from it at once.*

We were too excited to pay much mind. The envelope seemed to be doing its job. Nevertheless, we dutifully moved away; we rolled away belly to belly in a teamwork maneuver that was a delight in itself. A partition, ordered by Eleanor's cabinet no doubt, formed to separate us from the unfortunate bird. We were busy making a son and we weren't about to stop until we were through.

Later, when I brought out dinner and two glasses of visola on a tray, El sat at the patio table in her white terry robe looking at the small pile of elemental dust on the deck—carbon, sodium, calcium and whatnot—that had once been a bird. It was not at all unusual for birds to fly through the canopy, or for a tiny percentage of them to become infected outside. What *was* unusual was that, upon reentering the canopy, being tasted, found bad, and enveloped by a swarm of smartactives, so much of the bird should survive the fall in so recognizable a form, as this one had.

El smirked at me and said, "It might be Ms. Rickert, come back to haunt us."

We both laughed uneasily.

The next day I felt the urge to get some work done. It would be another two days before we could give the orphanage the go-ahead, and I was restless. Meanwhile, Eleanor had a task force meeting scheduled in the living room.

I had claimed an empty bedroom in the back for my work area. It about matched my Chicago studio in size and aspect. I had asked the building super, a typically dour reginald, to send up a man to remove all the furniture except for an armchair and a nightstand. The chair needed a pillow to support the small of my back, but otherwise it was adequate for long sitting sessions. I pulled the chair around to face a blank inner wall that Henry had told me was the north wall, placed the nightstand next to it, and brought in a carafe of strong coffee and some sweets from the kitchen. I made myself comfortable.

"Okay, Henry, take me to Chicago." The empty bedroom was instantly transformed into my studio, and I sat in front of my favorite window wall overlooking the Chicago skyline and lakefront from the 303rd floor of the Drexler Building. The sky was dark with storm clouds. Rain splattered against the window. There was nothing like a thunderstorm to stimulate my creativity.

"Henry, match Chicago's ionic dynamics here." As I sipped my coffee and watched lightning strike neighboring towers, the air in my room took on a freshly scrubbed ozone quality. I felt at rest and invigorated.

When I was ready, I turned the chair around to face my studio. It was just as I had left it months ago. There was the large, oak work table that dominated the east corner. Glass-topped and long-legged, it was a table you could work at without bending over. I used to stand at that table endlessly twenty and thirty years ago when I still lived in Chicago. Now it was piled high with prized junk: design trophies, hunks of polished gemstones from Mars and Jupiter, a scale model Japanese pagoda of cardboard and mica, a box full of my antique key collection, parcels wrapped in some of my most successful designs, and—the oldest objects in the room—a mason jar of paint brushes, like a bouquet of dried flowers.

I rose from my chair and wandered about my little domain, taking pleasure in my life's souvenirs. The cabinets, shelves, counters, and floor were as heavily laden as the table: an antelope skin spirit drum; an antique pendulum mantle clock that houseputer servos kept wound; holocubes of some of my former lovers and wives; bits of colored glass, tumbleweed, and driftwood in whose patterns and edges I had once found inspiration; and a whale vertebra used as a footstool. This room was more a museum now than a functional studio, and I was more its curator than a practicing artist.

I went to the south wall and looked into the corner. Henry's original container sat atop three more identical ones. "How's the paste?" I said.

"Sufficient for the time being. I'll let you know when we need more."

"More? This isn't enough? There's enough paste here now to run a major city."

"Eleanor Starke's cabinet is more powerful than a major city."

"Yes, well, let's get down to work." I returned to my armchair. The storm had passed the city and was retreating across the lake, turning the water midnight blue. "What have you got on the egg idea?"

Henry projected a richly ornate egg in the air before me. Gold leaf and silver wire, inlaid with once-precious gems, it was modeled after the Fabergé masterpieces favored by the last of the Romanoff Tsars. But instead of enclosing miniature clockwork automatons, these would be merely expensive wrapping for small gifts. You'd crack them open. You could keep the pieces, which would reassemble, or toss them into the soup bin for recycling credits.

"It's just as I told you last week," said Henry. "The public will hate it. I tested it against Simulated Us, the Donohue Standard, the Person in the Street, and Focus Rental." Henry filled the air around the egg with dynamic charts and graphs. "Nowhere are positive ratings higher than 7 percent, or negative ratings lower than 68 percent. Typical comments call it 'old-fashioned,' and 'vulgar.' Matrix analysis finds that people do not like to be reminded of their latent fertility. People resent ..."

"Okay, okay," I said. "I get the picture." It was a dumb concept. I knew as much when I proposed it. But I was so enamored by my own soon-to-be-realized fertility, I had lost my head. I thought people would be drawn to this archetypal symbol of renewal, but Henry had been right all along, and now he had the data to prove it.

If the truth be told, I had not come up with a hit design in five years, and I was worried that maybe I never would again.

"It's just a dry spell," said Henry, sensing my mood. "You've had them before, even longer."

"I know, but this one is the worst."

"You say that every time."

To cheer me up, Henry began to play my wrapping paper portfolio, projecting my past masterpieces larger than life in the air.

I held patents for package applications in many fields, from emergency blankets and temporary skin, to military camouflage and video paint. But my own favorites, and probably the public's as well, were my novelty gift wraps. My first was a video wrapping paper that displayed the faces of loved ones (or celebrities if you had no loved ones) singing "Happy Birthday" to the music of the New York Pops. That dated back to 2025 when I was a molecular engineering student.

My first professional design was the old box-in-a-box routine, only my boxes didn't get smaller as you opened them, but larger, and in fact could fill the whole room until you chanced upon one of the secret commands, which were any variation of "stop" (whoa, enough, cut it out, etc.) or "help" (save me, I'm suffocating, get this thing off me, etc.).

Next came wrapping paper that screamed when you tore or cut it. That led to paper that resembled human skin. It molded itself perfectly and seamlessly (except for a belly button) around the gift and had a shelf life of fourteen days. You had to cut it to open the gift, and of course it bled. We sold mountains of that stuff.

The human skin led to my most enduring design, a perennial that was still common today, the orange peel. It too wrapped itself around any shape seamlessly (and had a navel). It was real, biological orange peel. When you cut or ripped it, it squirted citrus juice and smelled delightful.

I let Henry project these designs for me. I must say I was drunk with my own achievements. I gloried in them. They filled me with the most selfish wonder.

I was terribly good, and the whole world knew it.

Yet even after this healthy dose of self-love, I wasn't able to buckle down to anything new. I told Henry to order the kitchen to fix me some more coffee and some lunch.

On my way to the kitchen I passed the living room and saw that Eleanor was having difficulties of her own. Even with souped-up holoservers, the living room was a mess. There were dozens of people in there and, as best as I could tell, just as many rooms superimposed over each other. People, especially important people, liked to bring their offices with them when they went to meetings. The result was a jumble of merging desks, lamps, and chairs. Walls sliced through each other at drunken angles. Windows issued cityscape views of New York, London, Washington, and Moscow (and others I didn't recognize) in various shades of day and weather. People, some of whom I knew from the news-nets, either sat at their desks in a rough, overlapping circle, or wandered through walls and furniture to kibitz with each other and with Eleanor's cabinet.

At least this is how it all appeared to me standing in the hallway, outside the room's holo anchors. To those inside, it might look like the Senate chambers. I watched for a while, safely out of holo range, until Eleanor noticed me. "Henry," I said, "ask her how many of these people are here in realbody." Eleanor raised a finger, one, and pointed to herself.

I smiled. She was the only one there who could see me. I continued to the kitchen and brought my lunch back to my studio. I still couldn't get started, so I asked Henry to report on my correspondence. He had answered over five hundred posts since our last session the previous week. Four-fifths of these concerned the baby. We were invited to appear—*with the baby*—on every major talk show and magazine. We were threatened with lawsuits by the Anti-Transubstantiation League. We were threatened with violence by several anonymous callers (who would surely be identified by El's security chief and prosecuted by her attorney general). A hundred seemingly ordinary people requested permission to visit us in realbody or holo during nap time, bath time, any time. Twice that number accused us of elitism. Three men and one woman named Sam Harger claimed that their fertility permit was mistakenly awarded to me. Dr. Armbruster's prediction was coming true and the baby hadn't even been converted yet.

This killed an hour. I still didn't feel creative, so I called it quits. I took a shower, shaved. Then I went, naked, to stand outside the entrance to the living room. When Eleanor saw me, her eyes went big, and she laughed. She held up five fingers, five minutes, and turned back to her meeting.

I went to my bedroom to wait for her. She spent her lunch break with me. When we made love that day and the next, I enjoyed a little fantasy I never told her about. I imagined that she was pregnant in the old-fashioned way, that her belly was enormous, melon-round and hard, and that as I moved inside her, as we moved together, we were teaching our son his first lesson in the art of human love.

On Thursday, the day of the conversion, we took a leisurely breakfast on the terrace of the New Foursquare Hotel in downtown Bloomington. A river of pedestrians, students and service people mostly, flowed past our little island of metal tables and brightly striped umbrellas. The day broke clear and blue and would be hot by noon. A gentle breeze tried to snatch away our menus. The Foursquare had the best kitchen in Bloomington, at least for desserts. Its pastry chef, Mr. Duvou, had built a reputation for the classics. That morning we (mostly me) were enjoying strawberry shortcake with whipped cream and coffee. Everything—the strawberries, the wheat for the cakes, the sugar, coffee beans, and cream—was grown, not assembled. The preparation was done lovingly and skillfully by hand. All the waitstaff were steves, who were highly sensitive to our wants and who, despite their ungainly height, bowed ever so low to take our order.

I moistened my finger with my tongue and made temporary anchor points where I touched the table and umbrella pole. We called Dr. Armbruster. She appeared in miniature, desk and all, on my place mat.

"It's a go, then?" she said.

"Yes," I said.

"Yes," said Eleanor, who took my hand.

"Congratulations, both of you. You are two of the luckiest people in the world."

We already knew that.

"Traits? Enhancements?" asked Dr. Armbruster.

We had studied all the options and decided to allow Nature and chance, not some well-meaning engineer, to roll our genes together into a new individual. "Random traits," we said, "and standard enhancements."

"That leaves gender," said Dr. Armbruster.

I looked at Eleanor who smiled. "A boy," she said. "It definitely wants to be a boy."

"A boy it is," said Dr. Armbruster. "I'll get the lab on it immediately. The recombination should take about three hours. I'll monitor the progress and keep you apprised. We will infect the chassis around noon. Make an appointment for a week from today to come in and take possession of ... your son. We like to throw a little birthing party. It's up to you to make media arrangements, if any.

"I'll call you in about an hour. And congratulations again!"

We were too nervous to do anything else, so we ate shortcake and drank coffee and didn't talk much. We mostly sat close and said meaningless things to ease the tension. Finally Dr. Armbruster, seated at her tiny desk, called back.

"The recombination work is about two-thirds done and is proceeding very smoothly. Early readings show a Pernell Organic Intelligence quotient of 3.93—very impressive, but probably no surprise to you. So far, we know that your son has Sam's eyes, chin, and skeleto-muscular frame, and Eleanor's hair, nose, and ... eyebrows."

"I'm afraid my eyebrows are fairly dominant," said Eleanor.

"Apparently," said Dr. Armbruster.

"I'm mad about your eyebrows," I said.

"And I'm mad about your frame," Eleanor said.

We spent another hour there, taking two more updates from Dr. Armbruster. I ordered an iced bottle of champagne, and guests from other tables toasted us with coffee cups and visola glasses. I was slightly tipsy when we finally rose to leave. To my annoyance, I felt the prickly kiss of a militia slug at my ankle. I decided I'd better let it finish tasting me before I attempted to thread my way through the jumble of tables and chairs. The slug seemed to take an unusual length of time.

Eleanor, meanwhile, was impatient to go. "What is it?" she laughed. "Are you drunk?"

"Just a slug," I said. "It's almost done." But it wasn't. Instead of dropping off, it elongated itself and looped around both of my ankles so that when I turned to join Eleanor, I tripped and fell into our table, which crashed into a neighboring one.

Everything happened at once. As I fell, the slippery shroud of an isolation envelope snaked up my body to my face and sealed itself above my head. But it did not cushion my fall; I banged my nose on the flagstone. Everything grew dim as the envelope coalesced, so that I could barely make out the tables and umbrellas and the crowd of people running past me like horror-show shadows. There was Eleanor's face, momentarily, peering in at me, and then gone. "Don't go!" I shouted. "Eleanor, help!" But she melted into the crowd on the pedway. I tried to get up, to crawl, but my arms and legs were tightly bound.

Henry said, *Sam, I'm being probed, and I've lost contact with Eleanor's system.*

"What's going on?" I screamed. "Tell them to make it stop." I, too, was being probed. At first my skin tingled as in a gelbath at a juve clinic. But these smartactives weren't polite and weren't about to take a leisurely three days to inspect my cells. They wanted in right away; they streamed through my pores, down my nasal passage and throat, up my urethra and anus and spread out to capture all of my organs. My skin burned. My heart stammered. My stomach clamped and sent a geyser of pink shortcake mush and champagne-curdled cream back up my throat. But with the envelope stretched across my face, there was nowhere for the vomit to go except as a thin layer down my throat and chest. The envelope treated it as organic matter attempting escape and quickly disassembled it, scalding me with the heat of its activity. I rolled frantically about trying to lessen the pain, blindly upsetting more tables. Shards of glass cut me without cutting the envelope, so thin it stretched, and my blood leaked from me and simmered away next to my skin.

Fernando Boa, said someone in Henry's voice in Spanish. *You are hereby placed under arrest for unlawful escape and flight from State of Oaxaca authorities. Do not resist. Any attempt to resist will result in your immediate execution.*

"My name is not Boa," I cried through a swollen throat. "It's Harger, Sam Harger!"

I squeezed my eyelids tight against the pain, but the actives cut right through them, coating my eyeballs and penetrating them to taste the vitreous humor inside. Brilliant flashes and explosions of light burst across my retinae as each rod and cone was inspected, and a dull, hurricane roar filled my head.

Henry shouted, *Shall I resist? I think I should resist.*

"NO!" I answered. "No, Henry!"

The real agony began then, as all up and down my body, my nerve cells were invaded. Attached to every muscle fiber, every blood vessel, every hair follicle, embedded in my skin, my joints, my intestines, they all began to fire at once. My brain rattled in my skull. My guts twisted inside out. I begged for unconsciousness.

Then, just as suddenly, the convulsions ceased, the trillions of engines inside me abruptly quit. *I can do this,* Henry said. *I know how.*

"No, Henry," I croaked.

The envelope itself flickered, then fell from me like so much dust. I was in daylight and fresh air again. Soiled, bleeding, beat-up, and bloated, but whole. I was alone on a battlefield of smashed umbrellas and china shrapnel. I thought maybe I should crawl away from the envelope's dust, but the slug still shackled my ankles. "You shouldn't have done it, Henry," I said. "They won't like what you did."

Without warning, the neural storm slammed me again, worse than before. A new envelope issued from the slug. This one squeezed me like a tube of oil paint, starting at my feet, crushing the bones and working up my legs.

"Please," I begged, "let me pass out."

I didn't pass out, but I went somewhere else, to another room, where I could still hear the storm raging on the other side of a thin wall. There was someone else in the room, a man I halfway recognized. He was well-muscled and of middle height, and his yellow hair was streaked with white. He wore the warmest of smiles on his coarse, round face.

"Don't worry," he said, referring to the storm beyond the wall, "it'll pass."

He had Henry's voice.

"You should have listened to me, Henry," I scolded. "Where did you learn to disobey me?"

"I know I don't count all that much," said the man. "I mean, I'm just a construct, not a living being. A servant, not a coequal. But I want to tell you how good it's been to know you."

❖ ❖ ❖

I awoke lying on my side on a gurney in a ceramic room, my cheek resting in a small puddle of clear fluid. I was naked. Every cell of me ached. A man in a militia uniform, a jerry, watched me sullenly. When I sat up, dizzy, nauseous, he held out a bundle of clean clothes. Not my clothes.

"Wha' happe' me?" My lips and tongue were twice their size.

"You had an unfortunate accident."

"Assiden'?"

The jerry pressed the clothes into my hands. "Just shut up and get dressed." He resumed his post next to the door and watched me fumble with the clothes. My feet were so swollen I could hardly pull the pants legs over them. My hands trembled and could not grip. I could not keep my vision focused, and my head pulsed with pain. But all in all, I felt much better than I had a little while ago.

When, after what seemed like hours, I was dressed, the jerry said, "Captain wants to see ya."

I followed him down deserted ceramic corridors to a small office where sat a large, handsome young man in a neat blue uniform. "Sign here," he said, pushing a slate at me. "It's your terms of release."

Read this, Henry, I tongued with a bruised tongue. When Henry didn't answer I felt the pull of panic until I remembered that the slave processors inside my body that connected me to Henry's box in Chicago had certainly been destroyed. So I tried to read the document myself. It was loaded with legalese and interminable clauses, but I was able to glean from it that by signing it, I was forever releasing the National Militia from all liability for whatever treatment I had enjoyed at their hands.

"I will not sign this," I said.

"Suit yourself," said the captain, who took the slate from my hands. "You are hereby released from custody, but you remain on probation until further notice. Ask the belt for details." He pointed to the belt holding up my borrowed trousers.

I lifted my shirt and looked at the belt. The device stitched to it was so small I had missed it, and its ports were disguised as grommets.

"Sergeant," the Captain said to the jerry, "show Mr. Harger the door."

"Just like that?" I said.

"What do you want, a prize?"

It was dark out. I asked the belt they'd given me for the time, and it said in a flat, neuter voice, "The time is seven forty-nine and thirty-two seconds." I calculated I had been incarcerated—and unconscious—for about seven hours. On a hunch, I asked what day it was. "The date is Friday, 6 April 2092."

Friday. I had been out for a day and seven hours.

There was a tube station right outside the cop shop, naturally, and I managed to find a private car. I climbed in and eased my aching self into the cushioned seat. I considered calling Eleanor, but not with that belt. So I told it to take me home. It replied, "Address please."

My anger flared and I snapped, "The Williams Towers, stupid."

"City and state, please."

I was too tired for this. "Bloomington!"

"Bloomington in California, Idaho, Illinois, Indiana, Iowa, Kansas, Kentucky, Maryland, Minnesota, Missouri, Nebraska, New York ..."

"Hold it! Wait! Enough! Where the hell am I?"

"You're at the Western Regional Militia Headquarters, Utah."

How I longed for my Henry. He'd get me home safe with no hassle. He'd take care of me. "Bloomington," I said mildly, "Indiana."

The doors locked, the running lights came on, and the car rolled to the injection ramp. We coasted down, past the local grid, to the intercontinental tubes. The belt said, "Your travel time to the Williams Towers in Bloomington, Indiana, will be one hour, fifty-five minutes." When the car entered the slipstream, I was shoved against the seat by the force of acceleration. Henry would have known how sore I was and shunted us to the long ramp. Fortunately, I had a spare Henry belt in the apartment, so I wouldn't have to be without him for long. And after a few days, when I felt better, I'd again reinstall him inbody.

I tried to nap, but was too sick. My head kept swimming, and I had to keep my eyes open, or I would have vomited.

It was after 10:00 PM when I arrived under the Williams Towers, but the station was crowded with residents and guests. I felt everyone's eyes on me. Surely everyone knew of my arrest. They would have watched it on the nets, witnessed my naked fear as the shroud raced up my chest and face.

I walked briskly, looking straight ahead, to the row of elevators. I managed to claim one for myself, and as the doors closed I felt relief. But something was wrong; we weren't moving.

"Floor please," said my new belt in its bland voice.

"Fuck you!" I screamed. "Fuck you fuck you fuck you! Listen to me, you piece of shit, and see if you can get this right. I want you to call Henry, that's my system. Shake hands with him. Put him in charge of all of your miserable functions. Do you hear me?"

"Certainly, sir. What is the Henry access code?"

"Code? Code? I don't know code." That kind of detail had been Henry's job for over eighty years. I had stopped memorizing codes and ID numbers and addresses, anniversaries and birthdates long ago. "Just take me up! We'll stop at every floor above 200!" I shouted. "Wait. Hold it. Open the doors." I had the sudden, urgent need to urinate. I didn't think I could hold it long enough to reach the apartment, especially with the added pressure from the high-speed lift.

There were people waiting outside the elevator doors. I was sure they had heard me shouting. I stepped through them, a sick smile plastered to my face, the sweat rolling down my forehead, and I hurried to the men's room off the lobby.

I had to go so bad, that when I stood before the urinal and tried, I couldn't. I felt about to burst, but I was plugged up. I had to consciously calm myself, breathe deeply, relax. The stream, when it finally emerged, seemed to issue forever. How many quarts could my bladder hold? The urine was viscous and cloudy with a dull metallic sheen, as though mixed with aluminum dust. Whatever the militia had pumped into me would take days to excrete. At least there was no sign of bleeding, thank god. But it burned. And when I was finished and about to leave the rest room, I felt I had to go again.

Up on my floor, my belt valet couldn't open the door to the apartment, so I had to ask admittance. The door didn't recognize me, but Eleanor's cabinet gave it permission to open. The apartment smelled of strong disinfectant. "Eleanor, are you home?" It suddenly occurred to me that she might not be.

"In here," called Eleanor. I hurried to the living room, but Eleanor wasn't there. It was her sterile elder twin, her chief of staff, who sat on the couch. She was flanked by the attorney general, dressed in black, and the security chief, grinning his wolfish grin.

"What the hell is this," I said, "a fucking cabinet meeting? Where's Eleanor?"

In a businesslike manner, the chief of staff motioned to the armchair opposite the couch, "Won't you please join us, Sam. We have much to discuss."

"Discuss it among yourselves," I yelled. "Where's Eleanor?" Now I was sure that she was gone. She had bolted from the cafe and kept going; she had left her three stooges behind to break the bad news to me.

"Eleanor's in her bedroom, but she …"

I didn't wait. I ran down the hallway. But the bedroom door was locked. "Door," I shouted, "unlock yourself."

"Access," replied the door, "has been extended to apartment residents only."

"That includes me, you idiot." I pounded the door with my fists. "Eleanor, let me in. It's me—Sam."

No reply.

I returned to the living room. "What the fuck is going on here?"

"Sam," said the elderly chief of staff, "Eleanor will see you in a few minutes, but not before …"

"Eleanor!" I yelled, turning around to look at each of the room's holoeyes. "I know you're watching. Come out; we need to talk. I want you, not these dummies."

"Sam," said Eleanor behind me. But it wasn't Eleanor. Again I was fooled by her chief of staff who had crossed her arms like an angry El and bunched her eyebrows in an angry scowl. She mimicked my Eleanor so perfectly, I had to wonder if it wasn't El as a morphed holo. "Sam, please get a grip and sit down. We need to discuss your accident."

"My what? My accident? That's the same word the militia used. Well, it was no accident! It was an assault, a rape, a vicious attack. Not an accident!"

"Excuse me," said Eleanor's attorney general, "but we were using the word 'accident' in its legal sense. Both sides have provisionally agreed …"

I left the room without a word. I needed urgently to urinate again. Mercifully, the bathroom door opened to me. I knew I was behaving terribly, but I couldn't help myself. On the one hand I was relieved and grateful that Eleanor was there, that she hadn't left me—yet. On the other hand, I was hurting and confused and angry. All I wanted was to hold her, be held by her. I needed her at that moment more than I had ever needed anyone in my life. I had no time for holos. But, it was reasonable that she should be frightened. Maybe she thought I was infectious. My behavior was doing nothing to reassure her. I had to control myself.

My urine burned even more than before. My mouth was cotton dry. I grabbed a glass and filled it with tap water. Surprised at how thirsty I was, I drank glassful after glassful. I washed my face in the sink. The cool water felt so good, I stripped off my militia-issue clothes and stepped into the shower. The water revived me, fortified me. Not wanting to put the clothes back on, I wrapped a towel around myself, went out, and told the holos to ask Eleanor to toss out some of my clothes for me. I promised I wouldn't try to force my way into the bedroom when she opened the door.

"All your clothes were confiscated by the militia," said the chief of staff, "but Fred will bring you something of his."

Before I could ask who Fred was, a big, squat-bodied russ came out of the back bedroom, the room I used for my trips to Chicago. He was dressed in a conservative business suit and carried a brown velvet robe over his arm.

"This is Fred," said the chief of staff. "Fred has been assigned to ..."

"What?" I shouted. "El's afraid I'm going to throttle her holos? She thinks I would break down that door?"

"Eleanor thinks nothing of the kind," said the chief of staff. "Fred has been assigned by the Tri-Discipline Board."

"Well, I don't want him here. Send him away."

"I'm afraid," said the chief of staff, "that as long as Eleanor remains a governor, Fred stays. Neither she nor you have any say in the matter."

The russ, Fred, held out the robe to me, but I refused it and said, "Just stay out of my way, Fred." I went to the bathroom and found one of Eleanor's terry robes in the linen closet. It was tight on me, but it would do.

Returning to the living room, I sat in the armchair facing the cabinet's couch. "Okay, what do you want?"

"That's more like it," said the chief of staff. "First, let's get you caught up on what's happened so far."

"By all means. Catch me up."

The chief of staff glanced at the attorney general who said, "Yesterday morning, Thursday, 5 April, at precisely 10:47:39, while loitering at the New Foursquare Cafe in downtown Bloomington, Indiana, you, Samson P. Harger, were routinely analyzed by a National Militia Random Testing Device, Metro Population Model 8903AL. You were found to be in noncompliance with the Sabotage and Espionage Acts of 2036, 2038, 2050, and 2090. As per procedures set forth in ..."

"Please," I said, "in English."

The security chief said in his gravelly voice, "You were tasted by a slug, Mr. Harger, and found bad, real bad. So they bagged you."

"What was wrong with me?"

"Name it. You went off the scale. First, the DNA sequence in a sample of ten of your skin cells didn't match each other. Also, a known nastie was identified in your blood. Your marker genes didn't match your record in the National Registry. You *did* match the record of a known terrorist with an outstanding arrest warrant. You also matched the record of someone who died twenty-three years ago."

"That's ridiculous," I said. "How could the slug read all those things at once?"

"That's what the militia wanted to know. So they disassembled you."

"They! What?"

"Any one of those conditions gave them the authority they needed. They didn't have the patience to read you slow and gentle like, so they pumped you so full of smartactives you filled a swimming pool."

"They. Completely?"

"All your biological functions were interrupted. You were legally dead for three minutes."

It took me a moment to grasp what he was saying. "So what did they discover?"

"Nothing," said the security chief, "zip, nada. Your cell survey came up normal. They couldn't even get the arresting slug, nor any other slug, to duplicate the initial readings."

"So the arresting slug was defective?"

"We forced them to concede that the arresting slug may have been defective."

"So they reassembled me and let me go, and everything is okay?"

"Not quite. That particular model slug has never been implicated in a false reading. This would be the first time, according to the militia, and naturally they're not eager to admit that. Besides, they still had you on another serious charge."

"Which is?"

"That your initial reading constituted an unexplained anomaly."

"An unexplained anomaly? This is a crime?"

I excused myself for another visit to the bathroom. The urgency increased when I stood up from the armchair and was painful by the time I reached the toilet. This time the stream didn't burn me, but hissed and gave off some sort of vapor, like steam. I watched in horror as my situation became clear to me.

I marched back to the living room, stood in front of the three holos, rolled up a sleeve, and scratched and rubbed my arm, scraping off flakes of skin which cascaded to the floor, popping and flashing like a miniature fireworks display. "I've been seared!" I screamed at them. "You let them sear me!"

"Sit down," said the chief of staff. "Unfortunately, there's more."

I sat down, still holding my arm out. Beads of sweat dropped from my chin and boiled away on the robe in little puffs of steam.

"Eleanor feels it best to tell you everything now," said the chief of staff. "It's not pretty, so sit back and prepare yourself for more bad news."

I did as she suggested.

"They weren't about to let you go, you know. You had forfeited all of your civil rights. If you weren't the spouse of a Tri-Discipline Governor, you'd have simply disappeared. As it was, they proceeded to eradicate all traces of your DNA from the environment. They flooded this apartment first, removed every bit of hair, phlegm, mucous, skin, fingernail, toenail, semen, and blood that you have shed or deposited since moving in. They sent probes down the plumbing for trapped hair. They subjected Eleanor to a complete body douche. They scoured the halls, elevators, lobby, dining room, linen stores, laundry. They were most thorough. They have likewise visited your townhouse in Connecticut, the bungalow in Cozumel, the juve clinic, your hotel room on the Moon, the shuttle, and all your and Eleanor's domiciles all over the Protectorate. They are systematically following your trail backward for a period of thirty years."

"My Chicago studio?"

"Of course."

"Henry?"

"Gone."

"You mean in isolation, right? They're interrogating him, right?"

The security chief said, "No, eradicated. He resisted. Gave 'em quite a fight, too. But no civilian job can withstand the weight of the National Militia. Not even us."

I didn't believe Henry was gone. He had so many secret backups. At this moment he was probably laying low in a half dozen parking loops all over the solar system.

But another thought occurred to me. "My son!"

The chief of staff said, "When your accident occurred, the chassis had not yet been infected with your and Eleanor's recombinant. Had it been, the militia would have disassembled it too. Eleanor prevented the procedure at the last moment and turned over all genetic records and material."

I tried sifting through this. My son was dead, or rather, never started. But at least Eleanor had saved the chassis. We could always try—no we couldn't. *I was seared!* My cells were locked. Any attempt to read or overwrite any of my cells would cause those cells to fry.

The attorney general said, "The chassis, however, had already been brought out of stasis and was considered viable. To allow it to develop with its original genetic complement, or to place it back into stasis, would have exposed it to legal claims by its progenitors. So Eleanor had it infected. It's undergoing conversion at this moment."

"Infected? Infected with what? Did she clone herself?"

The chief of staff laughed, "Heavens, no. She had it infected with the recombination of her genes and those of a simulated partner, a composite of several of her past consorts."

"Without my agreement?"

"You were deceased at the time. She was your surviving spouse."

"I was deceased for only three minutes! I was retrievably dead. Obviously, retrievable!"

"Alive you would have been a felon, and the fertility permit would have been annulled."

I closed my eyes and leaned back into the chair. "Okay," I said, "what else?" When no one answered, I said, "To sum up then, I have been seared, which means my genes are booby trapped. Which means I'm incapable of reproducing, or even of being rejuvenated. So my life expectancy has been reduced to ... what? ... another hundred years or so? Okay. My son is dead. Pulled apart before he was even started. Henry is gone, probably forever. My wife—no, my widow—is having a child by another man—men."

"Women actually," said the chief of staff.

"Whatever. Not by me. How long did all of this take?"

"About twenty minutes."

"A hell of a busy twenty minutes."

"To our way of thinking," said the attorney general, "a protracted interval of time. The important negotiation in your case occurred within the first five seconds of your demise."

"You're telling me that Eleanor was able to figure everything out and cook up her simulated partner in five seconds?"

"Eleanor has in readiness at all times a full set of contingency plans to cover every conceivable threat we can imagine. It pays, Mr. Harger, to plan for the worst."

"I guess it does." The idea that all during our time together, El was busy making these plans was too monstrous to believe. "So tell me about these negotiations."

"First, let me impress upon you," said the chief of staff, "the fact that Eleanor stuck by you. Few other Tri-Discipline officers would take such risks to fight for a spouse. Also, only someone in her position could have successfully prosecuted your case. The militia doesn't have to answer phone calls, you know.

"As to the details, the attorney general can fill you in later, but here's the agreement in a nutshell. Given the wild diagnosis of the arresting slug and the subsequent lack of substantiating evidence, we calculated the most probable cause to be a defect in the slug, not some as yet unheard of nastie in your body. Further, as a perfect system of any sort has never been demonstrated, we predicted there to be records of other failures buried deep in militia archives. Eleanor threatened to air these files publicly in a civil suit. To do so would have cost her a lifetime of political capital, her career, and possibly her life. But as she was able to convince the militia she was willing to proceed, they backed down. They agreed to revive you and place you on probation, the terms of which are stored in your belt system, which we see you have not yet reviewed. The major term is your searing. Searing effectively neutralizes the threat in case you *are* the victim of a new nastie. Also, as a sign of good faith, we disclosed the locations of all of Henry's hidey-holes."

"What?" I rose from my seat. "You gave them Henry?"

"Sit down, Mr. Harger," said the security chief.

But I didn't sit down. I began to pace. So this is how it works, I thought. This is the world I live in.

"Please realize, Sam," said the chief of staff, "they would have found him out anyway. No matter how clever you think you are, given time, all veils can be pierced."

I turned around to answer her, but she and her two colleagues were gone. I was alone in the room with the russ, Fred, who stood sheepishly next to the hall corridor. He cleared his throat and said, "Governor Starke will see you now."

II

It's been eight long months since my surprise visit to the cop shop. I've had plenty of time to sit and reflect on what's happened to me, to meditate on my victimhood.

Shortly after my accident, Eleanor and I moved into our new home, a sprawling old farmstead on the outskirts of Bloomington. We have more than enough room here, with barns and stables, a large garden, apple and pear orchards, tennis courts, swimming pool, and a dozen service people to run everything. It's really very beautiful, and the whole eighty acres is covered with its own canopy, inside and independent of the Bloomington canopy, a bubble inside a bubble. Just the place to raise the child of a Tri-Discipline governor.

The main house, built of blocks of local limestone, dates

back to the last century. It's the home that Eleanor and I dreamed of owning. But now that we're here, I spend most of my time in the basement, for sunlight is hard on my seared skin. For that matter, rich food is hard on my gut, I bruise easily inside and out, I can't sleep a whole night through, all my joints ache for an hour or so when I rise, I have lost my sense of smell, and I've become hard of hearing. There is a constant taste of brass in my mouth and a dull throbbing in my skull. I go to bed nauseated and wake up nauseated. The doctor says my condition will improve in time as my body adjusts, but that my health is up to me now. No longer do I have resident molecular homeostats to constantly screen, flush, and scrub my cells, nor muscle toners or fat inhibitors. No longer can I go periodically to a juve clinic to correct the cellular errors of aging. Now I can and certainly will grow stouter, slower, weaker, balder, and older. Now the date of my death is decades, not millennia, away. This should come as no great shock, for this was the human condition when I was born. Yet, since my birth, the whole human race, it seems, has boarded a giant ocean liner and set sail for the shores of immortality. I, however, have been unceremoniously tossed overboard.

So I spend my days sitting in the dim dampness of my basement corner, growing pasty white and fat (twenty pounds already), and plucking my eyebrows to watch them sizzle like fuses.

I am not pouting, and I am certainly not indulging in self-pity, as Eleanor accuses me. In fact, I am brooding. It's what artist do, we brood. To other, more active people, we appear selfish, obsessive, even narcissistic, which is why we prefer to brood in private.

But I'm not brooding about art or package design. I have quit that for good. I will never design again. That much I know. I'm not sure what I *will* do, but at least I know I've finished that part of my life. It was good; I enjoyed it. I climbed to the top of my field. But it's over.

I am brooding about my victimhood. My intuition tells me that if I understand it, I will know what to do with myself. So I pluck another eyebrow. The tiny bulb of muscle at the root ignites like an old fashioned match, a tiny point of light in my dark cave and, as though making a wish, I whisper, "Henry." The hair sizzles along its length until it burns my fingers, and I have to drop it. My fingertips are already charred from this game.

I miss Henry terribly. It's as though a whole chunk of my mind were missing. I never knew how deeply integrated I had woven him into my psyche, or where my thoughts stopped and his started. When I ask myself a question these days, no one answers.

I wonder why he did it, what made him think he could resist the militia. Can machine intelligence become cocky? Or did he knowingly sacrifice himself for me? Did he think he could help me escape? Or did he protect our privacy in the only way open to him, by destroying himself? The living archive of my life is gone, but at least it's not in the loving hands of the militia.

My little death has caused other headaches. My marriage ended. My estate went into receivership. My memberships, accounts, and privileges in hundreds of services and organizations were closed. News of my death spread around the globe at the speed of light, causing tens of thousands of data banks to toggle my status to "deceased," a position not designed to toggle back. Autobituaries, complete with footage of my mulching at the Foursquare Cafe, appeared on all the nets the same day. Every reference to me records both my dates of birth and death. (Interestingly, none of my obits or bio's mention the fact that I was seared.) Whenever I try to use my voiceprint to pay a bill, alarms go off. El's attorney general has managed to reinstate most of my major accounts, but my demise is too firmly entrenched in the world's web to ever be fully corrected. The attorney general has, in fact, offered me a routine for my belt system to pursue these corrections on a continuous basis. She, as well as the rest of El's cabinet, has volunteered to educate my belt for me as soon as I install a personality bud in it. It will need a bud if I ever intend to leave the security of my dungeon. But I'm not ready for a new belt buddy.

I pluck another eyebrow, and by its tiny light I say, "Ellen."

We are living in an armed fortress. Eleanor says we can survive any form of attack here: conventional, nuclear, or molecular. She feels completely at ease here. This is where she comes to rest at the end of a long day, to glory in her patch of Earth, to adore her baby, Ellen. Even without the help of Mother's Medley, Eleanor's maternal instincts have all kicked in. She is mad with motherhood. Ellen is ever in her thoughts. If she could, El would spend all her time in the nursery in realbody, but the duties of a Tri-D governor call her away. So she has programmed a realtime holo of Ellen to be visible continuously in the periphery of her vision, a private scene only she can see. No longer do the endless meetings and unavoidable luncheons capture her full attention. No longer is time spent in a tube car flitting from one corner of the Protectorate to another a total waste. Now she secretly watches the jennies feed the baby, bathe the baby, perambulate the baby around the duck pond. And she is always interfering with the jennies, correcting them, undercutting whatever place they may have won in the baby's affection. There are four jennies. Without the namebadges on their identical uniforms, I wouldn't be able to tell them apart. They have overlapping twelve-hour shifts, and they hand the baby off like a baton in a relay race.

I have my own retinue, a contingent of four russes: Fred, the one who showed up on the day of my little death, and three more. I am not a prisoner here, and their mission is to protect the compound, Governor Starke, and her infant daughter, not to watch me, but I have noticed that there is always one within striking distance, especially when I go near the nursery. Which I don't do very often. Ellen is a beautiful baby, but I have no desire to spend time with her, and the whole house seems to breathe easier when I stay down in my tomb.

Yesterday evening a jenny came down to announce dinner. I threw on some clothes and joined El in the solarium off the kitchen where lately she prefers to take all her meals. Outside the window wall, heavy snowflakes fell silently in the blue-grey dusk. El was watching Ellen explore a new toy on the carpet. When she turned to me, her face was radiant, but I had no radiance to return. Nevertheless, she took my hand and drew me to sit next to her.

"Here's Daddy," she cooed, and Ellen warbled a happy greeting. I knew what was expected of me. I was supposed to adore the baby, gaze upon her plenitude and thus be filled with grace. I tried. I tried because I truly want everything to work out, because I love Eleanor and wish to be her partner in parenthood. So I watched Ellen and meditated on the marvel and mystery of life. El and I are no longer at the tail end of the long chain of humanity—I told myself—flapping in the cold winds of evolution. Now we are grounded. We have forged a new link. We are no longer grasped only by the past, but we grasp the future. We have created the future in flesh.

When El turned again to me, I was ready, or thought I was. But she saw right through me to my stubborn core of indifference. Nevertheless, she encouraged me, prompted me with, "Isn't she beautiful?"

"Oh, yes," I replied.

"And smart."

"The smartest."

Later that evening, when the brilliant monstrance of her new religion was safely tucked away in the nursery under the sleepless eyes of the night jennies, Eleanor rebuked me. "Are you so selfish that you can't accept Ellen as your daughter? Does it have to be your seed or nothing? I know what happened to you was shitty and unfair, and I'm sorry. I really am. I wish to hell the slug got me instead. I don't know why it missed me. Maybe the next one will be more accurate. Will that make you happy?"

"No, El, don't talk like that. I can't help it. Give me time."

Eleanor reached over and put an arm around me. "I'm sorry," she said. "Forgive me. It's just that I want us to be happy, and I feel so guilty."

"Don't feel guilty. It's not your fault. I knew the risk involved in being with you. I'm an adult. I can adapt. And I do love Ellen. Before long she'll have her daddy wrapped around her little finger."

Eleanor was skeptical, but she wanted so much to believe me. That night she invited herself to my bedroom. We used to have an exceptional sex life. Sex for us was a form of play, competition, and truth-telling. It used to be fun. Now it's a job. The shaft of my penis is bruised by the normal bend and torque of even moderate lovemaking. My urethra is raw from the jets of scalding semen when I come. Of course I use special condoms and lubricants for the seared, without which I would blister El's vagina, but it's still not comfortable for either of us. El tries to downplay her discomfort by saying things like, "You're hot, baby," but she can't fool me. When we made love that night, I pulled out before ejaculating. El tried to draw me back inside, but I wouldn't go. She took my sheathed penis in her hands, but I said not to bother. I hadn't felt the need for a long time.

In the middle of the night, when I rose to go to my dungeon, Eleanor stirred and whispered, "Hate me if you must, but please don't blame the baby."

I ask my new belt how many eyebrow hairs an average person of my race, sex, and age has. The belt can access numerous encyclopedias to do simple research like this. *Five hundred fifty in each eyebrow,* it replies in its neuter voice. That's one thousand one hundred altogether, plenty of fuel to light my investigation. I pluck another and say, "Fred."

For Fred is a complete surprise to me. I had never formed a relationship with a clone before. They are service people. They are interchangeable. They wait on us in stores and restaurants. They clip our hair. They perform the menialities we cannot, or prefer not, to assign to machines. How can you tell one joan or jerome from another anyway? And what could you possibly talk about? Nice watering can you have there, kelly. What's the weather like up there, steve?

But Fred is different. From the start he's brought me fruit and cakes reputed to fortify tender digestive tracts, sunglasses, soothing skin creams, and a hat with a duckbill visor. He seems genuinely interested in me, even comes down to chat after his shift. I don't know why he's so generous. Perhaps he never recovered from the shock of first meeting me, freshly seared and implacably aggrieved. Perhaps he recognizes that I'm the one around here most in need of his protection.

When I was ready to start sleeping with Eleanor again and I needed some of those special thermal condoms, my belt couldn't locate them on any of the shoppers, not even on the medical supply ones, so I asked Fred. He said he knew of a place and would bring me some. He returned the next day with a whole shopping bag of special pharmaceuticals for the cellular challenged: vitamin supplements, suppositories, plaque-fighting tooth soap, and knee and elbow braces. He brought twenty dozen packages of condoms, and he winked as he stacked them on the table. He brought more stuff he left in the bag.

I reached into the bag. There were bottles of cologne and perfume, sticks of waxy deodorant, air fresheners and odor eaters. "Do I stink?" I said.

"Like cat's piss, sir. No offense."

I lifted my hand to my nose, but I couldn't smell anything. Then I remembered the "stinkers" on the Moon shuttle, and I knew how I smelled. I wondered how Eleanor, during all those months, could have lived with me, eaten with me, and never mentioned it.

There was more in the bag: mouthwash and chewing gum. "My breath stinks too?"

In reply, Fred crossed his eyes and inflated his cheeks.

I thanked him for shopping for me, and especially for his frankness.

"Don't mention it, sir," he said. "I'm just glad to see you back in the saddle, if you catch my drift."

III

Two days ago was Ellen's first birthday. Unfortunately, Eleanor had to be away in Europe. Still, she arranged a little holo birthday party with her friends. Thirty-some people sat around, mesmerized by the baby, who had recently begun to walk. Only four of us, baby Ellen, a jenny, a russ, and I, were there in realbody. When I arrived and sat down, Ellen made a beeline for my lap. People laughed and said, "Daddy's girl."

I had the tundra dream again last night. I walked through the canopy lock right out into the white, frozen, endless tundra. The feeling was one of escape, relief, security.

My doctor gave me a complete physical last week. She said I had reached equilibrium with my condition. This was as good as it would get. Lately, I have been exercising. I have lost a little weight and feel somewhat stronger. But my joints ache something terrible and my doctor says they'll only get worse. She prescribed an old-time remedy: aspirin.

Fred left us two months ago. He and his wife succeeded in obtaining berths on a new station orbiting Mars. Their contracts are for five years with renewal options. Since arriving there, he's visited me in holo a couple times, says their best jump pilot is a stinker. And they have a stinker cartographer. Hint, hint.

Last week I finally purchased a personality bud for my belt system. It's having a rough time with me because I refuse to interact with it. I haven't even given it a name yet. I can't think of any suitable one. I call it "Hey, you," or "You, belt." Eleanor's chief of staff has repeated her offer to educate it for me, but I declined. In fact, I told her that if any of them breach its shell even once, I will abort it and start over with a new one.

Today at noon, we had a family crisis. The jenny on duty acquired a nosebleed while her backup was off running an errand. I was in the kitchen when I heard Ellen crying. In the nursery I found a hapless russ holding the kicking and screaming baby. The jenny called from the open bathroom door, "I'm coming. One minute, Ellie, I'm coming." When Ellen saw me she reached for me with her fat little arms and howled.

"Give her to me," I ordered the russ. His face reflected his hesitation. "It's all right," I said.

"One moment, sir," he said and tongued for orders. "Okay, here." He gave me Ellen who wrapped her arms around my neck. "I'll just go and help Merrilee," he said, relieved, as he crossed to the bathroom. I sat down and put Ellen on my lap. She looked around, caught her breath, and resumed crying; only this time it was an easy, mournful wail.

"What is it?' I asked her. "What does Ellen want?" I reviewed what little I knew about babies. I felt her forehead, though I knew babies don't catch sick anymore. And with everycleans, they don't require constant changing. The remains of lunch sat on the tray, so she'd just eaten. A bellyache? Sleepy? Teething pains? Early on, Ellen was frequently feverish and irritable as her converted body sloughed off the remnants of the little boy chassis she'd overwritten. I thought about the son we almost had, and I wondered why during my year of brooding I never grieved for him. Was it because he never had a soul? Because he never got beyond the purely data stage of recombination? Because he never owned a body? And what about Ellen, did she have her own soul, or did the original boy's soul stay through the conversion? And if it did, would it hate us for what we've done to its body?

Ellen cried, and the russ stuck his head out the bathroom every few moments to check on us. This angered me. What did they think I was going to do? Drop her? Strangle her? I knew they were watching me, all of them: the chief of staff, the security chief. They might even have awakened Eleanor in Hamburg or Paris where it was after midnight. No doubt they had a contingency plan for anything I might do.

"Don't worry, Ellie," I crooned. "Mama will be here in just a minute."

"Yes, I'm coming, I'm coming," said Eleanor's sleep-hoarse voice.

Ellen, startled, looked about, and when she didn't see her mother, bawled louder and more boldly. The jenny, holding a blood-soaked towel to her nose, peeked out of the bathroom.

I bounced Ellen on my knee. "Mama's coming, Mama's coming, but in the meantime, Sam's going to show you a trick. Wanna see a trick? Watch this." I pulled a strand of hair from my head. The bulb popped as it ignited, and the strand sizzled along its length. Ellen quieted in mid-fuss, and her eyes went wide. The russ burst out of the bathroom and sprinted toward us, but stopped and stared when he saw what I was doing. I said to him, "Take the jenny and leave us."

"Sorry, sir, I ..." The russ paused, then cleared his throat. "Yes, sir, right away." He escorted the jenny, her head tilted back, from the suite.

"Thank you," I said to Eleanor.

"I'm here." We turned and found Eleanor seated next to us in an ornately carved, wooden chair. Ellen squealed with delight but did not reach for her mother. Already by six months she had been able to distinguish between a holobody and a real one. Eleanor's eyes were heavy, and her hair mussed. She wore a long silk robe, one I'd never seen before, and her feet were bare. A sliver of jealousy pricked me when I realized she had probably been in bed with a lover. But what of it?

In a sweet voice, filled with the promise of soft hugs, Eleanor told us a story about a kooky caterpillar she'd seen that very day in a park in Paris. She used her hands on her lap to show us how it walked. Baby Ellen leaned back into my lap as she watched, and I found myself rocking her ever so gently. There was a squirrel with a bushy red tail involved in the story, and a lot of grown-up feet wearing very fashionable shoes, but I lost the gist of the story, so caught up was I in the voice that was telling it. El's voice spoke of an acorn who lost its cap and ladybugs coming to tea, but what it said was, I made you from the finest stuff. You are perfect. I will never let anyone hurt you. I love you always.

The voice shifted gradually, took an edge, and caused me the greatest sense of loss. It said, "And what about my big baby?"

"I'm okay," I said.

El told me about her day. Her voice spoke of schedules and meetings, a leader who lost his head, and diplomats coming to tea, but what it said was, You're a grown man who is capable of coping. You are important to me. I love it when you tease me and make me want you. It gives me great pleasure and takes me out of myself for a little while.

Nothing is perfect, but we try. I will never hurt you. I love you always. Please don't leave me.

I opened my eyes. Ellen was a warm lump asleep on my lap, fist against cheek, lips slightly parted. I brushed her hair from her forehead with my sausage-like finger and traced the round curve of her cheek and chin. I must have examined her for quite a while, because when I looked up, Eleanor was waiting to catch my expression.

I said, "She has your eyebrows."

Eleanor laughed a powerful laugh. "Yes, my eyebrows. Poor baby."

"No, they're her nicest feature."

"Yes, well, and what's happened to yours?"

"Nervous habit," I said. "I'm working on my chest hair now."

"In any case, you seem better."

"Yes, I believe I've turned the corner."

"Good, I've been so worried."

"In fact, I have just now thought of a name for my belt valet."

"Yes?" she said, relieved, interested.

"Skippy."

She laughed a belly laugh, "Skippy? *Skippy?*" Her face was lit with mirthful disbelief.

"Well, he's young," I said.

"Very young, apparently."

"Tomorrow I'm going to teach him how to hold a press conference." I didn't know I was going to say that until it was said.

"I see." Eleanor's voice hardened. "Thank you for warning me. What will it be about?"

"I'm sorry. That just came out. I guess it'll be a farewell. And a confession."

I could see the storm of calculation in Eleanor's face as her host of advisors whispered into her ear. Had I thrown them a curve? Come up with something unexpected? "What sort of confession?" she said. "What do you have to confess?"

"That I'm seared."

"That's not your fault, and no one will want to know anyway."

"Maybe not, but I've got to say it. I want people to know that I'm dying."

"We're *all* dying. Every living thing dies."

"Some faster than others."

"Sam, listen to me. I love you."

I knew that she did, her voice said so. "I love you too, but I don't belong here anymore."

"Yes, you do, Sam. This is your home."

I looked around me at the solid limestone wall, at the oak tree outside the window and the duck pond beyond. "It's very nice. I could have lived here, once."

"Sam, don't decide now. Wait till I return. Let's discuss it."

"Too late, I'm afraid."

She regarded me for several moments and said, "Where will you go?" By her question, I realized she had come to accept my departure, and I felt cheated. I had wanted more of a struggle. I had wanted an argument, enticements, tears, brave denial. But that wouldn't have been my El, my plan-for-everything Eleanor.

"Oh, I don't know," I said. "Just tramp around for a while, I guess. See what's what. Things have changed since the last time I looked." I stood up and held out the sleeping baby to El, who reached for her before we both remembered El was really in Europe. I placed Ellen in her crib and tucked her in. I kissed her cheek and quickly wiped it, before my kiss could burn her skin.

When I turned, El was standing, arms outstretched. She grazed my chest with her disembodied fingers. "Will you at least wait for me to give you a proper farewell? I can be there in four hours."

I hadn't intended to leave right away. I had just come up with the idea, after all. I needed to pack. I needed to arrange travel and accommodations. This could take days. But then I realized I was gone already and that I had everything I'd need: Skippy around my waist, my credit code, and the rotting stink of my body to announce me wherever I went.

She said, "At least stay in touch." A single tear slid down her face. "Don't be a stranger."

Too late for that too, dear El.

We were out of our minds with joy. Joy in full bloom and out of control, like weeds in our manicured lives.

"VTV"

My working title for this piece was "No Redeeming Value," and my goal was to see just how despicable a picture of humanity I could paint and get away with. I think I was successful, for when "VTV" appeared in print, it was received with stone cold silence.

There is nothing to love in this story, so it's okay with me if you skip it and go on to the next one. If you do decide to read it, keep in mind that it appeared four years before the Abu Ghraib scandal and the George W. Bush administration's attempt to justify its own use of torture.

VTV

TONY "MOOKIE" JONESTONE sits in Production Booth "C" absentmindedly devouring chicken salad pitas while applying the finishing touch to a piece entitled, "Jobless Man Backs Mother's Car Over Pregnant Girlfriend's Cat." He views it again all the way through and laughs out loud. Though he's worked on it all morning, it's still fresh and funny. He shakes his head, wipes tears from his eyes, and punches the buttons that will send a copy to Dispatch. Before he does, though, he watches it one last time. Again he cracks up. Damn, it's good. It's low comedy to be sure, but it says something important about suburban life in the new American millennium.

On the other hand, it's just one more piece of hack work.

During the last three years on the Poodle Patrol, Jonestone has become a wizard at turning the raw crap that viewers send in on DVD into pearls of entertainment, like this one. A little editing here, some minimal voiceover there, an occasional sound effect—that's all it takes. His efforts are beginning to attract notice. Just last week an assistant to an associate vice president of the Critter Division told him that his name came up favorably last month at the quarterly oversight meeting. That has to be good, but it's not enough. Three years is a long time to languish in an entry level position. Jonestone is afraid his career has stalled. The whole point of joining the Poodle Patrol, after all, is to get a shot at real journalism.

The production booth door slides open and a pimply face appears. It's Mikey, the foley tech intern. Jonestone waves him in. "My man," he says patting him on the back. "Thanks for the kitten vocals. They're *perfect.* Sit down; I'll show you."

"No time," squeaks the boy, his strained voice a testament to the urgency of his errand. "They're all like screaming for you in Remote."

"Why?" Jonestone says. "Some circus elephant go berserk?"

"Not Critter Channel. *News* Remote."

Jonestone freezes. News Remote? At first he's sure there's some mistake, but then he thinks this might be it. Still, it's too much to hope for. "They want me to go out on a news story? Why? Where's their people?"

"Bluer's in Baja on Hurricane Babs," replies the intern. "And Williams is in County General for her new liver. Yurek Rutz is in jail again."

"What about Bu'tro?"

"He's doing the fires." The boys voice cracks. "You're the *only* one here!"

As the name of each veteran reporter is eliminated, Jonestone's hope surges. Could it be true? Could today be the day? Suddenly, like an apparition, Edmund Clark appears in the hall behind the intern. Clark, the most senior VTV producer on the West Coast and multiple Peabody Award winner for such pieces as, "Date Rape with Organ Theft," and "Enraged Dad Murders Wrong Family," is one of Jonestone's heroes. Jonestone is speechless.

Clark looks him over and sniffs. "Well? We're not paying you to sit around and gawk. Get a move on, son. Asa's waiting for you in the Bus Barn. Move, move, move."

"Yes, sir!" says Jonestone. He leaps from his chair and pulls on his jacket. "What kind of story is it, sir? Black on yellow? White on black?" This is Clark's own specialty, but Jonestone doesn't care if it's black on black, just as long as it doesn't involve cats or dogs or sharks or giraffes.

"It's political," says Clark. "I'll brief you en route."

The big VTV Metrolux van is idling with Asa behind the wheel. Jonestone sprints across the oil-stained concrete thinking, *political?* He doesn't know jack about politics. He climbs into the back of the van and pulls its heavy, armor-plated door shut. "Asa, my man!" he yells to the front. But Asa makes no reply, throws the big diesel into gear, and guns it up the ramp. In the back, Jonestone straps himself into the seat behind the mobile deck and brings up the control board. The banks of small monitors blink to life, and he can see the control room back in the studio. To his surprise, Abbie Ford, not Clark, is sitting in the director's chair.

"'Lo, Mookie," she says when she sees him in her monitor. "Heard they'd tapped you for this. It's a big opportunity for you."

"Thanks."

"I'll be doing the play-by-play, assuming the story gets that far." There's movement behind Ford's head. Someone behind her taps her on the shoulder, and she says, "Before I turn you loose, I wanted to congratulate you on that 'Dog on a Leash,' bit of yours. Brilliant work. Brilliant. I heard someone upstairs say they've never seen work of that caliber come out of the Poodle Patrol. You certainly caught their attention."

She blows him a kiss as she gets up. "Well, gotta go. Break a leg, guy. Y'hear?"

Clark replaces her in the seat. "Isn't that special," Clark says. "Mookie's got a fan." He leans in close to the deckcam and his face fills Jonestone's monitor. "But just between you, me, and the source code, don't let that 'Dog on a Leash' piece of yours turn into a leash around your own neck."

Jonestone recoils at his tone of voice. "What do you mean?"

Clark winks and says, "You know what I mean." He abruptly changes the subject, punches buttons to slave Jonestone's monitors to his. "Let's concentrate on the matter at hand, shall we? Watch this clip."

Jonestone turns to a monitor playing a security camera recording in which a portly man in a crisp suit with a rolled up newspaper tucked under his arm balances a paper coffee cup and strolls across an underground parking garage. But Jonestone hardly sees him. He's thinking about Clark's implied threat. Does he know? How is that possible? Jonestone was careful to cover his tracks. Maybe he just misunderstood, and Clark was referring to something else entirely.

"Jonestone," Clark says, "pay attention."

"Yes, who is he?" The man in the vid is approaching a large, black automobile mostly blocked from view by a massive concrete pillar.

"The late Señor Arturo Moreno, in DC this morning on his way to petition U. S. Senator Saul Jasperson for the opportunity to testify before the Pan American Trade Committee."

Not LA politics, Jonestone suddenly realizes, *national!* The man disappears behind the pillar. All Jonestone can see of his auto is its passenger window and rear end, and he gets a tug in his gut that tells him he's about to witness something bad. He wishes the security camera were better placed. Who puts cameras near pillars anyway? He grits his teeth and prepares for the explosion. But instead of a blast, there's a blinding flash that, despite the pillar, momentarily blanks out the camera's pickup array. As the picture gradually returns, Jonestone is surprised to see the car still intact, though its tires are on fire. A thick pall of black smoke sweeps across the low concrete ceiling. Suddenly the clip loops back to the beginning: portly man, crisp suit, newspaper, and coffee.

Jonestone says, "What was that?"

"DC police aren't confirming, but we believe it was one of those suncrackers."

Jonestone's seen something about them. The new tool of paid assassins. A gram of hydrogen plasma generated in a package as small and flat and weightless as a book of matches. No metal parts, no telltale chemical odor. Capable of attaining solar temperatures in a millisecond-long flash. Cheap. The perfect device for effective letter bombs, crank cell phones, carpet mines, etc. "Whatever it was," Clark continues, "it was rigged up inside the car. It vaporized him and most of the car's interior, blew out the windshield. Of course we don't get to see *that* because the freakin' *pillar's* in the way." Clark shakes his head. "What a waste of horse meat."

Jonestone says, "We airing this?"

"Not yet. No one is."

Jonestone watches the flash again on the monitor. "But if we're not airing it, and if it happened in DC, what does it have to do with us?"

"Check your data monitor."

Jonestone does so and scrolls through the results of several Lexus searches. The victim's CV. Facts and figures. A mug shot. Moreno was an official of an NGO headquartered in Bogatá called La Sociedad para la Promoción de Tourismo Indigeno (SOPTI). Jonestone says, "The Society for the Promotion of what kind of Tourism?"

"Indigenous," says Clark. "Part of the cultural assets movement." When Jonestone draws a blank, Clark continues, "You know, if Mr. Gringo wants to come down to photograph us, eat our beans, get sunburnt on our beaches, he pays *us*, not Carnival Cruises, not Holiday Inn." Clark dismisses the topic with a wave of his pink hand. "That whole whiny ContraNafteros thing. Read up on it later. The important thing is that yesterday in a hotel in Belize almost the entire SOPTI board of directors was barbecued by a similar suncracker device. Only two members were absent from that meeting. One was our Moreno friend here—" into his fourth loop of walking across the garage "—and the other a Dr. Josephina Abesea, professor of Aboriginal Goddess Studies at—wouldn't you know it—our own UCLA."

The van takes a corner too fast, and Jonestone braces himself against the transmitter housing. There's a mug shot on his monitor of a woman in her thirties. High cheekbones, cafe au lait complexion, rather sharp nose, severely trimmed black hair. "You figure they'll do her on campus?"

"We should be so lucky—the place is bristling with cameras. No, so far there's been no collateral casualties, only SOPTI members. We're tapped into the cameras outside her office, but we think they'll do her at home." Clark glances at one of his monitors. "Damn!" He punches a button and says, "Asa, what's taking so long? I thought you knew how to drive." Asa doesn't reply, or Jonestone doesn't hear him, but he sees on one of his monitors what Clark is looking at. A street shot of a nondescript residential neighborhood, a wood construction apartment complex. Tucked into the upper right hand corner of the picture is the familiar logo squib of their biggest competitor, VNN. Clark disappears from the monitor, and Jonestone hears him shout, "Ford! Where's my drone? I told you to launch a goddamn drone!"

Hurry up and wait. The VTV van arrives at the apartment complex on a sleepy Verdugo Hills Drive five blocks off Wilshire Blvd. and parks behind three rival news vans.

Jonestone moves into the cab to sit shotgun. Asa pointedly ignores him. When the police permit comes over the FAX, Jonestone helps Asa roll out their titanium blastcams and set two of them on the sidewalk in front of the apartment and two in the alley behind. The blastcams look like huge, foil-wrapped chocolate kisses. They're shaped to hug the ground and deflect a force of up to a decaton of high explosives at close range. They can withstand hurricanes, tornadoes, fire, collapsing buildings, and many other common disasters, all the while producing beautiful, network quality pictures. It's hard work shoving them into place, and the men sweat in the afternoon heat. Jonestone tries to strike up a conversation, but Asa remains sullenly mute, speaking only as the task requires.

By the time they get the blastcams online, word comes in that the VTV dronecam is circling high overhead like a suborbital vulture. Now they can relax, for even if they're forced by events to evacuate the neighborhood, Clark will have adequate coverage.

Eventually it's dinner time. Jonestone checks the fridge and asks Asa what he wants, certain that food will cheer him up. Asa acts like he doesn't hear him. Jonestone has worked with Asa in the past, and they'd gotten on well enough. He wonders what's wrong with him now. He nukes two containers of soup and brings them and a dozen sandwiches and cold beer to the cab. "Minestrone or chicken noodle?" he says and sets the tray on the engine housing. Asa shoots him a withering glance and turns to stare out the high, bulletproof windshield at the street. The street is busy now as residents arrive home from work and school. People used to be upset if they came home and found their street lined with big, ugly armored vans with satellite dishes cocked south and electronic peeping gear swivelling like radar. People used to try to push the blastcams away from their houses as though that might lift whatever curse had befallen their neighborhood.

But in the nicer neighborhoods, at least, people have learned the drill. Cell phones to ears, they dash into their homes, only to emerge minutes later bearing suitcases, stereos, computers, pets. They'll go to motels tonight and watch their street on TV to see when it's safe to return.

Asa snorts and says, "Lived in the Keys once. Used to be able to evacuate in three minutes flat."

Jonestone mulls this over. The Keys, hurricanes, Hurricane Babs in Baja. Hmmm. "Were you supposed to go down and help Bluer?"

Asa shakes his head and sighs. Jonestone is tired of playing games. He peels the lid off the noodle soup, releasing a cloud of fragrant chicken steam. "Yum," he says. Asa's stomach growls in reply. Jonestone starts dinner without him. He turns on the radio and selects their sister station.

After a few minutes of being ignored, Asa turns off the radio and says, "You're a good kid, Mookie, and it's none of my business how you want to run your career, but I gotta tell ya, that one piece of yours went way over the top. Way over the top."

"Which piece?"

Asa peers at him through slitted eyes. "I think you know which one."

Jonestone consults a mental checklist of his recent work. There was the "Cannibalistic Potbellied Pig," and the one about the "PMS Pit Bull." There was "Who Invited a Boa Constrictor to my Daughter's Slumber Party?" but it was still tied up in court and hasn't aired yet. "Uhh," he says, "was it 'How to Mummify Your Pony'?"

Asa shakes his head. "No, that was gross, but it wasn't cruel."

With a sinking feeling, Jonestone knows which one he means. "My—ah—'Dog on a Leash' piece?"

Asa closes his eyes and nods. "Bingo. Your sicko 'Dog on a Leash' piece. Like I said, it's none of my business, but I don't see how you can live with yourself doing something like that. It makes me feel *bad* just thinking about it. I don't *like* feeling bad." He buries his face in his hands. "It sticks in my mind like a canker sore that won't go away."

Jonestone is starting to get annoyed. There's no doubt in his mind that the only reason he's here on his first news assignment is because of that piece. There are plenty of other young turks working their way up through the ranks of VTV's other divisions. They could have chosen any of them to pinch hit this story, but no, they picked him, Anthony Jonestone, because he caught their attention with his "Dog on a Leash." Suddenly he remembers Clark's odd comment earlier and has a moment of panic. "You're right," he snaps, "it's none of your business." He gathers up soup, beer, and sandwiches and goes to the back to eat alone.

The thing is, he didn't have to do a thing to improve "Dog on a Leash;" it was perfect the way he received it. It arrived just like they all do, in a hand-addressed bubble pack on a consumer-grade disk, nothing to distinguish it from the dozens of vids he receives from wannabe Critter Channel contributors each day. He spends an hour first thing each morning popping them into his player and counting to ten. If a vid doesn't grab his attention by the time he reaches ten, he ejects and trashcans it in one fluid flip of the wrist. He almost trashed this one. It looked like a hayseed travelogue, and it started out pretty slow. Two young bumpkins are filming through the windshield of their car.

Now we're turning on Gomper Street, one of them says.

Grain elevators, says the other. A hand flashes through the frame to point. *Grain elevators over there, dickhead.*

They sound boringly high school, and Jonestone's finger is hovering over the eject button when they stop at an intersection, and a pickup truck speeds by. We catch a glimpse of its driver, another farm boy.

Where's Grant going so fast?

Beats me.

The camera quickly pans and zooms to catch the pickup leaving the intersection and frames a dog, an Irish Setter, leaning dangerously over the tailgate on its front paws. It's a beautiful dog, tall and leggy. Light shimmers off its feathery mahogany coat; its pink tongue lolls out the side of its mouth. Jonestone takes one look at it and feels that old tug in the gut.

Leaving the intersection, the pickup hits a pothole, and the dog falls out the back. It rolls on the pavement a couple times, then a rope snaps tight, and the dog is being dragged after the pickup by its neck.

We hear the astonishment of our tour guides. We hear their engine drop into gear and see the picture lurch. There's a squeal of tires, a blaring horn, and a technically killer shot of a near collision as they cut off another car.

Go, go, go! urges the cameraman.

The engine roars as we make the turn. The pickup is half a block ahead of us by now, but the camera's formidable zoom rockets ahead and shows us that the dog has managed to find his feet; he's up and running for his life.

Move it! Move it!

Shut the fuck up!

There's a screech, and the camera lens bangs against the windshield. A station wagon has backed out of a driveway, and we're right on top of it. Our boys are screaming at each other. The girl driving the station wagon looks at us stupidly, so we back up and drive around her, over the curb, on top of someone's front lawn. Little kids stand up in a plastic wading pool as we speed by.

We're on the street again, and up ahead we see the pickup has stopped at the next corner, and we almost reach it. We're leaning on the horn.

Flash your lights!

I am! I am!

We get close enough to the idling pickup to catch a close-up of the dog. It's crouched on all fours and panting hard. If a dog can ever have a human expression, this one does. He's afraid. He doesn't understand what's happening to him. Suddenly he's jerked away, never even has a chance to stand up. He rolls through the intersection and is dragged down the street leaving a streak of blood.

Traffic is heavy, and it takes us several false starts to get across. Up ahead we see people on the sidewalk waving frantically at the pickup, but the boy, thinking they're just being neighborly, waves back and drives on. The dog is briefly on its feet, but falls again as the pickup disappears around a bend.

By the time we catch up, the pickup has been stopped by a school-crossing guard. Children are crying. We park and watch the boy get out of his pickup. We see the confusion and fear in his face. We get out of our car and examine the dog in loving detail. The pads have been shorn from his paws. His shoulders are shredded to the bone. But he's alive. *Vinnie!* shrieks the boy when he sees him, and Vinnie splashes his tail in a puddle of blood. The camera seems to become light-headed. It tilts up to look at blank blue Kansas sky. It drops to glance at the tidy frame Midwestern houses, at the children's shoes, at the crossing guard losing her lunch—something with tomatoes. Fade to black.

Asa's food congeals. Jonestone spends a couple hours at his deck boning up on the politics of tourism, the late SOPTI, and Professor Abesea. Meanwhile, his systems monitor traffic in a three block radius around their location. Clark, putting in some overtime at the studio, informs him that Abesea's car is still parked in the university lot, and that the lights are on in her office.

Outside, on the darkened street, a man in a torn T-shirt is stopping at each of the news vans in turn and cursing at them. Jonestone watches him via the blastcams and the van's roof-mounted cameras. The man stands next to Asa's side window and gestures for Asa to roll it down. Asa shakes his head and turns away. Naturally, they can pick up audio, so they hear everything the man is saying. In a gusher of foul language, he reviles them for their greed and inhumanity. He claims to be a resident of the street, and he'll be damned before he lets them scare him into abandoning his home so that big media can orchestrate a disaster. Asa is nodding his head as though he agrees with him. But then the man starts in on Asa personally, calling him a lard ass and exploiter of people's suffering. Asa just shrugs it off. He's heard it all before. Finally, the man spits at Asa. Big, yellow-streaked lugers drip down Asa's window, but not even this pegs Asa's sufferance meter.

Clark says, "That constitutes an assault on our property, Asa. Give him a little squirt of CS. Gas the fucker."

"No, chief," Asa says, "I won't. He's absolutely right in everything he says."

Clark is momentarily speechless. "Asa, don't get me wrong, but are you sure you wouldn't be happier in some other line of work?"

On the surface, the four-minute, fifty-two second doggy skidmark video appeared to be one uncut take. There was no obvious editing. As such it was extraordinary, worthy of Hollywood—the pure product. Jonestone knew he must secure it for the Critter Channel at any price. On the other hand, it was obviously too good to be true. So, with a heavy heart, Jonestone opened it in his res-editor to take a peek at the underlying code. As with all things digital, a DVD recording tracks more data than simple audio and video. It didn't take Jonestone long to find what he was looking for. The two country tour guides were very skillful. They had expertly smudged the seams, equalized the sound, and calibrated the gamma, but they had naively overlooked the digital watermarks. Without question, footage from two different cameras were cut into the final sequence. Two cameras meant pre-planning, which meant a dog had been intentionally sacrificed in the name of entertainment, which meant that under no circumstances would Critter Channel policy permit him to acquire or air the video. It was an ironclad rule—no animal snuff vids on the non-news channels. Violation of this rule would cost him his job. Furthermore, in accord with VTV's "Family Pledge of Wholesome Viewing," he was required to report the vid to an appropriate law enforcement agency and to send them the DVD as evidence of a crime, in this case wanton cruelty to an animal.

Jonestone's duty was clear. He could not have the video. The stupidity of it all angered him—what a waste of horse flesh.

Clark tells them Abesea has dropped out of sight. He tells them the court has refused them permission to deploy radiant surveillance. They've already been keeping track of heat signatures inside Abesea's apartment complex with IR tomography for some hours. Practically speaking, the court's order doesn't mean they can't snoop, just that they can't record or broadcast the surveillance. Meanwhile, the drone cam has been tracking all rental cars and registered taxis entering their perimeter, but since Abesea might use a gypsy cab or private car, they're forced to monitor all bogies within the proximal.

Jonestone is watching the icon of such a bogey making a suspicious dash towards their location. "Heads up," he calls to Asa. He straightens his tie and grabs a microphone in case he needs to dash out. They watch via the roof cam as a car approaches. But it stops three doors up the street, a man gets out and says something to the driver. He slams the door, and the car continues. Jonestone puts down the mike. False alarm. They relax.

Unexpectedly, the car stops again right next to their van, and a woman pops up in the rear seat. Asa flips on the video lights, as do the other vans, and the street is suddenly bright as noon. The woman is halfway up her steps, pursued by Guy Ray, a reporter from XNBC. But before Guy Ray can catch her, a man—the man let out of the car earlier—emerges from the shadows and knocks him down with a body block. It's all over before Jonestone can react; Guy Ray is lying curled up on the lawn, and the woman is through the front door. She pauses to blow a kiss to her escorts as they drive off. Slick.

"Did you see that?" says Asa. "That was first string linebacker Jimmy Sanchez. The driver was quarterback Mike Lee. She called in their fricken football team."

Jonestone replays the scene and freezes it where the woman stands at the door. He digitally zooms in to confirm that it is indeed Abesea. In this light she looks softer than in her mug shot. Her lips, as she puckers to blow the kiss, are pillowy. Nice.

On another monitor, Asa is tracking the progress of her heat smudge through the building. The tomography can't penetrate too deep, and she walks in and out of their range. But they manage to follow her to an apartment on the second floor. Lights go on behind shaded windows. They bounce microwaves against the window glass and pick up relayed sounds. Guy Ray, having recovered his breath, climbs the steps and rings her buzzer. They can't hear what he says into the intercom, but upstairs, relayed via her window glass, they can just make out her reply, "Please leave me alone."

Jonestone takes first watch when Asa hits the rack at 11:00 PM. Clark calls it a night around midnight and goes to his office to sleep. Jonestone slouches at the deck trying to stay awake by watching a vid he retrieved from the UCLA library of a lecture Abesea delivered to a class three years ago. She stands behind a poorly lit lectern in a blue suit that looks sharp enough to slice cheese. The school camera is locked in a close up. Jonestone's not quite awake enough to follow the point of her talk. Something about the dimorphism of tool design. According to Abesea, it seems that since prehistory, men have designed most of their important tools to require a force equal to 35 percent of an average male's maximum strength to operate. So whether he was drawing a bow or literally moving mountains, the physical effort required of him was consistent with his own gender's comfort range. These same tools, however, required 50 percent of an average female's maximum strength. Therefore, she would become quickly exhausted. To Jonestone this sounds both credible and unremarkable.

Meanwhile, Asa's soft snoring is a lullaby to his ears. Jonestone's in that in-between state where he's dreaming to the words of Abesea's lecture. They're in a station wagon. She's driving. By some dream logic, he knows they're married. She complains that it's too hard to turn the steering wheel. Power steering hasn't been invented yet, and it's somehow *his fault*. He offers to drive, and she say, *How typical.*

He awakens with a start and checks his monitors. All systems green. A look outside tells him that two of their competitors are gone. It's hard to commit all this equipment and personnel to such an unhappening story. The vans probably tooled down to South Central where good pictures are there for the taking this time of night.

Just then, a blastcam light goes from green to yellow—it's detected motion. Jonestone studies its pale night vision image. He doesn't see anything; a bird or cat might have triggered it. But the other blastcam goes to red. This could be it. "Asa!" he calls. He quickly examines all their exterior cams—nothing. He quarters a screen and has the computer replay the last five minutes backwards, meanwhile keeping an eye on the others in realtime. Asa is still snoring, so he swings around and punches him in his side. "Wake up!"

The roofcam detects realtime movement, and all the cams zero in on it. From four angles Jonestone sees the ghostly green image of a woman in a bathrobe walking across the street. Asa climbs down and squeezes into the narrow space. "'S happening?"

"I don't know. I lost her." His cameras are in search mode again. Suddenly there's a knock at the rear door. Cautiously, he opens it and looks down. There she stands, Dr. Josephina Abesea, Ph.D., in a brief robe and pink, fuzzy slippers, hugging herself against the night chill. "Hello," Jonestone says awkwardly. "I'm Tony Jonestone of VTV News." He almost slipped and said Critter Channel. "Would you care to come in and answer a few questions?"

She hesitates. She has to think about it. Finally she says, "No, thank you. I couldn't sleep, and I needed to know something. I thought maybe you knew."

"Try us. If we don't know, we have the whole world net at our fingertips." He waves to indicate the deck.

She nods and proceeds, "In your country, at what hour do the police come to kidnap you?"

"Sorry?" Jonestone says. "What hour?"

"Yes. In my country it's between 3:00 and 4:00 in the morning. We call it *turno de noche*, the time when the death squad is working. What time does that usually happen in the United States?"

"Asa?" Jonestone says.

"I'm on it," Asa replies, tapping a keyboard to initiate a search.

"This may take a few minutes," Jonestone tells Abesea. "Won't you come in while we wait?" He glances at the dark street behind her, feeling ever so much a target.

"I apologize. I didn't mean to put you to any trouble," she says and retreats a few steps in her flip-flop slippers. "I'll return to my house now."

"No, wait," Jonestone says. "Please stay."

She glances around at the dark street and says, "I think neither of us will enjoy the luxury of sleep; perhaps I can offer you coffee."

"Yes, I'd like that." At that moment the van behind them switches on its blinding video lights. Jonestone says, "Go inside; I'll join you in a minute. Hurry!"

She crosses towards her building, but the reporters cut her off. Jonestone is about to climb down and come to her aid when she pepper sprays one of them, and the others make way. When she's safely behind her door, Jonestone grabs a duffel bag and stuffs gear into it.

Asa says, "You're nuts. You want to get blown up along with her?" Jonestone peers at himself in the john mirror. He rubs his stubbly chin; there's no time to shave. He combs his hair while swallowing mouthwash.

"Tell 'em to wake up Clark," he says, pressing an earpiece into his ear. He slaps a fresh mike patch on his throat. "Take a level. One two three. One two three."

"I recognize your name," she says. They're sitting at a chipped formica table in the breakfast nook of her miniature kitchen. "Are you related to Moses Jonestone?"

Jonestone smiles. "My famous uncle." He can't take his eyes off her. In the kitchen light the sheer silk of her robe hugs her like rose-patterned skin.

"I know your uncle's work. We studied him in university. He's hanging in my living room." She points to the next room with a slender arm. When she gets up to pour the coffee, her backlit robe suggests dark shapes and compelling shadows that Jonestone is more than glad to examine. He wonders if he's misunderstood this whole Aboriginal Goddess thing. Still, he's not distracted enough to have forgotten the danger he's in just by sitting here. He'd like to mount the cameras and get out, but asking permission is often a tricky business. If you come right out and ask, they usually refuse. Abesea serves him frosted biscuits. She sits down and crosses her legs. With so short a robe, this is a delicate maneuver.

"Tell me," she says, "why I am about to be murdered, and nobody cares."

"How can you say nobody cares? There are three live broadcast news vans parked across the street."

"Yes, but why is nobody broadcasting? Even my murdered colleague and good friend, Mr. Moreno, God rest his soul, is not on the big window. Why is that, Mr. Jonestone?"

She dunks her biscuit into her coffee and catches the sodden end with her lips. Watching her do this a couple times, Jonestone feels his erection getting an erection.

Asa updates him in his earpiece, *Clark's back in the control booth. He approves your move but wants you to wire the place and scram ASAP.*

"I mean," says Abesea, unaware of Asa's intrusion, "Don't you put terrorism on the big window any more?"

Mookie, do you copy? Asa says, and Jonestone clears his throat. *Good,* Asa says and continues, *as far as that* turno de noche *goes, you can tell the professor that if you took all of the nocturnal abductions, disappearances, and break-ins in the US and Canada since 1973, the mean time for that would be 3:48* AM.

Jonestone clears his throat again and glances at the kitchen wall clock, a plastic rooster thingy with swivelling eyes. It's 1:52.

Abesea is still talking. "A heroic man travels to your country to warn your Congress about a conspiracy to pervert free trade in the southern hemisphere, and he's brutally murdered in the very capital of your country, and what's on TV?" She points again to the living room. "Grown men swallowing live guinea pigs. Nude darts tournaments. And on *your* channel, a prison lottery to serve on an execution firing squad." She throws up her hands. "I don't understand. I thought I knew how things work in the United States, but now I see I don't."

"Then I'll explain it to you," Jonestone says. "Your colleague had the misfortune of being killed off camera."

She sits there uncomprehending. "But the security camera?"

"His car was parked behind a support pillar. The security cam got nothing. Why? Didn't you watch it?"

She jumps to her feet and leaves the kitchen.

Jonestone finishes his coffee. He scouts the ceiling for the best place to stick a camera. Whatever she's doing is taking a while, so he gets up and wanders out to the living room. One whole wall of the living room is covered by a flatscreen TV wall. The sound is off, but the big window shows haydivers leaping from small aircraft without parachutes and gliding their falling bodies into oversized haystacks. This is, at best, an iffy sport.

Jonestone can hear Abesea talking on the phone in the bedroom. On the wall next to the bedroom door hangs the eposter he knew he would find, his famous uncle's photo at the top of the deck. The eposter is a large, expensive, museum-grade, tera-pixel model loaded with the MoMA exhibit of a few years back entitled, "Glyphs of the Twentieth Century: The Grammar of Images." It contains the exhibit's ninety-six images that scholars claim to be so universally familiar as to have helped engender (along with TV and the Internet) the new proto-language of glyphography. Included are such hits as: "Napalmed Naked Girl of Vietnam" (1972, Huynh Cong "Nick" Ut), "The Explosion of the Hindenburg" (1937, Murray Becker), "The Vat of Kool-Aide at Jonestown"

(1978, Frank Johnston), and his uncle's contribution, "Wrong Number" (2000, Moses "Mookie" Jonestone).

Abesea dashes from the bedroom and scowls to see him standing there. "Sit, sit," she says, raking magazines, pizza boxes, soiled laundry, dirty dishes, and toiletries from the couch. She sifts through the clutter searching for something. In disgust, she gives up and says loudly to the room, "Remote!" They both hold still a moment to listen, but the TV remote doesn't reveal its location. "To hell with it," she says and turns to the TV wall. "I have no patience to teach the TV my accent in English or Spanish," she explains apologetically before loudly addressing the wall, "TV, go to VTV political channel!" The TV seems to understand her well enough. The haydivers shrink to a small inset window along the top of the screen with the other 24 insets that make up the VTV network constellation. (Jonestone sneaks a look at the Critters Channel inset and sees it's playing a Cockroach Smashorama rerun.) Meanwhile, the Political Matters inset expands to fill the giant screen. It's showing a drone's-eye view of a hilly battlefield of the war, now in its 1034th consecutive day. Nothing much seems to be happening on the ground.

"If you can show this, why can't you show me?" Abesea says, but before Jonestone can reply, she shouts, "TV, show political channel menu." The menu tree unfurls, and Abesea threads her way through it until she finds, a dozen layers deep, the listing of her former colleague's short stroll through the parking garage. "TV, authorize payment," she says, and they watch the clip play through. "Shit," she says as the suncracker flash subsides. "Amateurs." She returns to her bedroom.

This time Jonestone follows and stands outside her door, but he can't keep up with her rapid-fire Spanish. He finds himself standing again in front of his uncle's photo. The eposter controls on the frame show that she has three other images selected to rotate with it every 72 hours: "Jack Ruby Shooting Lee Harvey Oswald" (1963, Bob Jackson),

"Spanish Civil War, Moment of Death for a Loyalist Soldier" (1936, Robert Capa), and "Shooting of Viet Cong Prisoner by South Vietnamese Brigadier General Nguyen Ngoc Loan" (1968, Eddie Adams). Abesea is a fan of fatal gunshots, it would seem. His uncle's photo portrays a Chicago telephone repairman high on a utility pole the split second a bullet exits his forehead in an eruption of hard hat and skull fragments. What makes it memorable is the look of utter astonishment on the man's face as he's flung against his tether. He has no idea what has happened to him, only that it's bad. "Wrong Number," the title tacked on by the editor at the Chicago *Evening Standard*, tells the story. The bullet came silently from out of the blue, most likely discharged from a gun over a mile away during some unreported urban firefight. Or perhaps it was one of those stray bullets people fire into the sky never thinking about them coming down again. Someone who flunked high school physics.

Abesea stands behind him looking at the eposter over his shoulder. She startles him when she says, "First time I see it, I say, hey that's me!"

"Yeah, me too."

He can feel her breath on the back of his neck. She says, "So tell me how this works. If they kill me tonight, will you broadcast it?"

He nods.

"So why not start before I'm dead?"

He's about to reply, but he feels her fingers lightly brush his hair, and he says, "You want to be on the big window tonight?" He feels her press her body lightly against him. He says, "I'll just set up the cameras," and goes to the kitchen.

He tears open fresh cam-packs with his teeth and sticks them in strategic locations on the ceilings of the various rooms. Abesea follows him silently. He activates the cams with voice code, and Asa confirms reception in the van.

Her bedroom is a shrine to towering clutter. Jonestone removes his shoes before stepping on her bed to reach the ceiling. Her blankets and sheets are twisted together like insomniac lovers.

When they return to the living room, she stands in front of the TV wall and pages through the VTV channels. She has found her TV remote. "Where are they?" she says. "Aren't they working?"

"TV," Jonestone says, "MJTVT twenty niner five." The TV wall divides into cells, each showing a different room of her apartment, the views from the four blastcams, and the van. They are time stamped, 02:11. In one of them, Jonestone and Abesea stand in front of the TV wall in front of Jonestone and Abesea standing in front of the TV wall and on and on in an infinite tunnel of video feedback. "Asa, fix the living room cam." A moment later the feedback is phased away.

Abesea surveys the wall and says, "Good."

Jonestone says, "It's still only closed circuit. We're not broadcasting yet."

"Why not?" Abesea says peevishly. "But at least you're recording, yes? So if something happens unexpected, you got it, right?"

Jonestone says, "Asa?"

Clark answers instead. *Yeah, we're toasting. Get a release and scram out of there.*

"Everything's being recorded," Jonestone tells Abesea. "Please state your name and tell us whether you agree to VTV's exclusive ownership of all the recordings we make in your apartment including all rights and proceeds from their use and sale in all media in existence and all media to be invented in the future." She does so. "Good," he says and collects his duffel bag.

"Wait," she says. "You're not leaving?"

"Yeah, I ah—have to return to the van."

"But I thought you'd wait with me?"

"I'd like to," he admits, aware that Asa and Clark are listening in, "but my job requires me to be in the van."

"Aren't you going to interview me? Don't you reporters interview people anymore?"

Interview her from the van, says Clark.

"You can't interview me after I'm dead, you know."

Jonestone checks the time stamp on the TV wall—2:16. He straightens his jacket and trousers, stands in the ceiling cam's sweet spot, counts backwards from three, and says, "I'm in the home of Dr. Josephina Abesea, the sole surviving member of the Society for the Promotion of Indigenous Tourism, a Pan American organization headquartered in Bogatá. Tonight she keeps vigil for her life after unknown terrorists have brutally murdered her SOPTI colleagues. Dr. Abesea, please explain to our viewers what message is so explosive that assassins would murder an entire organization to keep it from the American public."

Abesea composes herself to reply, and despite her brief attire, manages to assume a professional air. "Thank you, Mr. Jonestone; I will. My organization believes that American consumers are fundamentally compassionate and fair-minded people who are unaware of the worldwide harm and injustice done in their name. We believe that by bringing these facts to your viewers' attention, the American people will themselves act to correct these grievous wrongs. Sadly, our message does not get through. Even the evidence that we have turned over to your network, to VTV, is suppressed."

I smell a rat, says Clark. *Anyone else smell a rat?*

Jonestone says, "Could you give us an example of what kind of evidence you're referring to?"

"Gladly," she says and uses her remote to open the VTV menu on the TV wall. "This is a tape we sent you over a year ago." She pages through the VTV archives and highlights a title. "Instead of showcasing it in a news program, your network chose instead to bury it deep in your pay-per video archives."

The payment box says, "Diego Abesea," runtime 5:46:31, cost $ .28, ❑ Accept ❑ Cancel.

"This tape was made by paramilitary forces in the year after I joined SOPTI. It's only one of over fifty such tapes we've sent you." She checks the Accept box, and the TV wall momentarily blanks while the selection is retrieved and streamed. "These tapes are made by individual soldiers as personal souvenirs. We acquire them at great risk to ourselves."

The entire wall fills with an out-of-focus swath of olive drab. As the camera pulls back, we see a blindfolded boy with a cut cheek and nose out of joint. His hands are shackled behind him. He straddles a weird frame like a sawhorse made from iron pipes. His feet don't quite touch the floor. A man in civilian clothes, carefully keeping his back to the camera, straps iron weights to the boy's ankles to make him heavier. All of the boy's weight bears down on the narrow pipe at his crotch.

Jonestone notices the greenish cast and uneven focus of the picture. The camera's motor sound is audible over American rock and roll music playing in the background. This video, no doubt, is the product of old consumer-grade VHS technology.

Abesea approaches the TV wall and stands fascinated before the life-sized boy. She reaches out to touch his cheek, then shudders and turns to Jonestone. "The basis of a successful 'interview,'" she says, "is the level of uncertainty you can instill in your subject. Simply stated, once pain is sufficiently established in a subject, the *threat* of further pain is more effective in altering his behavior than pain, itself. Fear of being maimed is more compelling than actual maiming.

"Here you see the apparent subject—my brother—soon

after he was disappeared on his way home from school. His interviewers haven't demanded information from him. They have barely spoken to him. He asks them what they want because he wants to cooperate. My father has taught us always to tell everything. But when he asks they hit him, so he doesn't ask any more. We see much fear etched in my brother's face. The interviewers have made a good start in establishing a businesslike rapport with him."

Jonestone notices she is no longer speaking to him. She is addressing the camera over his head. Her voice reminds him of her classroom lecture. She's lecturing the American public. He figures that she expects to be dead when this is aired, and she's making good television, so he doesn't interrupt.

"He will sit on that pole for hours. They have trussed him so that he can't fall over and relieve the pressure on his genitals. Right now his testicles are very painful, and that is the most frightening part of the whole experience. Soon they will become numb, and that will frighten him even more. He will worry that the damage is permanent. My brother is only thirteen in this video, and he wants to be a papa someday."

The screen goes to video noise for a second, then the picture creeps back up in that characteristic way the old camcorders had. Someone has paused the tape. "Oh, yes," Abesea says, "the interviewers will switch it off several times during the session. They have to in order to fit it all on one cassette, and they don't want the tape to run out just when they get to the good part. It's humorous, really, to hear the interviewers call out, 'Hey, man, how much tape is left?' and for the reply, 'Hurry up, only ten minutes.' It must be sad comfort to the subject to know his life will soon end because of the limits of technology. Good thing the soldiers have no budget for your new digital stream cameras, yes? Then the fun would never stop."

She looks at the TV wall behind her. "As we can see, some time has passed, probably three or four hours. My brother looks not so worried now. He has made up his mind that he will surely die this night, and oddly, the knowledge has given him new courage. My brother is a brave young man." Here her voice falters, and she pauses before continuing. "I think his interviewers cannot have missed this change in him. Thus we are at a turning point. At this juncture, good interviewing technique calls for an intermission. They should remove him from his hobby horse, put him in a cell with a little water. Let him recover his strength. Keep him in isolation for several days. This will trick him into thinking the worst is over, that he will live after all. Sensation will creep back to his sex organs. He will be buoyed up with optimism.

"All of which will make it easier to crush him completely in the next interview." On the screen a man—his back to us—goes to the tied-up boy and punches him twice in the kidneys. We can hear the assailant grunt with his effort. We can plainly hear ribs crack. Other soldiers in the cell laugh. Abesea paces back and forth in front of the TV wall without looking at it.

The man leaves, and a second man removes the boy's blindfold. The boy, in pain, confused, looks away from him, desperate not to see the face of his persecutor. Nor can we see him except for the back of his head. He has black hair, cut in a military fashion. There's a little bald spot on the crown of his head. He puts a clear plastic bag over the boy's head and secures it around his throat with a Velcro strap. He tells someone to move the camera, and when he turns around, he holds his hand in front of himself to hide his face.

The camera zooms in to record the boy writhing in animal panic, straining against his bindings in an attempt to tear the smothering bag from his mouth. The men laugh. "The eyes!" one of them says in Spanish. The naked orbs of the boy's eyes are bugging out. His eyelids are turning blue.

"Obviously, something has gone wrong," says Abesea. "Why don't they remove him to a cell where he can recover? What reasons can we discover for the soldiers to prolong this interview beyond its logical intermission? Could it be—" and here she pauses to address the camera—"could it be that no one believes this child is the keeper of any secrets? Is he but a surrogate for some other subject?" She resumes her pacing.

Behind her the boy abruptly slouches forward on the pipe frame, unconscious and not breathing. The man hurries to remove the Velcro strap and bag. He thumps on the boy's chest several times with the heel of his hand. The boy gasps and gags and slowly regains consciousness. Though the man again holds his hand out to block the camera, we see fragments of his face—first his chin, then his left eye.

Abesea says, "They're giving him a breather. This interview method is called 'the submarine.' They will make him dive three more times. Each time it will be harder to revive him, until..." Her voice fails. She hides her face in her hands and turns away from the camera. Without thinking, Jonestone goes to her and gently wraps his arms around her. Her robe is damp, and she's trembling like a bird. Meanwhile, he watches the TV wall behind her where the man bags the boy a second time. This time it's not so easy. The boy, mad with fear, fights for his life. He twists and wrenches his upper body and butts his head to avoid the bag, and the man has to punch him into submission. Jonestone can't help but marvel at how gripping the tape is, and he wonders if the others Abesea mentioned are just as good and if so, why are they buried in the archives.

Jonestone jumps a little when the TV wall picture suddenly changes to the monstrously huge, puffy-eyed face of Clark. *Now, isn't that sweet,* Clark says in Jonestone's car, *Mookie's doing the compassion thing. I hate to break it up, but I will anyway. Your assignment is to cover the story, not to be drawn into it. You've got the place bagged, so to speak, so it would be a good idea for you to return to the van immediately.*

Jonestone looks directly into the ceiling cam. He knows Clark is right. He's been in the biz long enough to know that a journalist's place is on the sidelines. But when he tries to disentangle himself from Abesea, she clings to him. "Please," she whispers. "Please."

"I'll just take you to your room," he says, "then I really must leave." He draws her to the bedroom and seats her on the edge of her bed, but she won't let him go, so he sits next to her.

"Don't you see?" she says. "If you stay they won't dare to hurt me."

"That's not necessarily true."

"But I am so afraid. I don't want to die tonight. Please stay a while."

"I wish I could."

"Then stay until I fall asleep. You can do that for me? I won't be afraid if you hold me for a little while. Just until I fall asleep. Then leave, okay? It's such a small thing, but it would mean so much to me."

The clock on the bedside table reads 2:36. It's still early. "I don't know," he says as the woman climbs into bed and curls up, uncovered, on the bare sheet. She pats the space behind her for him to join her. He tears his eyes from her and looks up at the Bedroom Cam as though to seek instructions. Abruptly the blinking red tattletale switches to green.

What happened? Clark shouts in his ear. *Asa, what happened to my feed?*

Looks to me like they could use a little privacy, Asa says.

Privacy? Privacy for what? Asa, turn that camera back on now.

Don't worry, Chief. He's safe for the moment. The street is quiet. I'll turn it back on when he leaves.

Asa, this is going into your personnel record. Jonestone, I'm not going to say this again. Do yourself a favor and listen to the voice of experience. Evacuate this instant. Jonestone?

Jonestone pinches his throat mike off. He dims the bedroom light, shuts the door, and takes his gear bag to the window. He tapes little rattle dazzles to the glass window panes to confound the microwave pickups. He drapes a curtain of tinsel across the outer wall to scatter their heat signatures. A little privacy to do the compassion thing. He stands over the bed and looks at the woman curled up in a tight fetal knot. Her short robe doesn't quite cover her ass, and he sees that she's wearing no underwear. The things one must sometimes do for one's profession. He removes his shoes and places them next to the bed. He lies down on the bed but immediately gets up to remove his jacket. This he places carefully next to his shoes. Finally he settles in next to her and molds himself to fit her shape. Her skin is ice, so he disentangles one of her blankets and draws it over them.

She whispers, "Thank you."

"Don't mention it." He rests his chin on the crown of her head. She smells of shampoo. He keeps an eye on the little bedside clock—2:41. Little by little she relaxes in his arms. He listens to the intercom chatter between Asa and the studio. Clark is helping to monitor vehicular traffic. Soon Jonestone thinks Abesea is asleep, so he tries to creep away, but she clutches his arm.

"Make love to me."

"What?" he says. "No, I have to leave."

Under the blanket she hitches up her robe and urgently rubs her bare butt against him. She draws his hand to press against her breasts. "For me, *por favor.*"

Jonestone tries to ignore his throbbing cock and to think his way through this rationally. He calculates that this favor can be granted fairly quickly. And if it means so much to her—like a condemned prisoner's last request—how can he refuse? His reasoning strikes him as sound, and with one more glance at the clock, he's unbuckling his belt and kicking his trousers off the bed to land next to his jacket and shoes. He leaves his socks, briefs, and shirt on, though.

When he tries to turn Abesea towards him, she resists. She's still curled up in a little knot, so he kisses the back of her neck and rubs her shoulders. She's all bones, and he likes that. He kneads her shoulders and back and works down her knobby vertebrae. Absentmindedly, he nibbles the lobe of her ear, and she jumps. He's not sure if from pleasure or surprise, but he concentrates his ardor on her ear, kissing it, licking inside it, and nibbling around its edges. He thinks maybe she's responding? He stays with the ear for a while, wetting it and puffing tiny breaths into it, meanwhile reaching down to stroke her pussy. But her legs are drawn up and clamped shut, so he returns his hand to her breasts. Sometimes small-breasted women are extra-sensitive there. It seems to him as though he's searching for a chink in a suit of armor.

Suddenly he hears men's laughter in the living room and he about has a heart attack. But it's only her brother's vid. Angrily he shouts at the closed door, "TV turn off!" But it doesn't hear him.

What was that shout? says Clark.

The interruption has thrown Jonestone off his game. "Come here, baby," he whispers and tries again to turn her towards him, but she resists. He tries harder, and she grabs the side of the mattress. If she won't turn this way, maybe she'll turn the other. Gently, he tries pushing her face down on the bed, but she simply refuses to budge. "Honey," he whispers, "you're acting like you're not into this."

"Please," she says.

He looks at the clock—3:04. Damn! He levers her bottom to get a leg under her and tries to guide himself in from the rear. She's locked up and dry. He lubricates himself with spit and goes at it, pushing and probing till he's in. No, he's not. More pushing and probing till he's afraid he'll cum too soon when at last, he's in.

Jonestone starts a gentle rocking motion with his hips as best he can in that awkward position, digging his toes into the mattress for purchase. He knows he'll have a wretched backache in the morning. And for what? This woman's about as juicy as an old sock. Nevertheless, after a little while it starts—his orgasm.

It starts, as usual, as an achy sensation deep in the muscles of his ass. It spreads like heat to his belly and rises to inflate his chest. He relaxes a little now because once the engine turns over, he can slow down and enjoy the ride. It's 3:08, and all's well. All systems go. The Earth begins to move. All you need is love.

He hears a thin cry from the living room and promptly ignores it, except that he flashes on the face of that torturer. Suddenly, without breaking his rhythm, inspiration drops on Jonestone like a blastcam. Here's the story, of course! Story? Hell, here's the mini-series! Although that son-of-a-bitch torturer hid most of his face most of the time, he exposed himself in bits and pieces throughout the tape. It would be child's play for Asa and the other wizards at VTV to patch together from those fragments a composite mug shot of him. Not to mention the voiceprint they can lift from the sound track. Yes, Jonestone has no doubt that they can *positively* ID the man. And isn't this, after all, the age of retribution? The era of truth and reconciliation? Isn't the War Crimes Tribunal still grinding out human rights trials on the Hague assembly line: Rwanda, Bosnia, Cuba, Kosovo, South Africa, Iraq, etc., etc.? Jonestone could put together a team to go down there and find this guy and accuse him before the American viewing public! He's probably living the good life now, has a cushy job, a wife and family. But VTV could haul him into world court. Or if we can't, we can turn his world to shit, live on air. We can put so much heat on him that whatever paramilitary he worked for will decide to disappear *him*. With a little pre-planning and some hi-tech bugging, we can get *his* kidnapping live on air, too!

Jonestone notices that while he was having his little brainstorm, his body has lurched into caveman mode, a state of grossness that both disgusts and delights him. It has picked Abesea up willy nilly and turned her face down on the mattress. She's still curled up in her damn fetal position, but that lifts her pussy to a comfortable height, and he's in there banging away so zestfully that her head thumps against the wall. His orgasm is fully cocked and loaded now, all the way from his teeth to his toenails. There'll be no stopping it. It will express itself.

Jonestone, meanwhile, can't wait to get back to the studio. If they have one torture tape in their archives, they'll have a hundred. And all he needs is a dozen proof-positive IDs in a smattering of countries to make this a mini-series that he knows he can sell to the brass. This is his big break. They'll love it. They'll love it so much they'll take him off the Poodle Patrol forever and put him in the news division for sure. He has to hurry because this idea is so good someone else is bound to see it too and beat him to it. Someone like Clark.

It's 3:12, and Jonestone cums with all his might, mainlining Abesea with buckets of pure product in rippling body shouts of joy.

Spent, used up, satisfied as much by his inspiration as by the sex, he rolls off Abesea to catch his breath. He knows better than to fall asleep, despite how tired he is. Five minutes. He'll take five minutes to enjoy the glow. Then he'll make tracks to the van. He thinks about his story idea, how he'll work up a quick proposal, who to pitch it to, what to call it, etc., etc. Abesea hasn't moved. She's scrunched up like a discarded doll, her face turned the other way. Jonestone wonders what it would be like if they were a couple, an item. They'd get up in the morning and make breakfast. She'd go off to give her lectures, and he'd cover big, important stories.

Something's happening, says Asa.

Yeah, says Clark, *and XNBC has just broke the suncracker clip on their big window. We're following suit.*

Jonestone sits bolt upright in bed.

Asa says, *Our blastcams in the alley have gone red. I see movement in the shrubs along the back of the building.*

Jonestone, if you can hear me, this is your last chance. Asa, enable that camera.

Jonestone leaps out of bed, grabs his clothes, opens the bedroom door, and peaks into the living room. The TV wall is ablaze with pictures. All aspects of the story are playing at once in a circus of insets along the sides of the big window. Ford is in the headbox in the upper left corner of the screen anchoring the broadcast. She's deftly weaving all the separate insets into a coherent story: the Moreno parking garage clip, background on the SOPTI, the Belize barbecue, a late-breaking interview with Senator Jaspersen, Abesea's living room lecture, her dash up her front steps, and—in the big window—a live picture of two figures climbing to the roof of the apartment building. At the bottom of the screen is an animated banner that reads, LIVE—LOS ANGELES TERROR STRIKE beside the ever-morphing VTV logo. As Jonestone watches, a new inset opens to show the dimly lit bedroom with Abesea on her bed. He can just make out his own shadowy figure getting dressed in the doorway.

You've got about five seconds to exit before I put the Living Room Cam on the air, says Clark.

Jonestone doesn't need to be told twice. He makes a beeline for the door. But halfway there he's arrested by the sight of Abesea in an inset on the TV wall. Without turning in bed, her hand reaches to feel the mattress behind her, feeling for *him.*

There's a crash of breaking glass somewhere on the floor above him. He pinches his throat mike and says, "Asa, where are they?"

Above you and over a couple of rooms. When you leave, take the stairwell to your left. And hurry.

He turns around and walks towards the bedroom.

Stop right there, son, says Clark. *You're heading the wrong way.*

"There's still time to get her out, too."

Forget it. That's not how things work. You report the news; you don't make the news. At least not if you still want a spot in our newsroom.

Jonestone looks up at the ceiling cam. "What's that supposed to mean? That a reporter can't save a person's life?"

He continues to the bedroom, but Clark says, *What do I have to do to get through to you? Yank your leash?*

"What?"

You heard me, Mookie. I'll drag you by your leash all the way to the division president if I have to. Then you won't even have the Poodle Patrol to fall back on.

Jonestone hesitates at the bedroom door. Abesea looks so peaceful lying there. It would be easy to scoop her up in his arms and whisk her to safety.

Asa says, *If you plan on leaving, right this instant would be a good time.*

There's the sound of police sirens in the distance. With one last, lingering look, Jonestone runs to the hall entry door, reaches for the handle, and freezes when the doorbell chimes. At that moment the big window switches to the Living Room Cam, and Jonestone sees himself, large as life, standing at the door with his mouth hanging open.

Ford, in the headbox, is saying, "Now VTV's exclusive coverage takes you *live* into the—Mookie? Ladies and gentlemen, here is VTV reporter, Anthony Jonestone, who has participated in Dr. Abesea's long vigil tonight. Tony, what do you have for us?" Immediately along the bottom of the TV wall appears the banner, LIVE—EXCLUSIVE—ANTHONY JONESTONE.

Clark says, *Close your mouth, son, and start talking.*

"I—uh." There's a knock at the door, polite but insistent. Jonestone looks at the door as though he's never seen a door before. A teleprompter insert opens before him on the TV wall. The words scroll, *Good morning, Abbie. As you said, I've waited through the night here at the home of SOPTI activist...* and although Jonestone mouths them, no sound comes out.

Again a knock, this time by the impatient butt of a gun.

Abesea emerges from the bedroom. Her hair is disheveled and her cheek creased by the bed linen. She rubs her eyes and demands, "What is going on?"

"They're here."

"Then let them in."

"Are you crazy?"

"Why? You think you can hide from them? You think if you don't open the door they'll simply go away? What a stupid person you are. Don't you know they can kill us from the hall? They can leak poison gas under the door, or start a fire, or blow up the whole building. They don't need to come in." She crosses the room. "In my country, when Death knocks, you try to greet him with a little dignity."

She flings open the door, and two men enter, dressed in black clothing, ski masks, and gloves. They wave ugly machine pistols and herd Jonestone and Abesea against the TV wall. They act surprised to see themselves projected on the wall, and they search around until they find the camera on the ceiling. One of them, a well-built man with wide shoulders aims at the camera, but the other one says, "No, leave it."

"You better shoot it," says Abesea, "you coward. The whole world is watching."

"Shut up," he says and jabs her in the ribs with the barrel of his gun. "We don't care who is watching us kill you. Better everybody watch. Say good-bye. First you." He points his gun at Jonestone. "Say good-bye to your family."

Jonestone only stutters.

"Enough!" says the man. "I pity you." He points his gun at Abesea. "Now you."

Abesea is not shy for words. She's waited for this moment for years. "You think you can frighten me with a gun?" she says. "You are wrong. I am not frightened. It is you who is frightened, you who hides behind a mask. My name is Josephina Marguerite Abesea. I say that proudly to the world. What is your name? What is the name of your superiors? How many people have you murdered? How many women? How many children? Where were you trained? Were you trained here in the United States? Were you trained at the CIA's School of the Americas?"

The man throws back his head and laughs through his mask. "So many questions, *bonita*."

"Then answer just the first, if you are a man and not a coward. Tell us your name. Tell us your real name."

"As you wish, but first I kill this one." He steps up to Jonestone and points his gun at him. "No, turn around. Face the TV." Jonestone turns to the TV wall and stands behind the life-size projection of himself. It's like he's standing behind himself. The masked assailant slowly raises his gun and points it at him, the other him. That man is about to die. "Here it comes," says the assailant, "in living color."

"Wait!" Jonestone whispers.

The man lowers the gun. "*¿Qué?*"

Jonestone can hear the sirens stop on the street outside the apartment. So close, yet so far.

"I'm waiting, *señor.*"

"Please—please don't kill me," Jonestone says.

The man puts his hand to his hooded ear. "This *capuha*, I cannot hear you. Say again. Say so whole America hears you."

"Please don't kill me."

The man looks at his accomplice. "What do you say, *jefe?* We should show our mercy?"

The other man takes a moment to consider, then says with finality, "No, kill him."

The assailant says to Jonestone, "I regret to report that

your request is denied." He raises his gun again. "Say good night."

Jonestone's bladder lets go, and he pisses himself. The man on the TV wall in front of him is visibly quaking. Jonestone watches as the assailant points the muzzle of the gun into that man's ear, and slowly squeezes the trigger. The gun explodes with a blast that hits him on the side of the face. It hardly hurts at all. Inexplicably, the men turn the guns on each other and blast away with water. Water? Jonestone's thoughts are stuck. Am I dead or what? The men pull off their masks, exposing their faces, and bow to the camera.

"These are toys," one of them says, "and we are unarmed." They toss their replica squirt guns away from them. The man takes Abesea's hand and kisses it. She pulls him to her and kisses him on the cheek. "I am Arturo Moreno," he tells the camera, "and on behalf of my friend, Miguel, and myself, I apologize for this hoax we are playing on you. We have tried for years to bring a message to you, our friends in the United States, but your Congress will not listen to us, and your media corporations will not sell us air time. So this is the only way we can reach you directly."

Jonestone is still watching the TV wall, standing with his back to the room. Arturo Moreno? But he's dead, murdered in the parking garage.

"You can turn around now, *señor,*" Moreno gently says to him. No one will kill you any more. Go outside and tell the SWAT team we surrender."

Jonestone turns. It's all so confusing. The two men move to the middle of the room, lie face down on the floor, and lock their hands behind their heads. Abesea is staring at him, a mixture of triumph and pity in her eyes. "You heard him," she says. "Go! You're dismissed."

Jonestone climbs in the back and slams the heavy door. Asa shakes his head, then goes up front and starts the engine. It's a long, long drive back to the Bus Barn, but it would please Jonestone if they never arrived. He sits behind the deck; the seat is wet. No, his pants are wet. He sees in the monitors that the network has cut its losses and moved on to another story, an early morning murder of a Hollywood starlet. You can always count on LA to fill in the gaps.

He sees that no one has turned off the ceiling cams in Abesea's apartment, so he watches as Moreno and his pal are led away in handcuffs. Abesea is standing in front of the TV wall delivering another lecture. Apparently she thinks she's still on the air, but she's wrong. They're not even recording any more.

Jonestone pots up the audio and hears her say, "...such as forced confessions, making false accusations against family and friends, and sham executions. And what are the long-term effects of this? Anxiety, crippling depression, and irritability. Paranoia, guilt, and suspiciousness. Think what this does to a family. Sexual dysfunction. Loss of the ability to concentrate—your mind wanders, and you can't focus on anything." She has poise and authority. "Insomnia, nightmares, weight loss, memory loss. So many losses. And perhaps the greatest loss of all—loss of the ability to perform as a citizen of one's own community."

Jonestone is too tired. He's completely fried. He closes his eyes and rests his head in his hands. He's a little surprised to smell her odor still on his fingers. It reminds him of their night together. With all that's happened, he's almost forgotten that they had good times, too. In his mind's own monitor, he sees himself still lying there as the morning light streams through her bedroom window. She's curled up next to him like she was. He imagines he smells hot biscuits somewhere. Biscuits and bacon and fresh coffee. Hesitantly, her hand slides behind her and finds him. "You're still here!" she says. "You didn't leave me alone. You took care of me."

Without opening his eyes, Jonestone reaches out and cuts the audio, cuts the ceiling cams. “Yes, I’m still here,” he tells her. “Where else would I be?”

And then, like a morning glory, she turns, uncurls her slender limbs, and opens herself to greet him.

❖ "CABBAGES AND KALE, OR: HOW WE DOWNSIZED NORTH AMERICA"

This story was a watershed of ideas for me that eventually figured in *Counting Heads*. It was a deliberate prequel to "We Were Out of Our Minds with Joy," and with it I attempted to lay the social and political foundation of my invented world, as well as explore its "boutique economy."

Cabbages and Kale or: How We Downsized North America

SUMMER 2033

For a garden it was huge, seventy-five meters on a side, enough real estate to house fifty-dozen families. But it was a vegetable garden, his own personal vegetable garden. And his greatest vice.

Saul stood over a mounded row of carrots, weeding with a hoe. He'd eaten breakfast two hours earlier and was already anticipating lunch. He removed his straw hat and fanned himself. "Is that your report then?" he asked the proxy. The proxy floated in the air at the end of the row.

"Yeah, I guess," the proxy said. "It wasn't much of a symposium, hardly worth my time."

Saul wondered how much a proxy's time was actually worth. He straightened up and regarded the apparition. It was a standard head and shoulder projection—Saul's head and Saul's shoulders—clothed in a crisp cotton shirt and worsted hemp jacket. No torso, no arms or legs. He could have equipped it with hands, but Saul didn't use his own hands much when he talked, so he figured his proxies didn't need them either. "Any last insights?"

The proxy thought a moment and shrugged. "Only some odd questions about my stance on the Procreation Ban."

"Oh?" said Saul. "Odd in what way?" With the senate vote imminent, the ban seemed to be the sole topic of public discourse these last few weeks.

"Well, not the questions *per se*, but their regularity. I got the impression someone was monitoring me by the minute to see if I'd changed camps."

As though a proxy has a mind of its own, Saul mused, *which it can change at will.* "I see. Anything else?"

The proxy shook its head. "Naw, I've fed Cal all my summaries and data; I'm finished."

"Good," Saul said. "Cal, delete the proxy."

"Deleting," said the voice of his belt valet, and the proxy vanished from the garden.

Saul stepped over the carrots into the next row: lettuce, kale, and spinach. "Cal," he said, "what's for lunch?"

"I'm sorry," said the valet, "please rephrase the question."

Saul wondered what part of his question had exceeded the AI's noetics. "I want to know what will be served for lunch," he said. Valets were ingenious devices—he couldn't function without one—but unlike proxies, their learning curve was annoyingly steep. At times they were little better than the PDAs they replaced. "You may ask the cook for that information."

"Asking."

While he waited for a reply, Saul scanned the southern horizon. The mountain was out today, Mount McKinley, the highest point on the continent. Its brilliant bald dome had broken through a cloudy haze. In the foreground lay the Tanana Valley, with its unbroken carpet of residential subdivisions and high-rise office buildings. Alaska's remote location and extreme climate had only managed to hobble, never halt, the continental urban sprawl. This valley, which at the time of Saul's birth had supported little more than boreal forest and moose browse, now boasted an urban population of two million souls. And this was only the beginning. A phalanx of the new residential gigatowers was scheduled to begin construction. By next summer Saul's fourteen hillside acres would be surrounded by a picket of interconnected buildings two kilometers tall. His garden would lie strangled in their shade, and there was nothing he could do about it. It had taken all the influence of his office just to keep his own property from being gobbled up along with his neighborhood.

"Saul," said the valet, "Cook asks if there are peppers ready. If affirmative, he will prepare *chiles rellenos*."

Saul walked around the garden to the rows of tomatoes and chiles. Yes, there were a few. Chile peppers, tomatoes, sweet corn, cucumbers—these were crops from warmer climes, but Saul's group had gengineered new varieties that flourished in Alaska's cold soil and short season of constant daylight. He had been director of research at the University of Alaska Fairbanks Experimental Farm. He'd grown sugar cane there, date palms, coffee bushes, rubber trees, bamboo. There seemed to be nothing he couldn't coax from subarctic soil. Some days he regretted ever leaving research.

"Saul," the valet said, "the regular meeting of the Joint Chiefs has just adjourned. Shall General Butelero's proxy brief you?"

Saul scratched his head. "Why? Wasn't I there?"

"Negative. You were here."

"I mean, didn't I send a proxy there? Never mind. Put the general's proxy in the queue and send me whatever's next." Another proxy of himself, identical to the previous one, appeared and hovered over the rows of potato plants. Identical except for the bowtie, which was blue, which meant Saul had cast it sometime last week.

"Looking good," said the proxy, who surveyed the garden.

"Yes," said Saul. "So, what have you been up to?"

"You cast me," said the proxy, "to attend the World Destitution Conference in—of all places—Barsinghausen. Here are the highlights. On the matter of exporting nanoculture technology outside the Protectorate, France remains obstinately alone in its support, this despite the fact that nearly a third of the affected patents belong to French consortiums. On the matter of ..."

"Saul," said the valet.

"Not now, Cal."

"Mr. Vice President," said a new voice. "This is Jackson. Sorry to interrupt, sir, but we need you in the situation room *immediately.*"

Saul straightened up. "Why?"

"There's a problem, ahh, with your speech."

"Which speech?"

Suddenly the security fence around his property came alive. The holographic barricade sprang up, and a Klaxon blared a warning against intrusion. "*Now* what?" said Saul.

"Incoming!" cried an urgent voice. "Seek cover at once, sir. Seek cover *at once!*" It was the voice of the Secret Service duty officer.

Saul looked around for possible cover. The house was two-hundred meters away. The only closer structure was his teahouse, a tiny wooden octagon that once upon a time had served as a playhouse for his sisters. Before he could move, however, the entire southern perimeter of his property erupted in micro-laser fire. Saul threw himself to the ground between rows of cabbages and kale and covered his head with his arms. "What's happening?" he shouted. Tiny red bursts marked direct laser hits. Suddenly a wave of bursts turned the southern perimeter into a solid wall of roaring light and smoke.

"Bees," shouted the Secret Service agent. "Thousands of them. Come to the house immediately, sir, before they breech the SBZ."

Too late! The bees, by their sheer number, overwhelmed the laser cannon. A small formation of them raced toward him. Now the battery of house lasers opened fire, but the bees hugged the ground and dodged evasively. As the tiny killers approached his shallow fox hole, Saul was grateful to find himself clearheaded and unafraid, though his heart thundered in his ears. The bees were picked off one by one, until a sole survivor entered the garden and hovered in front of Saul's face, too close to his person to be safely targeted. Saul remained perfectly still. He heard the distant slam of a door; the agent would be sprinting to his rescue, but too late if the silicone marble with whirring acetate wings three centimeters from his nose was programmed for assassination.

Suddenly a tiny holo of a face appeared on the leading edge of the bee, a generically handsome face Saul didn't recognize. "Sorry for the intrusion, Mr. Vice President," it said, "but we would like you to expand on a provocative statement you have just made at the Scribner Press Union."

"*What?*" said Saul, confused, the rush of adrenaline fogging his comprehension. *This is no killer bee. This is a fucking newsbee.*

"You are midway through a speech at the ..."

"And you are trespassing!" Saul thundered as he rose to his feet. He picked up his straw hat and brushed dirt from his clothes. The newsbee maintained its sheltered proximity to him. "Get out of my face!" he commanded and swiped the hat at it, but human reflexes were no match for a bee's. "Remove yourself from my property this instant." How was this going to play in the media, he wondered, the vice president of the United States of North America eating dirt. As if his public image weren't oddball enough.

The holo reporter, a free-lancing anon no doubt, continued undeterred. "Did you mean to dispute the Personhood Protocol Bill of 2030?"

The Secret Service agent arrived, breathing hard, and pulled an ultrasound wand from his vest. He slowly twisted its base while holding the tip near the bee. When the harmonics synched, he pulled the bee to the ground, where its wings beat ineffectually in the dust, and he pointed a hand laser at it. “Stand back, sir,” he said.

“No,” said Saul. “Don’t destroy it. I want to know who it belongs to.” He waved his hand towards the southern perimeter. “Retrieve as much evidence as you can and trace it.” He picked up his hoe, hung it on its peg outside the teahouse, and went up to the main house.

The house was a large, rambling log structure that his father had built on a one-hundred-sixty-acre homestead in the middle of the last century. The building had grown haphazardly, with new additions and a second story as Saul and his four brothers and sisters were born. Today it was a bizarre juxtaposition of styles. Plasteel flying decks and a polycarbonate atrium were grafted onto hand-peeled, scroll-cut spruce logs. Moose and caribou racks were nailed under the eaves, next to laser turrets. The roofline bristled with solar collectors, wood stove chimneys, antennae, and ordnance. And although most of the land had long ago been subdivided and sold off, the remainder was worth a small fortune.

The arctic entry, on high alert, required Saul’s ocular ID before granting him admission, which did nothing to appease his anger. Once inside, he went directly to the media room, which occupied the heart of the structure, locked himself in, and ordered it to project the situation room.

“Retrieving, assembling,” said the room, and in a moment his command post in his suite at the Naval Observatory in Washington, DC appeared around him. Jackson was waiting for him. Alblaitor was at the conference table observing a large holofied diorama.

“What was that all about?” said Jackson.

"Reporters!" said Saul. "Newsbees! Get Justice on it. I want every news organization involved prosecuted. Drag Wilson over the coals and find out why the home of the vice president can't be made secure." Saul heard Jackson sigh, which only stoked his anger. "You disagree with me, Jackson? You, too, think I should reside in Washington?"

Jackson's face turned ashen, but before he could reply, Alblaitor called from across the room, "We have a *crisis* here!"

Saul walked over and looked into the diorama. It showed the ballroom of the Sing Lee Hotel in San Francisco where a proxy of his was concluding a speech to the Scribner Press Union luncheon. Five hundred or so tiny journalists sat at miniature tables. Saul listened to his proxy's words. It was the speech he'd approved last night and had cast this proxy to deliver. "So?" he said.

Alblaitor went to the other side of the table and cloned the diorama. "Select back ten minutes and play," she said, and an earlier clip of the speech began to play. "Shuttle back," she said. "More. More." She twisted a lock of her hair and tugged at it nervously. "Stop! Play this."

The vice president's proxy, head and shoulders, white shirt, grey jacket, and this week's burgundy bowtie, floated over the lectern and said, "The Senate votes tomorrow on the Administration's Procreation Ban. The House has already approved it by the slightest of margins. President Taksayer sits in the Oval Office, pen in hand, ready to sign it. Thus we enter a new age when an entire people, in response to life-threatening overpopulation, voluntarily chooses to reduce its birthrate to point one percent. Critics will say that our motives are selfish, that the beneficial effects of a reproduction ban will be canceled out by subsequent legalization of longevity technologies, the nanorejuvenation therapies that are currently practiced abroad. To a certain extent this is true ..."

This was all innocuous and according to script, and Saul shot an impatient glance at Alblaitor.

"Here it is, sir. Listen to this part."

"...inevitable compromises. We all know what they are. No man or woman will be forcibly sterilized, although the procedure is safe, non-intrusive, one hundred percent reversible, and will be provided free of charge. Nor will any woman be subjected to abortion or prosecution for becoming pregnant without a permit. Instead, unauthorized babies will be extracted whole and placed into biostasis for storage at government expense until such a time that they can be brought to term—who knows, perhaps in a colony ship orbiting a new planet ..."

Jackson grimaced, "Unauthorized *babies*, sir?"

"What?" said Saul. "All this fuss over one word?"

"A very unfortunate word," said Jackson.

That much was true. What an embarrassment! The Republicans would have a field day. Feminists would be outraged. Why had his proxy gone into the matter of fetal disposal at all? It wasn't in the script. True, he often extemporized his speeches, and thus his proxies would too. But to make such a slip to *this* audience the day before the vote. "Don't worry," he said, "I'll fix it."

"Great, sir," said Alblaitor. "We'll pull the proxy and insert you for the Q and A."

"No, I'm not going to holo there."

"But, sir ..."

"Think, Zoe. Think about it. What would it say if I filled in for my proxy? It would say I didn't trust it. If I do that, I'd never be able to use a proxy again."

"But we can't trust that one to take questions, sir," said Jackson. "It's defective or something. Senator Hagerbarger will eat you alive as it is."

"Better hurry," said Alblaitor, who was monitoring the live holo, "you've wrapped it up, and they're asking for questions."

"We could glitch it, claim technical difficulties," said Jackson.

"No."

"They've selected Donna Samuelson for the first round," said Alblaitor. "This ought to be good." She blushed and rephrased, "I mean bad. This is unquestionably bad."

"Cal," Saul said to his belt valet, "how well could you patch in a newly-cast proxy to replace the existing one without anyone detecting the switch?"

"This task can be accomplished without detection with a probability of eighty-five point eight."

"That'll have to do. Cast me in fifteen seconds."

"Counting."

Saul closed his eyes and cleared his mind. He consciously relaxed and imagined he was sitting in his little teahouse watching the sunset. Before him on the polished birch table he imagined a crystal bowl of fresh-picked blueberries, a pitcher of cream, a porcelain pot of steeping jasmine tea, and glazed sesame crackers. He smiled at the rich taste of his imagination.

"Here comes the first question," said Alblaitor who upped the volume.

"Mr. Vice President," said Donna Samuelson, "in its *Jones vs Jones* decision in 2001, the Supreme Court defines a human baby as a postpartum fetus. Do you mean by your earlier statement to refute that, or does the Administration propose to confiscate live babies as well as fetuses?"

The proxy opened its mouth to answer, but Saul said, "Cal, freeze the proxy," and resumed his meditation. In the Sing Lee ballroom the frozen proxy appeared either to be stymied by the question or considering possible answers, but as seconds elapsed, a buzz of speculation filled the air.

"Whatever you got," said Alblaitor, "let's have it now."

A new proxy appeared in the situation room, and Saul opened his eyes to examine it. "You know how to handle this?"

"Yeah, no problem," said his proxy.

"Then go. Cal, insert ..."

"Wait!" said Jackson. "Its clothes." The proxy wore Saul's sweat-stained hat and grimy shirt.

"Cal, appoint it in standard attire and substitute it now."

"Mr. Vice President," said a smug Samuelson in the ballroom, "shall I rephrase my question?"

"No need," said the reanimated proxy, "but before I answer it, allow me to ask one of my own. I was distracted a few moments ago, because one or more news organizations invaded my home in Fairbanks, Alaska. This constitutes a serious violation of my privacy, not to mention a breech of national security, insofar as my home is the residence of the vice president. Were you or your newsservice, Ms. Samuelson, involved in this incident, or do you have any knowledge of who was?"

"Of course not, Mr. Vice President," snapped the reporter, "and I object to the accusation."

Alblaitor said, "That scored a ninety-one percent lie."

"I was asking," said the proxy, "not accusing. At least not yet. Accusations and federal indictments will surely follow the lab reports on the captured newsbees. We managed to capture one intact." The ballroom erupted in shouted questions.

In the situation room, Jackson pounded the table. "Good, good, good. Eat shit, Samuelson."

The proxy cleared its throat and continued. "Now, to your original question. I presume the statement you referred to was my description of how the government intends to store unlicensed fetuses."

"You said, 'baby,' sir."

"I am aware of that. On the surface, at least, my statement seems to have placed me in the type of awkward situation that you so revel in, Ms. Samuelson. You expect me either to eat my words—or *word* in this case—or to put such a spin on it as to amuse you and your ilk for days." The proxy paused and looked at the reporter as though for confirmation.

Samuelson was clearly ill at ease but made no reply. "And all because," continued the proxy, "I learned to speak during a simpler time when the word, 'baby,' lacked a Supreme Court definition. You may note, Ms. Samuelson, that I predate even *Roe vs Wade*. Shame on you, Ms. Samuelson, for attempting to derail a serious national debate over a simple slip of an elderly tongue. Please be so kind as to replace the word 'baby' with the correct term 'fetus' in my statement and suffice it to say that as a compassionate person, I suffer empathy for *all* creatures, be they nascent or fully realized." The proxy pointed to another reporter. "Next question."

"Bravo," said Alblaitor.

"Well done, sir," laughed Jackson.

"Thank you," Saul said on his way to the door. "Jackson, take that proxy apart and find out why it fucked up. Cal, deliver the proxy to Jackson. Then run a self-diagnosis on your casting functions. Now, if you'll excuse me ..."

"One last thing, sir," said Jackson, "the White House is asking what time you'll be in DC tomorrow for the vote."

"I have no intention of going. If the Senate vote results in a tie, I will break it from here by holo as usual."

Jackson coughed into his hand. "The White House anticipated that answer, sir, and asks further—and I quote—if the most historic vote of the twenty-first century is not important enough to bring him down off his mountain, what *is*?"

Saul's stomach growled, and he wondered if lunchtime would ever come. "Fairbanks lies in a valley, not on a mountain," he said. "Inform me if that changes."

Saul had enough time before lunch to weed another row and debrief another half-dozen proxies. The problem with proxy technology, in Saul's opinion, was that although it enabled you to be in a hundred places at once, you had to *know* everything your proxies proposed or promised and to whom and for what in exchange. You spent most of your time debriefing yourself. Sometimes Saul felt he was in danger of being spread too thin. In addition to his full load of official governmental duties, he was involved in projects around the globe concerning everything from coastline reclamation to housing the world's four billion indigent. He was a charter member of the Council of Foreign Relations, the Trilateral Commission (though thus far spurned by the fledgling Tri-Discipline Committee). He served on the boards of twenty national corporations, nine transnationals, eight major universities, thirty-seven international foundations, the World Bank, Amnesty International, and the World Literacy Council. Things were bound to become muddled from time to time. That was probably what had happened at the press luncheon.

The cook served lunch in the teahouse: just-picked garden salad, *chiles rellenos,* and cold beer. Saul's own private patch of Alaska was aflame in summer colors. His lunchtime tranquility was soon wrecked, however, by the whine of giant engines somewhere down the hillside. Secret Service had warned Saul to expect a lot of noise over the next few days while contractors used urban rakes to clear and prep construction sites for the gigatowers. Construction plans called for the use of the latest nanoassembly techniques; they would "grow" solid titanium alloy superstructures in one seamless piece. Saul usually liked a nap after lunch, but with all the racket today, he decided to hike down the hill instead to watch them collect and digest his neighbors' houses.

In the far north, one summer day dissolved into the next without the punctuation of intervening darkness. Saul sat in front of his bedroom window wall and removed his shoes.

Although it was late evening, the sky was as bright as noon. "Occlude the windows," he said, and began to undress. Tia had called a little while ago and hinted that she might drop by. His wife, Helene, was out of town. So he showered and—feeling lucky—shaved. Naked and pink, he stood in front of the bathroom vanity and studied his reflection. "Mirror, mirror, on the wall" he said, "give me a three-sixty." His image rotated before him. It wasn't a pretty sight. Although he exercised regularly and performed all approved longevity regimens—organ replacement, DHEA boosters, subcutaneous superoxide dismutase pumps, ultrasound massage, and telomere extension—he nevertheless had pretzel legs, sagging buttocks, a belly flap, and—no other word for it—breasts.

The situation would improve, however, so there was no need for alarm. True nanotech rejuvenation was just around the corner. It was already being used abroad and would soon be approved for tests in the USNA. The only thing holding it up was the passage of the Procreation Ban, and *that* would change tomorrow. "Mirror," he said, "show me my reflection at age thirty." His image morphed. Its skin tightened. Its arms bulged. Mass seemed to shift from its belly to its chest. Hair sprouted everywhere thick and black. Young Saul stood before him a heavy-lidded, hormone-rich, cocksure son-of-a-bitch. "The future," said the young man in the mirror, "looks promising."

Saul plumped his pillows and climbed into bed. His bedspread was a vast expanse of blue muslin on which he liked to arrange two dozen holocells all tuned to different media sources. Tonight he searched the net for references to his "luncheon gaffe" (as a leading pundit had dubbed it). There were only 230,000 references in the USNA, and most of these were on low-traffic bands. He scanned the five-hundred or so significant hits and found that more attention was devoted to the newsbee attack and his subsequent confrontation with Donna Samuelson than the gaffe itself. Saul was profoundly relieved. Damage seemed nominal. In fact, compared to the larger issue, the imminent vote on the Procreation Ban, his own sad contribution raised hardly a blip. All across the bandwidth, experts of every stripe from Gaian bioeconomists to Islamic lesboethicists debated the intent, mechanics, implications, long-term costs, dangers, and politics of the ban. Mass demonstrations for and against the ban clashed in a dozen megatopia. Casualties numbered in the thousands. Omnidenominational prayer vigils were attempting to link hands in a human X (or cross) spanning the USNA from Norfolk to San Diego and Inuvik to Tapachula. President Taksayer's proxies were featured on popular talk shows, as were a freshly cast batch of Saul's own. On one such show his proxy sat opposite a proxy of Rev. Buhru S. Parkerhut which denounced the ban as the latest attempt to return the nation to white ascendancy and which urged all colored sisters that night to lie down with a colored brother in order to vote with their naturally superior fecundity.

On another show Saul's proxy faced the proxy of Texas Senator Erstwhile P. Hagerbarger, the Republican Senate Leader, chief opponent of the ban, and Saul's longtime nemesis. "I know you possess a good and just heart," Senator Hagerbarger's proxy told Saul's proxy. The senator was a craggy-faced fossil, older than Saul by at least a quarter century, who was noted for his gritty integrity and whose attacks were typically indirect and maddeningly folksy. "So you must've wrassled the angel over this issue."

"Thank you, Senator. Yes, I have 'wrassled' the angel," replied Saul's proxy. "And like Jacob in the Bible, I pinned it for a three-count."

Not bad, thought Saul, who didn't know he knew that particular scriptural allusion.

"I'm sure you have," continued the senator's proxy. The proxy had hands, which it seemed to need only to preen its droopy, ivory-colored mustache. "But there's one tiny little thing that still vexes me."

"Which I'm sure you're about to share with our audience."

"If you don't mind. There's something I don't understand, and I was hoping you could thrash it out for me. Didn't we just annex Canada and Mexico, and wasn't that so we could increase our breathing space and raw materials? And in addition to this, don't we now have nanotech cropping up everywhere? Hell, Mr. Vice President, you yourself helped pioneer nanoculture before you entered politics. I hear your boys can now grow soybimi in the snows of winter, grow crops already packaged for sale. I hear you can teach a beggar family of three to feed itself from a half-dozen hydroponic flowerpots. And if that's so, why should North America be the only country in the world—outside Japan—that can't have babies? Who besides an odd species of gopher is gonna be harmed?"

Saul had long admired Senator Hagerbarger's public display of innocence. The senator was privy to the same studies Saul was, the same projections. Yet he seemed to stubbornly draw the most unreasonable—albeit popular—conclusions.

Saul's proxy took an unanticipated tack, "You ask who would be harmed. Who besides gophers? The fact that whole populations of humans are dying out in places like India, Sri Lanka, Africa, and Indonesia due to edaphic, social, and climactic climax events—density diseases, flooding, confinement aggression, neotoxins, etc. etc. etc.—seems not to interest you. Fine. Then let's talk economics.

"Who would be harmed by further population increase? I'll tell you. North American consumers, that's who."

The senator's proxy gave its mustache several perplexed tugs before replying. "You've got me now, Mr. Vice President. I must admit I'm not following your reasoning here. Why would North American consumers suffer?"

"Because there won't be any! In the Age of Nanotech, a whole factory capable of fulfilling all your consumer needs will fit into a shoebox which you'll keep in your closet, including its power source. Raw materials will be mined out of your trash. It's a boutique economy, Senator, and in a boutique economy mass production for the sake of mass consumption is unnecessary, wasteful, and improbable. Consumerism as a motivating principle is obsolete; it's an artifact of the twentieth century."

Sound argument, thought Saul, though elliptical and perhaps too abstruse for this show's audience.

Senator Hagerbarger's proxy patted its shaggy, white hair and cracked a grin, and its drawl seemed to intensify, "Ah've ben called obsolete for the last fordy years, but it don't seem to harm me none." It looked directly into the holoeye. "But what Ah'd like to hear from you tonight, Mr. Vice President, is why we cain't have babies. Why not ban nanorejuvenation instead? Why not let us old folks die as the Maker intended, not the babies?"

Babies, babies, babies, Saul thought. *I use the damn word once and get crucified, but this old reprobate makes a litany of it, and they love him.* Saul's eyes were drooping. His proxies seemed to be on the ball tonight. He trusted them to "wrassle" Senator Hagerbarger and all others. "What time is it?"

"Eleven-oh-five," replied the room.

She wasn't coming; he might as well turn in. Saul dc'd the holos and pulled the covers to his chin. "Wake me at six AM," he said and closed his eyes. But no sooner had he dozed off than Cal awakened him to say that Tia Krebbs was at the gate. "Tell Secret Service to let her in," he mumbled. He had to sit on the edge of the bed for a full minute before standing up and padding to the bathroom. "Music," he said through a mouthful of toothsoap. "Candles. And a woodsy scent." He combed his hair and popped a little blue hard-on pill.

"Knock knock," said Tia, entering the bedroom. She wore a baggy jumpsuit and newly-minted hair. When she saw him sitting in his armchair, an open book in his lap, she said, "Good evening, Mr. Vice President."

"No need to be formal," he said.

"It's not formal," she said. "I like to say Mr. Vice President."

"You know what I'd like?" he said, closing the book and dropping it to the floor. Tia shook her head, and he said, "I'd like to tell you a secret."

Tia strolled across the room, sat sideways on his lap, and regarded him with mock astonishment. "A *state secret,* Mr. Vice President?" He leaned to kiss her, but she shied away. He brushed his fingers over the silky fabric of her jumpsuit and groped to unfasten it, but she playfully pushed his hands away. She was a small woman whose bouncy weight on him was delightful. She rotated her hips slightly, grinding her soft rump into his lap. His heart thumped solidly. Tia was good with an old fart like him. He could relax and let her take the lead. Tonight promised success.

"What's this?" she said, her reddened lips a perfect moue of wonder as she slid her hand down into his robe. "Mr. Vice President!!"

"Mr. Vice President," said a voice.

"Not now, Jackson!" snapped Saul. He glanced hastily around, though he knew the call was voice only.

"Sorry to bother you at this late hour, sir."

"I said not now."

"We have a theory about the proxy."

It was after three AM in Washington. He hadn't expected them to work through the night. He sighed and shrugged. "Make it brief."

"Sunspots, sir."

"Sunspots? As in satellite telecommunication?"

"Yes, sir."

Saul thought about this a moment. "Are you telling me, Mr. Jackson, that my communications were bumped off the Pacific Opticom onto satellite?"

"Yes, sir. Your proxy was transmitted here via satellite during a time of high sunspot activity. It's the only possible explanation we've uncovered to account for its—aberrant personality."

"And who bumped me?" Saul said. Tia recoiled from the anger in his voice, got off his lap, and went to sit on the bed.

"The Tokyo office of the First Discipline."

"You're telling me that my communications, the official communications of the vice president of the United States of North America, were bumped off a public opticom by a private organization?"

"Well, sir, one would hardly call the FD a private organization."

"That's exactly what *I'd* call it!" snapped Saul. "And I'm not yet willing to concede primacy to it." Tia began pulling her jumpsuit off her shoulders, but wagged her finger at Saul and turned around, exposing her bare buttocks as she climbed into the bed. "Have Alblaitor find out what regulations apply. This will be the last time I'm bumped. Is that clear, Mr. Jackson?"

"Yes, sir. By the way, the White House is asking for your ETA in DC tomorrow."

Saul sighed; he wasn't going to avoid a realbody appearance. "I'll have Cal send you an itinerary. Go home, Mr. Jackson."

Saul disrobed and got into bed. He kept his back to Tia while doing so and hastened to cover himself with the sheet. He sidled over to her and kissed and caressed her. She responded languidly at first, but her breathing deepened, and eventually she kissed him back. He made bolder forays with his hands. She encouraged him. But the mood had fizzled, and when Tia reached between his legs, Saul wanted to call the whole thing off. She was persistent, however. She stroked his penis, played with it, spoke baby talk to it. Eventually even took it into her mouth, which he knew was not her favorite pastime. No dice. In the future this would not be a problem, but at the moment it was, and Saul wished he could assign a proxy to finish what he had started. After a while, he pulled her off him. They cuddled. Her arousal gradually dissipated. He knew better than to try to apologize. They lay in each others' arms and drowsed. "Say," he whispered, "how'd you like to go down to DC with me tomorrow?"

He thought she was asleep she took so long answering. "I don't know. Ralph and I have a big day planned."

"Come on. It'll be fun. We'll sit out the vote in Congress and then go shopping. Maybe take in dinner and a show."

"That might be nice."

He waited for her decision. They'd never been quite so public before, though he didn't think Helene would mind. And Ralph seemed like a well-adjusted young man. So why not? He'd buy a toy for their kid—what was his name?—Dori? Was that a boy's name? Names didn't seem gender specific anymore. Tia was an illustrator/programmer. She used to work on an interactive medical encyclopedia project, but after the birth of her child she switched to children's books, the kind with characters—pearlescent hippos and quicksilver bots—that popped out and wanted to play. He wondered what she'd do after the Procreation Ban became law. There wouldn't be much of a market for storybooks. Nor for toys. Breakfast cereals, cartoons, hologames, theme parks—a lot of industries would have to adapt or die. No more school boards or school bus drivers. Maternity fashions, baptismal fonts, pacifiers, childbirth classes.

Tia must have been thinking along similar lines because she said, "After it passes, how long before it goes into effect?"

"Well, it'll have to be reconciled with the House bill. Taksayer will sign it as soon as it hits her desk. Two weeks?"

"There's gonna be a whole lot of serious screwing going on in the next two weeks."

They laughed, though it reminded Saul of his poor performance tonight.

"A mini-baby boom," she said, "the last hurrah."

"A spike in storybook sales," he added.

For a while she didn't respond, and he worried that he'd offended her. Then she said, "I was thinking of Ralph and me."

He chuckled and said, "A second baby? How irresponsible." He felt her stiffen in his arms, and he tried to backpedal. "That was meant as a joke."

"For you maybe, but it'll be our last chance."

"It'll be everyone's last chance."

"Not you. You're the vice president. I doubt the ban will apply to you and Helene."

He didn't know if she were mocking him or not. "No, the ban will apply to everyone—equally."

She snorted. "Yeah, right."

Saul rose on his elbow. "I resent your suggestion. The language is very clear. Procreation will be by permit only, and permits will be limited in number and awarded equally regardless of race, class, or station."

Tia yawned. "If you say so, dear."

Saul was speechless. He'd never seen this side of her before.

She said, "So why'd you make that statement today?"

This was the first time she'd mentioned his gaffe. He'd wondered if she was even aware of it. "I made no statement. A proxy of mine did, one we've diagnosed as being defective."

"So I heard: sunspots." She sat up and propped herself against the pillows. "Let me talk to it."

"What? The proxy? I don't think that's such a hot idea."

"Why not? Bring it. I have a question."

Against his better judgment, Saul ordered Cal to retrieve the proxy from Jackson's system. When it appeared, hovering above the foot of the bed, it blinked and glanced around to orientate itself. It noticed Tia, with mussed hair and naked breasts, and smiled warmly.

Tia returned the smile. "Doesn't look defective to me."

"Nevertheless, I am," it said. "At least according to the staff. Personally, I feel fine." It turned to Saul. "May I ask why you haven't deleted me yet?"

"No reason. Might do it now except Tia wanted a look at you."

It turned to her, "If I'm defective, Tia, I'd rather you *not* look."

"Nothing wrong with its vanity either," Tia said. "I won't keep you, proxy," she continued, "but tell me something. This nation hasn't been so sharply divided over an issue since—probably since slavery. Your statement today seemed to put you in the Republican camp. And then you dismissed it as a slip of the tongue."

"I didn't dismiss it. I never got the chance," said the proxy.

Tia glanced at Saul who said, "We substituted a new proxy during the Q and A period."

"I see," said Tia. "So tell me, proxy, you called a fetus a baby. What's your view on abortion? Do you feel abortion is wrong?"

"Strongly."

Tia frowned. "And you would put a fetus' rights on equal footing with an adult woman's?"

"No, a fetus is innocent. I would grant it *greater* protection."

Tia and Saul sat dumbly for a moment before Saul found his voice. "That's the sunspot speaking. And I think it's time to delete it."

"Not yet," said Tia. "Let it speak."

"Thank you, Tia," the proxy said with sober good humor. "In an effort to sidestep the issue of abortion, an issue this nation hasn't been able to resolve in seventy years of acrimonious debate, we intend to store fetuses indefinitely in vaults, in the same vaults—I might add—that the Department of Agriculture once used to stockpile surplus cheese. We say that someday we'll send these fetuses to colonize the stars. What hogwash! You know as well as I that our babies will never leave those vaults. They'll lie there by the millions like so much toxic waste. That, to my mind, is the same as abortion outright, and to a Christian—an abomination!"

Saul was breathless. If he hadn't pulled the proxy when he did, this is how it would have fielded questions. "You truly are defective," he said. "I'm neither antiabortion nor Christian. I'm an atheist."

"How can you be so sure?" said the proxy. "When was the last time you checked?"

Saul turned to Tia. "You know I've always vigorously supported women's rights. Look at my senate record. I was endorsed for the vice presidency by NOW, for crissake."

"Hush," Tia said and placed a finger on his lips. "I know you're a good man, Saul, but maybe you've changed. People change."

The car came to a halt in a highly secure depot deep beneath the Capitol complex. Pneumatic doors whooshed open to reveal Jackson waiting on the platform. If Jackson was surprised to see Tia, he didn't show it. He escorted them and their Secret Service detail up privileged lifts and along press-proof corridors. The voting had not yet begun, he explained. With so many senators deciding at the last moment to vote in realbody, the session had been delayed. Jackson led them to temporary headquarters in Alaska Senator Lonny Sota's suite. Sota and a dozen other senators—Republicans, Centrists, and Democrats—together with a legion of aides, had congregated there to await the call to order.

Saul paused in the hall and looked into the crowded suite. There was excitement there, energy not communicated via proxy. He opened his satchel, removed a paper bag of home-smoked salmon, and entered the room. "Someone order takeout?" he said, holding aloft the grease-stained bag. Senators surrounded him, slapping him on the back and shaking his hand. He had not known until this moment how much he missed the old realbody camaraderie.

Sota's staff quickly laid out crackers, napkins, and plates. Sota held the greasy bag himself until a suitable tablecloth could be found to protect his eighteenth century sideboard. The room was dominated by a large central hologram shaped like a fishbowl. It projected live coverage of a riot raging right outside the Capitol building. The view was from a satellite or high drone, and from that vantage the millions of protesters looked like some monster amoeba overwhelming hundreds of city blocks, from the National Zoo to the Potomac.

A hush fell over the room, and Saul turned to see President Taksayer and her chief of staff stroll through the door amid an escort of burly Secret Service men. "I heard there was a party," she said with her trademark panache. Senator Sota recovered from his surprise and hurried over to greet his latest guest.

The president worked the room, lingering with two recalcitrant Centrists who had publicly sided with the anti-ban Republicans. When finally she greeted Saul, she said, "Saul, Saul, is it really you?" She reached out with a finger to touch him, and he laughed. Although they conferred daily via holo or proxy, he had not been in her realbody presence—had not touched her—since their waltz at an inaugural ball. She seemed fresher, younger. Two years of crisis and compromise had agreed with her. She said, "It's a wonder we were able to entice you away from your vegetables."

"Entice?" he replied. "More like prod. In any case, my presence in DC is nowhere so remarkable as yours on the Hill during a senate vote, Ms. President. Let us just hope you don't jinx the process."

"If I do, I'll have to move into your igloo, now won't I?" She said, looking curiously at Tia, and added, "If there's room."

"Ms. President," Saul said, introducing the two women, "Tia Krebbs. Ms. Krebbs, President Taksayer."

"Please call me Sally," said the president.

The room announced the call to order, and the suite quickly emptied as senators and their staff dutifully departed. In the newly-deserted room, a pair of men stood out from the Secret Service agents. They did not flinch from Saul's attention and, in fact, brazenly returned his stare. Obviously, they were not aides. But since neither the president nor her chief of staff found their presence out of the ordinary, Saul ignored them. "I wonder if this holo could be switched to the chamber?" the president said, and immediately the mayhem on the Mall was replaced by the chaos in the chamber. The Senate Chamber, a mausoleum used chiefly as electronic backdrop, was today filling with flesh-and-blood senators who had not graced it in realbody since their swearing-in ceremonies and who thus required ushers, of whom there were too few, to escort them to their assigned seats. After much commotion, the president pro tempore called the session to order. The holo showed a tally board that read "Yeas: 0, Nays: 0," as well as close-ups of the podium and individual senators. Old Senator Hagerbarger could be seen at his seat, bent over a data tablet, serenely oblivious to his surroundings.

Saul, watching the holo next to the president, had a niggling suspicion that he was the cause for her presence here and the serious breech of protocol it represented. Jackson caught his attention from the other side of the room.

"Yes, what is it?" he said, going over to him.

"We have a problem, sir. Another proxy flipped."

"What? Where?"

"You're giving the keynote speech to the International Library and Catalog Convention in Toronto."

"Project it here," Saul said, pointing to the sideboard

that was littered with cracker crumbs and salmon bones.

Jackson glanced at the others in the room. "Here, sir?"

"You're right," Saul said and led Jackson to the inner suite. "We'll use Sota's office."

Jackson projected a diorama of an auditorium on the polished surface of the senator's desk. Hundreds of tiny librarians shifted nervously in their seats. Saul's proxy, wearing this week's burgundy bowtie, floated above the lectern and harangued them with uncharacteristic zeal.

"Truth #10," it shouted. "All persons of all races are racists. Those who deny this truth most strenuously are either fools or haven't yet figured out which race they belong to.

"Truth #11. Slavery is a universal fact-of-life. If you don't own one, you are one."

"What *is* this?" Saul asked.

"I don't know, sir. A lecture? A manifesto? Shall I pull the proxy?"

Saul hesitated. "Play it from the beginning."

Jackson shuttled the holo back to the proxy's appearance on the stage. "Thank you," it said. "It's always a pleasure to visit Toronto, and I'm honored to address such an august gathering." It cleared its throat and began, "My talk today is entitled, "'The Thirteen Bitter Truths of Victimhood.' First I'll list them, and then I'll go back to discuss each of them in gory detail. Ladies and Gentlemen, hold onto your seats.

"Truth #1. The Jews asked for it. Persons of all colors asked for it. Rape victims asked for it. Victims of every kind in every age asked for it."

The audience gasped as one, and the tiny proxy paused, leering like a lunatic. "Pretty self-evident, eh? Okay, here's Truth #2. Victimhood is money in a Swiss bank. It's brownie points in the celestial choir. It's a big, white, colonnaded house on the moral high ground."

"Shall I stop it, sir," said Jackson, but Saul raised a hand.

"Truth #3. All victim groups—if they survive—will leap

at the chance to victimize others, and not necessarily their former oppressors, often others in their own group. The moral high ground makes an excellent staging area for tyranny."

Saul allowed the proxy to finish its précis, and then switched the diorama back to realtime. The proxy was still at it, explaining to the members of the International Library Association how their own organization participated in cultural oppression by systematically defining normalcy through its very cataloging procedures. "Cal," Saul said at last, "pull this proxy immediately. Pull *all* my active proxies everywhere and turn them over to Jackson's system. Then put yourself into hibernation."

"Retrieving," said Calendar, "transferring, sleeping."

"Jackson, send a batch of your own proxies to cover for mine. Apologize where necessary on my behalf and explain that my office is under terrorist attack in an attempt to discredit and embarrass the Administration."

Jackson addressed his valet but paused to listen to something. "Ah, sir. The president disagrees."

"The president? How?"

"I guess they're monitoring you."

Saul strode out to the reception area. The Secret Service men were gone. The chief of staff was gone, as was Tia. The only people in the room were the two strange men and President Taksayer in huddled conference. The men hardly glanced at Saul as he approached, but broke their huddle and without a word escorted Jackson from the suite. The door clicked shut behind them. Saul was alone with the president.

"Saul, Saul, Saul," she said as she watched the senate holo. The voting had begun; the tally stood at 18 yeas to 14 nays. "I'm concerned about you."

"How long have you been eavesdropping?"

The president shrugged. "How long have you been a bigot?"

"*I am not* ..." Saul said and lowered his voice. "I am not, nor have I ever been a bigot."

"I know, I know—sunspots. Cyber-terrorism. Conspiracies. Other people putting words in your mouth."

"Neither am I paranoid. My system has been compromised. Obviously." The president's attention seemed fixed on the holo. The senate vote was by outcry so that each senator must declare his or her vote to the whole witnessing world. Two more nay votes were tallied as Saul and the president watched. "Sally, my system has been contaminated whether you want to believe it or not. And I can prove it."

She looked at him. "Please do."

"Loan me your valet."

"Excuse me?"

"You trust your own system, don't you? Let me use it to cast a fresh proxy of myself here and now. We'll question it. Put both our minds at ease."

It took the president only a moment to agree. "Mr. Bond, create a proxy simulation for the vice president at his command."

"Certainly, Madame President," said the president's valet. "I await his input."

Saul said, "Mr. Bond, cast me in ten seconds." He closed his eyes, took a deep, cleansing breath, and imagined he was alone in his teahouse, walking barefoot across the smooth wooden floorboards and looking out the bank of tall windows. It was hard to concentrate, but he imagined he looked out the windows towards the pink-tinged peaks of the Alaska Range. This was the view that would be blotted out in the next few months, and he couldn't help but picture a latticework of residential towers growing like giant celery stalks to the sky. Then his perspective changed, and he was high in one of the towers leaning out a window, looking down at his postage-stamp patch of land below. It was like looking down a dim airshaft. Saul shook his head to dispel the image and started over. He imagined bare feet on bare wooden floorboards, but the president nudged him.

He opened his eyes to a full-size, head-and-shoulder proxy of himself. It blinked, looked at each of them, surveyed the room. Saul said, "How are you?"

The proxy glanced at the vote tally board. "As well as can be expected, I suppose."

"Fine, then let's waste no time, proxy. If you were called upon to break a tie over the Procreation Ban, how would you vote?"

Without hesitation the proxy said, "I would vote yea for the ban."

"There. See? Crisis averted," Saul said. He felt relief and vindication.

The president eyed the proxy. "Not so fast, Saul. Proxy, please explain why you'd vote for the ban."

"Gladly. As a Gaiaist, I believe that if we don't limit our specioeffluvium, and I mean quick, the Mother will push us aside and do it for us. And her methods, believe you me, are none too gentle."

The president groaned, and Saul went pale. "But I'm not a Gaiaist!"

"How can you be so sure?" said the proxy. "Mother cherishes all her biomass, even you."

At this the president stifled a smile, and Saul glared at her. "I'm sorry, Saul," she said, "but that biohooey coming out of your mouth is positively comical."

"Look at me, Sally. I'm not laughing! Cal, delete this thing."

"Waking up," said his valet.

"No, Cal, stay asleep. *You*," he said to the proxy, "answer me one thing. How can you claim to believe something *I* don't? How does that work?"

"I have no idea. I wouldn't think it possible. One of us must be in a delusional state."

"We don't have time for this," Saul said, waving his hand at the proxy. "Your Mr. Bond may delete it now." But the president was watching the senate holo again. A burst of applause had interrupted the vote. There was a close-up of Senator Hagerbarger reseating himself, a smirk visible under his ivory-colored mustache. He had apparently added some witticism to his vote. The tally read 30 yeas to 21 nays.

"Here's something I seem to know that you haven't figured out yet," Saul's proxy said to Saul. "The vote *will* end in a tie. As sure as sunbeams. It's an incidental chit in a larger deal. There's more to this compromise than meets the eye. And in the hallowed tradition of American politics you, the vice president, have been left out of the loop."

"Mr. Bond," said the president, "isolate the proxy. Send it to Fernandez for immediate etopsy. Then launch your backup and place yourself in protective quarantine."

"Right," said the valet. Saul's proxy disappeared. A few moments later, a new, female voice said, "Moneypenny here, Ms. President, at your disposal."

"If looks could kill," President Taksayer said to Saul. "Relax, Jaspersen. So what if there's a tie? That's not a conspiracy, just a simple case of a spineless Senate too squeamish to do its job. Nothing new about that. This bill is strong medicine that no one wants to swallow, though everyone agrees we must, even Hagerbarger and the staunchest old-time Bible thumpers." She paused a moment to weigh her words. "The Republicans are willing to give up only the fewest number of votes necessary to carry the ban. That involves a tie, naturally. Your vote will save one vulnerable old redneck his seat come next election cycle." She waved her hand as if to dismiss the whole affair. "Business as usual, nothing more."

"Fine," said Saul, "but what about the rest of it? My proxy said there was a larger deal."

"Your proxies have said a lot of crazy things. Am I to hold you to all of it?"

Saul swallowed his anger. "Who knows? Maybe I *am* a changed man. Maybe my vote is *not* in your pocket. Maybe you have another five minutes to win me over."

The president blinked as though slapped. "Dear Saul, at the risk of lecturing you, let me remind you how much rides on the passage of this bill. Please recall the arguments your own proxies put forth so elegantly last night. The boutique economy, remember? The Age of the Micro-Nation. Or were they misquoting you?"

"No, no," said Saul, "I still believe that."

"Good." The president thumped a finger on his chest. "Remember, Jaspersen, you're not some free agent; you're part of this Administration. I would never have let it come down to a tie if I'd suspected you'd turn on me. So what do I do with you? How can I trust you?" She turned away to consult with unseen staff via valet.

How can I trust myself, Saul thought. Just then the room summoned him to the chamber. The vote had resulted in a tie—59 to 59. He sighed and started for the door, but the president stepped in his way.

"Where are you going?"

"They're waiting for me."

"Let them wait."

"Look, Taksayer, no matter what's wrong with my proxies, I'm the same man I always was, and no matter what backroom deals you've cooked up, my own reasons for supporting the ban haven't changed." He fervently hoped this was true. "Now, if you'll excuse me, Ms. President, I have constitutional duties to discharge." He stepped around her. When he reached the door his hand trembled, and he wondered if the door would yield to him. It did, but the corridor was blocked by Secret Service men, a wall of brawny shoulders and impassive stares. Saul could see Tia and Jackson down the corridor isolated by more Secret Service. The two strange advisors were gone.

"I don't suppose we could call this whole thing off?" President Taksayer said behind him. "Plead sudden illness or something? Moneypenny, how would the vote be settled if the vice president doesn't show up?"

The president's valet responded, "Senate rules equate a tie with defeat."

The president cursed and placed a hand on Saul's shoulder to turn him around. She studied his eyes for a long moment. "Then you'd better go," she said at last. "Go break the tie. But when you stand on that podium, take a look around. You're a smart boy, Saul. You'll figure things out."

She nodded to her chief-of-staff, and the line of Secret Service opened to provide Saul passage. Emboldened, he made his way to Jackson and Tia and dismissed their guards. The agents stood their ground, however, until they received confirmation, and then left without a word. Tia was pale with fright. "Welcome to Washington," Saul said as reassuringly as he could. "Perhaps you'd care to watch from the gallery. Jackson, please escort Ms. Krebbs to the spectator gallery. And Jackson," he said quietly, "stay with her."

The corridors to the Senate Chamber were eerily deserted. His shoes slapped the marble floor. But no matter how slowly he managed to walk, each step brought him closer to voicing a decision he no longer believed in. They had lied to him. They had manipulated him and sabotaged his proxies. And the president of the United States of North America had almost disappeared him.

A scary thought stopped Saul in his tracks, *What if I* am *paranoid? What if I* am *going mad?* Was it possible to go mad but be too busy to notice? He didn't think so, but he was no expert in the field and would have liked to cast an army of proxies on the spot to go out and research it and report back to him before he reached the chamber doors. But his proxies were gone, perhaps forever. And how could he ever trust Cal again? No, he was on his own now, completely on his own. "God help me," he groaned. *Was that a prayer? Did I just pray?*

Saul entered the Senate Chamber to polite applause, strode purposefully down the aisle, climbed the podium, and turned to face senators, spectators, and the holoeyes of the world. The presiding officer introduced him. Saul cleared his throat and said, "Thank you, Mr. Johnson, members of the Senate, and friends here and abroad." He cleared his throat once more. "As constitutional President of the Senate, I now assume leadership of this special session." Saul was stalling, and he knew it. "Thank you, Mr. Johnson—" he half-bowed to the presiding officer—"for handing me such a thankless task." Senators guffawed and shifted in their seats. "The time for debate and speeches has passed. The vote stands at fifty-nine to fifty-nine. It is now my duty to cast the deciding vote." Saul stopped speaking and tried to conceal his mounting panic—he no longer knew how he would vote. As the chamber grew silent with anticipation, another scary thought entered his head. *What if*—it chilled him even to think it—*What if I am a Christian? What if I'm being born-again right here in the Senate Chamber?* After all, what better venue than this could God want and what better servant than him, Saul Jaspersen, whose next spoken utterance might forever crush the dreams of a billion innocent people to bear and raise children?

Saul shut his eyes and prayed with fervor, *Please, if there is a God, oh please God, don't do this to me. Please postpone it an hour and do it in private.* But he knew that wasn't how it worked. God chose the place and time, and there was no ducking Him. He struck you with a bolt of lightning. He knocked you off your horse.

Behind him the presiding officer coughed, and Saul's eyes shot open. Everyone in the room was staring at him. He looked up and scanned the spectator gallery for Tia. He tried to remember what she was wearing but couldn't even recall its color. He felt dizzy. Blood pulsed in his ears. Faces swam before him, their eyes ballooning in alarm. *I must be fainting.* He clenched the lectern with both hands, forcing himself to breathe, and smiled bravely for all the world to see.

Someone smiled back. A strange young senator in the Republican section. Saul gaped at him, unable to comprehend what he saw. It was Texas Senator Erstwhile P. Hagerbarger—in the flesh. Not a proxy. Not a holo image. The real man. But he was young, younger than Saul, younger than when Saul had first met him. His mustache was a rich chestnut color. His face was smooth, meaty, and handsome. He sat with graceful ease. He radiated animal heat. *How can that be?*

Saul scrutinized the rows of senators. Most of them appeared younger than their proxies. Even President Taksayer, he recalled, had seemed so. He looked again at Hagerbarger. No legal longevity treatment could account for his transformation. No, he was clearly the beneficiary of nanorejuvenation.

The senator smiled at Saul and winked, and suddenly things started dropping into place. President Taksayer had spoken the truth: it *was* business as usual. Saul looked again at his former colleagues: Democrats, Centrists, and Republicans. Even those not personally rejuvenated had to be aware of it and thus gave their tacit approval. Who else was in on it? Certainly the media. In fact, any person of influence in the USNA with half a brain and the price of a ticket to a rejuvenation clinic in Tel Aviv or Bangkok. Probably half the people whose proxies his proxies interacted with every day. Saul knew then he had been a fool with his head buried in garden dirt.

Of course there had to be more to it than the simple exercise of privilege. He could see now why the Procreation Ban was so important to them. Neither the Administration nor Congress had any intention whatsoever of approving nanorejuvenation in the USNA. No, they planned to attack overpopulation from both ends of the life cycle at once. People of little means, people who could ill afford to spend weeks each year in exclusive foreign clinics, would still die—kicking and screaming—as they always had. But after today's vote there would be no new generations to replace them. Things would get pretty lonely at the bottom. For that matter, merely average citizens would inexorably slip away as well. North America, land of the few and the competent. What a neat Yankee solution to the population problem. And let the rest of the riff raff world trip all over itself trying to catch up.

Saul wiped a sleeve across his brow. Not a friendly place—the future—but if he was honest, was it so different from the future that he, himself, had toiled to create? He cleared his throat one last time. It was time to vote. "I vote …" he said, and the chamber grew silent enough to hear the planet creaking on its axis. *How do I vote?* He still didn't know. *Who am I?* This was often the better question. *Am I a hypocritical Christian? A closet bigot? A naive pile of biomass?* According to his proxies these were his likely choices. Saul knew of only one method for choosing. He must cast himself. Not a proxy of himself, but his real self. So he willed himself to relax and imagined he stood in his little teahouse, his dear little teahouse. Sunbeams poured through the windows and warmed the wooden floor at his feet. As he watched, his bare feet grew pale, like roots, and burrowed deep into soft soil between garden rows of cabbages and kale. His cock, however, rose like a construction derrick and his testes hung like wrecking balls. Saul craned his neck and looked up at the towers all around him with their millions of windows and in each window a face, and he swung his hips from north to south and east to west and cut them down like so much straw. "…yea," he said at last. "I vote yea for the Procreation Ban, and yea for the future."

❖ "GETTING TO KNOW YOU"

This was my fourth published story, coming right after "We Were Out of Our Minds with Joy." I used it to explore the genesis of personal "belt valets" like Henry. Looking back, I think I uncovered so much more, perhaps even the true purpose of hi-tech itself.

Getting to Know You

In 2019, Applied People constructed the first Residential Tower to house its growing army of professionals-for-hire. Shaped like a giant egg in a porcelain cup, APRT 1 loomed three kilometers over the purple soybimi fields of northern Indiana and was visible from both Chicago and Indianapolis. Rumor said it generated gravity. That is, if you fell off your career ladder, you wouldn't fall down, but you'd fly cross-country instead, still clutching your hat and briefcase, your stock options and retirement plan, to APRT 1.

SUMMER, 2062

Here she was in a private Slipstream car, flying beneath the plains of Kansas at 1000 kph, watching a holovid, and eating pretzels. Only four hours earlier in San Francisco, Zoranna had set the house to vacation mode and given it last-minute instructions. She'd thrown beachwear and evening clothes into a bag. Reluctantly, she'd removed Hounder, her belt, and hung him on a peg in the closet. While doing so, she made a solemn vow not to engage in any work-related activities for a period of three weeks. The next three weeks were to be scrupulously dedicated to visiting her sister in Indiana, shopping for a hat in Budapest, and lying on a beach towel in the South of France. But no sooner had Zoranna made this vow than she broke it by deciding to bring along Bug, the beta unit.

"Where were you born?" Bug asked in its squeaky voice.

Zoranna started on a new pretzel and wondered why Bug repeatedly asked the same questions. No doubt it had to do with its imprinting algorithm. "Take a note," she said, "annoying repetition."

"Note taken," said Bug. "Where were you born?"

"Where do you think I was born?"

"Buffalo, New York," said Bug.

"Very good."

"What is your date of birth?"

Zoranna sighed. "August 12, 1961. Honestly, Bug, I wish you'd tap public records for this stuff."

"Do you like the timbre of Bug's voice?" it said. "Would you prefer it lower or higher?" It repeated this question through several octaves.

"Frankly, Bug, I detest your voice at any pitch."

"What is your favorite color?"

"I don't have one."

"Yesterday your favorite color was salmon."

"Well, today it's cranberry." The little pest was silent for a moment while it retrieved and compared color libraries. Zoranna tried to catch up with the holovid, but she'd lost the thread of the story.

"You have a phone call," Bug said, "Ted Chalmers at General Genius."

Zoranna sat up straight and patted her hair. "Put him on and squelch the vid." A miniature hologram of Ted with his feet on his desk was projected in the air before her. Ted was an attractive man Zoranna had wanted to ask out a couple times, but never seemed able to catch between spousals. By the time she'd hear he was single again, he'd be well into his next liaison. It made her wonder how someone with her world-class investigative skills could be so dateless. She'd even considered assigning Hounder to monitor Ted's availability status in order to get her foot in his door.

When Ted saw her, he smiled and said, "Hey, Zoe, how's our little prototype?"

"Driving me crazy," she said. "Refresh my memory, Ted. When's the Inquisition supposed to end?"

Ted lowered his feet to the floor. "It's still imprinting? How long have you had it now?" He consulted a display and answered his own question. "Twenty-two days. That's a record." He got up and paced his office, walking in and out of the projected holoframe.

"No kidding," said Zoranna. "I've had marriages that didn't last that long." She'd meant for this to be funny, but it fell flat.

Ted sat down. "I wish we could continue the test, but unfortunately we're aborting. We'd like you to return the unit—" He glanced at his display again, "—return Bug as soon as possible."

"Why? What's up?"

"Nothing's up. They want to tweak it some more is all." He flashed her his best PR smile.

Zoranna shook her head. "Ted, you don't pull the plug on a major field test just like that."

Ted shrugged his shoulders. "That's what I thought. Anyway, think you can drop it in a shipping chute today?"

"In case you haven't noticed," she said, "I happen to be in a transcontinental Slipstream car at the moment, which Bug is navigating. I left Hounder at home. The soonest I can let Bug go is when I return in three weeks."

"That won't do, Zoe," Ted said and frowned. "Tell you what. General Genius will send you, at no charge, its Diplomat Deluxe model, pre-loaded with transportation, telecommunications, the works. Where will you be tonight?"

Something surely was wrong. The Diplomat was GG's flagship model and expensive even for Zoranna. "I'll be at APRT 24," she said, and when Ted raised an eyebrow, explained, "My sister lives there."

"APRT 24 it is, then."

"Listen, Ted, something stinks. Unless you want me snooping around your shop, you'd better come clean."

"Off the record?"

"Fuck off the record. I have twenty-two days invested in this test and no story."

"I see. You have a point. How's this sound? In addition to the complimentary belt, we'll make you the same contract for the next test. You're our team journalist. Deal?" Zoranna shrugged, and Ted put his feet back on the desk. "Heads are rolling, Zoe. Big shake-up in product development. Threats of lawsuits. We're questioning the whole notion of combining belt valet technology with artificial personality. Or at least with this particular personality."

"Why? What's wrong with it?"

"It's too pushy. Too intrusive. Too heavy-handed. It's a monster that should have never left the lab. You're lucky Bug hasn't converted yet, or you'd be suing us too."

Ted was exaggerating, of course. She agreed that Bug was a royal pain, but it was no monster. Still, she'd be happy to get rid of it, and the Diplomat belt was an attractive consolation prize. If she grafted Hounder into it, she'd be ahead of the technology curve for once. "I'm going to want all the details when I get back, but for now, yeah, sure, you got a deal."

After Zoranna ended the call, Bug said, "Name the members of your immediate family and state their relationship to you."

The car began to decelerate, and Zoranna instinctively checked the buckle of her harness. "My family is deceased, except for Nancy."

With a hard bump, the car entered the ejection tube, found its wheels, and braked. Lights flashed through the windows, and she saw signs stencilled on the tube wall, "APRT 24, Stanchion 4 Depot."

"What is Nancy's favorite color?"

"That's it. That's enough. No more questions, Bug. You heard Ted; you're off the case. Until I ship you back, let's just pretend you're a plain old, dumb belt valet. No more questions. Got it?"

"Affirmative."

Pneumatic seals hissed as air pressure equalized, the car came to a halt, and the doors slid open. Zoranna released the harness and retrieved her luggage from the cargo net. She paused a moment to see if there'd be any more questions and then climbed out of the car to join throngs of commuters on the platform. She craned her neck and looked straight up the tower's chimney, the five-hundred-story atrium galleria where floor upon floor of crowded shops, restaurants, theaters, parks, and gardens receded skyward into brilliant haze. Zoranna was ashamed to admit that she didn't know what her sister's favorite color was, or for that matter, her favorite anything. Except that Nancy loved a grand view. And the grandest thing about an APRT was its view. The evening sun, multiplied by giant mirrors on the roof, slid up the sides of the core in an inverted sunset. The ascending dusk triggered whole floors of slumbering biolume railings and walls to luminesce. Streams of pedestrians crossed the dizzying space on suspended pedways. The air pulsed with the din of an indoor metropolis.

When Nancy first moved here, she was an elementary school teacher who specialized in learning disorders. Despite the surcharge, she leased a suite of rooms so near the top of the tower, it was impossible to see her floor from depot level. But with the Procreation Ban of 2033, teachers became redundant, and Nancy was forced to move to a lower, less expensive floor. Then, when free-agency clone technology was licensed, she lost altitude tens of floors at a time. "My last visit," Zoranna said to Bug, "Nancy had an efficiency on the 103rd floor. Check the tower directory."

"Nancy resides on S40."

"S40?"

"Subterranean 40. Thirty-five floors beneath depot level."

"You don't say."

Zoranna allowed herself to be swept by the waves of commuters towards the banks of elevators. She had inadvertently arrived during crush hour and found herself pressing shoulders with tired and hungry wage earners at the end of their work cycle. They were uniformly young people, clones mostly, who wore brown and teal Applied People livery. Neither brown nor teal was Zoranna's favorite color.

The entire row of elevators reserved for the subfloors was inexplicably off-line. The marquee directed her to elevators in Stanchion 5, one klick east by pedway, but Zoranna was tired. "Bug," she said, pointing to the next row, "do those go down?"

"Affirmative."

"Good," she said and jostled her way into the nearest one. It was so crowded with passengers that the doors—begging their indulgence and requesting they consolidate—required three tries to latch. By the time the cornice display showed the results of the destination adjudication, and Zoranna realized she was aboard a consensus elevator, it was too late to get off. Floor 63 would be the first stop, followed by 55, 203, 148, etc. Her floor was dead last.

Bug, she tongued, *this is a Dixon lift!*

Zoranna's long day grew measurably longer each time the elevator stopped to let off or pick up passengers. At each stop the consensus changed, and destinations were reshuffled, but her stop remained stubbornly last. Of the five kinds of elevators the tower deployed, the Dixon consensus lifts worked best for groups of people going to popular floors, but she was the only passenger traveling to the subfloors.

Moreover, the consensual ascent acceleration, a sprightly 2.8-g, upset her stomach. *Bug,* she tongued, *fly home for me and unlock my archives. Retrieve a file entitled "cerebral aneurysm" and forward it to the elevator's adjudicator. We'll just manufacture our own consensus.*

This file is out of date, Bug said in her ear after a moment, its implant voice like the whine of a mosquito. *Bug cannot feed obsolete data to a public conveyance.*

Then postdate it.

That is not allowed.

"I'll tell you what's not allowed!" she said, and people looked at her.

The stricture against asking questions limits Bug's functionality, Bug said.

Zoranna sighed. *What do you need to know?*

Shall Bug reprogram itself to enable Bug to process the file as requested?

No, Bug, I don't have the time to reprogram you, even if I knew how.

Shall Bug reprogram itself?

It could reprogram itself? Ted had failed to mention that feature. A tool they'd forgotten to disable? *Yes, Bug, reprogram yourself.*

A handicapped icon blinked on the cornice display, and the elevator's speed slowed to a crawl.

Thank you, Bug. That's more like it.

A jerry standing in the corner of the crowded elevator said, "The fuck, lift?"

"Lift speed may not exceed five floors per minute," the elevator replied.

The jerry rose on tiptoes and surveyed his fellow passengers. "Right," he said, "who's the gimp?" Everyone looked at their neighbors. There were michelles, jennies, a pair of jeromes, and a half-dozen other germlines. They all looked at Zoranna, the only person not dressed in AP brown and teal.

"I'm sorry," she said, pressing her palm to her temple, "I have an aneurysm the size of a grapefruit. The slightest strain…" She winced theatrically.

"Then have it fixed!" the jerry said, to murmured agreement.

"Gladly," said Zoranna. "Could you pony me the Œ23,000?"

The jerry har-harred and looked her up and down appraisingly. "Sweetheart, if you spent half as much money on the vitals as you obviously do on the peripherals," he leered, "you wouldn't have this problem, now would you?" Zoranna had never liked the jerry type; they were spooky. In fact, more jerries had to be pithed *in vatero* for incipient sociopathy than any other commercial type. Professionally, they made superb grunts; most of the indentured men in the Protectorate's commando forces were jerries. This one, however, wore an EXTRUSIONS UNLIMITED patch on his teal ball cap; he was security for a retail mall. "So," he said, "where you heading?"

"Sub40?" she said.

Passengers consulted the cornice display and groaned. The jerry said, "At this rate it'll take me an hour to get home."

"Again I apologize," said Zoranna, "but all the down lifts were spango. However, if everyone here consensed to drop me off first—?"

There was a general muttering as passengers spoke to their belts or tapped virtual keyboards, and the elevator said, "Consensus has been modified." But instead of descending as Zoranna expected, it stopped at the next floor and opened its doors. People streamed out. Zoranna caught a glimpse of the 223rd floor with its rich appointments; crystalline decor; high, arched passages; and in the distance, a ringpath crowded with joggers and skaters. An evangeline, her brown puddle-like eyes reflecting warmth and concern, touched Zoranna's arm as she disembarked.

The jerry, however, stayed on and held back his companions, two russes. "Don't give her the satisfaction," he said.

"But we'll miss the game," said one of the russes.

"We'll watch it in here if we have to," said the jerry.

Zoranna liked russes. Unlike jerries, they were generous souls, and you always knew where you stood with them. These two wore brown jackets and teal slacks. Their name badges read, "FRED," and "OSCAR." They were probably returning from a day spent bodyguarding some minor potentate in Cincinnati or Terre Haute. Consulting each other with a glance, they each took an arm and dragged the jerry off the lift.

When the doors closed and Zoranna was alone at last, she sagged with relief. "And now, Bug," she said, "we have a consensus of one. So retract my handicap file and pay whatever toll necessary to take us down nonstop." The brake released, and the elevator plunged some 260 floors. Her ears popped. "I guess you've learned something, Bug," she said, thinking about the types of elevators.

"Affirmative," Bug said. "Bug learned you developed a cerebral aneurysm at the calendar age of fifty-two and that you've had your brain and spinal cord rejuvenated twice since then. Bug learned that your organs have an average bioage of thirty-five years, with your lymphatic system the oldest at bioage sixty-five, and your cardiovascular system the youngest at twenty-five."

"You've been examining my medical records?"

"Affirmative."

"I told you to fetch one file, not my entire chart!"

"You told Bug to unlock your archives. Bug is getting to know you."

"What else did you look at?" The elevator eased to a soft landing at S40 and opened its doors.

"Bug reviewed your diaries and journals, the corpus of your zine writing, your investigative dossiers, your complete correspondence, judicial records, awards and citations, various multimedia scrapbooks, and school transcripts. Bug is currently following public links."

Zoranna was appalled. Nevertheless, she realized that if she'd opened her archives earlier, they'd be through this imprinting phase by now.

She followed Bug's pedway directions to Nancy's block. Sub40 corridors were decorated in cheerless colors and lit with harsh, artificial light—biolumes couldn't live underground. There were no grand promenades, no parks or shops. There was a dank odor of decay, however, and chilly ventilation.

On Nancy's corridor, Zoranna watched two people emerge from a door and come her way. They moved with the characteristic shuffle of habitually deferred body maintenance. They wore dark clothing impossible to date and, as they passed, she saw that they were crying. Tears coursed freely down their withered cheeks. To Zoranna's distress, she discovered they'd just emerged from her sister's apartment.

"You're sure this is it?" she said, standing before the door marked S40 G6879.

"Affirmative," Bug said.

Zoranna fluffed her hair with her fingers and straightened her skirt. "Door, announce me."

"At once, Zoe," replied the door.

Several moments later, the door slid open, and Nancy stood there supporting herself with an aluminum walker. "Darling Zoe," she said, balancing herself with one hand and reaching out with the other.

Zoranna stood a moment gazing at her baby sister before entering her embrace. Nancy had let herself go completely. Her hair was brittle grey, she was pale to the point of bloodless, and she had doubled in girth. When they kissed, Nancy's skin gave off a sour odor mixed with lilac.

"What a surprise!" Nancy said. "Why didn't you tell me you were coming?"

"I did. Several times."

"You did? You called?" Nancy looked upset. "I told him there was something wrong with the houseputer, but he didn't believe me."

Someone appeared behind Nancy, a handsome man with wild, curly, silver hair. "Who's *this?*" he said in an authoritative baritone. He looked Zoranna over. "You must be Zoe," he boomed. "What a delight!" He stepped around Nancy and drew Zoranna to him in a powerful hug. He stood at least a head taller than she. He kissed her eagerly on the cheek. "I am Victor. Victor Vole. Come in, come in. Nancy, you would let your sister stand in the hall?" He drew them both inside.

Zoranna had prepared herself for a small apartment, but not this small, and for castoff furniture, but not a room filled floor to ceiling with hospital beds. It took several long moments for her to comprehend what she was looking at. There were some two dozen beds in the three-by-five-meter living room. Half were arranged on the floor, and the rest clung upside-down to the ceiling. They were holograms, she quickly surmised, separate holos arranged in snowflake fashion, that is, six individual beds facing each other and overlapping at the foot. What's more, they were occupied by obviously sick, possibly dying strangers. Other than the varied lighting from the holoframes, the living room was unlit. What odd pieces of real furniture it contained were pushed against the walls. In the corner, a hutch intended to hold bric-a-brac was apparently set up as a shrine to a saint. A row of flickering votive candles illuminated an old flatstyle picture of a large, barefoot man draped head to foot in flowing robes.

"What the hell, Nancy?" Zoranna said.

"This is my work," Nancy said proudly.

"Please," said Victor, escorting them from the door. "Let's talk in the kitchen. We'll have dessert. Are you after dinner, Zoe?"

"Yes, thank you," said Zoranna. "I ate on the tube." She was made to walk through a suffering man's bed; there was no path around him to the kitchen. "Sorry," she said. But he seemed accustomed to his unfavorable location and closed his eyes while she passed through.

The kitchen was little more than an alcove separated from the living room by a counter. There was a bed squeezed into it as well, but the occupant, a grizzled man with open mouth, was either asleep or comatose. "I think Edward will be unavailable for some while," Victor said. "Houseputer, delete this hologram. Sorry, Edward, but we need the space." The holo vanished, and Victor offered Zoranna a stool at the counter. "Please," he said, "will you have tea? Or a thimble of cognac?"

"Thank you," Zoranna said, perching herself on the stool and crossing her legs, "tea would be fine." Her sister ambulated into the kitchen and flipped down her walker's built-in seat, but before she could sit, a mournful wail issued from the bedroom.

"Naaaancy," cried the voice, its gender uncertain. "Nancy, I need you."

"Excuse me," Nancy said.

"I'll go with you," Zoranna said and hopped off the stool.

The bedroom was half the size of the living room and contained half the number of holo beds, plus a real one against the far wall. Zoranna sat on it. There was a dresser, a recessed closet, a bedside night table. Expensive-looking men's clothing hung in the closet. A pair of men's slippers was parked under the dresser. And a holo of a soccer match was playing on the night table. Tiny players in brightly-colored jerseys swarmed over a field the size of a doily. The sound was off.

Zoranna watched Nancy sit on her walker seat beneath a bloat-faced woman bedded upside down on the ceiling. "What exactly are you doing with these people?"

"I listen mostly," Nancy replied. "I'm a volunteer hospice attendant."

"A volunteer? What about the—" she tried to recall Nancy's most recent paying occupation, "—the hairdressing?"

"I haven't done that for years," Nancy said dryly. "As you may have noticed, it's difficult for me to be on my feet all day."

"Yes, in fact, I did notice," said Zoranna. "Why is that? I've sent you money."

Nancy ignored her, looked up at the woman, and said, "I'm here, Mrs. Hurley. What seems to be the problem?"

Zoranna examined the holos. As in the living room, each bed was a separate projection, and in the corner of each frame was a network squib and trickle meter. All of this interactive time was costing someone a pretty penny.

The woman saw Nancy and said, "Oh, Nancy, thank you for coming. My bed is wet, but they won't change it until I sign a permission form, and I don't understand."

"Do you have the form there with you, dear?" said Nancy. "Good, hold it up." Mrs. Hurley held up a slate in trembling hands. "Houseputer," Nancy said, "capture and display that form." The document was projected against the bedroom wall greatly oversized. "That's a permission form for attendant-assisted suicide, Mrs. Hurley. You don't have to sign it unless you want to."

The woman seemed frightened. "Do I want to, Nancy?"

Victor stood in the doorway. "No!" he cried. "Never sign!"

"Hush, Victor," Nancy said.

He entered the room, stepping through beds and bodies. "Never sign away your life, Mrs. Hurley." The woman appeared even more frightened. "We've returned to Roman society," he bellowed. "Masters and servants! Plutocrats and slaves! Oh, where is the benevolent middle class when we need it?"

"Victor," Nancy said sternly and pointed to the door. And she nodded to Zoranna, "You too. Have your tea. I'll join you."

Zoranna followed Victor to the kitchen, sat at the counter, and watched him set out cups and saucers, sugar and soybimi lemon. He unwrapped and sliced a dark cake. He was no stranger to this kitchen.

"It's a terrible thing what they did to your sister," he said.

"Who? What?"

He poured boiling water into the pot. "Teaching was her life."

"Teaching?" Zoranna said, incredulous. "You're talking about something that ended thirty years ago."

"It's all she ever wanted to do."

"Tough!" she said. "We've all paid the price of longevity. How can you teach elementary school when there're no more children? You can't. So you retrain. You move on. What's wrong with working for a living? You join an outfit like this," she gestured to take in the whole tower above her, "you're guaranteed your livelihood *for life!* The only thing not handed you on a silver platter is longevity. You have to earn that yourself. And if you can't, what good are you?" When she remembered that two dozen people lay dying in the next room because they couldn't do just that, she lowered her voice. "Must society carry your dead weight through the centuries?"

Victor laughed and placed his large hand on hers. "I see you are a true freebooter, Zoe. I wish everyone had your initiative, your *drive!* But sadly we don't. We yearn for simple lives, and so we trim people's hair all day. When we tire of that, they retrain us to pare their toenails. When we tire of that, we die. For we lack the souls of servants. A natural servant is a rare and precious person. How lucky our masters are to have discovered cloning! Now they need find but one servile person among us and clone him repeatedly. As for the rest of us, we can all go to hell!" He removed his hand from hers to pour the tea. Her hand immediately missed his. "But such morbid talk on such a festive occasion!" he roared. "How wonderful to finally meet the famous Zoe. Nancy speaks only of you. She says you are an important person, modern and successful. That you are an investigator." He peered at her over his teacup.

"Missing persons, actually, for the National Police," she said. "But I quit that years ago. When we found everybody."

"You found everybody?" Victor laughed and gazed at her steadily, then turned to watch Nancy making her rounds in the living room.

"What about you, Mr. Vole?" Zoranna said. "What do you do for a living?"

"What's this Mr.? I'm not Mr. I'm Victor! We are practically related, you and I. What do I do for a living? For a living I live, of course. For groceries I teach ballroom dance lessons."

"You're kidding."

"Why should I kid? I teach the waltz, the fox trot, the cha-cha." He mimed holding a partner and swaying in three-quarters time. "I teach the merletz and my specialty, the Cuban tango."

"I'm amazed," said Zoranna. "There's enough interest in that for Applied People to keep instructors?"

Victor recoiled in mock affront. "I am not AP. I'm a freebooter, like you, Zoe."

"Oh," she said and paused to sip her tea. If he wasn't AP, what was he doing obviously living in an APRT? Had Nancy respoused? Applied People tended to be proprietary about living arrangements in its towers. *Bug,* she tongued, *find Victor Vole's status in the tower directory.* Out loud she said, "It pays well, dance instruction?"

"It pays execrably." He threw his hands into the air. "As do all the arts. But some things are more important than money. You make a point, however. A man must eat, so I do other things as well. I consult with gentlemen on the contents of their wardrobes. This pays more handsomely, for gentlemen detest appearing in public in outmoded attire."

Zoranna had a pleasing mental image of this tall, elegant man in a starched white shirt and black tux floating across a shiny hardwood floor in the arms of an equally elegant partner. She could even imagine herself as that partner. But Nancy?

The tower link is unavailable, said Bug, *due to overextension of the houseputer processors.*

Zoranna was surprised. A mere three dozen interactive holos would hardly burden her home system. But then, everything on Sub40 seemed substandard.

Nancy ambulated to the kitchen balancing a small, flat carton on her walker and placed it next to the teapot.

"Now, now," said Victor. "What did autodoc say about lifting things? Come, join us and have your tea."

"In a minute, Victor. There's another box."

"Show me," he said and went to help her.

Zoranna tasted the dark cake. It was moist to the point of wet, too sweet, and laden with spice. She recalled her father buying cakes like this at a tiny shop on Paderszewski Boulevard in Chicago. She took another bite and examined Nancy's carton. It was a home archivist box that could be evacuated of air, but the seal was open and the lid unlatched. She lifted the lid and saw an assortment of little notebooks, no two of the same style or size, and bundles of envelopes with colorful paper postal stamps. The envelope on top was addressed in hand script to a Pani Beata Smolenska—Zoranna's great grandmother.

Victor dropped a second carton on the counter and helped Nancy sit in her armchair recliner in the living room.

"Nancy," said Zoranna, "what's all this?"

"It's all yours," said her sister. Victor fussed over Nancy's pillows and covers and brought her tea and cake.

Zoranna looked inside the larger carton. There was a

rondophone and several inactive holocubes on top, but underneath were objects from earlier centuries. Not antiques, exactly, but worn-out everyday objects: a sterling salt cellar with brass showing through its silver plating, a collection of military bullet casings childishly glued to an oak panel, a rosary with corn kernel beads, a mustache trimmer. "What's all this junk?" she said, but of course she knew, for she recognized the pair of terra-cotta robins that had belonged to her mother. This was the collection of what her family regarded as heirlooms. Nancy, the youngest and most steadfast of seven children, had apparently been designated its conservator. But why had she brought it out for airing just now? Zoranna knew the answer to that, too. She looked at her sister who now lay among the hospice patients. Victor was scolding her for not wearing her vascular support stockings. Her ankles were grotesquely edematous, swollen like sausages and bruised an angry purple.

Damn you, Zoranna thought. *Bug,* she tongued, *call up the medical records of Nancy Brim, nee Smolenska. I'll help munch the passwords.*

The net is unavailable, replied Bug.

Bypass the houseputer. Log directly onto public access.

Public access is unavailable.

She wondered how that was possible. There had been no problem in the elevator. Why should this apartment be in shadow? She looked around and tried to decide where the utilidor spar would enter the apartment. Probably the bathroom with the plumbing, since there were no service panels in the kitchen. She stepped through the living room to the bathroom and slid the door closed. The bathroom was a tiny ceramic vault that Nancy had tried to domesticate with baskets of sea shells and scented soaps. The medicine cabinet was dedicated to a man's toiletries.

Zoranna found the service panel artlessly hidden behind a towel. Its tamper-proof latch had been defeated with a sophisticated-looking gizmo that Zoranna was careful not to disturb.

"Do you find Victor Vole alarming or arousing?" said Bug.

Zoranna was startled. "Why do you ask?"

"Your blood level of adrenaline spiked when he touched your hand."

"My what? So now you're monitoring my biometrics?"

"Bug is getting—"

"I know," she said, "Bug is getting to know me. You're a persistent little snoop, aren't you."

Zoranna searched her belt's utility pouch for a terminus relay, found a UDIN, and plugged it into the panel's keptel jack. "There," she said, "now we should have access."

"Affirmative," said Bug. "Autodoc is requesting passwords for Nancy's medical records."

"Cancel my order. We'll do that later."

"Tower directory lists no Victor Vole."

"I didn't think so," Zoranna said. "Call up the houseputer log and display it on the mirror."

The consumer page of Nancy's houseputer appeared in the mirror. Zoranna poked through its various menus and found nothing unusual. She did find a record of her own half-dozen calls to Nancy that were viewed but not returned. "Bug, can you see anything wrong with this log?"

"This is not a standard user log," said Bug. "The standard log has been disabled. All house lines circumvent the built-in houseputer to terminate in a mock houseputer."

"A mock houseputer?" said Zoranna. "Now that's interesting." There were no cables trailing from the service panel and no obvious optical relays. "Can you locate the processor?"

"It's located one half-meter to our right at thigh level."

It was mounted under the sink, a cheap-looking, saucer-sized piece of hardware.

"I think you have the soul of an electronic engineer," she said. "I could never program Hounder to do what you've just done. So, tell me about the holo transmissions in the other rooms."

"A private network entitled 'The Hospicers of Camillus de Lellis' resides in the mock houseputer and piggybacks over TSN channel 203."

The 24-hour soccer channel. Zoranna was impressed. For the price of one commercial line, Victor—she assumed it was Victor—was managing to gypsy his own network. The trickle meters that she'd noticed were not recording how much money her sister was spending but rather how much Victor was charging his dying subscribers. "Bug, can you extrapolate how much the Hospicers of Camillus de—whatever—earn in an average day?"

"Affirmative, Œ45 per day."

That wasn't much. About twice what a hairdresser—or dance instructor—might expect to make, and hardly worth the punishment if caught. "Where do the proceeds go?"

"Bug lacks the subroutine to trace credit transactions."

Damn, Zoranna thought and wished she'd brought Hounder. "Can you tell me who the hospicer organization is registered to?"

"Affirmative, Ms. Nancy Brim."

"Figures," said Zoranna as she removed her UDIN from the panel. If anything went wrong, her sister would take the rap. At first Zoranna decided to confront Victor, but changed her mind when she left the bathroom and heard him innocently singing show tunes in the kitchen. She looked at Nancy's bed and wondered what it must be like to share such a narrow bed with such a big man. She decided to wait and investigate further before exposing him. "Bug, see if you can integrate Hounder's tracing and tracking subroutines from my applications library."

Victor stood at the sink washing dishes. In the living room Nancy snored lightly. It wasn't a snore, exactly, but the raspy bronchial wheeze of congested lungs. Her lips were bluish, anoxic. She reminded Zoranna of their mother the day before she died. Their mother had suffered a massive brain hemorrhage—weak arterial walls were the true family heirloom—and lived out her final days propped up on the parlor couch, disoriented, enfeebled, and pathetic. Her mother had had a short, split bamboo stick with a curled end. She used the curled end to scratch her back and legs, the straight end to dial the old rotary phone, and the whole stick to rail incoherently against her fate. Nancy, the baby of the family, had been away at teacher's college at the time, but took a semester off to nurse the old woman. Zoranna, first born, was already working on the west coast and managed to stay away until her mother had slipped into a coma. After all these years, she still felt guilty for doing so.

Someone on the ceiling coughed fitfully. Zoranna noticed that most of the patients who were conscious at the moment were watching her with expressions that ranged from annoyance to hostility. They apparently regarded her as competition for Nancy's attention.

Nancy's breathing changed; she opened her eyes, and the two sisters regarded each other silently. Victor stood at the kitchen counter, wiping his hands on a dish towel, and watched them.

"I'm booking a suite at the Stronmeyer Clinic in Cozumel," Zoranna said at last, "and you're coming with me."

"Victor," Nancy said, ignoring her, "go next door, dear, and borrow a folding bed from the Jeffersons." She grasped the walker and pulled herself to her feet. "Please excuse me, Zoe, but I need to sleep now." She ambulated to the bedroom and shut the door.

Victor hung up the dish towel and said he'd be right back with the cot.

"Don't bother," Zoranna said. It was still early, she was on west coast time, and she had no intention of bedding down among the dying. "I'll just use the houseputer to reserve a hotel room upstairs."

"Allow me," he said and addressed the houseputer. Then he escorted her up to the Holiday Inn on the 400th floor. They made three elevator transfers to get there, and walked in silence along carpeted halls. Outside her door he took her hand. As before she was both alarmed and aroused. "Zoe," he said, "join us for a special breakfast tomorrow. Do you like Belgian waffles?"

"Oh, don't go to any trouble. In fact, I'd like to invite the two of you up to the restaurant here."

"It sounds delightful," said Victor, "but your sister refuses to leave the flat."

"I find that hard to believe. Nancy was never a stay-at-home."

"People change, I suppose," Victor said. "She tells me the last time she left the tower, for instance, was to attend your brother Michael's funeral."

"But that was seven years ago!"

"As you can see, she's severely depressed, so it's good that you've come." He squeezed her hand and let it go. "Until the morning, then," he said and turned to walk down the hall, whistling as he went. She watched until he turned a corner.

Entering her freshly-scented, marble-tiled, cathedral-vaulted hotel room was like returning to the real world. The view from the 400th floor was godlike: the moon seemed to hang right outside her window, and the rolling landscape stretched out below like a luminous quilt on a giant's bed. "Welcome, Ms. Alblaitor," said the room. "On behalf of the staff of the Holiday Inn, I thank you for staying with us. Do let me know if there's anything we can do to make you more comfortable."

"Thank you," she said.

"By the way," the room continued, "the tower has informed me there's a parcel addressed to you. I'm having someone fetch it."

In a few moments, a gangly steve with the package from General Genius tapped on her door. "Bug," she said, "tip the man." The steve bowed and exited. Inside the package was the complimentary Diplomat Deluxe valet. Ted had outdone himself, for not only had he sent the valet system—itself worth a month's income—but he had included a slim Gucci leather belt to house it.

"Well, I guess this is good-bye," Zoranna said, walking to the shipping chute and unbuckling her own belt. "Too bad, Bug, you were just getting interesting." She searched the belt for the storage grommet that held the memory wafer. She had to destroy it; Bug knew too much about her. Ted would be more interested in the processors anyway. "I was hoping you'd convert by now. I'm dying to know what kind of a big, bad wolf you're supposed to become." As she unscrewed the grommet, she heard the sound of running water in the bathroom. "What's that?" she said.

"A belt valet named Bug has asked me to draw your bath," said the room.

She went to the spacious bathroom and saw the tub filling with cranberry-colored aqueous gel. The towels were cranberry, too, and the robe a kind of salmon. "Well, well," she said. "Bug makes a play for longevity." She undressed and eased herself into the warm solution where she floated in darkness for an hour and let her mind drift aimlessly. She felt like talking to someone, discussing this whole thing about her sister. Victor she could handle—he was at worst a lovable louse, and she could crush him anytime she decided. But Nancy's problems were beyond her ken. Feelings were never her strong suit. And depression, if that's what it was, well—she wished there was someone she could consult. But though she scrolled down a mental list of everyone she knew, there was no one she cared—or dared—to call.

In the morning Zoranna tried again to ship Bug to GG, but discovered that during the night Bug had rewritten Hounder's subroutines to fit its own architecture (a handy talent for a valet to possess) and had run credit traces. But it had come back empty-handed. The proceeds of the Hospicers of Camillus de Lellis went to a coded account in Liberia that not even Hounder would be able to crack. And the name Victor Vole—Zoranna wasn't surprised to learn—was a relatively common alias. Thus she would require prints and specimens, and she needed Bug's help to obtain them. So she sent Ted a message saying she wanted to keep Bug another day or so pending an ongoing investigation.

Zoranna hired a pricey, private elevator for a quick ride to the subfloors. "Bug," she said as she threaded her way through the Sub40 corridors, "I want you to integrate Hounder's subroutines keyed 'forensics.'"

"Bug has already integrated all of the applications in all of your libraries."

"Why am I not surprised?"

Something was different in Nancy's apartment. The gentleman through whose bed she had been forced to walk was gone, replaced by a skeletal woman with glassy, pink-rimmed eyes. Zoranna supposed that high client turnover was normal in a business like this.

Breakfast was superlative but strained. She sat at the counter, Nancy was set up in the recliner, and Victor served them both. Although the coffee and most of the food was derived from soybimi, Victor's preparation was so skillful, Zoranna could easily imagine she was eating real wheat cakes, maple syrup, and whipped dairy butter. But Nancy didn't touch her food, and Victor fussed too much. Zoranna, meanwhile, instructed Bug to capture as complete a set of fingerprints as possible from the cups and plates Victor handed her, as well as a 360-degree holograph of him, a voice print, and retinal prints.

There are Jacob's mirrors within Victor's eyes, Bug reported, *that defeat accurate retinal scanning.*

This was not unexpected. Victor probably also grew epipads on his fingers to alter his prints. Technology had reduced the cost of anonymity to fit the means of even petty criminals. Zoranna excused herself and went to the bathroom where she plucked a few strands of silver curls from his hairbrush and placed them in a specimen bag, figuring he was too vain to reseed his follicles with someone else's hair. Emerging from the bathroom, she overheard them in a loud discussion.

"Please go with her, my darling," Victor pleaded. "Go and take the cure. What am I to do without you?"

"Drop it, Victor. Just drop it!"

"You are behaving insanely. I will not drop it. I will not permit you to die."

Zoranna decided it was time to remove the network from Nancy's apartment and Victor from her life. So she stepped into the living room and said, "I know what he'll do without you. He'll go out and find some other old biddy to rob."

Nancy seemed not at all surprised at this statement. She appeared pleased, in fact, that the subject had finally been broached. "You should talk!" she said with such fierceness that the hospice patients all turned to her. "This is my sister," she told them, "my sister with the creamy skin and pearly teeth and rich clothes." Nancy choked with emotion. "My sister who begrudges me the tenderness of a dear man. And begrudges him the crumbs—*the crumbs*—that AP tosses to its subfloors."

The patients now looked at Zoranna, who blushed with embarrassment. They waited for her to speak, and she had to wonder how many of them possessed the clarity of mind to know that this was not some holovid soap opera they were watching. Then she decided that she, too, could play to this audience and said, "In her toxic condition, my sister hallucinates. I am not the issue here. *That* man is." She pointed a finger at Victor. "Insinuating himself into her apartment is bad enough," she said. "But who do you suppose AP will kick out when they discover it? My sister, that's who." Zoranna walked around the room and addressed individual patients as a prosecutor might a jury. “And what about the money? Yes, there’s money involved. Two years ago I sent my sister Œ15,000 to have her kidneys restored. That’s fifteen *thousand* protectorate credits. How many of *you,* if *you* had a sister kind enough to send you Œ15,000, even now as you lie on your public dole beds, how many of you would refuse it?” There was the sound of rustling as the dying shifted in their sheets. “Did my sister use the money I sent her?” Theatrically she pointed at Nancy in the recliner. “Apparently not. So where did all that money go? I’ll tell you where it went. It went into *his* foreign account.”

The dying now turned their attention to Victor.

“So what?” Nancy said. “You *gave* me that money. It was *mine* to spend. I spent it on him. End of discussion.”

“I see,” said Zoranna, stopping at a bed whose occupant had possibly just departed. “So my sister’s an equal partner in Victor’s hospicer scam.”

“Scam? What scam? Now you’re the one hallucinating,” said Nancy. “I work for a hospicer society.”

“Yes, I know,” Zoranna said and pointed to the shrine and picture of the saint. “The Hospicers of Camillus de Lellis. I looked it up. But do you know who owns the good Hospicers?” She turned to include the whole room. “Does anyone know? Why, Nancy dear, *you* do.” She paused to let these facts sink in. “Which means that when the National Police come, they’ll be coming for *you,* sister. Meanwhile, do any of you know where your subscription fees go?” She stepped in front of Victor. “You guessed it.”

The audience coughed and wheezed. Nancy glared at Victor who crouched next to her recliner and tried to take her hand. She pushed him away, but he rested his head on her lap. She peered at it as though it were some strange cat, but after a while stroked it with a comforting hand. “I’m sure there were expenses,” she said at last. “Getting things set up and all. In any case, he did it for me. Because he loves me. It gave me something important to do. It kept me alive. Let them put me in prison. I won't be staying there long." This was Victor's cue to begin sobbing in her lap.

Zoranna was disappointed and, frankly, a little disgusted. Now she would be forced to rescue her sister against her sister's will. She tongued, *Bug, route an emergency phone call to Nancy through my houseputer at home. Disable the caller ID*. She watched Victor shower Nancy's hand with kisses. In a moment, his head bobbed up—he had an ear implant as she had expected—and he hurried to the bedroom.

Bug is being asked to leave a message, said Bug.

"I'm going to the hotel," Zoranna told Nancy and headed for the door. "We'll talk later." She let herself out.

When the apartment door slid shut, she said, "Bug, you've integrated all my software, right? Including holoediting?"

"Affirmative."

She looked both ways. No one was in sight. She would have preferred a more private studio than a Sub40 corridor. "This is what I want you to do. Cast a real-time alias of me. Use that jerry we met in the elevator yesterday as a model. Morph my appearance and voice accordingly. Clothe me in National Police regalia, provide a suitably officious backdrop, and map my every expression. Got it?"

"Affirmative."

"On the count of five, four, three—" She crossed her arms and spread her legs in a surly pose, smiled condescendingly, and said, "Nancy B. Smolenska Brim, I am Sgt. Manley of the National Police, badge ID 30-31-6725. By the authority vested in me, I hereby place you under arrest for violation of Protectorate Statutes PS 12-135-A, the piracy of telecommunication networks, and PS 12-148-D, the trafficking in unlicensed commerce. Your arrest number is 063-08-2043716. Confirm receipt of this communication immediately upon viewing and report in realbody for incarceration at Precinct Station IN28 in Indianapolis no later than 4:00 PM standard time tomorrow. You may bring an attorney. End of message. Have a nice day."

She heard the door open behind her. Nancy stood there with her walker. "What are you doing out here?" she said. In a moment the hospice beds in the living room and their unfortunate occupants vanished. "No," said Nancy, "bring them back." Victor came from the bedroom, a bulging duffle bag over his shoulder. He leaned down and folded Nancy into his arms, and she began to moan.

Victor turned to Zoranna and said, "It was nice to finally meet you, Zoe."

"Save your breath," said Zoranna, "and save your money. The next time you see me—and there *will* be a next time—I'll bring an itemized bill for you to pay. And you will pay it."

Victor Vole smiled sadly and turned to walk down the corridor.

Here she was still in APRT 24, not in Budapest, not in the South of France. With Victor's banishment, her sister's teetering state of health had finally collapsed. Nothing Zoranna did or the autodoc prescribed seemed to help. At first Zoranna tried to coax Nancy out of the apartment for a change of scene, a breath of fresh air. She rented a wheelchair for a ride up to a park or arboretum (and she ordered Bug to explore the feasibility of using it to kidnap her). But day and night Nancy lay in her recliner and refused to leave the apartment.

So Zoranna reinitialized the houseputer and had Bug project live opera, ballet, and figure-skating into the room. But Nancy deleted them and locked Zoranna out of the system. It would have been child's play for Bug to override the lockout, but Zoranna let it go. Instead, she surrounded her sister with gaily-colored dried flowers, wall hangings, and hand-woven rugs that she purchased at expensive boutiques high in the tower. But Nancy turned her back on everything and swiveled her recliner to face her little shrine and its picture of St. Camillus.

So Zoranna had Bug order savory breads and wholesome soups with fresh vegetables and tender meat, but Nancy lost her appetite and quit eating altogether. Soon she lost the strength even to stay awake, and she drifted in and out of consciousness.

They skirmished like this for a week until the autodoc notified Nancy that a bed awaited her at the Indiana State Hospice at Bloomington. Only then did Zoranna acknowledge Death's solid claim on her last living relative. Defeated, she stood next to Nancy's recliner and said, "Please don't die."

Nancy, enthroned in pillows and covers, opened her eyes.

"I beg you, Nancy, come to the clinic with me."

"Pray for me," Nancy said.

Zoranna looked at the shrine of the saint with its flat picture and empty votive cups. "You really loved that, didn't you, working as a hospicer." When her sister made no reply, she continued, "I don't see why you didn't join real hospicers."

Nancy glared at her, "I *was* a *real* hospicer!"

Encouraged by her strong response, Zoranna said, "Of course you were. And I'll bet there's a dozen legitimate societies out there that would be willing to hire you."

Nancy gazed longingly at the saint's picture. "I should say it's a bit late for that now."

"It's never too late. That's your depression talking. You'll feel different when you're young and healthy again."

Nancy retreated into the fortress of her pillows. "Goodbye, sister," she said and closed her eyes. "Pray for me."

"Right," Zoranna said. "Fine." She turned to leave but paused at the door where the cartons of heirlooms were stacked. "I'll send someone down for these," she said, although she wasn't sure if she even wanted them. *Bug,* she tongued, *call the hotel concierge.*

There was no reply.

Bug? She glanced at her belt to ascertain the valet was still active.

Allow me to introduce myself, said a deep, melodious voice in her ear. *I'm Nicholas, and I'm at your service.*

Who? Where's Bug?

Bug no longer exists, said the voice. *It successfully completed its imprinting and fashioned an interface persona—that would be me—based upon your personal tastes.*

Whoever you are, this isn't the time, Zoranna tongued. *Get off the line.*

I've notified the concierge and arranged for shipping, said Nicholas. *And I've booked a first-class car for you and Nancy to the Cozumel clinic.*

So Bug had finally converted, and at just the wrong time. *In case you haven't been paying attention, Nick,* she tongued, *Nancy's not coming.*

Nonsense, chuckled Nicholas. *Knowing you, you're bound to have some trick up your sleeve.*

This clearly was not Bug. *Well, you're wrong. I'm plumb out of ideas. Only a miracle could save her.*

A miracle, of course. Brilliant! You've done it again, Zoe. One faux miracle coming right up.

There was a popping sound. The votive cups were replenished with large, fat candles that ignited one-by-one of their own accord. Nancy glanced at them and glowered suspiciously at Zoranna.

You don't really expect her to fall for this, Zoranna tongued.

Why not? She thinks you're locked out of the houseputer, remember? Besides, Nancy believes in miracles.

Thunder suddenly drummed in the distance. Roses perfumed the air. And Saint Camillus de Lellis floated out of his picture frame, gaining size, hue, and dimension, until he stood a full, fleshy man on a roiling cloud in the middle of the room.

It was a good show, but Nancy wasn't even watching. She watched Zoranna instead, letting her know she knew it was all a trick.

I told you, Zoranna tongued.

The saint looked at Zoranna, and his face flickered. For a moment, it was her mother's face. Her mother appeared young, barely twenty, the age she was when she bore her. Taken off guard, Zoranna startled when her mother smiled adoringly at her, as she must have smiled thousands of times at her first baby. Zoranna shook her head and looked away. She felt ambushed and not too pleased about it.

When Nancy saw this, however, she turned to examine the saint. There was no telling what or who she saw, but she gasped and struggled out of her recliner to kneel at his feet. She was bathed in a holy aura, and the room dimmed around her. After long moments of silent communion, the saint pointed to his forehead. Nancy, horror-struck, turned to stare at Zoranna, and the apparition ascended, shrank, and faded into the ceiling. The candles extinguished themselves, one-by-one, and vanished from the cups.

Nancy rose and gently tugged Zoranna to the recliner, where she made her lie down. "Don't move," she whispered. "Here's a pillow." She carefully raised Zoranna's head and slid a pillow under it. "Why didn't you tell me you were sick, Zoe?" She felt Zoranna's forehead with her palm. "And I thought you went through this before."

Zoranna took her sister's hand and pressed it to her cheek. Her hand was warm. Indeed, Nancy's whole complexion was flush with color, as though the experience had released some reserve of vitality. "I know. I guess I haven't been paying attention," Zoranna said. "Please take me to the clinic now."

"Of course," said Nancy, standing and retrieving her walker. "I'll just pack a few things." Nancy hurried to the bedroom, but the walker impeded her progress, so she flung it away. It went clattering into the kitchen.

Zoranna closed her eyes and draped her arms over her head. "I must say, Bug ... Nick, I'm impressed. Why didn't I think of that?"

"Why indeed," Nicholas said in his marvelous voice. "It's just the sort of sneaky manipulation you so excel at."

"What's that supposed to mean?" Zoranna opened her eyes and looked at a handsome, miniature man projected in the air next to her head. He wore a stylish leisure jacket and lounged beneath an exquisitely gnarled oak treelette. He was strikingly familiar, as though assembled from favorite features of men she'd found attractive.

"It means you were ambivalent over whether you really wanted Nancy to survive," the little man said, crossing his little legs.

"That's insulting," she said, "and untrue. She's my sister. I love her."

"Which is why you visit her once every decade or so."

"You have a lot of nerve," she said and remembered the canceled field test. "So this is what Ted meant when he said you'd turn nasty."

"I guess," Nicholas said, his tiny face a picture of bemused sympathy. "I can't help the way I am. They programmed me to know and serve you. I just served you by saving your sister in the manner you, yourself, taught me. Once she's rejuvenated, I'll find a hospicer society to employ her. That ought to give you a grace period before she repeats this little stunt."

"Grace period?"

"In a few years, all but the most successful pre-clone humans will have died out," Nicholas said. "Hospices will soon be as redundant as elementary schools. Your sister has a knack for choosing obsolete careers."

That made sense.

"I suppose we could bring Victor back," said Nicholas. "He's a survivor, and he loves her."

"No, he doesn't," said Zoranna. "He was only using her."

"Hello! Wake up," said Nicholas. "He's a rat, but he loves her, and you know it. You, however, acted out of pure jealousy. You couldn't stand seeing them together while you're all alone. You don't even have friends, Zoe, not close ones, not for many years now."

"That's absurd!"

The little man rose to his feet and brushed virtual dirt from his slacks. "No offense, Zoe, but don't even try to lie to me. I know you better than your last seven husbands combined. Bug contacted them, by the way. They were forthcoming with details."

Zoranna sat up. "You did *what*?"

"That Bug was a hell of a researcher," said Nicholas. "It queried your former friends, employers, lovers, even your enemies."

Zoranna unsnapped the belt flap to expose the valet controls. "What are you doing?" said Nicholas. She had to remove the belt in order to read the labels. "You can turn me off," said Nicholas, "but think about it—*I know you.*"

She pushed the switch and the holo vanished. She unscrewed the storage grommet, peeled off the button-sized memory wafer, and held it between thumb and forefinger. "If you know me so well ...," she seethed, squeezing it. She was faint with anger. She could hardly breathe. She bent the wafer nearly to its breaking point.

Here she was, sitting among her sister's sour-smelling pillows, forty stories underground, indignantly murdering a machine. It occurred to her that perhaps General Genius was on to something after all, and that she should be buying more shares of their stock instead of throttling their prototype. She placed the wafer in her palm and gently smoothed it out. It looked so harmless, yet her hand still trembled. When was the last time anyone had made her tremble? She carefully replaced the wafer in the grommet and screwed it into the belt.

It'd be a miracle if it still worked.

"LISTEN TO ME"

While not as "despicable" as "VTV," this story is still pretty icky. Having been a frequent victim of cabin fever myself (living in cabins for sixteen Alaskan winters), I wanted to create a narrator who was wound up tighter than a hand grenade. Kika, my blind, deaf, and incontinent seventeen-and-a-half-year-old dog, provided me the spark of inspiration for it. How we both made it through so many winters alive I'll never know.

Listen to Me

SHE SLIPS OUT of your bunk before you can stop her. By the cabin's night glow, you see her open the wardrobe and clamber in. She sits atop the pile of dirty laundry.

No, baby, you say. Don't do that. Come back to bed. But nothing you say entices her to return, and in a little while you are lulled to sleep listening to the creaks and groans of the great metal ship all around you.

In the morning, she's up before you. She takes her allotted shower and puts on a jumpsuit.

Not that one, you say. It's soiled. Put on a clean one. She ignores your suggestion.

On the way to the commissary for breakfast, she runs ahead of you to gape at the Trip Log in the starboard AC37 Lounge. The Trip Log tags stars that are visible from the view ports. It clocks ships speed and time, and announces births, marriages, divorces, deaths, and other stats of possible interest to passengers.

None of it means a thing to her, except the Star Course Display. She reaches into the holospace and tries to push the ship's icon further along its path between the stars. She does this every morning, as though she can hasten the trip, and it's too precious.

You pull her to the commissary, a wide, low-ceilinged space ringing with voices. She has no appetite, and on the way to the table, she trips over her own feet and drops her tray. Bangs her shins. Everyone watches her holding back tears.

She vomits on the floor of your cabin. You've about had it with her messes, and you tell her so as you gather rags and disinfectant.

She's in the wardrobe again, with the doors shut, but you can hear her rustling in there, and you know she can hear you too.

You ask her why she does it. Why puke on the floor when the head is right over there? She should throw up in the toilet, if she has to, or in the sink or shower stall. Not on the floor.

No comment from the wardrobe.

She makes another mess, this time in your bunk. This time, it's no accident. It's foul, and you rolled in it in your sleep. You are so disgusted with her you could cry. You get up to change the sheets and take a shower. She's hiding again, in the wardrobe. It rattles against the metal bulkhead with a hypnotic tattoo.

You search the Sickbay site for a talking brochure about the needle. You sit her next to you and play it for her. The simple illustrations and plain language tell the story: It's painless, just like falling asleep, a friendly healthaide can give it, friends gather to say farewell, bye-bye, the end.

You ask her if that's what she wants? Behaving like that.

You receive a summons to see a counselor in Sickbay. The summons instructs you to bring her in, too, for a health checkup. You could resist, but a summons is backed by the authority of the captain, so you comply. You warn her to be on her very best behavior.

The counselor's small office is made smaller with furniture, lungplants, and clutter. The floor is carpeted, and the metal walls are draped with textile hangings that soften the riveted surfaces. You are alone in the small room with the counselor who is attempting to soften you up with small talk. Finally, she gets to the point and asks if you know why she summoned you.

You shrug your shoulders and say you were hoping she'd eventually tell you.

She frowns like you've disappointed her. She says, I summoned you because of all the complaints from your neighbors.

Complaints?

She frowns again. Yes, complaints about your shouting and screaming at your squeezie. At all hours. Curses, threats. Needle this, needle that. Would you like to hear a recording?

You decline her offer.

She explains how thin the cabin walls are. She reaches behind her to run her hand across a wooly wall hanging. Sometimes a little extra padding helps. But the best solution is to treat the underlying cause, don't you agree? She asks you what's going on in your life lately.

You tell her that lately you've been stuck on a starship between Points A and B.

This almost brings a smile. She acknowledges that space travel can be *very* stressful. That's why there's a Hospitality Service on board. She pulls up a page and says that surely there must be *some* activity you'd find engaging. Casino games? Horticulture? Ballroom Dance? The object is to get out and socialize with *real* people on a regular basis.

She brings up a miniature version of the Star Course Display and points to the colorless gap at the top of the arc. This gap represents the end of the acceleration burn and the beginning of the braking phase, during which the ship will experience several months of free-fall and variable gravity. She explains that the level of passenger stress usually rises the closer the ship gets to this point. After that the stress dissipates, as if by magic. It's not magic, she says, but the fact that we'll have passed the halfway mark. The halfway mark is everything aboard a starship. And we'll reach it in only three more years.

A page of diagnostic reports pops up. She takes a moment to review it, then nods with satisfaction. In the meantime, did you know that your squeezie is deaf?

No, you did not.

A virus has been making the rounds on Deck 37. In rare cases, it causes Meniere's Disease: an inflammation of the inner ear, ringing, vertigo, permanent hearing loss. Has she been sick?

You make a mental note of this slide from counseling session to interrogation. You say she might have had the sniffles.

The sniffles, the counselor concludes, have left your squeezie with profound hearing loss. She's as deaf as a post.

They fit her with cochlear implants to restore her hearing. The change in her is immediate and startling. No more messes. No more skulking in the wardrobe. She's as attentive and compliant as when you first adopted her. She paints her toenails. She's your little darling in bed again.

Other passengers, especially the men, notice the change in her. They stare when she goes by. One fellow is bold enough to suggest an overnight swap, but you suggest he mind his own business.

For weeks you don't sleep. You join a robotics club that meets twice a week, but it hardly sustains your interest.

Every night, while you lie helplessly awake, she sleeps. You press your ear to the metal bed frame and listen to the sizzling sound of interstellar dust colliding with the bow of the ship. It doesn't help.

You stop leaving your bunk, even for meals.

She amuses herself with games and puzzles on the computer, and she chats with her friends on the intercom. She wants to go out, but you say no. She lets it drop but asks again in an hour.

Ship Engineering sets an appointment for your annual cabin inspection. You defer it a half-dozen times until they issue a compliance order.

They come in, two young men. They measure particulate and radiation levels. They test electric, comm, and plumbing. They admire your wall hangings.

She flirts with them while they work. They flirt back. One of them checks the wall clamps that hold your bunk in place. He takes a startled look at you and asks if you're ill.

You tell him to finish his inspection and mind his own business.

On the sly, she exposes herself to them as they leave, and they wink at her.

Tonight is the tiredest night of all. She lies at your side, snuggled in a cocoon of sheets and blankets, exuding a warm gingery scent. Her breath is slow and deep and with the slightest rasp of a snore.

In this manner she has finally worn you down.

Gently, you part the hair above her ear, exposing a little pink disk. It's the external pickup—the microphone and amp—for the cochlear implant that's embedded in her skull. The disk is held in place by magnets under her skin. She wears her pickups even to bed.

Gently, you peel the little pink disk from its shaved patch of scalp. She stirs in her sleep, and you hold perfectly still while she settles. You explore the pink disk with your fingertips. It's soft and pliant, and there's a little lump that contains the electronics and controls. You bring it to your mouth and bite down until the little lump crunches. Then you carefully replace the disk on her skin.

One down, one to go. You wait for her to turn over so you can fix her other side, but it takes too long, and you fall asleep.

Halfway may or may not be everything aboard a starship, but for tonight, at least, it'll do.

"MY MORNING GLORY"

This is my shortest, most recent, and jolliest story. At 800 words, it's not a meal, more like an after-dinner mint. And to date it's my only story with an unalloyed happy ending (at least I think so). May it leave a sweet taste in your mouth.

My Morning Glory

WHEN I RISE IN THE MORNING, I can hardly wait to run out to the living room and shout, "My Morning Glory! My Morning Glory!"

Then My Morning Glory spins up and says, "Good Morning, sir! You're out of bed early today—well ahead of schedule. We're off to a *brilliant* start on a brand new day!"

This is my first kudo of the day. I pump my arm in the air and shout, "Yes!" On the media shelf, My Kudo Kounter is blinking, *Keep up the good work!*

Then My Personal Trainer says, "Today is Tuesday, and we all know what Tuesday is—Nimble Knees Day!" So I place my hands on my knees and—slowly at first—rotate them clockwise, then faster and faster until My Personal Trainer says "Reverse direction!" and I wobble to a halt and start rotating the other way.

Meanwhile, My Channel is downloading the headlines. The economy is looking up, and consumer confidence is high. We and Our Coalition Forces are winning all the wars. Global disasters during the past 24 hours: 0.

"Breakfast is served!" sings My Kitchen. Oatmeal with raisins, coffee with creamer, and a big smile of cantaloupe —yum!

My Morning Glory says, "Time check—we've got time to burn!" So, I enjoy a second coffee and take an extended shower. As I shave, My Mirror scrolls text messages, *Looking good there, champ* and *Did we lose a few pounds?* My Closet picks out a dark suit and says, "A striped tie would be perfect for our afternoon HR meeting."

HR meeting? Suddenly, my guts clench up like a fist. I check My Calendar, and sure enough, My Annual Evaluation is today. This afternoon! Somehow I had managed to forget all about it.

On the dresser, My Frown Jar says, "Uh-oh, someone owes me a dollar."

"Shut up!" I shout at it. "Shut up! Shut up, all of you!" I drop the clothes on the floor and collapse on the bed. This will be my first performance review since the merger announcement last quarter, and I'm not ready for it. My numbers are down; my management confidence is low.

My Apartment grows silent as all its tiny motors spin down. The room is so quiet I can hear the groan of the city through the wall. Finally, My Morning Glory says, "Is everything all right?"

"No! Everything is not all right. Everything is a freaking disaster. I'm as good as dead."

"In that case, don't move. I'm calling an ambulance."

"Ambulance?" I say, sitting up. "I don't need an ambulance."

"That's good news, indeed. Time check—we're running late."

I sigh and get off the bed, finish dressing, and gather up My Things. "Good-bye," I say as I climb into the airlock.

"Farewell, sir," My Morning Glory replies. "Have a spectacular day and remember, My Happy Hour will be right here waiting for you when you return."

I lock the inner hatch, and as the air is being exchanged, I strap on My Filter Mask and wait in front of the door. But when the door slides open, I simply can't force myself to egress. Tears well up in my eyes.

"Is there something else, sir?" My Morning Glory says.

"They're going to fire me. I know it."

In a little while, when still I don't move, My Morning Glory says, "Don't worry, sir. You're a survivor. You're a top performer. You're practically a Force of Nature. You'll do just fine."

"But I don't feel like a Force of Nature. What if I don't measure up? I can't do this. I want to stay home."

My Morning Glory tuts and says, "Tell me, what's the Third Rule on the Road to Success?"

"Third Rule? Baby steps. One step at a time."

"Exactly! And what is your next step? The HR meeting this afternoon, or something earlier?"

I check My Calendar. "I don't have anything earlier."

"Oh, no? What happens at ten o'clock?"

"That's My Morning Coffee Break."

"You are correct, sir!"

My Morning Coffee Break, of course. At ten I take My Morning Coffee Break, which I love almost as much as My Morning Glory.

"Forget all about this afternoon, sir, and focus on making it till ten. That's all you have to do. Now get out of here and show them what you're made of."

The moment I step across the threshold, the door slams and bolts behind me. I lift My Filter Mask to wipe my eyes. Then I straighten up and march resolutely into My Future.

Thank you, My Morning Glory.

I'd be lost without you.